SPARKS

BOOK 2 OF THE BLACKOUT DUOLOGY

KIT MALLORY

Kit Mallory

SPARKS

© 2020 Kit Mallory

Cover design by Jane Dixon-Smith

First edition

ISBN (Print): 978-1-9999697-9-0
ISBN (eBook): 978-1-9999697-8-3

Contact the author:
Email: kitmallorywrites@gmail.com
Twitter: @kitkattus

To my parents, with love and thanks.

CONTENTS

AUTHOR'S NOTE

This book is set against a backdrop of considerable trauma. Whilst I have done my best to approach these topics responsibly and sensitively, please be aware that this book contains a number of themes and scenes that some may find distressing or triggering. I encourage readers to be mindful of this and to exercise self-care whilst reading. A full list of content and trigger warnings can be found on my website: www.kitmallory.wordpress.com.

1

RIPPLES

Faith almost didn't answer her phone when it rang.

It was ten at night and she'd been working since well before sunrise; breaks weren't in Hahn's frame of reference, either for herself or her subordinates. Faith had been stifling yawns for hours, limbs heavy with the pull of sleep – and she would be up before dawn tomorrow to do it all again.

One evening to herself. Was that really too much to ask?

Evidently it was, because the second she collapsed onto her bed, her phone buzzed in her pocket.

Just this once, maybe she wouldn't answer. It might not even be urgent.

It was always urgent.

Swallowing a curse, she answered the call.

"Yo, you still working?" It was Hakima from comms: permanently perky, minimal regard for social niceties.

"Actually –"

"Ha, just kidding. Like you ever stop."

Hakima was actually okay, or at least not the most annoying person in the Agency, but occasionally it was hard to remember that. Faith pinched the bridge of her nose. "This better not be like that time you called me at two AM because you wanted doughnuts."

"If you want to bring me doughnuts you're welcome, but nah. I'm sending you something. It came through to all the big news agencies at once. DR, TV2, a bunch of national papers –"

"Just Danish ones?"

"Nope. CNN, Al Jazeera..."

Faith reached for her laptop. "What is it?"

"Just look, then call me back and tell me what Hahn says. *Then* you can bring me doughnuts."

Oh. Of course that was why Hakima was calling her. "Hahn's busy."

"Yeah, but you're her favourite."

You're not supposed to tell your colleagues to fuck off. You're not supposed to tell your colleagues to fuck off. "That's not –"

"Yeah yeah yeah. Just look at the stuff."

Her eyes stinging behind her glasses, Faith squinted at the email Hakima had forwarded. The first attachment was titled *The Final Report of the Northern Containment Committee.*

The dry heaviness behind her eyes vanished. "Holy *shit.* This is from the UK government."

"You're welcome. You're always banging on about how we should do something over there."

2

"I don't *bang on*," Faith said distractedly, scrolling through the document. "It's just pretty messed up that they've got some insane dictatorship thing going on and nobody's –" A section highlighted in red grabbed her attention. She sat bolt upright. "*Fuck.*"

"You got to the good stuff, then."

"Is this *real*? This is the Board talking about exterminating half their country. Wiping out the North. This is genocide. Who *sent* this?"

"Watch the video."

Faith opened the video and her stomach gave a sharp pang. The girl on the screen looked about sixteen, with dark blonde hair in an untidy plait and a pale face swollen with bruising. A long cut, stitched closed, traced the bottom of her left eye socket. She looked like she was in... a kitchen, perhaps. With a boarded-up window behind her.

"Jesus," Faith breathed.

"I know, right? And presumably the Board hadn't even caught up with her at that point. God only knows what state she's in now."

Faith pressed play.

"Uh –" the girl on the screen began. She stopped, scowled, squared her shoulders. "So we just blew up a laboratory..."

Her English accent was flat, exhausted. Like she didn't expect anyone to care about what she was saying; like she wasn't sure why she was bothering at all. But then, she was British – and, apparently, Northern. And something terrible was happening in the North, and if

3

she was thinking nobody had come to their rescue so far, she was right.

But in the video's final seconds she leaned towards the camera, and an edge of steel glimmered in her words. "We're just people," she said. "We're just like you, and we need your help. Please. If you're listening... Don't let them do this to us."

Faith played the recording again, mental cogs spinning furiously. Who *was* this girl? Where was she now? What was happening to her?

"Clara reckons it's fake," Hakima supplied. "She said to sit on it till it's verified."

No. You couldn't fake that kind of world-weary exhaustion. The girl was flat in the way someone could only be when the weight of the world had crushed them entirely.

"Clara's an asshole," Faith said. "And by *sit on it*, she means keep it away from Hahn, right?"

"Right."

Maybe Hakima wasn't so bad after all. "What do you reckon?"

"Well, we're still trying to find out if they really did blow up a government lab."

"Would've thought that'd be easy enough to find out."

"You'd think. But domestic power's out across the South, and the virus in the Board's computer system's *definitely* real. Their whole network's fucked – all their comms, everything. Ayodele tried to get in and his computer got scrambled too."

"So they've got a hacker."

"Yep. At least as good as any of ours. Ayodele said he might as well just set fire to his laptop, the state it's in. I reckon that's her in the video. Looks like she recorded it and sent the whole package straight out."

Faith jumped to her feet. She wouldn't be sleeping tonight. Suddenly it didn't matter. "We have to do something."

"Settle down, Supergirl. I wouldn't get your cape out just yet. This stuff has to go to panel, remember? They'll spend the next day and a half arguing, and that girl and her friends will be riddled with bullets by the time everyone's made up their minds."

Faith grabbed her laptop. "I'll take it to Hahn."

"I thought Hahn was busy." There was a smile in Hakima's voice.

"Yeah. Never mind."

There was no point knocking on Hahn's office door. In fact, when Faith tried it, it was locked. But that was okay. She had a key, even if she'd never actually dared use it.

Her legs were strangely wobbly as she fished it out. "Keep it for emergencies," Hahn had instructed. Well, this was definitely an emergency for the girl in the video, whoever she was.

Faith had half-wondered whether she might catch Hahn eating a sneaky packet of biscuits and watching sitcoms with her feet up on her desk. But it was almost impossible to imagine her boss needing something so human as a little respite, and when Faith edged guiltily into the office Hahn was seated, as usual, behind a desk

5

swamped with paperwork, her hair still pinned as neatly as it had been sixteen hours earlier, typing furiously and glaring at her computer as though it had insulted her mother.

"Faith," she said, without lifting her eyes from the screen. "Is the building on fire?"

"Um, no." Faith took her glasses off and polished them on her shirt, laptop tucked awkwardly under one arm. "I, uh –"

"Is someone dying?"

"No." *No one in this building, anyway.* Emboldened, Faith stepped forward. "I think you should –"

Hahn looked up at last, with an expression so withering her continued inattention would have been preferable. "Have the words 'Do not disturb me until morning' taken on a meaning I'm unaware of?"

"Uh, no." Faith straightened her back, crossed the office, and set her laptop down on the paperwork explosion. "Julia. Listen. I think you're going to want to see this."

2

PURGATORY

Angel's feet thudded on frozen mud, her breath coming hard, ghostly in the first light of the rising sun. She'd been running too much, if the blisters were anything to go by, but she couldn't stop. The soles of her trainers were wearing thin and that was going to be a problem soon – it wasn't like it would be easy to find a new pair up here – but she would have run in her bare feet if she'd had to.

It was the only thing that helped.

Two months since they'd crossed the Wall, and of all the ways she'd imagined life in the North, she'd never thought it would be like this.

For one thing, she'd always thought Skyler would be here too.

But Skyler wasn't here, and her absence was a constant ache, a yawning chasm of a wound that threatened to swallow Angel whole. If she trained long enough, hard enough, she could almost outrun it.

Almost.

She slowed to a jog as she reached her tent, one of hundreds crammed onto the hillside, the ground between them slick with mud. Some were tiny, like hers, while others housed entire families. Few people were up and about this early. Someone would be tending the fire pit at the top of the hill if she'd wanted company, but she didn't.

She barely registered the pain that stabbed at her feet as she wiped sweat out of her eyes. When she unzipped her tent, though, wrongness prickled on her skin like needles.

She stiffened.

Pulling a small knife from her belt, she ducked inside the canvas.

Mackenzie, propped on his elbows on top of her sleeping bag, stretched and yawned. "Morning, sunshine."

Angel re-sheathed the knife, trying not to grit her teeth. "Why are you here?"

"Just thought I'd come for a chat."

"How is it you're so damn anxious about everything else, but you never listen when I tell you not to take me by surprise?"

"Hey." He sat up. "Come on. I've been better recently."

This was true, sort of. He'd stopped washing his hands so much, at least, though maybe that was only because it was impossible to keep anything clean in this muddy, rain-washed environment. The counting had got worse, though. Some days he counted everything:

8

his footsteps, trees, people, even the words out of his mouth.

It would be petty to point this out. It was hardly like he didn't know. Instead she sat beside him and eased her trainers off, trying not to wince. "How come you're up so early, anyway?"

"Looking for you. You've been avoiding me."

A stab of guilt, sharper than the pain in her feet. "That's not –"

"Oh, please. You run and you work in the infirmary, that's all you do. And every time you see me, you run the other way."

So perhaps that was true. Angel sighed. "I'm sorry."

"You don't have to apologise."

"No. I am." She was being unfair. He needed someone to talk to, even if she didn't.

He peered at her feet. "You're bleeding."

"So?" She didn't think she could stand it, though. She knew what he wanted to talk about, and the very idea was like stepping onto a high wire in a howling gale.

"*So* your medical supplies aren't gonna last forever. *So* you know the Board are coming for us eventually, and when they do it'd probably help if you could run away without limping."

When she said nothing, he sighed. It was the first time in months she'd heard something approaching exasperation in his tone. "Angel."

She made herself glance at him.

"You miss her."

I can't do this. "Don't you?"

9

"Of course! I mean, if *miss* is the right word for someone who's rude and grumpy ninety percent of the time." When she didn't smile, he laid a hand on her shoulder. "I think about her all the time. Of course I do. But... Angel. It's like you're broken. I mean, I feel like if I picked a fight with you right now, I'd kick your arse. How messed up is *that*?"

Despite herself, Angel almost grinned. "Yeah, right, Mack. You wish."

His bright bird's eyes watched her face. She looked away.

"You need to talk to someone," he said. "You're gonna go crazy otherwise."

"I'm pretty sure if I talk about this I'll go crazy."

"Nah. I don't think that's how it works."

But when she opened her mouth her heartbeat filled her throat, choking her. She got to her feet instead.

Mackenzie rolled his eyes. "What, you're gonna go for another run? Sit down, Angel. You're not a machine."

"No," Angel said under her breath. "But I wish I was."

He waited.

"It's everything." She sat back down, digging her nails into her palms. "We've got no idea what we're doing here, what's happening in the South. I mean, great, we stopped the Board releasing the virus. Now what?"

"Everyone here would be dead if we hadn't blown up that lab," Mackenzie reminded her gently. "And lots more, too."

"And we might all still get blown up tomorrow. I *hate* not having any control. I can't stand it."

"Yeah, I know. Me either. But... Angel..."

She screwed her eyes shut. "I don't need to talk about this."

"Bollocks."

"Mack –"

"It's not really about that, is it? It's about her."

She tried to focus on her burning feet, like the pain could stop her disintegrating. "It's not just –"

"Yeah, it is. How could it not be?"

Angel's ears rang. For a moment there was nothing but darkness: a vortex of rage and grief and the aching hole in her chest where her heart should have been. Any second now she was going to lose her grip on the world, she was going to open her mouth and scream at Mackenzie, who was only trying to help, who was the closest to understanding, if anyone possibly could, how she felt: *how is talking going to help? Will it bring her back? Will it make me want to keep breathing?*

She pressed her bloody feet into the groundsheet and kept her mouth and her eyes shut.

Mackenzie's voice, soft. "Angel..."

The tent canvas rattled. "Angel? You there?"

Thank God. She blinked, slowly. "Come in."

An olive-skinned young man with a Roman nose and an untidy ponytail stuck his head in: Jake, a couple of years older than her at twenty-one, who'd worked as a healthcare assistant in what the community referred to as

'Before'. Before the Wall went up. Before everything they knew had been obliterated.

"Susie needs you in the infirmary," he said. "Soz."

"Col?"

"Yeah."

"Okay."

He ducked out. Angel pulled her trainers back on, swallowing the pain.

Mackenzie sighed. "And you're off again."

"I can hardly say no, Mack."

"He's really sick, huh?"

She nodded.

"Off you go, then. Save some lives."

"Sorry." She didn't mean it. Col and his tooth infection had saved her.

"Angel," Mackenzie said, as she was leaving. Reluctantly, she looked back.

"I'll be here," he said. "When you're ready. I'll be here."

Outside, Jake was stamping his feet and rubbing his hands together; early April, and the mornings still dawned with a biting chill. He gave Angel a grateful nod as she jogged towards the barn that housed the infirmary.

The settlement had been here two years by the time she, Mackenzie, Col, Joss and Lydia had arrived eight weeks ago on a freezing February night. The North had had no electricity, fuel or clean water for a year before that. In contrast to the festering devastation of the towns, this remote corner of the Yorkshire Dales was a haven: the land was fertile, sheep and wild animals roamed the hillsides, and a clear, rocky stream – a precious resource – flowed through the valley. The community had pooled their skills, learned to work together. And to be fair, they'd done all right. There had even been a few babies, though why anyone would want to bring a child into this post-apocalyptic nightmare was beyond Angel.

But the North was just emerging from a bitter winter and the nearest other settlement was at least a day's walk away. Here, you could die from an infected blister or the flu. And people did.

The community had worked hard to make the infirmary habitable. They'd even installed a wood-burning stove, making it easily the settlement's most comfortable spot. Camp beds were arranged in neat rows, and the sick and injured were tended to by a handful of former doctors and nurses. Their unofficial boss was Susie, a pink-cheeked woman with a pleasant, lined face and grey-streaked hair.

Susie smiled as Angel edged into the barn, but her brow was even more furrowed than usual. "Hiya, love. How're you doing?"

Angel sidestepped the question. "How is he?"

Susie grimaced. "He was having seizures, and then he stopped. He hasn't come round. I doubt he will now."

Angel crossed to the dim corner where Col lay, grey-faced, one cheek shiny red and swollen. He was unrecognisable as the person he'd been only two weeks ago.

He'd developed an abscess on his tooth, but hadn't mentioned it until one night around the fire when Angel had noticed he was picking at his food and shivering despite the flames. He'd brushed away her concern – "Just toothache. I'll swill a bit of saltwater, it'll be right."

It hadn't been right. The next day he'd collapsed, and though they'd dragged him to the infirmary and pumped him full of antibiotics, it hadn't done any good.

"The infection's in his brain," Susie murmured at Angel's shoulder, and Angel jumped. "His organs are shutting down."

Angel pressed her fingers into her eyes. "Can we do anything?"

"Probably not. Even if he lived, he wouldn't be the same. What'd we do with him then? Is that even what he'd want?"

Modern medicine was a distant memory up here. The community's initial suspicion of their new arrivals had been tempered by Angel's backpack of medical supplies. When those were gone there would be no more, and giving Col antibiotics had been a contentious decision in the first place. "He's too sick," Fiona, a former cardiac nurse, had argued. "Those could save loads of other lives."

She was right, and Angel didn't even like Col, but guilt had driven her to appeal to Susie regardless: "We have to at least try." She hadn't pulled out the bigger weapon: *if it weren't for us, you wouldn't have any meds to decide what to do with.*

Susie had backed her up, but Col was dying anyway.

"We need to make a decision," Susie said quietly, now.

Angel picked at her thumb. It started to bleed. "You're the doctor."

"I know what I'd do. I'm askin' if you're okay with that."

Angel didn't know Col well, outside of blowing up a building together, but she was certain he would hate the idea of losing control of himself. She took a deep breath. "No more treatment."

Susie squeezed her arm. "Good lass."

Angel pulled her sleeve over her thumb to hide it from Susie's pointed glance. "Can we make him any more comfortable?"

"I don't think anything'd touch him. We just have to wait." Susie steered her towards a rickety table beside the glowing stove. "You look a right waif, girl."

"I eat my share."

Susie gave her a sharp look. "Then you're doin' too much. D'you think I haven't seen you, running all over the bloody hills at all hours?" She laid a small, flat loaf in front of Angel. "Here."

The words on the tip of Angel's tongue, waiting to fall, were: *you're not my mother*. She bit the inside of her cheek hard. It would be beyond cruel to let them slip out. Susie had been kind, let Angel help in the infirmary even though she had no proper medical training, taught her new things.

She'd lost people. She never talked about it. She just bustled around, alternately fussing over people and barking orders. When she emerged from the infirmary she ground wheat or washed clothes in the stream or

15

stoked the fire pit, keeping up a cheerful chatter the whole time.

And occasionally, in the depths of the night when the infirmary was shadowy and still, Angel would see her across the barn rubbing her hands over her face, her shoulders heaving like she was trying to relieve them of an unbearable, unshakeable weight.

Any time they skirted the edge of a personal conversation, Angel took off running. She wouldn't have been able to bear Susie's kindness.

She nudged the bread away. "Someone else'll need it."

"You need it, you daft creature. Get it down you."

Arguing would be pointless. Angel picked up the bread and tried to smile.

3

FUNERAL

Col died in the afternoon. Susie sat sponging his sweat-sheened face, patting his hand as his breath rattled in and out, slower and slower until at last it disappeared altogether. Angel stayed away, tending to a young woman named Cara with food poisoning. "My own fault," Cara croaked with a weak grin, between heaves. "Should've known the meat was off."

Susie materialised and touched Angel's shoulder. Angel flinched.

"He's gone," Susie murmured. "Go get some muscle, there's a good lass. We need to get him out of here."

The dead were burned on a hilltop well away from the camp. Funerals were frequent enough that the ridge was scorched black and grey, the vegetation long gone. Tonight they would build a pyre for Col and light it with torches, and the adults would drink the horrible eye-watering alcohol brewed with whatever fruit and vegetables were to hand, and maybe someone would say a few words.

Angel went to find Joss and Lydia. They'd come here together, the five of them, after all. It would be cruel to ask Mackenzie to help; handling a dead body would send his anxiety through the roof. Besides, he and Col had not been fond of each other.

Lydia was butchering a sheep, wrapped in a blood-stained sheet and wielding an alarmingly large knife. "All right, kid?" she asked as Angel approached.

"Col's dead."

Lydia lowered the knife. "Ah, shit." She shook her head. "Shame."

Angel pressed her feet into the bloody ground.

"Someone gettin' the fire going?"

"Some of the guys have gone for wood. Can you help me move the body?"

Lydia nodded. The temperature was barely in double figures but she was in a vest under the sheet, muscles rippling under scarred skin as brown as the earth around them. "Go grab Joss." She lifted the sheep by its hind legs. "I'll be right with you."

Joss was chopping wood at the bottom of the hill. When Angel told him about Col he just sighed, wiped the sweat out of his eyes, and followed her to the infirmary.

The whole community was there when they lit Col's pyre at sunset. Not because he'd been especially popular

– though he'd pulled his weight, he hadn't exactly had a knack for making friends. Perhaps it wasn't so surprising the community had struggled to warm to them, what with Col stomping around like a surly raincloud and Angel not speaking at all if she could help it. There was only one person she wanted to talk to now, and she couldn't.

At least Mackenzie and Joss tried, chatting to their neighbours, even playing with the kids. But no – few people were actually mourning Col tonight. The funeral was an excuse to gather in the firelight, eat and drink, sing and dance: a diversion from the relentless, numbing pressure of everyday life.

Angel's preferred strategy on these occasions was to hole up with the sickest person she could find until the fire died down and the last of the group stumbled back to their tents. But Susie had banned her from the infirmary tonight – "It's been a rough day, and you can't be in here all the time. Where's the harm in bein' sociable for a few hours?"

And if she hid in her tent Mackenzie would come to find her. At least this way she could claim to be making an effort. So the plan was to stick near Lydia, who wasn't much of a talker either, look busy if Mackenzie approached, and hopefully get so blackout drunk on the horrible home brew that she wouldn't have to think about anything until morning.

Unfortunately, she only managed a few mouthfuls of the home brew – at least this batch was made with apples, it was better than Jake's carrot experiment – before Nadira made a beeline for her.

Reluctantly, Angel handed the bottle to Lydia. It would not be a good idea to get too drunk to stand whilst talking to Nadira, who along with her partner Rhys appeared to view herself as some sort of community figurehead and made clear at every opportunity that she considered Angel and the others an inconvenient and disruptive presence.

"Angel, hi." Nadira still talked like the business development manager – *what even was that?* – she'd been Before. "We don't normally see you at these things."

"Susie gave me the night off," Angel said. "Col was a friend. Sort of."

Nadira patted her arm and Angel recoiled before she could stop herself. "This must be hard for you."

Angel bit back a bark of laughter. "Yeah. You know."

Lydia had wandered off. *Damn.* She and Joss were silhouetted against the pyre, talking to a couple Angel didn't know. Mackenzie, further from the flames, appeared to have a small child on his shoulders.

"I'm glad I caught you," Nadira barrelled on. "I wanted to check in about your Board issue."

She always made it sound like some inter-office squabble she'd been called in to adjudicate. "You mean the *issue* with the Board trying to massacre everyone here?" Angel said. "You know as much as I do, Nadira."

Nadira huffed a little sigh through her nostrils as though Angel were being needlessly dramatic. "I just wondered if you'd heard anything."

"What, on my secret bat phone?"

"No, I just thought –"

"What did you think?"

Nadira's eyes narrowed. Angel bit her tongue. *You're on the same side. Stop making things worse.*

Like things could possibly get any worse.

"I'm sorry." She tried to sound like she meant it. "It's... been a tough day."

Nadira adopted an air of magnanimous sympathy. "Of course." She patted Angel's arm again. Angel made herself stand still this time and tried to look grateful. "It's just – people are anxious. You show up in a big flap about the Board and an explosion and a virus, and since then – well, everything's just carried on as normal."

"What exactly did you expect? It'll be months before the runners you sent to other settlements come back. Even then, we still need to decide what we're actually going to do. Nobody said this would be easy."

"I'm just saying, it would be nice to have *some* sort of plan –"

"*Nadira* –" Too late, Angel realised she'd shouted. She clamped her mouth shut, her heart thumping like it might punch through her ribcage.

"Everything okay?" Rhys, freckle-faced, built like a rugby player, materialised behind Nadira, his hand resting easily on her shoulder.

Out of nowhere, Lydia slung an arm around Angel. "All right, kid?"

Angel made herself unclench her fists.

"We're fine," Nadira said sweetly. "Aren't we, Angel? We were just talking."

Rhys looked Angel up and down. "We did say we needed a chat, didn't we?"

"Maybe now's not the best time," Lydia said, surreptitiously tightening her hold on Angel. "What with us payin' our respects to Col and all. Emotional day, right, Angel?"

Angel couldn't move. Lydia gave her a gentle wobble. "C'mon, kid. Let's go sit down."

"We'll catch up soon," Nadira said. "Good talking to you, Angel."

She and Rhys turned away, murmuring to each other. Angel watched them, trying to make out their words, until Lydia steered her away. "Don't get stroppy, kid. You'll only have to apologise later."

Angel groaned and sat down on a log with a bump, digging her knuckles into her eyes. The smoke was making them sting. "I don't think I can face it."

"Tough shit. You can't go pickin' fights with our *community leaders.*" Lydia's last two words were redolent with sarcasm. "Just stay away from 'em for tonight and we'll go and make nice tomorrow. I'll even come with you, how does that sound?"

Angel peered at her from between her fingers. "It sounds bloody awful."

Lydia laughed, a deep, throaty chuckle. "Yeah, well, never mind. Now, you gonna eat something?"

Angel shook her head. "I'll have a drink, though, if there's some going."

Lydia squinted dubiously at her. "Not sure that's the

best idea, kid. Don't want you startin' on someone else 'cos they looked at you funny."

"Fine." Angel stood up. "I'll go to bed."

Lydia sighed. "C'mon, Angel –"

But Angel was already walking away.

She heard people return to their tents, a trickle and then a flood. Tears from over-tired children and their parents trying to soothe them. Low voices, snatches of song, the odd thud when someone fell over a guy rope.

At some point, Mackenzie's worried voice: "Did she seem okay?"

And Lydia: "Eh, we all know she's not. Honestly, I thought she was gonna nut Nadira."

More rustling, whispers, giggling that turned into quiet moans and groans. There was no privacy here. Everyone heard everything, and everyone knew everything about each other.

Finally, quiet settled. Angel stared into the blackness, counting her breaths. In, out. In, out.

Don't fall asleep. Don't fall asleep.

At some point, she stopped thinking.

Next thing, she was bolt upright, drenched in sweat. She gasped for air, but it was like someone had a plastic bag over her face. She wrestled her way out of a sleeping bag that had become an over-heated, stifling cocoon, and her head hit the canvas, closing her in.

When she pulled her trainers on her fingers felt

clumsy, like they didn't belong to her. A high-pitched whine rang in her ears.

Someone crashed into her tent. Angel leapt up, her hand already at the knife in her belt. Outside, Mackenzie called, breathless: "Angel? Angel!"

She wanted to ignore him, but he would just let himself in again.

"*Angel!*"

"All *right*! Jesus." She wrenched the tent open. "What is it, like six in the morning? Last night wasn't *that* bad, for God's sake —"

Mackenzie was trembling, his face as pale as the sun-bleached horizon. He grabbed her arm. "*Listen.*"

What was he on about? "I can't hear any —"

And then she could.

The whining drone wasn't inside her head. It was a rhythmic, far-off whir, moving steadily closer.

People started scrambling out of tents, sleep-rumpled and frantic. "What is that? What's going on?"

Mackenzie was still clutching her arm. "D'you think it's the Board?" he whispered.

He was practically vibrating with terror. Angel knew she should be too, but she couldn't feel anything at all.

"Come on," she said, because she knew he needed her to. "I suppose we should go see."

Mackenzie screwed his eyes closed, his lips moving frantically. Angel waited in silence for him to finish counting. If she interrupted he'd have to start all over again, and while she didn't think it was helpful to encourage him to live life around his rituals, now was probably not the time to address that.

All around them, people craned towards the distant speck of the helicopter. "It's coming closer –"

"It's gonna land over there –"

"Should we run?"

Cara, the girl with food poisoning, was crying quietly. Susie put a weary arm around her. "There, now. Let's not panic yet."

Joss, standing behind Susie with Lydia, gave Angel a sort of resigned grimace.

Mackenzie opened his eyes, looking sick. "Okay. Let's go."

He squinted at the helicopter, now hovering two hilltops over. A frown spread across his face.

"Angel...?" he said. "I... don't think that's the Board."

An icy stab, piercing and numbing. Terror. Disbelief. And the faintest treacherous, irrepressible trickle of hope.

"And... there's only one. Wouldn't the Board send lots?"

Angel stopped thinking.

She didn't feel her feet as she ran, didn't wonder whether Mackenzie would follow her – though he did, she could hear him crashing through the frost-encrusted nettles behind her. She couldn't slow down for him.

She couldn't breathe again as she reached the crest of the hill, and it had nothing to do with the running.

The helicopter touched down. The spinning blades slowed and stopped.

Angel faltered. Now what?

She lurched forward. Mackenzie caught up with her, gasping, and grabbed her wrist. She spun to face him. "Mack –"

"Just – wait," he said quietly. "Please. I can't watch you get shot."

At least one of them still had some sense. She fumbled for his hand, squeezed tight.

The helicopter door opened.

The figure it revealed was slight, pale, dressed in black, her dark-blonde hair pulled into a plait. She hovered at the top of the steps, scanning the hillside uncertainly.

Angel's vision blurred. The world spun like a whirlpool.

This isn't real.

It can't be.

But she flew towards the helicopter anyway, and as she did so the other girl flung herself down the steps, the uncertainty swept from her face in a starburst of joy and relief. They collided, laughing and sobbing, and there was warm, solid flesh under Angel's hands as she gasped, "You're alive, you're alive –" and then Mackenzie flung himself on them too, so that all three of them landed in a heap on the frozen ground.

And Skyler, her eyes over-bright, struggled to sit up under their combined weight and said, deadpan, "Did you miss me?"

Mackenzie sat up too. "Nah," he said, grinning at her. "Not really."

And then he burst into tears as well.

4

BARGAINING

Two hours.

Two hours since they'd hurtled through the Wall into the barren blackness of the North. Two hours of jolting over cracked roads, of listening for aircraft, of waiting for gunfire, for the world to explode into light.

Two hours of Skyler's skin, icy cold. Of her blood soaking their clothes. Of fumbling for the weakening flutter of her pulse. Of waiting, in agony, for every next breath to come.

Angel, white-faced right down to her lips, hands stained crimson in the light from Lydia's torch, words clipped as though she was afraid a scream might escape instead: "Pass me the gauze. The tape. Hold that. Don't move."

Mackenzie, clinging to Skyler's hand, willing her to open her eyes, to sit up and demand to know what the fuck he thought he was doing: *she'll be all right as long as I don't think the wrong words. She'll be all right as long as*

I count to fifty before Angel speaks again. She'll be all right. She'll be all right. She'll be –

"She's not breathing properly," Angel said flatly.

Mackenzie jerked his head up. "What? What do you –?"

"She's bleeding into her chest cavity. Her lung can't inflate." Angel began to feel along Skyler's ribcage. "Lyd, I need a scalpel and a plastic tube. Mack, hold her still."

"I – I don't – what do you want me to –?"

"Hold her still, Mackenzie!"

Mackenzie gripped Skyler's shoulders, choking down a sob. Angel raised the scalpel and sliced between two of her ribs.

Blood spilled out – more blood, surely she couldn't afford to lose any more? – and Angel, with a shuddering breath, took the plastic tube and shoved it into the incision.

Mackenzie had been terrified Skyler would scream, but the ragged sigh she gave instead was so much worse. She didn't open her eyes.

Blood trickled from the tube onto the floor. Angel dropped back and buried her face in her hands.

Mackenzie looked frantically between her and Lydia. "Did it work? Is she gonna be okay?"

Angel stared dully at the new pool of blood. "It worked."

"Is she gonna be –"

He was almost relieved to be cut off, because of course Skyler wasn't going to be okay. But his relief was short-lived, because the interruption came in the form of the deafening clack of all-too-close helicopter blades and the blinding whiteness of a massive spotlight.

The truck swerved. "Jesus!" Joss yelled from the driver's seat.

"Fucking *hell*," Lydia muttered.

An unnaturally amplified voice boomed from overhead. "STOP THE VEHICLE. COME OUT WITH YOUR HANDS UP."

Joss accelerated, but the spotlight kept pace with them. In its glare, Skyler's face was more grey than white.

"PULL OVER OR WE OPEN FIRE. YOU HAVE TEN SECONDS TO COMPLY."

Joss slammed on the brakes and turned to the rest of them. Mackenzie looked at Angel, but she was blank-faced, staring at Skyler. She might as well have been carved out of stone.

"FIVE SECONDS."

Well, they were probably all dead anyway. "Screw it," Mackenzie mumbled, and slid out into the freezing night.

Behind him, Lydia sniffed. "Dunno if he's brave or stupid. C'mon, then, Joss."

The twins emerged, followed by Col. Mackenzie raised his hands, screwed his eyes shut against the desperate staccato of his pulse, and waited for the lights to go out.

When, sixty seconds later, he wasn't dead, he decided to risk opening his eyes.

The helicopter had landed. Two strangers stood in front of them: a willowy Caucasian woman with a smooth bun, and a slim man of East Asian descent with square glasses and slicked-back hair. Both of them carried handguns, but – and this was the important bit – the guns weren't actually aimed at anyone.

Their matching expressions of supreme disapproval, however, definitely were. "Where are the others?" the woman demanded. "The girl who sent the video?"

Mackenzie frowned. Her accent wasn't British; it might have been German. Which meant these people weren't Army. Nor, from their crisp white shirts and dark suits, were they the Board's special agents, the greycoats.

The woman cocked her pistol. "In case anyone is in doubt, that question wasn't optional."

She looked far too much like she meant it. "They're in the truck," Mackenzie blurted, before anyone else got shot. "They can't come out. She's – Skyler's – hurt. Like, really hurt."

The strangers exchanged glances.

The woman lowered her gun a fraction. "Well, you're covered in blood, so we'll give you the benefit of the doubt. Any sudden moves, though, and we *will* shoot."

"Understood," Mackenzie mumbled.

"So," the man said. "You're the terrorists."

"Fuck off," Lydia snapped. "We're not terrorists."

This whole not-getting-shot endeavour was off to a great start.

"Tell that to the Board," the German woman said.

There was a puzzled silence.

"Huh?" Mackenzie said.

Joss scratched his chin. "Just so we're clear... you're sayin' you're *not* Board?"

The suited man looked genuinely offended. "Of course not. We're an autonomous international agency. We're here to offer you a deal. Work for us, and we'll help you clear up the mess you've made."

Mackenzie glanced at Lydia, whose twitching fingers suggested there was a moderate chance she was about to shoot someone.

"Can I just point out," Joss said, in the tone of someone determined to be reasonable in the face of extreme provocation, "that you were threatening to blow us up not five minutes ago?"

"Well, you wouldn't have pulled over otherwise. It would have been difficult to explain all this from mid-air."

"Yeah," Col said, beside Lydia. His stance suggested he wouldn't have minded a fight, though there was nothing particularly remarkable about that. "Thanks but no thanks. This is our fight. We don't need your help."

The German woman looked him up and down. "I'm sure your sophisticated approach of head-butting things into submission is exactly what the North needs. Tell us. Did it occur to any of you geniuses that the Board might just react to your stunt by, say, flattening what's left of the North?"

Mackenzie felt like he'd swallowed a lump of freezing concrete. "Is – is that what they've done?"

"Luckily, not yet. India and the Scandinavian Coalition have threatened retaliation if they do. That seems to have deterred them for now, but it's hard to say how long that will last. My point stands. If you want to do anything more with the Board than punch things or run them over, you need our help."

Mackenzie's head was threatening to explode. These strangers were possibly mad, possibly lying, certainly didn't give a shit that they were about to goad someone into some sort of irreversible action – and none of that mattered, because Angel and Skyler were still in the truck, alone, and by now Skyler might be –

Nonononono. Don't. Don't think that.

They were out of time and out of options. He had to do *something*.

He gestured at the truck. "Please. If you really mean it – if you really want to help us – Skyler needs help. Like, right now."

"What happened?" the man asked.

"She got shot in the stomach. I –" The words stuck like fish bones in his throat. "I think it's really bad."

The woman sighed as though this was a substantial inconvenience, pulled out a radio and had a short, terse exchange in a language Mackenzie didn't understand. A few moments later, another woman and man emerged from the helicopter, dressed in green and manoeuvring a stretcher laden with medical equipment. The man had an oxygen cylinder under one arm. They looked the part, at least.

The German woman strode towards the truck. Mackenzie, eyeing her gun, hurried to get there first. "Uh. Could you maybe, like... hang back a bit?"

There was no sound from inside the truck.

Mackenzie would have given anything not to have to open the door.

"If things are so critical," the woman said in his ear, "you'd better get on with it."

She was right, unfortunately. Mackenzie reached for the truck door, bracing himself, but before he got there, it flew open.

Angel's pale face was smeared with blood, her eyes wide and wild like a cornered animal's. She crouched in front of them, pistol in hand. "What's going on, Mackenzie?"

Mackenzie stared at Skyler's motionless form. "Is – is she –?"

"She's... holding on. Who the hell are these people?"

"Er. They're some kind of international... something. They're –"

"Currently your only chance of survival," the agent said from behind him. "Come out. Now."

Brilliant. Thanks, random woman, that was really super helpful. Mackenzie glanced at Angel's fingers, which were white around her gun. "This really might not be the best way to –"

"I really don't care. And your friend is dying. You'd better let our medics see her."

Mackenzie took a deep breath and held out a cautious hand to Angel. "C'mon. It's okay. They're gonna help her."

Angel climbed out, her eyes fixed on the woman. Mackenzie exhaled quietly. "Okay. Okay. Let's just –"

Angel levelled her pistol at the male paramedic's head. "If you hurt her –"

The safety catch on the agent's gun made a quiet, definitive *click*. "You will not threaten my staff. Stand down *now*, or we'll let your friend die."

Mackenzie dived between them, hands raised. "She's not gonna shoot," he babbled over his shoulder at the woman. "She's not gonna shoot." He swung back to Angel, his heart pounding. "Angel – please. Please. I know it's scary, but – I think we need the help. *She* needs help."

Angel looked through him.

"Please, Angel. Put the gun down. Look – we'll stay here, okay, where we can see them. They're not gonna hurt her."

For a moment he wasn't even sure she could hear him. At last, slowly, she lowered her weapon.

Mackenzie's legs shook with what was probably, in the circumstances, somewhat premature relief as the agent lowered hers too and the medics moved towards the truck.

"I don't get it," he said to the agents, keeping one eye on Angel as they rejoined the rest of the group. "Why would you want to help us? You don't know anything about us."

"You've pulled off something impressive," the man said. "Reckless, mind, and not exactly sophisticated – but clearly you did the best you could with what you had. Our agency sympathises with your cause, and we're always looking for talented staff."

"I think," Lydia said, "we might need to know a bit more about this agency of yours."

"Isn't there some British saying about beggars and choosers?"

"Well, forgive us for havin' a few reservations, but we were just in the middle of fleeing one despotic organisation. Wouldn't mind making sure we're not walkin' straight into another one."

"You get the details once you're on board," the man said. "No pun intended. That's kind of the point of a secret organisation. Take it or leave it."

Lydia shifted her weight in a way that suggested her patience was fraying into threads. Mackenzie shook his head frantically at her. Angel was so close to the edge, one wrong move might push her over. Lydia, seeming to understand this, defused a couple of notches.

What now? Mackenzie couldn't read the twins, past 'not impressed'. Angel was still staring at the medics as they flurried around Skyler, now laid on a stretcher. The only two opinions he really wanted might as well have been a thousand miles away.

So... what would Skyler do now?

He pointed at the stretcher. "Save her first."

The German agent's eyebrows shot into her hairline. "You are in no position to make demands."

"You reckon we could be useful to you. Useful enough for you to come all the way here and risk the Board shooting you out of the sky, apparently. Well, I can't speak for the others, but Sky and Angel and me – we come as a package. So if she lives, then we'll talk."

The eyebrows stayed raised. "Or what?"

The hell with it. If Skyler – if they lost her, none of this would matter anyway. "There's no negotiation without Sky. If that means the Board get me instead – so be it."

The woman turned to the twins and Col. "And the rest of you?"

Joss and Lydia shared a long look.

Joss' mouth twitched.

Lydia gave a very small nod.

"We're with them," Joss declared.

Col just threw up his hands.

The male agent shrugged. "Then I guess we're doing it your way."

One of the medics hurried over, her brow furrowed. "We need to get her in the air," she told the agents in a low voice.

At this, finally, Angel stirred. "I'm going with her."

The German agent's lips thinned. "I'm afraid you are not."

Mackenzie would never understand how Angel had managed to hold herself together up to that moment, but that was the point at which she disintegrated. She flung herself in front of the stretcher, her voice rising to a wail: "You can't take her! You can't! I have to stay with her!" She swung to Mackenzie. *"Tell* them! I promised her –"

The medic edged towards Angel. Mackenzie tensed, but the medic stopped at a safe distance, holding up her hands. "Of course you're scared," she said. "Of course you don't want to leave her. And you've done a good job.

You've kept her alive – but she's dying. We can save her, but you have to let us leave *now*."

Everything went still.

Mackenzie held his breath. The Angel he knew would have stepped aside. He had no idea what this Angel might do.

Then she collapsed onto her knees, sobbing into her rust-red hands. Mackenzie sprang forward and pulled her into his arms as the medics hurried to load Skyler into the helicopter.

Angel lifted her head and stared as they carried her past, but Mackenzie couldn't bear to watch. She looked so fragile, so very un-Skyler-like, that she might as well have been a stranger.

The German agent pulled out a phone and started tapping irritably at it. "We're going to need another helicopter."

Col cleared his throat. Mackenzie groaned. Of course it was too much to hope that they get through this whole interaction without Col engaging fight mode.

The woman gave him a flat stare. "Yes?"

"What happens to the rest of us now, then? Are you getting us out of here?"

"Why would we do that? You've been perfectly clear there's no alliance yet."

Mackenzie risked a glance over his shoulder, which confirmed his suspicion that Col was glaring at him like he wanted to murder him. "Then what?" Col snarled. "Are we even gonna live long enough to find out whether she does?"

The agent shrugged as if she didn't much care either way. "According to your own terms, negotiations resume if the girl survives. In the meantime, we'll take you to one of the Northern settlements. The Board can't take on India and Scandinavia single-handed. You should be safe enough until they come up with a new strategy."

"*Should* be? What if we're not?"

"Perhaps you should have thought of that before you started blowing things up. We'll be back. Assuming the girl lives."

5
_____

REUNION

He'd really, really thought she was dead.

For two months, a constant battle had been waging in Mackenzie's head: *there's no way she could've survived.*

They said they could save her.

You're kidding yourself.

She might be okay if I get the rituals right. If I don't picture her like that. If I don't think she might be –

But it had been impossible not to think about it. About her.

He hadn't dared voice any of this to Angel, who was so clearly hanging on by the most insubstantial of threads. She needed to prepare for the worst; they all did. But if they'd talked about it, Angel would have snapped, and Mackenzie wasn't strong enough to hold on alone; he would have gone hurtling down into the void with her.

But now Skyler was laughing and sobbing in Angel's arms on the frosty ground, squeezing Mackenzie's hand like a vice – something she wouldn't have done in a million years under any normal circumstance. She was as pale as ever, but less skinny than she'd been back in the South. The mysterious agency had evidently taken reasonable care of her.

Speaking of which –

The Asian man in his square glasses and the German woman with the air of a headteacher about her were standing over them. This time, they'd brought a friend. She was younger than the others, maybe not much older than Mackenzie himself, with golden-brown skin, a cloud of tight black curls, and kind eyes behind thick-rimmed glasses which she fiddled with as she hovered behind her colleagues.

"Well, we held up our end of the bargain," the man said.

Skyler threw the agents an unfriendly look. "Oh yeah. Apparently we had some sort of deal with this lot."

Angel's jaw tightened almost imperceptibly as her gaze landed on the German woman. Mackenzie winced. *That* relationship would take some radical surgery to repair.

He scrambled to his feet. "You'll want the twins too?"

"Yes," the woman said dryly. "Apparently you come as a package."

"And the other one," the man added. "Angry-looking guy."

Mackenzie hesitated. "He's... not with us anymore."

The woman frowned. "Meaning?"

There were certain words the poisonous little worm

in his brain really didn't like – *it's bad luck, you'll make it happen to someone else* –

"He's dead," Angel said flatly.

The youngest agent's expression wavered into something like sympathy, but the older woman merely flapped a hand. "Fine. Fetch the twins and take us somewhere private."

Mackenzie considered their surroundings, which were mostly mud, a scattering of rather forlorn trees, and chilly-looking sheep. And, hovering just over the ridge of the hill, a cluster of Northerners bursting to know what the hell was going on.

"There's a barn?" he suggested.

The youngest agent's mouth twitched. At least one of them might be a human being.

Mackenzie hurried towards the waiting group, which included the twins, a visibly agitated Nadira and a more phlegmatic Susie. "What's happening?" Nadira demanded, before anyone else could get a word in. "Who are those people?"

"It's fine," Mackenzie said. "They're on our side. Er, probably. They're not Board, anyway."

A ripple of sighs and relieved mutters rolled through the crowd.

"Time to talk business?" Lydia said.

Mackenzie nodded.

Joss rubbed his chin. "Well, they did bring Skyler back. Which is a bloody miracle, considering she had a hole all the way through her. Guess we owe them an audience."

Nadira puffed out her chest. "I do think Rhys and I should be a part of –"

Susie patted her on the back. "Settle down, lass. I'm pretty sure this don't concern us."

Nadira opened her mouth indignantly.

"Oh, shush." Susie turned to Mackenzie. "That's Angel's girl, then? That's your Skyler?"

Mackenzie blinked. "She told you –?"

"Nah, don't be daft. It were just bloody obvious." Susie stared up the hill at the little figures, still clinging together. "About bloody time someone round here got some good news."

The chosen barn was crammed with tools and nearly-exhausted food supplies, all meticulously arranged. Most of this was Mackenzie's doing. Lydia took the piss, but that was fine. Nobody but he and Angel needed to know that this was one of the least harmful ways of shutting up the insidious whine of the worry for a few precious minutes at a time.

He and Joss dragged crates into a circle, but the gathering still ended up with a somewhat adversarial feel. The twins' folded arms and poker faces rivalled the older agents', but Angel's attention was still glued to Skyler, like she was the only important thing in the world.

Mackenzie fidgeted on the edge of his crate, his body buzzing with an all-too-familiar warning hum. The strangers had saved Skyler and, crucially, brought her back. And they were offering something, but they also wanted something in return.

"About our agreement," the German woman began.

Joss raised a hand. "How about you start by introducing yourselves?"

She gave him a flat stare. "Julia Hahn. My colleagues are Ren Kimura" – indicating the man – "and" – with a nod at the younger woman – "Faith Jackson."

"Work experience kid?" Lydia said.

Kimura raised an eyebrow. "Rich, considering you seem to have raided a creche to put your team together."

Joss snorted.

Lydia grinned. "Fair point."

"As we told you before," Kimura said, "we work for an agency without borders, without sovereign control. We keep people safe. Destabilise oppressive regimes. Take down criminals official law enforcement can't touch."

"Great," Skyler said. "This is all news to me, by the way. These fuckers wouldn't even tell me what country I was in." Her eyes narrowed at the agents. "So where the hell have you been until now, if you care so much? Were you not bothered about the Board, or are you just not very good at your jobs?"

There was an uncomfortable pause. Faith and Kimura glanced at Hahn, whose face set momentarily in a way that reminded Mackenzie of his own feelings on the occasions he'd had to restrain himself from trying to strangle Skyler.

Faith frowned. "That's –"

"We're *very* good." Hahn met Skyler's stare head on. "There have been... significant barriers to intervening. But now we have a chance to change that."

43

"Between you, you have some remarkable talents," Kimura interjected. "We're proposing a mutually beneficial agreement."

Skyler was still underwhelmed. "And how much say do we get in this *agreement*? Because I get the distinct impression that you lot think I owe you."

The agents looked nonplussed. Mackenzie found himself caught between suppressing a snort and hoping Skyler wouldn't actually goad these people into shooting them.

Kimura's gaze darted towards Angel, then, when she gave no reaction, to the twins.

Joss chuckled. "She's only sayin' what we're all thinking. Best answer her."

"Think of our actions so far as a... gesture of good faith," Kimura said, with impressive smoothness. "You've already made it clear we can't force you to do anything you don't want to."

"Have we?" Skyler said. "How'd we do that?"

Kimura nodded at Mackenzie. "Your friend's quite the negotiator."

"He is?"

"No need to sound so surprised, Sky," Mackenzie said.

Lydia cracked her knuckles. "Well, that's a lovely sentiment, but we're gonna need specifics. Where'd your Agency come from? How does it work? How do you decide who the good guys are?"

Hahn gestured imperiously at Faith. "Explain."

Faith pushed her glasses up her nose. "The Agency

was co-founded in the sixties by an American and a Russian, right after the Cuban Missile Crisis. They basically just didn't want anyone to get blown off the face of the planet. Our agents come from all over the world, but we're not affiliated with a government or state. Governments are corruptible. We're not."

"Very noble," Joss said dryly.

"We like to think so," Kimura agreed.

"So where *have* you been?" Skyler asked. "'Cause it'd have been a lot more useful if you'd shown up, like, five years ago."

"Well, we're here now," Kimura said. "So unless you've got a time machine, I suggest you get over it and think about how we move forward."

"The fact is," Faith said, "the Board did a great job of cutting the UK off before they put the Wall up. They withdrew from NATO, closed the borders, told the rest of the world – including the South – that the North voted for devolution. People know full well the Board do terrible things, but getting the evidence to intervene is another story."

"Like anyone's bothered trying," Mackenzie muttered.

She met his eyes. "You're absolutely right." There was a heat to her words that cut through the older agents' cool detachment. "People let them get on with it. Out of sight, out of mind. And it's messed up. But now there's a spotlight on the Board, because of you. It won't last long. People will move on soon – so now's the time to act. And we can help you."

"If we work for you," Angel said.

She looked calm, sort of. But she was so flat, so unreadable, that she was almost frightening. "Doing what, exactly?"

"I was under the impression you were bright enough to work that out," Hahn said.

"I want us to be clear."

Hahn sat back. "Skyler's a genius. With an ego to match, apparently. I'm sure she won't be surprised to hear none of our staff can match her –"

"Nope," Skyler said.

"Thomas Mackenzie, meanwhile –"

Mackenzie's stomach lurched. Nobody had called him that in – Christ. Everyone who'd ever known him by that name was –

"Is brilliant." Hahn made this sound rather tedious. "I doubt we have anywhere near your full portfolio, either. And Lydia and Joseph are, evidently, multi-talented. Holding your own in a city run by a particularly ruthless crime lord took... considerable tenacity."

Lydia nudged Joss. "Hear that, *Joseph*? We'll add it to our CVs, eh?"

"And you." Hahn turned back to Angel. "We don't know nearly enough about you, not even your real name. But try as we might to avoid it, we'll always need people like you."

Something dangerous flashed in Skyler's eyes. "What do you mean, *people like her*?"

"I just called you a genius. Please don't embarrass both of us by making me revise my assessment so soon."

Skyler opened her mouth, almost certainly to put herself in the running for some kind of international diplomacy award. As Mackenzie tried frantically to work out how to intervene without pissing her off even more, Angel reached out and touched her hand. Skyler subsided.

"What if I don't want to do that anymore?" Angel said quietly.

Hahn shrugged. "You've been killing people for years. Why stop now?"

There was a long silence.

"Violence is always a last resort," Kimura said eventually, with the manner of someone trying to plaster over a pile of rubble. "We rarely go into operations intending to kill."

"But sometimes you do." Lydia leaned forward. "What if you want us to do something we don't agree with?"

Another shrug from Hahn. "Sometimes we all have to do things we don't want to do."

"That's not an answer."

"Decisions are made by consensus," Kimura said. "But ultimately, we expect... mutual co-operation."

"We do as we're told or you might just decide the Board's not that important, that kind of thing?"

Faith winced.

"Office junior says yes." Lydia folded her arms. "Might want to work on that poker face, kid."

Faith stared at the floor like she wanted it to open up and swallow her. Mackenzie felt a pang of sympathy for her. He knew all about riding in the wake of someone who didn't care what anybody thought of them.

He sighed. This conversation wasn't going to get any easier. "We need to talk things through."

Joss heaved himself to his feet. "Agreed. C'mon, kids. Let's give the agents the VIP lounge."

Outside, the sky had grown dull and heavy. As they headed down the hill to the shelter of a small cluster of trees, fat raindrops began to spatter on the branches.

"Interesting bunch, aren't they?" Joss nudged Angel. "You're proper quiet, kid. What're you thinking?"

Angel picked at her thumb, then covered it with her sleeve when it started to bleed. Skyler watched her, her perennial scowl softening and sharpening at once: care and worry, the same leaden weight Mackenzie dragged around every waking moment. He'd figured that as soon as Angel saw Skyler, the fog of grief and uncertainty and terror would burn away and underneath would be the old Angel, solid and unshakeable. But she still looked like a ghost.

Skyler touched her arm. Angel blinked.

"I... don't like them," she said. "But that doesn't mean we shouldn't work with them. You've spent the last two months with them, Sky. What do you think?"

Skyler's face pinched. "I was in some hospital the whole time. I didn't have a clue what was happening for the first couple of weeks, and after that the only people I saw were nurses and doctors who couldn't tell me a bloody thing. Hahn turned up eventually to try and shut me up. She told me you guys were okay the last time she saw you – which was *super* fucking reassuring – and then she fucked off again till last night. I only met Kimura and Faith today. Kimura's a smartarse, but he's fine. He got that all I wanted was to see you guys. Faith just does what she's told. She's some sort of assistant, I think." She sighed. "Don't get me wrong, I'm all grateful I didn't die and stuff, but I don't think we should do anything bad for them. How'd you even convince them to help me, anyway? I think Hahn's still pissed about it."

"You can thank Mack for that." Angel smiled, sounding something like her normal self for the first time. "He told them if they didn't save you, he'd turn himself over to the Board."

Skyler looked startled. "You did that for me?"

"Yeah." Lydia yawned. "It were proper heartwarming."

"And they say they want to help us." Angel was picking her thumb again, a bright crimson bead welling at the bed of the nail. "But which way round is it? Do they want to take down the Board and our skills are a bonus? Or are they just out for what they can get, and this is the carrot to convince us?"

"I can answer that," a quiet Canadian voice said behind them.

As one, they spun to face the youngest agent.

"Jesus," Joss said. "What're you, some sort of bloody ninja?"

Faith's dark blazer was pulled tight against the rain, droplets gathering on her glasses and in her hair. She smiled. "I came down because – well, Hahn and Kimura

49

aren't always exactly personable, right? And I figured you should know the whole story."

Lydia rolled her eyes. "Do we really have to hear the whole thing about there being a heart of gold in there somewhere?"

"No," Faith said flatly. "But you should hear this. We knew nothing about your skills when we set out looking for you that night. Yes, it helps that you've got something to offer, and you'll be expected to pull your weight. But – no offence – none of you are worth taking on an entire regime for. Hahn and Kimura got in that helicopter because they care. The Board needs to go. We want to take it down."

Nobody spoke. Skyler and Lydia's expressions were both more scathing than sceptical. Angel's blankness was, if possible, even more unnerving. Even Joss looked dubious.

But Mackenzie believed Faith. She wasn't cold and steely like Skyler, but her conviction was a force, none-theless.

If he said that aloud, Skyler would definitely call him a soft touch.

"Maybe you won't believe me," Faith added. "Maybe you'll just think they sent the work experience kid down to play good cop. I would, probably. But the fact is – you sent out a plea for help, and we answered. As far as I can tell, we're the only ones who did. So... how bad do you want this?"

Without waiting for an answer, she turned and walked away.

"Ugh." Skyler wrinkled her nose. "I hate to say it, but she might have a point."

"They do want stuff from us, though." Mackenzie chewed his lip. "And what they want from Angel isn't like breaking into a building or writing a virus."

Skyler reached for Angel's hand. "Well, they can't actually force us to do anything, right? So what if, whatever they ask, we decide as a team whether it's okay? We look after each other. No matter what."

Angel nodded slowly. "I... think I could do that. Mack?"

A team. "Aw, hell." Mackenzie rubbed his eyes, trying not to grin too hard. "Yeah, let's do that."

"Beautiful." Joss clapped his hands. "Let's all get matching friendship bracelets too. What d'you reckon, then, Lyd? Are we with them?"

"I dunno. I mean, they talk a good talk, and they did save Skyler's life. But..." Lydia cracked her knuckles. "I'm not dead keen on the idea of working *for* anyone, to be honest."

"Aye," Joss agreed. "And this is all well and good, but what if this lot turn out to be the evil overlords after all?"

Mackenzie glanced between them. "You're not coming, are you?"

"Let's be real," Joss said. "Lyd and that Hahn woman'd end up killing each other in about three days. And really, it don't seem like a great idea to put all our eggs in one basket."

Mackenzie would have felt a lot better with the twins on board, especially considering how absent Angel had been. But Skyler could take on a bunch of fancy suits any day.

He sighed. "Maybe you're right."

Joss clapped him on the shoulder. "You three should go. Skyler'll be able to do all sorts of fancy computer shit. But there should be a plan B. Just in case."

"And you guys are okay with that?"

The twins grinned at each other. "We like a challenge," Lydia said.

Skyler jerked her head up the hill. "We've got company."

Hahn was indeed marching through the wet grass towards them. "Well?" she demanded.

"Me and Joss aren't comin'," Lydia said.

"Fine. And the rest of you?"

Skyler raised her chin. "We'll work with you, if you're serious about bringing down the Board. But we work as a team. No exceptions."

Hahn gave a very faint, stiff smile. "You're stubborn people."

"Yep."

"Some people would be so grateful to be alive they'd agree to anything."

"Yeah," Skyler said. "That's not really our style."

"Evidently. Collect your things. We leave in thirty minutes."

"Where are we going?" Mackenzie asked.

Hahn was already striding away. "Copenhagen."

6
___

SAFE

Half an hour later, they were in the air.

Everything was happening too fast. All Angel wanted was to be alone with Skyler, to cling to her, to ask, *Are you sure you're okay? Are you really better?* She'd thought she was dreaming when Skyler first appeared, that her brain, knowing how close she was to letting go of everything, had conjured a mirage to trick her into holding on. She'd believed that right up to the moment she'd fallen into Skyler's arms.

But the relief, the certainty, kept slipping through her fingers like oil. And she couldn't read Hahn or Kimura. Usually she could see straight through anyone, every shift in stance, every tensing muscle; now she didn't know anything. They'd placed their trust in these cold, clinical people who claimed they wanted to help and wanted her to kill for them, and Angel had no idea how catastrophic a mistake she'd made.

"So what's the deal?" Skyler demanded, as the Dales

dwindled beneath them. "How do we take down the Board?"

Kimura held up a pacifying hand. "There's no need to dive straight in. We'll discuss it nearer the time."

"How much time do you think we've *got*?"

Hahn regarded Skyler dispassionately. Mackenzie, clearly registering the emergence of Skyler's trademark *I'm-not-taking-this-shit* scowl, interrupted hastily. "What happens in Copenhagen?"

"One of our biggest bases is there, including accommodation," Kimura said. "You'll work from there for now."

"There are ground rules that apply to all employees," Hahn added. "The office's cover is as an investment bank, so you'll need to stay inside until we're confident you won't draw attention locally. No wandering out looking like you've been dragged through a hedge backwards, in other words. Certain areas, like the basements, are restricted. *No* illegal activity once you get internet access" – this to Skyler, who rolled her eyes – "and," with a fleeting glance at Angel, "absolutely no physical violence."

"Unless you're telling us to do it," Skyler said.

Hahn didn't miss a beat. "Yes."

Her gaze kept darting towards Angel. Angel might as well have been made of glass: every flicker of uncertainty, every flaw in her foundations felt like it was on display.

This woman's not your enemy.

So why did it feel like she was scouring for cracks in Angel's armour?

"You'll have a few days to settle in," Kimura said. "It will take time to adjust to being safe and comfortable. We'll ask for your help on smaller ops so we can get to know you while we work out a strategy for the Board."

"Can we go back to the 'employee' thing?" Skyler said. "Traditionally, employees get paid."

"Consider your payment for now to be your room and board, plus your rather significant medical expenses," Kimura said. "As well as protection from the UK government, who, in case you've forgotten, would still very much like a word with you."

"So... we get fed?"

Hahn's nostrils flared. "Yes, you get fed."

Two hours later, the helicopter landed on a flat rooftop in bright, chilly sunshine.

"Welcome to Copenhagen," Kimura said.

Skyler wrapped her arms around herself. "If this place is so top secret, how do you explain all the helicopters?"

"Investment bank, remember?" Faith said, as Kimura ushered them down a set of metal steps into the building. "Those people love their helicopters."

Angel could still feel Hahn's eyes on her back. Then she stepped inside and let out an involuntary groan as a wave of warmth hit her.

"Holy shit." Mackenzie's eyes were wide. "Actual central heating. I bet you guys have, like, hot water and showers and everything."

"We do." Hahn sounded underwhelmed.

Faith offered them a more encouraging smile. "We'll show you to your rooms and leave you to settle in."

They were shepherded down two floors – "In a *lift*," Mackenzie marvelled – to a silent, spotless corridor that could have belonged to a hotel chain, lit with too-bright electric strip lights that stung Angel's eyes. They were handed keys, shown to three adjacent rooms, and left alone.

Angel's thoughts were still moving too slowly. How was any of this possible?

Mackenzie took stock of himself and pulled a face. "We must smell awful to you," he said to Skyler.

She grinned. "I didn't like to say anything."

Angel dug her nails into her palms. *Focus.* "Well. I guess I'll go see if I can remember how a shower works."

"Right." Mackenzie ran a hand through his hair. "Yeah. Good plan."

Skyler glanced between them uncertainly. "Knock for me when you're done?"

Wake up. Come on. Angel reached for her hand. "Come in and wait for me?"

Skyler's face brightened.

Angel's room was another mirage. Cream walls. A double bed with a mattress, made up with a duvet and pillows. It was at least four years since Angel had slept on a proper mattress. When she perched on it, it was unnervingly comfortable, like a marshmallow that might swallow her whole.

And Skyler, hovering by the door, twisting a strand of

hair round her fingers. "You're probably gonna have a headache for the first few days," she offered.

Angel had yearned for this moment with the bottomless, tearing ache of longing for something she knew would never come. Skyler was safe, they were alone together, and Angel could finally release all the words she'd thought would be forever trapped in her head like insects in amber, relics of a past she could never return to. But she felt like a stranger watching herself through a glass wall.

"I'm going for a shower," she said at last, picking up the clean linen without looking at Skyler. "I don't dare touch anything right now."

The bathroom was so clean and bright it hurt. Angel's own face in the mirror was a shock: still pale, freckled, but dirt-smudged, thinner than she remembered, than she'd expected, with fine lines under her eyes and a crease in her brow that she didn't remember either. Mackenzie had done a surprisingly good job of cropping her reddish-gold hair. Her eyes were the same colour, the green of a deep forest – but they were different, too. She recognised the same look in Skyler's eyes, and Mackenzie's: the look of someone who might as well have lived for a thousand years.

Her hands were reddened, callused. No matter how long she'd spent scrubbing them in the infirmary, they were always dirty again in minutes. Against this startling, clinical whiteness, they looked filthy.

She turned on the shower, discarded her ragged, dirt-stiffened clothes, and stared at the rising clouds of steam.

She'd spent years strip-washing with a bucket that was luke-warm at best, and usually freezing. Now, when she stepped under the hissing stream, the heat felt like it would strip away her skin. Hastily, she turned down the temperature. Luke-warm would do for now.

Weeks of grime and mud swirled into the drain until the water ran clear, until her skin was pink. The idea that she could stand here as long as she wanted, that this water didn't have to be painstakingly rationed, seemed unbelievable – but then so did everything about this new world.

She tried to anchor herself by touching things: the cold smooth tiles, the shiny taps, the unexpectedly soft towels, the clothes that smelled like washing powder instead of sweat. Still this new reality felt only surface-deep, as though if she pushed too hard she would punch through into a void.

When she couldn't put it off any longer, she opened the bathroom door, bracing herself for darkness.

Skyler was sitting on the edge of the bed, shoulders rigid. Angel tried to smile through a dizzy rush that was half relief, half terror: *you can't trust yourself, it's not okay, you're going to lose everything. Again.*

"I can't believe all I can smell is soap." She tried to make her voice normal. "It's so weird."

Skyler looked at the ceiling, kicking her feet together. Carefully, Angel sat beside her. "Are you okay?"

Skyler shook her head furiously as though trying to banish a wasp. Panic hardened like a rock in Angel's chest. "Sky? Talk to me."

Skyler turned away. "I don't want to talk."

"Please." Angel touched her shoulder. "What's wrong?"

Skyler jerked round, her cheeks streaked with tears. "Where were you? Where *were* you?"

"I – what?" Angel felt like Skyler had punched her. "You know where I was!"

"Right." Skyler scrubbed her face angrily with her sleeve. "In the North, with Mack and the others. Why, Angel? Did you think they needed you more than I did?"

"Do you think I *wanted* to leave you? Do you think I wasn't scared out of my mind the entire time?"

"I don't know," Skyler snapped, and for a moment all Angel could see was the only Skyler most people ever saw, the bulletproof shell she wore as armour against the world. "You weren't there. What was I supposed to think?"

"You should know I would never have wanted to leave you –"

"Then *why did you*?"

"They wouldn't let me go with you!"

"You should've made them." Skyler's fists clenched. "Or didn't you care?"

The jagged rock in Angel's chest was tearing a hole in her. "How can you say that? You know how I feel about you!"

"I thought I did! And then I woke up God knows fucking where and nobody would tell me anything and you were *gone*! How could you do that? You promised me –"

The rock in Angel's chest turned molten. She leapt to her feet. "Jesus Christ, Sky. How *dare* you."

"Is that what you do now, then?" Skyler's voice was small, choked. "Walk away from me?"

Angel froze. She was halfway to the door. She hadn't even realised.

"I'm sorry," Skyler whispered. "I didn't mean –"

Stiffly, Angel turned and sat back down.

"You were dying," she said, and the words were flinty, because it was the only way she could get them out. "I knew as soon as I saw the wound there was no way you were going to make it. But... I tried. You held on for a couple of hours, and I did everything I could... and I knew it wasn't going to be enough. I knew I was going to have to watch you die."

Skyler sniffed and gulped.

Angel scuffed her toe across the striped carpet. "And then they said they could help you. And I wanted to go with you, but they said no. And maybe I should've pushed harder – but the truth is, Sky, you had minutes left, and there was nothing else I could do for you."

Her throat tightened. "I'm sorry I left you. I'm so sorry. I couldn't lose you. And I couldn't fight anymore."

Skyler held out her hand. When Angel's fingers found hers, she shifted closer.

"I was so scared," she said softly, resting her head on Angel's shoulder. "I kept asking for you, and the hospital staff didn't have a clue what I was on about. I thought you and Mack must both be dead. I thought I was never going to see you again."

Angel buried her face in Skyler's hair. "Me either."

Skyler sat up and pressed her forehead against Angel's, thawing the ice Angel was trapped in, pulling her into the room, into her body. "You should've known I'll always come back for you."

Angel smiled.

"Can I kiss you now?"

Angel closed her eyes. "God, yes."

7

NEW WORLD ORDER

Kimura sprawled into an armchair in front of Hahn's desk. "This might have been a mistake."

Hahn's scowl suggested she might agree. Faith perched on the arm of the chair next to Kimura's. "What are you talking about?" The Northerners had only been there five minutes. Literally.

"The hacker's a loose cannon. She has no respect for authority. And no sense of gratitude either, apparently."

Hahn shot him a reproving look. "I distinctly recall you saying she'd be worth the hassle."

"Because I've never seen talent like that. I just didn't expect her to be so..."

"Forthright?" Faith offered. Really, though, what had Kimura expected? People who respected authority didn't usually go around blowing up government buildings.

"It's not her I'm concerned about," Hahn said. "Unless you're worried she's too smart for you, Ren?"

"She's too smart for all of us. And the boy... Is he

really the South's best thief? You can feel the anxiety pouring off him."

Kimura wasn't wrong, but Faith had a strange urge to defend Mackenzie. "Well, there's no doubt he is. So he must have found a way to manage it." Perhaps he did what she did: used his work to act like the person he wanted to be, not the person he feared he was deep down.

"He's obviously functional," Hahn said. "How he manages that is his business. The other girl, though... she's a mess."

That was, unfortunately, hard to dispute. People all over Birmingham told the same story about Angel: she was fierce, fearless, powered by rage and adrenaline, with a focus that never cracked. But the Angel they'd found in Yorkshire was brittle, dazed, unsettled. She held her arms wrapped around herself, her gaze flitting like a sparrow from point to point.

Hahn was right. Angel was not okay. But really, it was hard to imagine that any of them would be.

Kimura sighed. "Well, we've got them now. We've committed to going into the South."

"Once we're sure they can cope," Hahn reminded him. "We're not sending anybody on a suicide mission. If they can't prove they can handle it, we're not touching the Board."

"Are you going to tell them that?"

"Don't be such a baby, Ren. You're not scared of the hacker already?"

"She could melt down all our systems in her sleep."

"Well, then you'd better keep her busy."

"And Angel?" Kimura asked. "What do we do about her?"

Hahn drummed her fingers on her desk. "Keep an eye on her. She needs to prove she's functional."

"They don't trust us." Faith had caught enough of the conversation on the hillside – and the suspicion in their eyes – to be certain of that. And why would they? All they'd had from authority figures was pain and persecution – and though Kimura was occasionally known to act more or less like a human being, neither he nor Hahn would ever be in the running for the congeniality award at the Agency Christmas party.

Hahn raised an eyebrow at Kimura. "I think Faith's offering to go and do some public relations."

Kimura grinned. "What a good idea. Why don't you show them round, Faith? Try to convince them we're the good guys."

"We... *are* the good guys?"

He stood up and patted her on the shoulder. "Something like that. But perhaps with a little more conviction."

They really could be assholes sometimes, both of them.

That was how Faith found herself hovering outside the Northerners' bedrooms, feeling stupid. She felt even more stupid when she knocked on first Skyler's and then Angel's door and no one answered. Skyler was probably elbow deep in their systems already.

She tried Mackenzie's room. From inside came a scrambling noise and a thud that sounded like someone landing heavily. The door flew open to reveal a slightly guilty-looking Mackenzie.

"Oh," he said, brushing a lock of dark hair out of his eyes. "Um. Hi?"

"Hey. Are you all in here?"

He went pink. "Uh, no. Sky and Angel are next door. I think they're, er... busy."

Faith suppressed a smile. She'd wondered, when she saw the way they looked at each other. Hahn and Kimura didn't seem to have picked up on that. "Got it."

"Oh, God. I don't mean they're – I just –"

She took pity on him. "You can breathe. I'm not here for gossip."

He kept eyeing her warily.

"I thought you might want a tour," Faith said quickly. "And some food?"

Mackenzie brightened at once. "Yes, please. I'm bloody starving. How does food work here?"

"The canteen's open twenty-four hours. You don't have to pay."

His eyes widened. "There's really... Seriously? We can just get food whenever we want?"

Faith almost smiled again, until she remembered why he was so awed by something she'd never given a second thought to. "Seriously." She tried to keep her tone light. "You should make the most of it. Especially since they're not even paying you yet."

Mackenzie grinned. "I'm not gonna argue with that."

His whole face changed when he smiled; suddenly, a spark of mischief lit his dark eyes. Somewhere behind the weariness and the hunger and the crushing weight of the world on his shoulders was a boy who would have liked to laugh, if only there'd been anything for him to laugh about.

"Let's give the others a couple more minutes," he suggested. "They've got... a lot to catch up on." He ran a hand through his hair, standing it on end. "Anyway. So you're like... What do you do, exactly?"

"Oh, you know. Sidekick. General minion." Faith rolled her eyes, to show she was half joking. "I'm Hahn's minion, specifically. I'm an analyst. I find and collate information and help plan our ops."

"So you work for her all the time? Wow. Sorry about that."

Faith laughed, then cut herself off guiltily. "It's really not that bad."

"Not sure I believe you. Is she always that scary?"

Public relations, remember? "I mean... a bit. But she's not a psychopath. She just has high expectations."

"Not a psychopath? That's quite a bar. So she's probably not gonna murder us in our sleep?"

"Nah. If Hahn ever murdered someone, she'd do it to their face."

"Awesome. I've never felt safer."

He wasn't at all what she'd expected. She'd collated most of the Agency's information on the Northerners while Skyler was recovering; she had a whole file on Mackenzie and his escapades in the South, which felt a lot weirder now he was right in front of her. 'He's got a smart mouth,' one goon had commented, which seemed to be the universal consensus. 'He'd have got his head kicked in a long time ago if he weren't so bloody brilliant.'

No one had mentioned the nervous edge that danced through his movements like sunlight on water. She'd expected him to be stony, all business; surely he'd had to be, navigating the perilous terrain of the Southern underworld. But instead he had bright, kind eyes and a quirk to the corner of his mouth that was half humour, half sadness. His face softened when he talked about his friends. He'd cried when he was reunited with someone he thought he'd lost.

Bravery, Faith had always thought, looked like Hahn and Kimura – and Skyler and Angel, come to that: coldness and sharp edges, the way she'd always assumed she would have to become if she ever wanted to be proud of herself. "You're not thinking critically," Hahn had chided her, the night Faith had tiptoed into her office carrying her laptop like a grenade and launched into the argument she'd been rehearsing the whole way there – *they need our help, we have to stop this, we have to do what we were designed for.* "Use your head, not your heart."

But surely what your heart had to tell you was just as important?

Mackenzie cocked his head. "How old are you, anyway?"

"Nineteen. You?" Admitting that she already knew would definitely make things awkward.

"Uh... what month is it?"

"April. 2033."

He blinked. "Then I'm – Huh. I'm eighteen, I guess. I didn't even realise." He gave her a lopsided grin. "I honestly didn't think *that* was ever gonna happen."

Before Faith could think of a response beyond, 'Jesus, that's awful,' he groaned. "God, how embarrassing. I can't believe I said that. World's smallest violin, right?"

"Oh, I don't know. I'd say that's at least a medium-sized violin."

Mackenzie laughed. "Thanks. I feel validated."

"Want to go celebrate making it to adulthood by eating all the food in the canteen?"

This time, when his eyes met hers, the shadow of wariness in them had all but vanished. "Hell, yes."

8

THE FIRST STAR

Although Skyler supposed the canteen trip with Mackenzie and Faith had been a necessary diversion, all she really wanted was to be alone with Angel. By the time they returned to their rooms Mackenzie was stifling yawns, and she found herself guiltily grateful when he wished them a weary goodnight.

And then at last she and Angel were safe inside her room, and the words came out so easily, after years of calculating the risk every time she opened her mouth: "I don't want to be away from you again."

Angel had been quiet and solemn the whole time they'd been in the canteen. Now, a rare true smile blossomed. "Me either."

But something wasn't right. Skyler frowned. "You're not okay, are you?"

She had no idea how to have these conversations. She'd always avoided talking about feelings with Mackenzie because Angel was so much better at it. But she'd never seen Angel like this before, on edge, radiating misery. And maybe she didn't have a clue how to help, but she needed to try anyway.

"I..." Angel's face clouded. She shook her head. "I'm fine."

"You're bloody not."

Angel gave a not-quite laugh. "Is it that obvious?"

"Little bit, yeah."

"I was just... scared. And today's been a lot to process. I just need to get used to believing everything's really okay."

"What's gonna help you do that?"

Angel took her hand and pulled her close. "This might."

Her embrace was as steady and solid as it had always been. And the warmth of her body, the softness of her cheek against Skyler's, made Skyler's heartbeat quicken the way it always had; made her long for something more.

She brushed her lips against Angel's cheek. "How about this?"

Angel pulled back to meet her eyes, and now there was something alive in them that mirrored the spark in Skyler's veins, that magnetic pull that was longing and excitement and possibility and need, all at once. "That definitely works."

Skyler reached up into a soft, tentative kiss. "And this?"

In answer, Angel kissed her back.

They fell onto the bed, talking and kissing and laughing. A slow, joyful exploration unfolded: fingers tracing cheeks and lips, arms and shoulders, necks and backs, and then, at last, under shirts, and Skyler marvelled at every new inch of skin, every shiver and smile and soft gasp from Angel, and at Angel's ability, like magic, to elicit those same responses from her.

She'd stumbled into a world she hadn't been able to even begin imagining. And now she was here she wanted to know everything: every place she could trail her fingers that would make Angel's breath quicken, make her wriggle against Skyler; what would happen if she replaced the touch of her hands with kisses instead; what it was she wanted from Angel in those dizzy, delicious moments when Angel's hands slid over her skin and her lips brushed Skyler's neck and Skyler thought her heart might stop beating.

"I didn't know," she whispered.

Angel looked up, smiling. "Didn't know what?"

"That it was possible to feel like this. I never imagined..." Skyler shuddered at a sharp flash of unwelcome memory. "I always thought my body was my enemy. It got me hurt so many times." She ducked her head. "Sorry. I'm kind of ruining the mood."

Angel coaxed her chin up. "You're not ruining anything." Her eyes searched Skyler's. "Do you want to talk about it?"

"No. I don't want to think about that now."

"Do you want to stop?"

Skyler smiled. "No."

Angel stroked a strand of hair from her cheek. "You

set the pace, okay? If you're even a tiny bit not sure, we'll stop. Can you do that? Can you tell me?"

Skyler nodded. "I don't want to give them any more of my life," she said into Angel's neck. "They took enough. They don't get to have this."

In reply, Angel kissed the top of her head.

Skyler looked up at her. "Angel?"

"Mm?"

Her heart was suddenly beating even faster. "What if I wanted to take my shirt off?"

Angel gave her a gentle, glowing smile. "That would be more than okay with me."

"I –" Skyler's cheeks flushed. "This is stupid, but –"

"Not stupid. What is it?"

"I got shot. There's a massive scar."

Angel laughed softly. Skyler's face grew hotter still. "Why are you laughing?"

"Because you're beautiful. The scar means you survived. It means you're still here with me. Why would I do anything but love it? Besides – have you forgotten who you're talking to? Wait till you see all my scars."

She brushed Skyler's arm. "I mean it, though," she murmured. "We don't need to rush anything. I only want this if you're sure you do too."

With a tiny, excited shiver in her stomach, Skyler sat up and pulled her shirt over her head. The shiver coiled into squirming uncertainty as Angel studied the angry red snarl of scar tissue that spread over half her abdomen: *what if she thinks I'm repulsive after all?*

Carefully, Angel touched the raised edge of the scar with a fingertip. "Does it hurt?"

"Not usually. Only a bit inside sometimes, if I eat too much or move too fast. Probably don't want anyone to punch me in the stomach anytime soon, though."

Angel's hand hovered over the scarring. "Can I...?"

Skyler nodded, her breath catching in her throat.

Gently, Angel laid her palm against the scarring. "Is that okay?"

The warmth of her hand dissolved the nervous twist in Skyler's stomach. "It's very okay." The words came out breathless.

"See?" Angel kissed her gently. "You're beautiful."

Later, in the depths of the night, Skyler lay in Angel's arms staring into the darkness. It was always like this. Stillness and silence were not her friends. She knew how Angel felt after all: everything was okay, but some sharp, urgent instinct that ran deeper than rational thought insisted it wasn't.

She shifted, and Angel stirred at once. "You okay?"

"Mm. Were you asleep?"

"Sort of. What's up?"

Skyler hesitated. Angel rolled over and switched the bedside lamp on. "Talking is good, as Mackenzie's spent the last two months reminding me."

"Ha. Bet you didn't listen, though."

"That..." Angel flapped a hand. "That is irrelevant."

Skyler didn't *do* talking, but she could already feel

that this was going to eat away at her. She might as well try. What was the worst that could happen?

Better not pull too hard at that thread.

"Did you ever wish..." she began, "...when I was away, when you thought I was... gone... Did you ever wish you'd never met me? That we'd never –?"

Angel studied the ceiling, a tiny crease between her brows. "I thought it," she said eventually, and Skyler's pulse raced sharp and sickly, because that was the insidious fear burrowing inside her, because they still weren't safe, they might never really be safe, and if Angel couldn't bear that, it meant –

"But I didn't mean it," Angel added.

Skyler's sigh of relief came out louder than she'd intended. Angel laughed. "Did I just scare the crap out of you?"

"What?" Skyler reached for her poker face. "Of course not."

Angel nudged her. "Liar."

"Yeah, yeah. Just because you know me or whatever." But Skyler was smiling too. Years of hiding every last emotion, bad or worse or – rarely, so rarely – a flicker of good, and finally she didn't have to. It wasn't scary that Angel could read her, could know her. It was a gift. Even if it did feel really weird.

"My life wasn't a life, before." Angel laid her hand over Skyler's. "When you and Mack showed up at my door with that flash drive, you gave me something I didn't think I'd ever have again. If pain is the trade-off... well, that's how you know something matters, right? We'd never fight to keep anything if we didn't grieve its loss. And that's part of being alive too. So if the choice is between existing or feeling alive – then I choose living."

"You wouldn't always have."

"No," Angel conceded. "But I don't feel like that anymore. And I knew that, even when I thought I'd lost you. I wouldn't have traded that time for anything."

She glanced at Skyler. "What about you? You thought we were gone too. Did you ever wish the same? Do you –?"

Skyler gripped her hand. "I'm not walking away from this." She'd thought about it, over and over, weighing up the checks and balances: would she have been better off never letting herself feel, never letting anything matter? God knew she'd fought hard enough not to let so many things matter.

"It was awful," she said. It hadn't been, of course; there wasn't a word to describe how it had felt. "Like when I went back to Leeds and saw our flat. When I realised Mum and Sam were gone. I thought I'd never be able to breathe again." She still did, sometimes: three years later, and sometimes she caught herself thinking, *I'll tell Sam about* – and suddenly it was like she was in the middle of a sandstorm, skin scoured raw, no air in her lungs. "But when I think about it – really think about it – I think about who I'd have been, what I'd have been, if I'd never had them. If I'd never let them matter."

Angel smiled, soft and sad. "I'd have liked to meet your brother."

"I wish you could have."

"You think he'd have approved of me?"

"I reckon he'd have liked you. Not sure what you'd have made of him, mind. He was a total know-it-all, he'd have tried to debate a million things with you. You'd definitely have given him a run for his money, though. And..." A bittersweet lump rose in her throat. "And he'd have been so happy that you make me happy."

Angel rested her head on Skyler's shoulder. "I'm glad."

"Me too."

Quiet.

"I'd like to tell you about my family one day," Angel said, not looking at her. "I'm just... not ready."

"Well, when you are, I'll be here."

"So we're doing this?" Angel looked up at her. "Even though it's scary as hell?"

"We're doing this." Skyler held her tighter. "Because otherwise, why even bother with all this shit?"

9

FREE SOLO

Mackenzie spent a strange, restless night in his room.

Everything felt wrong. The glaring intensity of the lights – left on even in empty rooms, like power shortages and rations didn't exist – had given him a headache. And, worse, an acute awareness of exactly how long it was since he'd had a proper wash or clean clothes. That had triggered a panic so physical it was like being electrocuted. It had taken him three attempts to get out of the shower.

At least Angel and Skyler were only next door. He wasn't ready to be away from them. Which was odd, really, because he'd spent most of the last three years on his own. It was only in the last few months they'd been thrown together, forced – and it had certainly felt like that at times – to work as a team. There had been many occasions in the not-too-distant past when he'd have paid good money for a break from Skyler. But what hit him now, with a painful clarity, was just how much he wanted not to be alone anymore.

Not that he had much choice right now; it had been clear the whole time they were eating that Angel and Skyler needed some time to themselves. So Mackenzie had done some theatrical yawning when they left the canteen, figuring at least he'd enjoy his best night's sleep in years.

Instead, of course, he was wide awake assessing his surroundings.

His room was on at least the tenth floor. The windows, like ones he'd seen in hotels another lifetime ago, only opened a couple of inches. He examined the hinges to see how easy they would be to unscrew: not very, it appeared. Outside were no visible drainpipes, no handholds, no other windows or ledges within reach.

What was he *doing*? So far the most menacing thing the Agency had done was give him access to a shower and clean clothes. And here he was scoping out escape routes.

You're not safe. You don't know anything about these people.

He could feel himself winding up, tighter and tighter. *Run. Get out of here.*

He dragged his hands through his hair. He just needed to sleep. He'd feel better in the morning.

But the room was too warm, the bed too comfortable. Mackenzie drifted between clamouring thoughts and strange, urgent dreams, and over and over he jolted awake, flailing for a candle before he remembered the light was there.

In the small hours of the morning, sick of himself, he filled the bathroom basin with cold water and splashed his face, hoping the chill would chase away the spectral discomfort that clung to him. But as he tried to leave the bathroom, an all-too-familiar creeping itch stirred: *go back. Wash your hands. Something terrible's going to happen.*

His brain and body buzzed like an electricity pylon. On autopilot, his feet took him back to the sink.

He'd given up trying to keep his hands clean in the North, because it was both impossible and irresponsible to wash them as often as the hissing itch demanded. It had been unbearable at first, day after day spent hiding in his tent, too terrified to eat, while his brain screamed at him: *you're contaminated, you're going to die, you're going to infect the others –*

But Angel had refused to leave him, even when he yelled at her. "You're not going to make me sick," she'd repeated, over and over. "And I'm not leaving you." She'd eaten food off the ground, even licked the bottom of her shoe, trying to prove the poisonous voice in his head was lying. 'Exposure,' she'd called it. It had sounded like bollocks. How could making himself even more terrified possibly help?

But incredibly, over time, the gnawing panic had subsided. The hiss grew easier to ignore. He'd started eating again, stopped noticing when his hands weren't spotless. It had been such a *relief.* He'd been proud of himself.

Less than a day with access to soap and clean water, and the fear was back. Mackenzie wanted to kick himself.

He gripped the tap. The hiss grew louder: *you'll make Skyler and Angel sick. You can't risk it. You're being selfish.*

The voice is lying. It's always lying.

It's not. It's reminding you of something you can't afford to forget.

If I didn't make anyone sick in the North, I'm not going to here.

But you did, didn't you?

No. That wasn't my fault.

A putrid lump hardened in his throat. *This is your responsibility. Your fault if something bad happens.*

He stared at the tap for a long, long time.

I'm not going to hurt them.

I'm not going to live like this.

He pulled his hand from the tap, turned, and went back to bed.

The next morning dawned crisp and bright, with no sign of Angel or Skyler. Mackenzie had no idea what to do with himself.

As he dithered in the corridor, quiet footsteps padded behind him. He spun round, his heart pounding the way it always did when he was teetering on a knife edge, inches from being caught.

Faith, bright-eyed and alert in a purple shirt and

black trousers, raised a quizzical eyebrow at him. "You okay?"

Mackenzie's face burned. God. He must look nuts, whipping round like he'd been shocked, hands raised against an imaginary attacker.

After an excruciating pause, he managed a nod.

Faith's eyebrows stayed raised. "Super convinced right now, honestly."

Mackenzie reached for his voice. Thankfully, it hadn't gone too far. "Hi. I'm fine. Thanks."

"If you say so. Want some breakfast? Most important meal of the day and all."

If he had breakfast with Faith instead of Skyler and Angel, he'd have to act like a normal person. On the other hand, he was starving. "Sure you don't mind?"

"You kidding? I'm dying to hear some of your stories first-hand. C'mon."

"First-hand?" Mackenzie said, as they set off towards the lifts. "There's a borderline creepy implication there."

"Ah. Yeah. Sorry. I kind of forget that a lot of Agency stuff probably seems insane to outsiders."

"What, like having a whole dossier of information on people you've never met?"

"Dude." Faith grinned. "If you think that's gonna be the weirdest thing about working here, I've got bad news."

"How long've you been here, then?"

"With the Agency? Two years. Hahn turned up on my doorstep when I was seventeen with a scary folder containing my entire life story, so trust me, I get the weirdness."

Seventeen seemed impossibly young. Of course, Mackenzie had also spent his seventeenth year doing plenty of frankly insane stuff, but in his case nobody sensible had actually suggested it was a good idea. "She obviously convinced you. How? Did you piss off a totalitarian regime too?"

Faith laughed. "Nothing nearly so dramatic."

"Where are you from, anyway?"

"Vancouver. Lived there my whole life. Hahn was based in Seattle back then, but she was just about to transfer here. I'd always wanted to see Europe. Never really thought I'd have the chance. So, you know. That was pretty cool."

"You moved halfway across the world at seventeen?" That seemed the most incredible choice of all. He'd have given anything to be at home with his family now.

Faith shrugged. "Seemed like the thing to do."

"Was it tough moving away?"

She shot him a glance, but she seemed amused, not annoyed. "What's with all the questions?"

Because you're interesting, he wanted to say. Instead, he waved an airy hand. "Just levelling the playing field. Unless you fancy showing me your scary file instead?"

"Hmm. I'm not sure you could handle that." The corner of Faith's mouth twitched. "I'll allow a few more questions."

"Very gracious of you."

The canteen was a dizzying whirlwind of smells.

Mackenzie's mouth started watering before he was even through the door; he wasn't sure he'd ever be able to play it cool again when it came to food. A clatter of plates and a buzz of chatter rose from the two dozen or so people dotted around the long tables, peering at tablets and laptops in varying states of alertness. At least half of them eyed Mackenzie with a distinct lack of subtlety.

Faith handed him a tray. "Ignore the staring. I'll fend them off."

The servery, fortunately, proved a good distraction. Mackenzie piled his plate with a bit of everything that looked even remotely edible and slid into a seat opposite Faith in an empty corner.

"It wasn't too bad moving away," she said casually, buttering toast and piling scrambled egg on top. "I needed to get out of Vancouver. Hahn gave me the opportunity."

They didn't know each other anywhere near well enough for him to ask why she'd needed to get out of Vancouver. In a world where any sort of normal social rules still applied, this would normally be the point where Mackenzie asked about her family. But it was entirely possible her choice not to mention them so far had been a careful and deliberate one. This was something Mackenzie understood only too well. The last thing he wanted to do with his first potential new friend in years was clumsily knock scabs off an old wound.

"How come Hahn wanted you?" he asked instead.

"Because I'm really, really smart," Faith said, deadpan. She giggled at Mackenzie's expression. "We don't value modesty here. If you're good at something, why shouldn't you own it?"

He grinned. "Skyler'll fit right in, then."

A young, round-faced East Asian man with floppy hair and a rather rumpled suit dived into the seat beside Faith. "I heard a rumour," he announced, offering Mackenzie his hand. "I'm Jie. I already know your name."

Apparently the Agency's list of valued skills didn't include basic interpersonal ones. Mackenzie shook Jie's hand uncertainly. "Er. Hi."

A tall, pale woman with an angular face and a mass of wavy dark hair plonked herself down beside Jie. "This is Clara," Jie said cheerfully.

Mackenzie gave her an awkward wave. "Nice to meet you."

Clara gave him a terse nod. "So you're the famous Mackenzie," she said, in an accent that might have been Scandinavian. It sounded rather like an accusation.

"Oh, stop it, you guys," Faith said. "You're making him uncomfortable."

She was right. Mackenzie was beginning to feel like he'd transferred to a new school halfway through term.

Clara, undeterred, kept examining him as though he were a lab specimen. "You look scared shitless. Have you been given an assignment yet?"

"He's only just got here," Faith said through her toast.

Clara's sniff implied this was a poor excuse. "What do you actually do, anyway?"

Jie's eyes sparkled. "I heard you blew up a government lab."

Mackenzie sighed. Blow up one building and apparently you never heard the end of it. "Well, it wasn't just me. But... yeah. We didn't have a choice."

Clara made a comment to Jie in a language Mackenzie didn't understand. Jie replied in kind, though rather more cheerfully. While Mackenzie tried to maintain an expression of polite interest, Faith retorted sharply in the same language, before switching to English: "Don't do that. It's rude."

"I was only saying" – pointedly, in Mackenzie's general direction – "that I find it hard to understand how Hahn's mind works sometimes." Clara picked up her tray. "Jie, we're due to meet with Kimura."

Jie stood too. "It was a pleasure, Mackenzie."

"Don't take her personally," Faith said, when Clara and Jie were probably not quite out of earshot. "She's got kind of a thing about Hahn. They're always picking holes in each other's decisions."

"Like intervening in the UK?"

"Uh... sort of. It doesn't matter, though. Clara doesn't get a say in this. And she's a jerk, anyway."

"That whole language thing was a test, wasn't it? What were you speaking?"

"Mandarin. And you're right, unfortunately. Remember how I'm really smart? Well, everyone here is. Only some people forget there's different kinds of smart."

Good thing they wouldn't be working directly with Clara. She and Skyler would get on like a house on fire, possibly in the most literal sense.

Faith turned back to her breakfast. "Want to know a secret?"

Mackenzie wasn't entirely sure he did. "Okay?"

"Clara and Jie? Totally getting it on."

"For real?"

"Yup. The consensus seems to be that he makes her a slightly nicer person, but personally I don't think it shows much. Also, although they're doing a terrible job of it, they're trying to keep it quiet."

"My lips are sealed," Mackenzie said solemnly. "How come? Are relationships not allowed here?"

"Oh, no. God, everyone here's sleeping with everyone else. Have to do something for fun in amongst all the saving the world. It's just pretty hard to keep people out of your business."

Mackenzie took in the significant number of people still eyeballing him. Faith spread her hands. "What did I tell you?"

"For a super-secret agency full of super-secret agents, none of this lot seem very discreet."

"You've got a point." She drained the last of her coffee and bounced upright. "C'mon. I don't have to be anywhere for another hour. Want to see where I go when I need some peace?"

"Don't you just go to your room?"

"One breakfast and you're already angling for an invite up to my room, huh?"

"Oh, God." Mackenzie's face went hotter than the sun. He'd wished many times for the power of invisibility, but none more fervently than just then. "Sorry. No. God. I didn't mean –"

"Relax, Mackenzie, I'm messing with you. Agency 101: your room's the first place they look. No one ever looks here, though."

They reached the lifts and Faith pressed the button for the basement. Panic twanged in Mackenzie's chest like an elastic band. "We're not allowed down there –"

She grinned. He couldn't remember when he'd last seen someone smile so freely. It made him want to smile too, and there hadn't been much to smile about lately. There hadn't been much to smile about for a long bloody time.

"Don't worry," she said. "This wasn't what they had in mind."

The lift opened onto a wide white corridor uncomfortably reminiscent of the lab Mackenzie had – as people kept reminding him – blown up. Faith strode to the end of the corridor and flung a door open. "Behold."

Mackenzie stared at the rows of shelves laden with neatly folded linen. "This is… not what I expected."

Faith led him to the shelves at the far end of the room, ducked under the lowest one and made herself comfortable on a pile of towels. "Don't look so nervous. Sit down."

Maybe this was a test. Maybe Hahn was about to burst out of a heap of pillowcases and demand to know why Mackenzie had allowed himself to be led into both breaking the rules and messing up the clean laundry in less than twenty-four hours.

Talk about paranoid. Gingerly, he settled onto the towels beside Faith. "Sorry. Still trying to get my head around – well, everything, really."

"Sure. This must be so different to what you're used to."

"It literally feels like a different world. I mean, I sort of remember what life was like before the power rationing, but that was like six, seven years ago. Since the Wall went up, I've pretty much only been in places with proper electricity when I was breaking in. I feel like I shouldn't even be here." Was that why his brain kept howling at him? Perhaps eventually he would stop feeling like he was trespassing.

"Well, that makes sense," Faith said gently. "You haven't even been here a day."

"Everyone's gonna stop staring soon, right?"

"Sure. In a month or two."

She didn't look like she was joking, unfortunately. "There's no way Skyler's gonna put up with that for even a couple of days."

"Ha. Yeah, I can see that." Faith cocked her head. "You guys must be pretty close after everything you've been through."

Mackenzie had to think about this. He'd known Skyler for years, but although he'd always admired her tenacity and the phrase 'been through a lot together' seemed like a major understatement, up until recently he wouldn't have described her as a friend unless you stretched the meaning of the word to include anyone in the small minority of people in the South who didn't actively want him dead.

But maybe things were different now.

"Yes," he said, realising he'd been quiet too long. "I think we are."

"You must've been so worried about her."

"You know about that?" He remembered the scary file. "Oh. Of course you do."

She winced. "Sorry."

"I really thought she was... gone," Mackenzie confessed. "The whole time, I was just trying to figure out how we'd cope when we found out. Or if we just never heard anything at all."

"That..." Faith bit her lip. "I can't even imagine how that must've felt."

"Yeah. She's not the easiest person to get on with, Sky, but... you know."

"You're a package." She didn't say it sarcastically, like Hahn had. She said it like she understood.

He grinned. "Whether either of us like it or not. And – well. Angel. She... I don't know what she'd have done if Skyler had – if she hadn't come back." He squeezed his hands together. "That was the scariest bit. When Sky was gone... it was like Angel wasn't even herself anymore."

What was he doing, telling this almost-stranger all the terrible thoughts and fears he'd fought and failed to banish? He inspected his hands, suddenly afraid he'd given too much away. What if Faith went back and relayed all this to Hahn?

"It's okay, Mackenzie." She touched his arm and he

looked up in surprise. "You're allowed to talk about what you're thinking."

He shook himself. "Sorry. I'm used to it just being the three of us, and Sky's not exactly the touchy-feely type. And before her and Angel, there was no one." *God. Would you listen to yourself?* "Sorry. I don't mean to sound so pathetic."

Faith laid her hand over his. "I think we might have different benchmarks for excessive self-pity," she said as Mackenzie froze, trying to figure out what exactly he was supposed to do with himself. "So how about you assume you're good unless I do... this?" She tipped her head sideways, screwed up her face and stuck her tongue out.

Mackenzie found himself laughing. When had he last laughed over something small and normal and sweet? He had no idea, but his head was somehow quieter for it. "That's pretty disturbing."

"I promise I'll only deploy it in emergencies." She checked her phone. "I'd better go. Heads up, you're getting an op tomorrow. Don't worry. I expect it'll be easy compared to what you're used to."

10

LEVEL UP

"So let me get this straight," Angel said. "You want us to steal from an arms dealer?"

Their second morning at the Agency had been considerably less relaxed. So far it had consisted of a two-hour lecture in Hahn's office on the political climate of Eastern Europe and the activities of a Finnish businessman named Virtanen, who had spent the last decade pretending to run a product design company whilst quietly nurturing his real passion, which was selling weapons to people who definitely shouldn't have been allowed them.

Kimura gave Angel a thumbs up. "Glad you've been paying attention."

Skyler's arms had been folded for at least ninety minutes. "When are we going to talk about the Board?"

"When we're ready," Hahn said. "Which means after we've assessed your skills and understand how we can use you."

"You *know* what we can do. You've got a creepy file full of shit we've done. Why are we wasting time on this guy?"

"Because plunging in half-baked to try to topple a dictatorship is how wars start."

Skyler scowled. Mackenzie nudged her. "Sky."

She managed to temper the scowl very slightly before turning it on him. "What?"

"Let's just... talk about this job, okay? It's gonna take more than a day to work out how to take the Board down."

For a moment Angel thought Skyler was going to argue with him too, but she just heaved an irritable sigh. "Fine."

Hahn nodded at a door across her office. "Use that room. Don't keep us waiting."

They piled into the smaller office. Angel leaned against the door, listening to the sharp note of annoyance in Hahn's voice as she murmured to Kimura. Mackenzie hoisted himself onto the desk and glared at Skyler. "D'you think you could wait like five minutes before you start winding them up?"

Skyler plopped into an office chair and spun it in a lazy circle. "You're right. It *is* gonna take more than a day to figure this out. They're wasting time."

"And you're gonna waste our best chance to save the North. This lot are used to being in charge. Pissing them off won't make them move any quicker."

"You don't know that."

Mackenzie started tapping the desk in a rapid, steady

rhythm. He looked away when Angel caught his eye, but didn't stop tapping.

Nearly forty-eight hours together before they'd started bickering. That had to be a record. Angel waved at them. "Focus, guys. What do you think about this job?"

"We're gonna get murdered," Mackenzie said.

Skyler rolled her eyes. "You always say that."

"I think it's valid here, don't you? This Virtanen guy is a psychopath."

"Which would be a good reason to take the job, time-wasting bullshit aside. Selling automatic weapons to self-appointed militias is like the definition of 'villain'."

"Except for the bit where we're gonna get murdered."

Skyler stopped spinning. "At what point in the last three years have we *not* been at risk of getting murdered?"

"It's one thing trying to cross a busy road," Mackenzie snapped. "It's another thing to stand in front of a moving lorry. And it's not gonna be you in front of the lorry, is it? It'll be me breaking into his hotel room and stealing his shit."

Angel pinched the bridge of her nose. There was a real danger this could go on all day. "Mack, are you saying you don't want to do it?"

He deflated. "No," he muttered, kicking his heels together. "I was just kind of enjoying the whole not facing an imminent horrible death thing. This guy sounds like Redruth but worse."

Redruth. The word was an unexpected lance through the weak point of Angel's armour. After Erin, after she'd lost everything, when she'd decided that if she was going to keep on living she would dedicate every heartbeat to hunting Redruth down, Angel had forced herself to repeat his name until it lost all meaning. It had worked, sort of; she could hear it spoken unexpectedly without bolting like a frightened deer. It still felt like the twist of a knife, though, deep in her stomach.

"Right," Skyler agreed, and Angel wrenched herself back to the room. "Which is even more reason to take him out."

Mackenzie scowled. "I hate it when you're right."

Skyler grinned and spun herself in another circle. "Unlucky. You know I'm always right."

"You won't be on your own, Mack," Angel said. "I'll be there."

He managed a half-hearted smile. "Then there's no reason to be scared, is there?" He sighed. "I'm sorry. It just... felt good to be safe. Even if it was only for two days."

Unexpectedly, Skyler's expression softened. "I get it, Mack. I don't want anything to happen to you guys either. Or to me, obviously. But if this is the Agency's idea of easing us in, we'd better get used to people like Virtanen."

"Great," Mackenzie mumbled, echoing Angel's own thoughts.

"Hey." Skyler prodded his knee. "We can totally handle this." She touched Angel's hand. "What do you think?"

In the South, Angel had gone after men like Virtanen

without hesitating. He was no more a threat than any of a dozen people she'd killed. And Skyler was right, assuming the Agency's account was truthful. He definitely fit the definition of 'villain'.

She shrugged. "I think we should do it."

"How very gracious of you," Hahn said, when they delivered their verdict. "Skyler, go with Kimura. You have a lot to do."

"I want to use my own computer," Skyler said immediately.

Kimura smiled. "I thought you would. We've got programs you might find useful, though. And you need access to our records."

"You two will work with Faith," Hahn told Angel and Mackenzie, as Skyler left with Kimura. "But first, Angel – I need to speak with you alone."

Her words were a shark's fin, gliding through seemingly serene water. Angel didn't let herself react. "Okay."

Mackenzie caught her eye, raising his eyebrows in a question. She gave him a very slight nod, and he backed out of the room.

Angel was alone with a woman she couldn't read, treading water in a vast, empty ocean.

Hahn gestured to a chair in front of her desk. "Have a seat."

Angel couldn't sit. She couldn't relax, not with Hahn scrutinising her like that. Angel was displaying her discomfort, her weakness, and it made her want to claw at herself.

"I'm fine here," she said.

"Suit yourself."

Nothing bad is going to happen. She can't hurt you.

"I have a question for you," Hahn said pleasantly, folding her hands on her desk. "And I'd appreciate an honest answer."

"Okay."

"Recruiting the other two was a no-brainer. They're both prodigiously talented. They have skills no one here can match. It's different for you."

Because you're nothing but a weapon. A murderer. Your value is that you can kill without blinking.

"That wasn't a question," Angel said.

"It's different for you," Hahn continued, as though Angel hadn't spoken, "because violence affects people in unpredictable ways. All our agents undertake rigorous assessments before going out on an op with the expectation that they might harm someone. We don't rely on rumour as an endorsement of their capabilities."

A thread of pain wove across Angel's rigid shoulders. Hahn was saying that not only was she no more than a thug, she couldn't even do that right. "That's not a question either."

Hahn leaned forward. "In the South your reputation precedes you, and I'm afraid I don't mean that in a good way. It's not your skills that are in question, it's how you use them. Now, the three of you have made it clear you come as a package" – said with an edge of distaste – "and that package needs to be functional *now*. The North doesn't have time to waste while you learn to regulate yourself. So let me be clear. This op is an assessment. It's small scale stuff, but lives depend on it. I am taking a risk with you, and I need to know: can you cope?"

What did Hahn know about Angel's emotions? And why couldn't she shut them off, bury them as she had for so long? Why was she unravelling now, in front of a woman who posed no threat? When she was the safest she'd been in years?

"There's no point lying," Hahn added. "I won't throw you out if you tell me you can't handle this right now. You've been through –"

That was *enough*. "You've got no idea what I've been through."

"I know what I saw the night I met you. I know you spent two months not knowing whether someone you cared about was dead or alive."

A flare of anger, dark and ugly like spilled blood. "Yes. Which you could have done something about, if you'd wanted." Hahn had put them all through weeks of suffering. Was she sadistic, or just indifferent?

"We'd both be naïve to imagine that hasn't affected you," Hahn went on, as easily as if she were discussing the weather.

"I can do the job."

"You've got a good poker face."

Not compared to usual. "I know."

"I don't know if I should believe what you tell me."

Angel drew a long breath. This was what she did.

What she'd become, when she'd collected the remaining fragments of herself and her existence and scraped them together to construct an approximation of a life. "I get how important this is. People like Virtanen... I know people like him."

"Yes. That's what I'm worried about."

"What's *that* supposed to mean?" Angel kept telling herself not to react. She kept failing. What was wrong with her?

"That this is not an assassination. I don't want you to get... carried away."

"*Excuse* me?"

Was that satisfaction that darted across Hahn's face, quick as a minnow? "You know exactly what I mean. No *accidents*. No heat of the moment decisions that you know best. Virtanen lives."

Another deep breath, and one more, like it would help. Hahn's stare drove straight through Angel as though she could see every ugly thought, every treacherous feeling; as though Angel's every move was utterly predictable.

"You think I lose control so easily?" Angel said.

"I think you didn't need to control yourself before. You were a renegade, with no one to answer to. If you wanted to kill out of vengeance, anger, even amusement – you could."

A bitter surge of nausea rose in Angel's throat. Anger. Amusement. She had never been driven by those things. But she knew someone who had been.

Was Hahn saying she was like *him*?

"In the South, you killed people you thought deserved it. Violent thugs, rapists, sadists. You were careful about the jobs you accepted, by all accounts."

"Yes. I was."

"But you also set up situations that allowed you to justify acting how you wanted. You were vengeful. Here, you don't get to decide who deserves to live or die."

"Right." Too late, Angel realised her fists were clenched. She had to force them to loosen. "Here *you* do that. How is that different, exactly?"

"The Agency considers assassination to be a last resort."

"Oh, of course. Because I always had plenty of other options." Angel could hear her own voice, cutting, sarcastic, like a stranger's. "Maybe I should've tied the bad guys up and left them outside the police station? Well, guess what? Half the time, the police *were* the bad guys – and the rest of the time, they worked for them. That's what the South was like. No relationship between law and morality. No one to help, except me. Don't you make me out to be a monster. I helped people."

"Yes. And now you have to learn to do so differently."

Angel wasn't even in her body anymore. She couldn't make herself do what she needed to do.

"You don't know me," she said at last. "Whatever it says in that folder, you don't know anything about me."

"We agree on that, at least. I don't know nearly as much as I'd like." Hahn flipped the file shut. "Go find Kimura. You have a lot of preparation to do."

"That's *it*? You just wanted to tell me you think I'm some sort of vigilante thug and warn me to behave?"

Hahn shrugged. "If that's how you want to look at it."

It took Angel too long to make herself move. Every moment she stayed stuck intensified the heat inside her, shrivelling her into something small and twisted.

When, too many seconds later, she had control of herself again, she turned, careful and mechanical, and left the office.

11

MASKS

"Okay." Faith sat on her desk, swinging her legs. "Once more. C'mon."

Her office, a few doors down from Hahn's, was so small there was barely room for Mackenzie to sit in front of her desk. With them sitting like this, their knees were almost touching. For some reason, this wasn't helping Mackenzie's concentration.

Mackenzie screwed up his face, focused, and produced what even he could recognise as a hideously mangled version of the Polish phrase she'd spent the last three hours teaching him.

"Oh, come on," he protested, as Faith dissolved into giggles. "It wasn't *that* bad."

She took off her glasses and wiped her eyes. "It really was. Sorry. Maybe it's just that I've never heard Polish in a Yorkshire accent before. Is there, uh, any chance...?"

"That I could tone down the accent?" Mackenzie

grinned. "Sky's been telling me for years it's gonna get me shot. You'd think that'd be enough incentive."

"I mean, would it help if I put a gun to your head?" Faith said, and immediately clapped a hand over her mouth. "Shit. I'm so sorry. That was –"

Mackenzie burst out laughing. "Honestly, it might be the only way."

Faith relaxed. "Maybe we'll keep that in reserve. Let's try phonetically. Give me a sec."

Mackenzie never normally had trouble making eye contact with anyone he didn't think might try to kill him, and macabre jokes aside, Faith probably didn't fall into that category. So why did he keep forgetting how to make his face work? And why had he been so simultaneously pleased and terrified to hear they'd be working together?

"Right." Faith clapped, and he shook himself. Shit. Had he been staring at her? Oh, God, he'd been staring.

"Let's try it this way," she said. "Repeat after me..."

Another painstaking hour of practice and he had it down. Well, sort of.

Faith high-fived him. "Like a pro. I knew you could do it."

"Well, that makes one of us. Now show me how it's actually meant to sound?"

She reeled off a string of flawless, fluid Polish. Mackenzie's mouth fell open. "That's amazing."

She ducked her head, her smile widening. "It's no big deal. I mean, look at all the stuff you've done."

She was really pretty when she smiled. She was

really pretty all the time, actually. "Er, how many languages are you fluent in again?"

"Uh... Russian, Polish, Spanish, Mandarin and French. My Arabic's not so good, but I'm working on it. And Kimura's taught me quite a bit of Japanese... What? Why are you laughing?"

"Because you're basically a genius, and you're impressed I can pick a couple of stupid locks."

"So I'm smart. I wouldn't have the nerve to do half the things you've done."

Mackenzie shrugged. "If you'd told me four years ago I'd end up breaking into drug dealers' houses or government offices, or that I'd *blow up a building*, I would've laughed in your face." It still sounded ridiculous. Often when people talked about jobs he'd pulled, his first reaction was, *what kind of nutter would do that?*

"How'd you even learn to do all that stuff?" Faith asked.

"I... taught myself."

"How come?"

Because the alternative had been starving to death. This was the thing about Skyler and Angel: even though talking to either of them could be rather like conversing with a brick, they *got* it. Especially Skyler. They'd been in the North together, spent all those years fighting to survive as fugitives in the South; he never had to fumble for explanations or worry that she'd think him over-dramatic. But how could he possibly explain to Faith?

Composing an answer that wasn't excruciatingly self-pitying would be a good start. "Well, I couldn't get a proper job in the South, obviously. I started off shoplifting and pick-pocketing, and then only when I got desperate. But it turned out I was good at it." He gave Faith a wry smile. "I never liked getting that close to people, though. So I bought some cheap tools from a guy in a bar and started burgling houses. I was lucky, I guess – I did athletics at school, and lots of rock climbing, before..." His throat tightened. He coughed. "Got into a few places other people thought were too difficult, and before I knew it I was getting approached."

His cheeks burned. He looked away. A common thief. That was all he was.

"Do you enjoy it?" Faith asked.

Huh. She didn't sound disdainful, disappointed. Only curious. "I like the challenge. I felt bad about breaking into people's homes, but the better I got, it was less personal, more business. The gangs and enforcers paid me to steal from rivals, that sort of thing. I preferred that."

"Really? That sounds way more dangerous."

"Ha. True. Those guys weren't very forgiving. I always made it clear I was neutral. Never asked who I was working for, never learned which heavies worked for who." He half-chuckled. "One time this gang paid me to steal a load of pills from another gang. Then the rival gang employed me to steal them back... It got a bit ridiculous. Every so often someone offered to put me on a retainer, but most of the people I worked for... they weren't good people."

"You are, though." She said it like it wasn't even a

question. He didn't know if it made him want to smile or cry.

All those people who'd come home to find their space invaded, their belongings gone. The drugs he'd helped get onto the streets. The money he'd made for people like Redruth.

"I try to be," he said. "But that doesn't really mean anything, does it?"

She touched his hand, just for a moment. "It means everything."

Seriously, what was wrong with him? Was his face ever going to go back to its normal colour?

"I'd never be brave enough to do anything like that," Faith added.

"I'm not brave. I was scared shitless the entire time."

"Yeah, but you did it anyway."

Mackenzie pretended to have developed a sudden extreme interest in his knees. Except Faith was so close it probably looked like he was staring at her knees. Christ.

He cleared his throat. "People are capable of all sorts when they're desperate enough. Doesn't make me brave."

"Brave and scared aren't mutually exclusive, Mackenzie. You can be both at once."

"That makes zero sense."

"Hey. You just called me a genius. I think that means you should trust me, don't you?"

Mackenzie and Angel – or Rosie, according to her passport; he'd never met anyone who looked less like a Rosie in his life – were, ostensibly, travelling to Armenia separately. Angel's cover story was that she was on a business trip. Mackenzie, whom Kimura had professed too young to pass for a businessman, was pretending to be on a school exchange. In some bizarre parallel universe, this was actually plausible. If he really had grown up in Poland, he might be in his final year of school now, with no idea how to pick a lock or scale a ten-storey building. Perhaps, perhaps.

Preparing for the op with Faith had been surprisingly fun, even if she had spent half the time teasing him about his accent. She'd even managed to distract him from the fact that he was, once again, throwing himself into a situation he might well not survive. In return, he'd taught her some phrases from his hometown, ones he'd never dared use in the South in case they slipped out in front of the wrong person, marking him as dangerously other, illegal, unwelcome.

He'd never been on a plane before. The urge to count, to bargain with some unseen entity, seized him the instant he set foot in Copenhagen airport. *You're allowed twenty-five steps from here to the next doorway. Angel will be okay if you count to seven before the security guard looks up.*

But it was impossible to stick to all those rules without making his behaviour obvious to Kimura, which would have been both risky and shameful, and every mistake, every incomplete ritual, ratcheted up the tightness in Mackenzie's chest until he felt like he was made of clockwork wound tight enough to snap.

Incredibly, though, the passport control officer in Copenhagen gave him only a cursory glance, and although the Armenian officer looked twice at his photo, she too waved him through. By then, his legs were so wobbly he could barely put one foot in front of the other.

While Angel and Kimura checked into Virtanen's hotel, Mackenzie ducked into a public toilet and emerged wearing navy overalls and carrying a large toolbox: the universal outfit of the maintenance man. Immediately, the tension drained from his body and he could walk with his head up, without calculating every step. Years of experience had taught him that an outfit like this made him virtually invisible.

Hefty, smartly-dressed doormen stood stiffly outside the hotel's sparkling glass doors. Adopting the air of slightly dim-witted helpfulness that had eased his path into so many such places, Mackenzie ambled up the marble steps.

The doorman thrust out a meaty hand, directing a rapid stream of what sounded like fairly unfriendly Armenian at him. Mackenzie allowed just the right amount of puzzlement to trickle across his features. "Sorry," he said in Polish. "I don't speak Armenian."

The unfamiliar syllables still felt strange in his mouth. The doorman's scowl intensified.

"Polish," Mackenzie offered with an apologetic smile, in English this time.

The doorman grunted. "ID."

Mackenzie fumbled for the badge Faith had made him. The doorman scrutinised his photo for longer than either of the passport control officers had, then grunted again. "Speak to front desk."

The hotel lobby *gleamed*, all polished chrome and glass and a glossy black floor Mackenzie could see his reflection in. He felt tiny, scruffy, like a flea-ridden stray cat wandering in. Arranging his features into a suitably hopeful expression, he approached the concierge, who regarded him over her severe glasses as if he'd come bearing a dead rat.

"What do you want?" she demanded in accented English. She peered at his ID, keeping her hands tucked behind the desk as though she might catch something. "Ah. Showers on fourth floor. I thought your people fixed those."

"Needed extra parts." Mackenzie showed her the holdall, offering up a silent apology to all Polish people everywhere for his accent.

She jerked her head. "Lifts are that way. Do not get dirt on carpets."

He scurried away, dodging the steely, dark-suited people dotting the lobby. They must be Virtanen's body-guards. No hotel needed *that* many bouncers.

Fourth floor. That was good; that was where Angel and Kimura were, though Mackenzie had mentally checked the room number so many times he was somehow less certain of it than ever. He was unsteady again, full of the humming urge to flee as he shifted from foot to foot outside the door. Finally, thank God, Angel opened it, slight and oddly formal in her tailored grey suit and the faint frown that seemed to permanently haunt her features these days.

The room was enormous, with a deep, soft carpet and more shiny black and chrome everywhere. "Bloody hell," Mackenzie said, staring. "Does this Virtanen have expensive tastes or what?"

Kimura was hunched in a leather armchair, his nose buried in his laptop. "He can afford them," he said, without looking up. "He's one of the richest men in the world."

Mackenzie looked at Angel. "Did you clock the number of bodies on the floor?"

She fiddled with her shirt cuffs. "Yes. It's not going to be easy to get past that much muscle."

Kimura's half-suppressed grimace suggested he agreed. But he said, "Hahn says you're the best. That's why you're here."

"Even so, I counted five just between here and the lobby. There'll be more on the top floor, and I'm sure you know that when it comes to knocking people out, it's basically go big or go home. If you want them unconscious for more than a couple of minutes, I can't guarantee they'll survive."

Mackenzie had expected a snide retort, but Kimura seemed unruffled. "It's Virtanen we need alive, not his entourage. He's probably paid off the hotel staff not to call the police, but gunshots would still draw attention. That aside, do what you need to do." He glanced up. "There's a plan, don't forget. I know you're used to winging it. That would really not be advisable here."

"No shit," Mackenzie muttered.

Two hours later, Kimura's computer pinged. Skyler appeared on the screen.

"Right," she declared. "Virtanen's got fifteen body-guards, all suitably menacing. Seven are patrolling the hotel. Three are on the top floor where his rooms are. The rest – the scariest ones – go wherever he goes. He's at some fancy diplomat party across town tonight. So all that muscle's going with him, and I" – she flashed them a winning smile – "am going to get the rest of them out of your way. He's got a secret code word that means he needs all hands on deck. If I send it from two or three phones it'll look nice and convincing, most of the muscle in the hotel will lumber over to him, and you can head on up to the top floor."

Angel picked at her thumb. "How many of his people will still be up there, do you think?"

"I reckon two. Which should be no trouble, right?" For the first time, there was an edge of anxiety to Skyler's voice.

"I think I can handle that."

"Good." Skyler peered severely into the camera. "You're both to come back in one piece, understand?"

"I'm impressed," Kimura commented.

Skyler attempted what was probably meant to be a modest shrug. "Yeah, well. I am really good at this. Oh – and he's doing a deal tomorrow, right?"

"Indeed."

"Well, I figured we might as well screw that up too, so I told his buyer the time's changed to four hours later."

Kimura gave a startled cough. "Did you clear that with Hahn?"

"Why, do you think I should have?"

"It would have been... uh, protocol."

"It was a good idea though, right?" Skyler cocked an eyebrow. "Right? Admit it."

"...Perhaps. In future, though, stick to the script."

"I'll take that as a thank you." She sat back, looking satisfied. "Good luck, guys. Be careful." She signed off.

Mackenzie looked at Angel. "You ever think about what the three of us could've got done if we'd spent the last few years working together?"

Kimura massaged his temples. "Is she always like that?"

"Afraid so," Mackenzie said cheerfully.

Kimura got to his feet. "Excuse me a minute."

Mackenzie grinned at Angel. "He's gone to warn Hahn that Sky's started taking the law into her own hands. And it only took her three days."

Angel almost smiled, but then her face fell.

Mackenzie frowned. "Angel, you know I keep asking if you're okay?"

"Mm?"

"D'you realise it's because I know full well you're *not* okay? Have you talked to Sky about it?"

She shook her head.

"Is something up with you two?"

Her expression had turned into one he recognised,

unfortunately. It suggested she was about to go somewhere else in her head; probably nowhere good. He touched her arm. "Angel?"

She blinked at him, but then her gaze slid away again. She stared at the carpet like she had no idea how she'd found herself there.

"No," she said at last. "Everything's fine with us."

Carefully, Mackenzie sat on the bed. He liked Angel. She was kind, she was patient – she was, in fact, much easier to get on with than Skyler. And although he still had a healthy respect for the fact that she could have killed him with both hands tied behind her back, over the past few months he'd come to consider her a friend.

But sometimes a switch would flip and suddenly she'd be a million miles away. He'd assumed she would be okay now they had Skyler back – because she was Angel, she was always okay. They needed her to be okay.

Maybe he'd been naïve, though. They were all still wrestling with stuff, after all, and they would probably all be in the ring for the rest of their lives.

"You don't have to talk to me about it," he said gently. "But I think you should talk to one of us."

Angel dragged her hands over her face. "You'll think it's stupid."

"Don't be daft."

She sat beside him, rubbing her hands together. "I... feel like there's something off about Hahn. I don't trust her."

"For what it's worth, I'm not sure I do either. I mean,

aside from the fact that she's obviously a literal robot, how many people do you really trust?"

"Sky. You. The twins."

"Yep, my count's about the same. And it took a long time to add Sky in after she knocked me out and stole that bloody memory stick. As far as I'm concerned, we take this whole Agency thing with a massive pinch of salt." He squeezed her shoulder. "But Angel... you have to *talk* about this. You know what Sky's like. If it's to do with feelings you pretty much have to spell it out, but she'll definitely want to hear it."

Angel rubbed her eyes. "Bloody hell, Mack, when did you get so wise?"

"I've always been wise. What aren't you telling us? What did Hahn say to you the other day?"

"She..." Angel fiddled with a loose thread in her jacket.

Mackenzie put out a hand. "Careful. That's a five-hundred-pound suit you're pulling apart."

"She said..." Angel's fists clenched. "She said she doesn't trust me not to kill Virtanen just because I feel like it. She basically called me a vicious murderer with no self-control."

Mackenzie winced. Evidently Hahn knew how to push people's buttons. He was glad she hadn't had a go at his yet. "Well, she's talking bollocks." He put an arm around Angel. "Birmingham was a better place with you in it."

Angel tried to smile again, but it was clear her heart wasn't in it.

12

ECHOES

Later that night, a courier delivered a suitcase to Angel. "Your missing luggage, ma'am." It had, of course, been impossible to carry her weapons on a commercial airline. There were local arrangements in place instead.

Mackenzie's lock-picking tools had survived airport security. Angel had watched him sag with relief when he checked his bags afterwards. His tools were custom-made and deeply personal; she'd never seen a finer set. She felt similarly about her own weapons; after all these years she knew their weight, their fit in her hands, like they were an extension of her own bone and muscle.

But the Agency had supplied a decent set for her: solid, well-crafted, the blades as sharp as she kept her own. And if they didn't feel quite perfect in her grip – well, she'd improvised plenty of times, too.

In a quiet moment, figuring she might as well take advantage of the Agency's resources, she'd asked Faith for a couple of other items she'd always wanted to experiment with but had never been able to source in the South. Faith had been surprisingly helpful, and surprisingly willing to accept the explanation, "I just think it might come in handy."

Angel loaded her pistols carefully, adjusting to their weight. She hadn't shot at anyone since the night they'd crossed the Wall. Over the last few days, while Skyler was busy showing Kimura how much better she was than all their other hackers and Mackenzie picked his way through the most complicated locks Faith could find, Angel had spent hours in the shooting range proving to herself she hadn't lost her touch.

She'd sparred with Joss and Lydia in the North – an unforgiving challenge – but she hadn't fought hand-to-hand for real either since the day before they'd blown up the lab. The day Redruth had turned up to exact his revenge on Skyler.

The fight itself was nothing but a bloody blur in her memory now. What she remembered, in the moments when she couldn't stop herself, was the single thought that had ricocheted around her mind as she'd hurtled towards the twins' house: *he's going to take her away like he took everyone else.*

You're too late.

You won't be able to stop him.

This can't be happening again.

The first time she'd felt real terror since –

Another front door, except she hadn't known what was waiting behind this one.

Flying into the house, sobbing. *Mum. Mum.*

Dinner cooking. Shepherd's pie. Hattie's favourite.

She burst into the living room, and he was there.

What's going on?

Blood soaking the carpet. It smelled like copper and meat. She hadn't known that before.

I don't understand –

Hattie's schoolbooks scattered on the floor, crimson seeping into her spelling homework.

Screaming. So much screaming.

Her throat constricting, drying like old paper. *Stop. Please. I'm sorry, I'm sorry.*

Can't move. Can't speak. Can't save them.

They don't understand. They don't understand why this is happening to them.

They only know it's my fault.

If I'd moved –

If I'd said something –

Anything –

I could have stopped him.

I should have stopped him sooner.

This can't be happening again.

It's my fault.

"Angel?"

A distant voice, at the end of a long tunnel. It didn't belong there.

"Angel?"

Pressure on her shoulders. Her hands flew out.

"Jesus –"

A rasp of fabric under her hands. She blinked.

A head of untidy dark hair and a thin, pale face swam

into view. "It's okay," Mackenzie said hoarsely. "It's just me, Angel. It's okay."

She blinked again. Mackenzie was up against a wood-panelled wall, his face taking on an unusually colourful hue. Her own arm, clad in expensive dark grey fabric, was across his throat.

Her thoughts moved with glacial slowness.

No screaming.

No blood.

Her legs shook. Her heart hammered like she'd been running for miles.

"Any time you fancy letting go of me," Mackenzie croaked.

She dropped him and staggered backwards, hands over her face. "Sorry," she mumbled.

He coughed. "Not gonna bother asking if you're okay. What happened?"

You have to look up. Remember where you are.

It took everything she had to make herself lower her hands. She stared around the room, slotting pieces into place. *This is Mack. You know him. You blew up a lab together.*

You're in Armenia, working for the Agency.

Redruth's not here.

That's in the past.

She wiped her forehead. Her hand came away damp.

Mackenzie rifled through the mini bar and handed her a glass bottle of water. Angel clutched it gratefully, using the cold as an anchor. *You're in Armenia. Redruth's dead.*

"Is – is Sky okay?" she whispered.

Mackenzie frowned. "She's fine. She's in Copenhagen, pissing everybody off."

Of course she is. She's safe.

Mackenzie guided her towards the bed. "You should sit down."

"I'm fine."

"Bollocks."

Angel ran her fingers over the silky bedspread. "What did I do?"

"Nothing, really. I came in and you were flat against the wall with your hands over your face. Did you even know I was there?"

She swallowed the rising acid of humiliation. "Did I – say anything?"

"Nope. Not a word."

Her shoulders were so stiff they'd cramped. When she wriggled them, pain rippled down her back.

"I've never seen that happen before..?" Mackenzie sounded like he was trying to find a good way to ask what the hell had just happened and couldn't think of a single one.

Angel gulped half the water and held the bottle to her cheek. "It hasn't happened for ages."

"It was like... a flashback?"

She nodded. She'd never spelled out to him what Redruth had done to her family because she'd dared to fall in love with his daughter. He wasn't stupid, though. He understood enough.

A shameful thought twisted round her insides, withering her into something small and pathetic. "Did Kimura see –?"

"No, don't worry. He's next door, talking to Sky."

"Oh. Okay."

"What helps? When this happens?"

"Uh..." She didn't want to talk about this. She wanted to seal it back in the terrible box she kept stuffed in the darkest corner she could shove it into. She wanted Mackenzie to forget what he'd seen.

But it was a sensible, if unwelcome, question.

"Cold," she said slowly. "Really strong smells – mint, or something. Knowing where I am. Knowing it's over."

"If I talked to you, would that help?"

"I don't know. There's not usually anyone else around." Reluctantly, she tried to recall the last few minutes. "But I think it helped just now, yes."

They sat in silence while Angel gulped the water and flexed her fingers, willing herself to stop shaking.

"D'you know what sets it off?" Mackenzie asked eventually.

He was asking all the right questions, the ones she'd asked him quietly, patiently, on the nights he couldn't leave his tent or he'd scrubbed his hands raw. She sighed. "Lots of things used to." For the longest time, dozens of things had had the power to catapult her back into the past. Eventually, she'd forced herself to list them all. Even that had felt impossible, unbearable. She'd been afraid she'd go crazy, that she would tear apart from the inside.

But once she had the list, what came next was a thousand times worse. Because then, one by one, she'd made herself face every item on it, over and over until she could see a blood-soaked carpet or hear *his* name or smell shepherd's pie cooking and stay anchored, know where she was, know what was happening.

It's just a memory, that's all.

And the thing that had driven her on, had held her together while every cell in her body was screaming at her to fall apart, was a single, piercing thought:

I'm going to stop him.

I'm going to make him pay.

"Angel?" Mackenzie said gently.

She shook herself. "I was thinking... about the last day at the twins' house. The day..."

"The day *he* turned up."

Her hands clenched around the water bottle. "Yes."

"Something specific?"

A surge of black ink, thorns and barbed wire, the taste of metal in her mouth, more blood, she was going to suffocate, she'd never claw her way back up –

"I – I can't –" Her voice caught, small and weak and frightened. She gritted her teeth. *Remember who you are.*

"It's not important," she said. "We've got a job to do."

Mackenzie squinted doubtfully at her. "Sure you're good for this?"

She didn't insult him by forcing a smile. "It happened most days for the best part of two years. I kicked plenty of ass during that time."

He patted her on the shoulder. "That's the spirit."

13

FALL

Whatever she said, though, Angel definitely did not look all right. Mackenzie wondered briefly whether he should talk to Kimura, let him decide whether Angel was in the right place to take on an arms dealer's posse. But he couldn't do that. It would have been a betrayal.

His own task was to retrieve a notebook from a safe locked inside another safe. If this seemed underwhelming, Faith had assured him that the notebook's contents would lead them to Virtanen's stock of weapons, waiting to be merrily distributed to anyone willing to pay. Apparently these were not the sort of people who could reasonably be trusted with a big pile of machine guns.

By the time Skyler sent the SOS message to Virtanen's people, Angel was, at least on the surface, back to normal: quiet, focused and armed to the teeth. Her footsteps made no sound on the plush carpet as Mackenzie and Kimura followed her up the stairs to the top floor.

Mackenzie made a mental note to ask her for stealth lessons.

As she opened the door onto the landing, a shadow moved on the wall opposite.

"Oh, sorry." Angel was all apologetic innocence. "Wrong floor –"

"Hester!" a male voice yelled.

Angel darted onto the landing. Through the glass in the door, Mackenzie watched her strike out at the male bodyguard. He'd never seen her fight before – he'd never seen *anyone* fight like this, spinning and ducking and pirouetting, every movement clean and fluid. It was a work of art.

But though the bodyguard couldn't land a hit on Angel, he shook off every blow she delivered. And then Hester arrived.

She was taller than Angel and much more solid, in a way that appeared to be pure muscle. Angel's onslaught stayed neat and precise and relentless – but how long could she keep this up for? She'd spent the last two months existing on rations, half of which she'd given away. Beside Virtanen's solid, well-fed people, she looked like a ghost.

Hester's fist slammed into Angel's rib cage with a sickening *crack* and Angel doubled over. She unfolded almost instantly, but Hester had already hit her again.

This time, Angel went rigid. And for the first time, it occurred to Mackenzie that this might not be a fight she could win.

Both bodyguards lunged forward, expressionless,

expert, professional. Angel came back to life just in time with a spinning kick to the man's kneecap. As he yelled and staggered, her foot slammed against his head. He crashed into the wall and slumped to the floor.

Hester flew at Angel, metal glinting in her outstretched hand. Angel grabbed her wrist and jerked. There was a *snap* of bone, and Angel snatched the knife and forced Hester up against the wall, pressing the blade to her throat.

And then Angel did... nothing.

Mackenzie pressed himself against the glass, his heart pounding furiously. What was Angel *doing*? Was she hurt? Hester wasn't fighting back. Angel had just... stopped.

He cast a desperate glance at Kimura. Surely he was about to step in?

But Kimura just watched, impassive, as Hester swung her unbroken arm around, slammed her fist into Angel's jaw and grabbed her by the throat. Angel made a horrible choking noise and dropped the knife, and –

Mackenzie launched himself onto the landing and had somehow managed to hook an arm around Hester's neck before he realised quite how stupid he was being. Hester reacted to this the way she might have to the appearance of a large wasp – annoying, perhaps capable of inflicting a little pain, but ultimately no more than a brief inconvenience. If she'd had two working arms, Mackenzie was pretty sure he would already have been smeared on the floor. As it was, though, he got in a blow to her windpipe. As Hester spluttered, Angel wrenched herself free, snatched up the knife, and plunged it into Hester's chest.

Everything went still.

Hester stood, blinking at the blood spreading bright and viscous across her shirt.

Mackenzie considered this was probably a reasonable time to let go of her.

As Hester collapsed, Angel turned away, white-faced. "That took too long," she muttered.

Mackenzie hurried after her, suppressing the urge to bombard her and Kimura with questions like "What just *happened*?" and "Hey, Kimura, didn't you feel like actually doing anything helpful there?"

Now they had a new problem. All ten rooms on this floor were booked under Virtanen's name. All ten contained identical safes. "You just need to work out which room's his," Faith had said breezily. "He's a control freak, he wouldn't trust anyone else."

It was going to be really bloody inconvenient if she was wrong.

"Wardrobe's your best clue," Angel murmured as Mackenzie groaned at the sight of the first immaculate, impersonal room.

It was a good call. The first three contained only black suits and white shirts. The fourth, however, boasted an array of vibrant, staggeringly expensive shirts.

Angel frowned. "We should still check the other rooms." Hester's finger-marks on her neck were already livid purple, but she'd recovered her composure. She seemed to have, anyway. That was what Mackenzie had thought earlier, too.

"Why?" he asked.

"Could be a decoy."

This, unfortunately, made sense. They checked the next few rooms, only to discover an equally lively wardrobe three doors down.

"Fuck." Mackenzie ran a hand through his hair. "I haven't got time to crack four safes."

"Here." Angel, rummaging through a drawer, held up something small and sparkling. "Diamond cufflinks. Look like the real thing."

"This one, then?"

She hesitated, then nodded.

"Right."

Angel stationed herself at the door. Mackenzie had no idea where Kimura had got to. It didn't matter. It wasn't like he'd been much bloody use so far.

He set to work.

He *loved* this part. Every time he picked up his tools, the humming tension in his muscles faded into pure, blissful clarity. No matter how complex the locks were, they were always an oasis of glorious simplicity. There was no point rushing or fumbling or worrying, reaching for rituals or trying to jump impossible mental hoops. They offered a certainty that didn't exist anywhere else in his world: there was one solution, and when he found it, the lock would open.

And the pride, the sheer exhilarating buzz when all that painstaking care and precision paid off – what a joy.

He'd been paid a fortune to pick locks designed by some of the world's greatest locksmiths. He'd stolen devastating secrets and items of inconceivable value. He had never – with the single exception of the Board drive – kept anything he'd stolen for himself. The thrill of knowing that he alone had conquered those impeccably crafted safeguards was its own reward.

Skyler had asked him once how he knew what to do. He just *knew*. And after so many years, so many locks, came a confidence that didn't exist anywhere else in his world either: if one tactic didn't work, that was fine. He would learn from it, and he would try something else, and then he'd learn from *that*, and eventually it would just... happen.

Still, this lock was taking *quite* a long time.

The first safe was fine: it was hefty and well-made, but to a familiar specification. The second, however, was custom-designed, probably by someone much more experienced than Mackenzie, and it was built *into* the first safe, so there was no way to remove it without taking half a wall with you.

He closed his eyes, tuned out the chatter of his thoughts. Just him and the lock. The tiny clicks and tremors, the tension in his tools, the rasp of metal against metal. Nothing else mattered.

One last click, and the door swung open.

"Good," Kimura said in his ear. Mackenzie yelped and dropped his tools. "Virtanen will be here in five minutes."

Mackenzie grabbed the three leather-bound notebooks from the safe and shoved them into his holdall. "Shit. What do we do?"

"Leave through the service exit on the lower ground floor. There's a car two streets away. *Walk*, don't run. We mustn't give anyone reason to question us."

Mackenzie looked at Angel's suit, which was stiff with drying blood. "Like that, you mean?"

She wrenched off her jacket and stuffed it into his holdall. It didn't help much. Mackenzie tried not to think about his tools getting covered in Hester's blood.

"I'll say it's wine, if anyone asks," she said. "*Then* I'll run."

As they scrambled down the stairs, Mackenzie knew they were moments from being caught, that he should be focused on escaping and absolutely nothing else – but he couldn't shake the thought that kept banging up against the forefront of his mind.

Angel froze.

They weren't going to make the getaway vehicle. The nagging wrongness in Angel's chest insisted, and her instincts were rarely wrong. She tried to ignore the thought that they had not been serving her well today.

Kimura and Mackenzie hurried out of the service exit into an alley and headed for the main street. As they disappeared, Angel hung back.

The alley was empty save for five industrial-sized bins. She slipped between two of them, readying a pistol in each hand. She wasn't going to waste time convincing herself she could do this. She *had* to do it.

The service door crashed open. Dark-suited body-guards – male, female, slim, heavy, black, white – spilled into the alley. Angel didn't always shoot to kill, but these were professionals; mercy would be the last mistake she ever had the chance to make. By the time the last ones standing realised where the shots were coming from, it was already over.

The alley was a mess. She felt nothing, taking in the scene she'd created, but it would take some effort to get out without leaving footprints.

Right now, though, that was the least of her worries.

Virtanen's bodyguards dressed with neat, expensive anonymity; Virtanen dressed with flair. He was a foot taller than Mackenzie, with blonde hair swept back from a high forehead, and he had slender hands – pianist's hands – one of which was pressing a knife to Mackenzie's throat. His sole remaining bodyguard, an Asian man with a deeply humourless expression, was holding a gun to Kimura's head.

A razor slash of fear, hot and sharp. Angel gritted her teeth. *Hold on.*

Why hadn't Virtanen just killed them? But of course, it was in the poise of his blade at Mackenzie's throat. He wanted to revel in it, eke out every last drop of suffering. But if he had to do it fast, he wanted to be soaked in it, immersed in it.

Just like Redruth.

She'd expected the fear again, was ready to stamp on

it, but instead it was rage, dark and jagged, that sprang to life inside her. And that was all right. She knew what to do with rage.

The bodyguard waited, stony-faced. Kimura was equally unreadable. Mackenzie looked rather resigned.

"Well," Virtanen mused. His gaze roved over Angel like a promise: *I'll remember you.* "Who are you, little girl? The angel of death?"

Angel said nothing.

Virtanen waggled his eyebrows in a way many people had probably found endearing, to their detriment. "I think you and I should have a little chat."

"It doesn't look like I've got much choice," Angel said.

He beamed. "Indeed! And you seem a smart girl, so I'm sure you know exactly how much I'll enjoy taking your friend's eye out if you upset me. Lay down your weapons – slowly, please – and come upstairs."

"Okay." Angel crouched carefully, holding eye contact with him. "I'm putting them down."

Gently, she laid her pistols in front of her. As she did so, she dislodged a small glass vial tucked into her left sleeve. It rolled out onto the ground just behind one of the guns.

"There's a knife in my belt," she said. "Can I reach behind me and take it out and put that down too?"

He nodded benevolently.

Angel reached behind her, inching her left foot forward. The vial crunched under her boot. She closed her eyes, swung the third gun out of her waistband, and the alley burst into brilliant, blinding light.

Virtanen yelled. There was a scuffle of feet and a grunt that suggested someone had taken an elbow straight to the stomach. With her eyes still screwed shut, Angel aimed her pistol and fired twice.

The shots died away. Angel lowered the gun, her heart beating as fast as a hummingbird's wings.

"Er," a Yorkshire accent said, and the surge of relief almost buckled her knees. "You can probably open your eyes now."

The searing flare of the magnesium had faded, leaving strange bright after-impressions. Mackenzie was picking himself up and still had both eyes. Kimura was standing over the dead bodyguard looking like he didn't know whether to be pleased or furious.

And Virtanen was on the ground, his immaculate suit perfectly at odds with the graceless sprawl of his limbs, a single bullet hole in the centre of his forehead.

Mackenzie winked at Angel. "Show off."

Kimura's lips pursed so tight they all but disappeared. "I think we'd better get the hell out of here," he said.

14

CRACKS

By the time Hahn got off the phone to Kimura, the temperature in her office seemed to have dropped below freezing. Faith's pulse had begun to quicken, a counterbalance to the deepening chill of the atmosphere, several seconds into the call. "What's happened?" she asked. "Did – did something go wrong?" Oh, God. Had they underestimated Virtanen? Had she given Mackenzie bad advice?

Hahn's face was a mask. The sort that featured in films Faith had always been too scared to watch as a kid. "Virtanen's dead."

"...Oh."

"The girl shot him."

Oh. "Well – she must've had a good reason, right?"

"Presumably she thinks so. That's irrelevant." Hahn tapped her pen against her desk. "She was warned."

"Do you know why –?"

"I don't care why. She needs to learn she can't behave like this."

Hahn's idea of a lesson was not a gentle reflection on what one might do differently next time. "What... uh, what are you going to do?"

Taptaptaptaptap. "Put her in her place."

Well, that was sure to go down brilliantly. "Julia –"

"No. She sits there claiming she doesn't want to kill anyone, and then we send her out and the first thing she does is put a bullet in someone's head. This was her chance to show she could solve problems without violence, and she's failed. She might not want to be a killer, but she doesn't know how not to be one."

Faith steeled herself. "I... think maybe you're being unfair."

The full force of Hahn's glare swung towards her and Faith immediately regretted her decision. "Explain."

"I don't think she's violent by nature. She doesn't enjoy hurting people. The way the South is... I think she genuinely didn't have much choice."

"And she needs to understand that the rules have changed. If she sees her behaviour as innate, rather than something she can adapt, there'll be trouble for her and everyone who comes into her orbit. Unless" – with a sarcastic edge – "you think we should let her keep running around killing at will?"

"I just think maybe *putting her in her place* isn't the way to handle this. She doesn't seem to be her usual self."

"If she's so fragile, that's also a problem."

The back of Faith's neck prickled. It wasn't that she

couldn't challenge Hahn. Hahn had always encouraged it, even if her standard response was to circle back around and go in for the kill. *If you don't have enough conviction in your ideas to defend them,* she told Faith, often, *what good are they?*

"If Angel's struggling," she tried, "shouldn't we help her deal with that? Not pile it on to see how much she can take before she cracks."

"The fault lines are already there. If we tried to *help her*" – Hahn's lip curled – "we'd just be papering over them, and all that means is that we wouldn't see when she was about to fall apart. You never know what someone's truly capable of, Faith – in the best and worst of ways – until they're at breaking point. Would you rather that happened now, or when she's halfway through saving an entire country?"

"But surely this isn't the only way to –"

Hahn slammed her pen down. "As Skyler keeps reminding us, the North has very little time. We've got weeks, maybe, before the Board reaches an agreement with the US. Once they do, the North will be bombed into oblivion within days. I will not have another failed mission over there, Faith."

Faith bit her lip. This was why she'd brought this to Hahn, after all. She had known Hahn wouldn't be able to resist.

"It's my biggest failure." Hahn straightened a pile of papers and smoothed her hair. "And look what the cost has been. So if we have to rule the girl out of the op – even if we have to let her get herself killed – then that's what we'll do. Right now she's stuck, and we can't pull her out of that mess. She's got to get through it herself. So either we push her through it, or we leave her behind."

* * *

They were late.

Angel and Mackenzie should have been back by lunchtime. But mid-afternoon arrived with no sign of them and a thousand terrible possibilities were burrowing inside Skyler, poison-tipped needles creeping under her skin.

She didn't *do* worry. Oh, she was used to *fear*, the howl of the alarm – *run, you're in danger* – but that was always an in-the-moment reaction. Worrying about what *might* happen seemed like a waste of energy that could be better spent trying to survive everything that actually *was* happening.

But now all she could think of were the ways she might lose Angel and Mackenzie. And every time she pictured a blade in Angel's stomach, a bullet in Mackenzie's chest, she didn't know whether she wanted to cry or throw up or smash something.

After the Wall had gone up, through all the endless years in Daniel's cellar when danger had been her constant shadow, Skyler had survived by refusing to feel anything at all. Now suddenly she had far, far too many feelings, and there seemed to be no way of shutting them off again.

This was incredibly inconvenient.

Skyler stared at her laptop without seeing it, twisting a strand of hair around her fingers. Usually her work could distract her from pretty much anything, but she couldn't even remember what she'd spent the last half hour doing.

She needed answers, but she might as well consult a fortune cookie as try to get them from Hahn. Besides, the idea of showing Hahn her anxiety set the alarm in Skyler's brain pinging urgently. Kimura seemed okay, but he was with the others. She'd barely exchanged a handful of words with anyone else.

There was Hahn's assistant, though, Faith. Mackenzie seemed to like her. And despite his bizarre insistence on seeing the best in people, he wasn't stupid.

She found Faith's office door ajar. When she pushed it open, Faith looked up from behind her desk, surprise flitting across her face.

Maybe Skyler should have knocked. Oh well.

Faith, to her credit, didn't comment. "Hey." She closed her laptop. "How're you doing?"

Skyler clenched her fists. Having feelings was one thing. Sharing them with an almost-stranger, even as a secondary function, felt almost as dangerous as the images taunting her.

But she had to know. She had to.

"Have you heard anything?" she asked, before she could change her mind. "They should've been back by now, right?"

Faith hesitated. A caustic wave of dread rose in

Skyler's throat: *something's wrong, someone's hurt, someone's dead* –

"What?" she demanded. "What's wrong?"

"They're fine," Faith said, and Skyler's legs shook with relief. "But things didn't quite go... according to plan. They couldn't come back on a commercial flight. They had to drive into Turkey to get picked up."

So something *had* gone wrong. "Why? What happened?"

Faith polished her glasses absentmindedly on her shirt. "Everyone's in one piece, don't worry. I can't give you all the details right now."

"Why the hell not?"

"Well, I don't actually know them, for one. It's *okay*, Skyler. They'll be back tonight, and no one's badly hurt."

Skyler was tempted to plant herself in front of the desk until Faith told her exactly what she *did* know, but Mackenzie and Angel would probably both point out this wasn't the most diplomatic course of action. "Right," she said instead, reluctantly. "Okay." She turned towards the door, then remembered herself. "Oh. Thanks."

"I get it," Faith said. "It's not easy waiting behind."

That was more than enough sharing feelings for one day. "Okay." Skyler turned away again. "See you later."

But the hours dragged into the evening, and Skyler still couldn't lose herself in her work. What did Faith mean, no one was *badly* hurt?

Finally, just when she thought she really might go

mad, someone knocked at her door. She leapt up and flung it open.

"Their helicopter's landing," Faith said, before Skyler could broadcast her disappointment. "D'you want to come up?"

Hahn was already on the roof when they arrived. She ignored Skyler but shot Faith a pointed glare. Skyler wondered briefly what that was about – but then the helicopter touched down and she forgot to care.

Mackenzie looked fine, if a little dishevelled. But Angel –

Skyler drew a sharp breath. Angel's eye was swollen, the left side of her jaw bluish-purple, her clothes rusty with blood. Her shoulders were hunched, making her look smaller than usual.

Skyler scrambled towards her, but Hahn stepped between them. "My office," she told Angel curtly. "Now."

"For fuck's sake," Skyler snarled. "Can't you –"

Hahn spared her a contemptuous glance. "No."

"You can't just –"

A hand caught at Skyler's sleeve. "*Don't*," Faith whispered urgently as Skyler rounded on her, fizzing with rage. "Seriously."

"She may need to see a doctor," Kimura said.

Angel straightened her back. "I'm fine."

Skyler caught her eye and mouthed, *I'll be waiting for you.* A little of the grimness ebbed from Angel's face as she followed Hahn.

15

ABYSS

"Explain," Hahn said.

Her desk, with its mountain of paperwork, was between her and Angel like a moat. Angel was so exhausted the room felt like it was tilting sideways. She was going to have to choose between staying on her feet and lining up a coherent sentence.

"I... had to," she managed at last.

"No," Hahn snapped, "what you *had* to do was not shoot Virtanen. And instead you created such a bloodbath that Kimura had to drive you all to the next country. Few governments can ignore the matter of twelve bodies behind the country's most expensive hotel."

Angel could feel her patience wearing down to the bone. "I was protecting Mackenzie and Kimura."

"You were told not to kill Virtanen."

"Are you seriously telling me you'd rather I'd saved that piece of shit than them? I don't believe you. And if it's true, I don't want to work for you."

"You could have found another solution."

"There was hardly time for a conference call!"

"I was very clear that Virtanen's death was not an option. And yet you still decided it was. Can you honestly not see how much of a problem that is?"

Every nerve in Angel's body was buzzing, urging her to turn and walk away. But it wasn't just her future at stake, but Skyler's, Mackenzie's and every single surviving Northerner.

If she hadn't already jeopardised all of that.

She screwed up her eyes. "Perhaps it would help," she said slowly, "if I understood *why* it was so important. Surely he'd have been almost impossible to prosecute? His lawyers must be as good as his bodyguards."

"Better," Hahn murmured. "It was never about that."

Angel blinked. "I... don't understand."

"You're right. He'd have murdered and bribed his way through the witnesses and the prosecution. We'd never have put him away."

This didn't make sense because Angel was tired and shaken and frustrated. That was all. "Then why did you want him alive?" Her stomach lurched. "Unless – you *wanted* him to keep selling weapons?"

"Oh, don't be dramatic. Of course not."

Angel was going to scream. "Then *why* –?"

"It was a test," Hahn said calmly. "To see if you could handle a difficult situation without resorting to murder. And it would appear that you can't."

* * *

Skyler was in her room with Mackenzie when Angel arrived, white-faced, her movements heavy with misery. Mackenzie jumped to his feet at once.

"You don't have to –" Angel began.

He squeezed her shoulder. "It's all good. I'll see you in the morning."

Skyler shot him a grateful look as he slipped out. She held out a hand to Angel. "Are you okay? What's –?"

Angel collapsed into a ball on the bed, her body heaving with huge, wracking sobs. A lump hardened in Skyler's throat. Uncertainly, she curled herself around Angel. "It's okay. It's okay. I've got you."

But it wasn't okay. She had no idea how to help. And Angel just kept sobbing into the duvet like her heart was broken, like she might never stop.

"I can't do this anymore," Angel mumbled at last. "I can't, Sky."

"You don't have to." Skyler rubbed her back. "You don't have to do anything you don't want to."

"I do –" Another sob. "It's all I'm good for. Hahn basically said so."

"What does she know?" With an effort, Skyler kept her tone gentle. What had Hahn done? Skyler would kill her. If she could kill to protect herself, she could certainly do it for Angel. "She doesn't know anything about you."

"She knows I'm a monster."

"Angel, no." Skyler held her tighter. "That's not true."

"It is." Angel sniffed. "Did Mack tell you what happened today?"

"Uh... He said you had a... bad moment, before the op. And that during the fight..."

"I froze," Angel said flatly. "I *froze*. That's never happened before."

Skyler hesitated. But Angel seemed to want to talk; maybe it was okay to ask. "Why do you think it happened today?"

"I –" Angel gulped. "D'you know what I thought when Kimura told me I could kill the bodyguards? I thought: *good, that makes my life easier*. I was about to cut this woman's throat, and it was like... like I woke up, right then. I woke up and realised I'm someone who kills people to make their life *easier*. I've spent the last five years fighting monsters, and I didn't even notice I'd turned into one."

Skyler sat up and pulled Angel into her lap, rocking her the way she remembered her mum doing for her when Skyler was small and grieving over something so much less important than this.

"My family," Angel said bitterly. "They'd be so sick if they could see what I've become."

"I don't believe that. We're all different now, Angel. We had to be." Skyler stroked Angel's hair, searching for the words to convey this most important of things. It was like trying to speak a foreign language, but Angel needed to hear it, so she had to get it right.

"You saved me," she said at last. "You didn't even know me the first time you saved my life. You did so much to protect me when I lived in the cellar. You helped me when I stole the drive from Mack even though you both thought I was being a brat." Angel gave a tiny, choked laugh. "You figured out what to do about the virus when it would've been so much easier to walk away. You came to rescue me that day at the twins' even though I was being an asshole." She coaxed her fingers under Angel's chin. "You sat up all those nights with Mack. Remember?"

Angel nodded.

"Well, then. If that's your idea of making your life easier, you're doing a bloody terrible job of it."

Another wobbly almost-laugh. Skyler took a deep breath. "All those years in that cellar and I never let myself hope, I never wished for anything good, because I knew it would never come. And now –" Her voice cracked, because it was true, where would she be without Angel? At the bottom of the canal or in the ground, or worse, maybe – lost and wandering, breathing but not alive, with no idea what safety or joy or hope felt like. "And now here you are."

She bent her head. "Angel. Look at me."

"I can't."

"You need to." Skyler lay down and tilted Angel's chin up to meet her eyes. "If you believe anything," she whispered, "believe this. I need you. I don't know how to do any of this without you. You're the furthest thing from a monster, and I don't care what anyone says, and I don't care why the Agency thinks you're here. You can be whatever you want to be, and I won't ever let anyone tell you otherwise."

Angel was crying again, tears running down her nose and onto Skyler's pillow. "What did I do to deserve you?"

"You were just you. That's kind of the point." Skyler kissed her carefully on the forehead. "C'mon. Let's get you cleaned up."

16

CHAOS THEORY

Faith was halfway to Mackenzie's room before she'd thought about what she was doing. She had no idea what she was going to say to him. She just wanted to know if he was okay.

Something strange fluttered in her stomach as she knocked at his door. Was she nervous? About talking to Mackenzie? That would be ridiculous, wouldn't it?

The door opened. She looked up.

"Oh," Mackenzie said. "Hi."

She hadn't expected *that* little enthusiasm. She stepped back. "Hello yourself."

He grimaced. "Sorry. I didn't mean –" He ruffled his hair. "I thought you were someone else."

"I came..." Was this a stupid idea? People did this all the time, right? It was no big deal. "I just wondered – do you fancy a drink?"

"Uh..."

"Or, you know, not. I just figured – it's traditional to celebrate a success, right?"

His brow wrinkled. "Not really where I'm from, to be honest."

"Well, I promise you this way's much more fun." But evidently this had, after all, been an epically stupid idea. Faith backed away, willing the heat from her cheeks. Why was she so mortified? Because she'd thought maybe he liked her? That they understood each other, somehow? This was exactly why she didn't do the feelings thing: she obviously didn't have a clue what she was doing. And it was kind of pathetic, really, moping around wondering what a boy thought of her. "Seems like you'd rather be on your own, though. I'll see you later."

"No – I didn't mean –" He reached after her and she turned before she could stop herself. "Sorry. I didn't mean to be rude. This is all just... very new."

There were shadows under his eyes and a tiny nick at his throat. Perhaps she'd expected too much, imagining he'd be in the mood to celebrate.

"Are you okay, Mackenzie?" she asked.

"I... yeah. Sort of. I don't know. I'm fine."

"Well, that's super convincing."

He made a noise that was part sigh, part weary, humourless laugh. "Virtanen was pretty nuts."

"I heard."

"He told Angel he was gonna take my eye out. Pretty sure he meant it."

"That..." What the hell did you say to that? *Oh well, good job he didn't?* "You must've been terrified."

145

He gave her one of those sweet, lopsided smiles that did confusing things to her stomach. "I dunno what this says about my life, but I'm not sure that even makes the top five scariest shit. Angel was there, anyway. She wouldn't have let anything bad happen."

Angel had been rather too erratic for comfort, by the sound of it. "You must really trust her."

"I do," he said simply. "More than anyone I know."

"She... kind of went off-script today, right?" Perhaps if Faith understood what had happened, she'd be able to fend Hahn off Angel. "D'you have any idea why –?"

But she'd made a mistake. Mackenzie's expression closed down like a shutter slamming. "She did what she had to do. She saved me and Kimura."

"Was there really no other way?"

"No. She shouldn't be in trouble. She got us out alive."

"Mackenzie –"

"You didn't have to invite me out to do this, you know." There was hurt in his dark eyes.

"I'm not! That's not what I – I just –"

Mackenzie stood, studying the carpet as though trying to solve some complex equation. At last, he glanced up. "Do you guys really want to help us? Is this really –? We're trusting you. Should we?"

Unexpectedly, that hurt. "Why would we do all this if we didn't want to help? I was just worried about you and Angel. Kimura said she choked up, and –"

Another mistake. Mackenzie gripped the doorknob. "She was fine. She handled it."

"I'm just trying to understand –"

"I don't want her to get into trouble."

"I'm not going to get her into trouble!" Exasperation sharpened Faith's tone. She took a deep breath.

Mackenzie shook his head. "I shouldn't be talking to you about this. I'm sorry I – I'm sorry. I can't do this."

Do *what*? Though she would definitely rather not be doing this weird, stumbling, cross-purpose dance either. She sighed and turned to leave. "I'll go. Sorry I disturbed you. I hope you're okay."

"Kimura didn't help," he said.

Faith stopped dead. "Excuse me?"

She turned back. Mackenzie's shoulders were slumped, a crease between his brows that added years to his face. "Kimura didn't help," he repeated. "Angel got into trouble with the bodyguards, and he just stood and watched her get beaten."

He met Faith's eyes. "Would he have stepped in? Or was he just going to let them kill her?"

"Mackenzie..."

"Goodnight, Faith." His voice was achingly weary.

"Mackenzie –"

He closed the door.

"How did Angel take the debrief?" Kimura asked the next morning in Hahn's office.

Hahn, as usual, was doing four things at once. She glanced up from her typing. "Well, she didn't throw anything or punch anything, so that's a start."

Faith dragged her hands through her hair. She'd spent the night with Mackenzie's words running on a loop in her brain: *Kimura didn't help.* And this morning she'd walked into Hahn's office to find the pair of them merrily debating the best way to get a rise out of Angel.

"They'll never trust us if we keep acting like this," she said. "They'll think we're deliberately fucking with them." Which, to be fair, was exactly what was happening.

"I don't care whether they trust us," Hahn retorted. "I want to know if we can trust *them*."

"Is this really going to encourage them to be trustworthy?"

"They need to understand they can't just run around doing whatever they want."

"What, so this is some weird dominance thing now?"

Hahn stopped typing. "That's *enough*." She didn't raise her voice even a fraction, but her words had the finality of a steel door. "This is not about everyone being friends. This is about taking down a totalitarian regime. Those three think they know what they're doing – they have no idea it's only through blind luck they haven't already got the North wiped off the map. They are not the experts here. And neither are you."

Faith fought the instinct to recoil, to make herself smaller. She could argue with Clara or Hakima or even Kimura all day long, but Hahn's chastisement never failed to make her feel three inches tall.

"At least Angel's shown she can be creative under pressure," Kimura offered cheerfully.

"By disregarding a direct order." Hahn's attention was, unfortunately, back on Faith. "That's another thing. You didn't think to mention she'd asked you for extra kit?"

"Uh –" Truthfully, Faith knew she should have run that past Kimura. But, she'd figured, where was the harm? She'd reasoned that Angel needed to see she had at least one ally here. "I... didn't think it was a big deal."

"Doubtful. But now you know better."

Kimura stretched his arms over his head. "Don't be too hard on her, Julia. That magnesium did save my life."

"I'm sure there's a blessing in there somewhere."

Faith had never been out on an op with Kimura, but every agent she knew talked about how reassuring he was, how supportive. *He didn't help*, Mackenzie had said. But she couldn't imagine him just watching someone get beaten to a pulp.

Hahn, maybe. But not him.

She took a deep breath. "Ren?"

"Oh, she's not done." Kimura raised his eyebrows. "That desperate to get back in the firing line?"

Not really. But she couldn't let this go. "Mackenzie said... when Angel got into trouble... he said you didn't step in." She wasn't accusing him. He just needed to know, so he could help the Northerners understand what had really happened. The look in Mackenzie's eyes the night before had been that of a wild animal that had just started to consider trusting someone and then spotted the cage. If they weren't careful, he and the others would bolt into the shadowy depths of the woods and never come close enough to risk another betrayal.

"I didn't," Kimura said.

Faith snapped her head up. "*What?*"

"Imagine what we'd get from Clara and her lot if I'd had to intervene on their very first op. Besides – this was an assessment. I needed to see if she could handle it."

"They kicked the shit out of her!"

"And she handled it. With some help from the boy, anyway. He's not exactly a fighter, that one."

"But –"

"I would have stepped in if I'd had to. I wouldn't have let her get seriously hurt."

It made sense, in an Agency robotic sort of way. But it didn't feel right.

Hahn sighed. "Faith. Am I going to have to reassign you?"

"What? No!" This was *her* op. She was meant to be here.

"Then you need to remember your place. Which is not to be these people's friend. Kimura and I aren't here to be *nice* to them –"

– like that wasn't abundantly clear –

"And nor are you. You're not on their side."

Faith started to retort that she'd thought they were all on the same side, and then caught Hahn's eye and closed her mouth instead.

17

TEAMWORK

Three days after Armenia, they were back in Hahn's office.

They'd been more or less left alone in the meantime. Angel was trying to act like she was back to normal, but she was on the edge of her seat, gripping her knees with white knuckles.

Reluctantly, Skyler examined the file Faith had handed her. She'd promised Mackenzie she wouldn't start any arguments, even though they'd just been handed another total waste of time mission that had nothing to do with the North.

"This one's in Denmark," she said. "Does that mean I get to go?"

"Yes," Hahn said. "Try not to get over-excited."

God, she was itching to tell Hahn to fuck off, though.

Angel flipped through the pages. "What's the job?"

"An Iranian couple, Leila and Amir Yousefi, are passing through Aarhus. They're human traffickers – not as sophisticated as Virtanen, but just as unpleasant. They've sold thousands of people into slavery."

"And you want them arrested?"

"No." Hahn met Angel's eyes. "We want them killed."

Angel stiffened.

Skyler held up a hand. "Hang on. Why are these guys different?"

"There's no point trying to bring them to trial," Faith said. "They'd just disappear."

"What are you, her PR rep? Who *makes* these decisions?"

"That's not your concern," Hahn said.

"Bollocks." Skyler leaned forward. "You're asking us to murder two people and you don't think we need to know who decided that and why?"

Kimura coughed, looking pained. "Hahn and I came to this conclusion in consultation with our colleagues in Iran. Faith's right. Interpol are nowhere near catching these two."

"The rationale's in that file," Hahn added. "Rest assured a good deal more thought went into it than most of the decisions you three have made."

"Assuming that's true, you've got a building full of agents. Why are you asking us?"

"You need to earn your keep."

Skyler barked a laugh. "Is *that* what you think?"

"Sky –" Mackenzie began.

He was way too patient. Fair enough, she'd promised no arguments, but these people were taking the piss. "No,

Mack. We came here because this lot said they'd help us take down the Board and we literally haven't heard a word about that since we arrived. They're wasting time the North doesn't have, and they expect us to just be grateful and do as we're told? People are dying over there every day we sit around doing nothing."

Kimura sighed. "Skyler. That's not –"

Hahn got to her feet, slow and elegant. "I don't care if you're grateful. You have two options: return to the North and try to take on the Board with no intelligence, no technology, no resources – or stay here and do it our way. That means remembering yours aren't the only people who need help. You seem to think the world revolves around you. It doesn't."

Hot with fury, Skyler opened her mouth to tell Hahn to go fuck herself. But then she caught Hahn's expression. It was the expression of someone who was looking forward to watching their opponent dig their own grave.

Skyler shut her mouth. Beside her, Mackenzie breathed what might have been a very small sigh of relief.

"We haven't forgotten the UK," Kimura said gently, ignoring Hahn's scathing glance. "After this op, we'll attend to it. There's no immediate threat, I promise. But the Yousefis will only be in Denmark for another couple of days, and we have a real chance to save a lot of lives and prevent a lot of misery. Please will you help us?"

Skyler turned to Angel, whose face was carefully blank. "It's your call. Are you okay with this?"

Angel nodded.

"Angel –"

"I think we should do it." Angel glanced at Mackenzie. "How about you?"

He hesitated. "If you're okay with it –"

"I can shoot," Skyler told Hahn. "It doesn't have to be Angel."

For a deeply satisfying instant, incredulity cracked through Hahn's composure. "I... don't think that's a good idea."

"How would *you* know?"

Angel touched her arm. "You're not killing anyone for me, Sky."

Kimura almost looked relieved, but he recovered well.

"Good." Hahn snapped her laptop shut. "We'll run the op tomorrow. Faith will help you prepare."

"Uh." Mackenzie rubbed his neck. "When you say *we* –"

"I'm your handler this time." Hahn's stare was a challenge. "Faith's coming too. It will be a learning experience for her."

Kimura got to his feet. "Skyler, come with me, please. We need to discuss how you access the Yousefis' phones."

They really didn't. "I can do it myself."

"Stop being a drama queen. You'll do it faster with my help. And the sooner this is done, the sooner we move onto the North."

"I don't –" But she did care, of course. She knew perfectly well how petty she was capable of being, but that didn't extend to putting actual lives at risk.

Kimura's office was more cramped than Hahn's, a little less like an android's, with a couple of photos of people Skyler supposed were relatives and a slightly forlorn potted plant. She plonked herself in front of his desk, scowling. "What've you got, then?"

He slid into a chair opposite her. "Nothing. Just some advice."

"Are you fucking kidding? As if you were just on about *me* wasting time –"

"Skyler. Shut up."

Skyler's mouth fell open. "What did you just say to me?"

"You know very well I can't get into those phones any quicker than you. But let me give you some advice in a language I think you'll understand. Knock the attitude the fuck off."

"*Excuse* me?"

"You've already started a war with the Board. Don't start one with Hahn too."

"Kimura, she's deliberately fucking with Angel. You know she is! Kill people, don't kill people – what's she playing at?"

"Her job. Which is making sure her team are capable."

Skyler folded her arms. "Bullshit." She'd thought Kimura was all right, but he was obviously as much under Hahn's thumb as everyone else in this bloody place.

Kimura smiled. "Listen. I can't say I always agree with Julia's methods, but I know her. She's as stubborn as you, but with twenty years' more experience. I can help you – and Angel – but not if you keep this up. She'll only dig her heels in, and trust me, you don't want that."

"Has anyone ever told you lot that you're psychopaths?"

"And you, as I believe I mentioned, are a drama queen. This will blow over if you just play the game, Skyler – but if you try to change the game, she'll change it too. You won't win. Don't forget we're on the same side here."

"It doesn't bloody feel like it."

"You and Hahn are more similar than you think. You're both control freaks."

"Fuck off."

Kimura just shrugged serenely. "The best way you can help Angel is to not piss Julia off. Which – let's be honest – probably means keeping your mouth shut."

18

ONE OF THE GOOD ONES

They left Copenhagen at midnight in a van that reminded Angel uncomfortably of the one they'd escaped North in. In a moment of particularly unhelpful paranoia, she'd wondered whether Hahn had chosen it for its resemblance. At least Hahn was driving and ignoring them as they sat in the back like they were embarking on the world's weirdest school trip.

Angel didn't want to think about the job. *Her* job, because while Skyler was hacking the Yousefis' phones and Mackenzie would be breaking into their apartment, it would be Angel pulling the trigger. Who else? Mackenzie's aim was average at best, and besides, killing wasn't in his nature. The staff who'd died in the lab explosion, the greycoat he'd shot to save Skyler – they were necessary sacrifices, but they weighed on him. They wouldn't even have registered as a blip on the radar of Angel's conscience.

Skyler was a better shot, and she would only think of

the lives saved, the misery spared. She would have taken the burden without flinching, and for a moment Angel had been tempted to give it to her. Skyler was strong; perhaps she could bear it. But Angel couldn't ask her to step onto that path, to become a person with half a soul. A person who thought of human life in terms of convenience.

Besides, it was bad enough that Skyler was even here. If something were to happen to her –

The truck rattled to a halt, interrupting the escalating staccato of Angel's pulse. It was five in the morning and the clouds had cleared, revealing a starlit sky and a crescent moon glowing gently above the empty car park at Aarhus Harbour. To their right was a jumble of buildings, from red brick to Gothic stonework to a collection of bright white structures with jagged roofs like icebergs, gleaming in the city lights. To the left, vast concrete platforms stretched out to meet the ships in the water.

Something in Angel's chest gave a longing tug at the sight of the sea. She was seized with a fierce urge to jump out of the truck, savour the salty air, even dip a hand into the water; let the chill chase away the frantic clamour of her heartbeat. Hahn would think she'd lost her mind.

Skyler brushed her arm. "You like the sea, right?"

"I love it. I always have."

"We're not on holiday," Hahn snapped. "Pay attention."

Skyler rolled her eyes. Angel could have kissed her.

"Leila and Amir Yousefi." Faith held up her tablet to show their faces. "Twenty-five and twenty-nine years old.

They've been selling people into slavery for the last six years – promise to get them abroad, then take away their passports and hand them over to anyone who'll pay for free labour. She's the brains. They both have nasty reputations, but she's particularly ruthless."

She glanced at Angel. "The expectation is that... uh... you'll kill on sight."

Angel was well aware of that. She'd already promised, obediently, that she would follow orders.

"And we don't have all day," Hahn added, restarting the engine.

The Yousefis had rented a high-rise apartment in a district called Gellerup. Skyler had her laptop out as they approached, quietly monitoring the couple's phones. She seemed absorbed, but as they passed tall concrete buildings shielded by the budding branches of trees, she touched Angel's hand and motioned at the laptop. *Sure about this?* the screen read.

Angel nodded.

Hahn stopped the truck outside the apartment block and turned to Skyler. "Are they definitely in there?"

Skyler's gaze flitted towards Angel: one more chance to pull out.

Angel gave a tiny nod.

"Yes," Skyler said.

"You're sure?"

"Of course I'm bloody sure."

"Then it's time."

Ignore her looking at you like you're a child. Do what you came to do. Angel raised her chin. "I'm ready."

Faith cleared her throat. "Just – be careful. Leila's good at playing the innocent, but she's vicious. Don't give her a chance. She won't give you one."

It was kind of sweet that she was worried.

"Mackenzie will open the front door and leave before he can get in the way," Hahn said. "The rest of us will wait here."

Skyler sat bolt upright. "No we bloody won't."

Faith frowned. "Mackenzie's already been a human shield once this week."

Angel laid a hand on Skyler's knee. "She's right, Sky."

"No," Mackenzie said. "We agreed. You're not going in alone."

"Fine," Hahn said. "Then we all go."

Mackenzie's head snapped towards Faith. "But –"

"Enough." Hahn got out of the truck. "We're wasting time."

Skyler caught at Mackenzie's arm. "Thank you, Mack."

He didn't smile. "We made a deal."

What was Hahn playing at? Five people was too many for Angel to cover without making herself a target. And there was a persistent, barbed little worm burrowing into her brain: *what if you freeze again? What if you have another flashback?*

It was bad enough that it had happened in front of Mackenzie. The idea of Hahn seeing her like that – terrified, defenceless – was unbearable.

She had to be okay. She had no choice.

The location of the Yousefis' apartment couldn't have

been less convenient, with neighbours on all sides and miles from the fire exit. Predictably, their group drew puzzled looks from the few inhabitants of the block already leaving for work.

"They've only been in a couple of hours," Skyler murmured, as they crept towards the apartment. "Hopefully asleep."

Angel had some rudimentary lock-picking skills, but more often than not she lost patience and resorted to a well-placed kick instead. Mackenzie's silent work, by contrast, looked effortless. He was too absorbed to notice Faith watching intently as he studied the lock, nodded to himself and selected his tools. A few seconds later, the door was open.

But only a couple of inches. It was chained from the inside.

Faith inhaled sharply, but Mackenzie didn't even blink. Taking a rubber band and a small roll of tape from his pouch, he wrapped a piece of tape around the band, looped it carefully around the chain, slipped his hand inside the gap and pulled the door closed. The chain slid out with a quiet rattle. Angel gave him an approving nod as she stepped inside and assessed her surroundings.

Clothes spilled from a large designer suitcase in the middle of the floor, at odds with the neutral tidiness of the rest of the open-plan living space. A door to Angel's left led to the bedroom and bathroom. Drawing her gun would be pointless; not worth the attention it would attract. She unsheathed a knife instead as she opened the hallway door and held up a hand to the others: *stay here.*

She hoped they would. None of them were very good at doing as they were told.

As she tiptoed towards the bedroom, mattress springs creaked inside. Angel pressed her back to the wall beside the door. There was a faint thud and a muffled curse in a male voice: Amir, then, presumably heading to the bathroom. Either he didn't know she was there, or stealth was not his strong suit.

The bedroom door opened. Amir stumbled out, wearing a pair of shorts. Angel stepped forward, grabbed his arm and twisted it behind his back.

He was taller and heavier than she was, but though fear had pricked him into alertness, he didn't seem to know what to do. He grunted and struggled. Angel dug the point of her knife into his lower back, a warning, and he froze.

So did Angel.

It would be so *easy*. She could drive the blade into his kidney and be in and out of the bedroom before Leila ever knew what had happened.

Her heart thundered like a prisoner raging against a cage. Her muscles sang with tension.

But she was still herself. Still in control.

As she swung Amir around and forced him back into the bedroom, a light flared on inside.

Leila Yousefi was sitting up in bed. She was small, a little plump, with rounded features and glossy dark hair cascading across her shoulders. Big dark eyes; a pretty, pouty mouth. And a gun in her hand, aimed squarely at Amir and Angel.

"Hello, sweetpea," she said. Her English was clear and faintly accented. "Honestly, Amir, you really are *absolutely* useless." She shot Angel a dazzling smile. "Do excuse my manners. To what do we owe the pleasure? Are you here to rob us?"

"...No." Angel still didn't know what to do. *Decide, you have to decide* now.

Leila rolled her eyes. "*Don't* tell me you're some sort of vigilante. You're too young to die, little one." She leaned forward. "Listen. You're cute, and you've taught my idiot husband a valuable lesson, so how about we let you tiptoe out of here?"

Angel stared at her. Leila gave a tinkling laugh. "Oh, I know, this isn't how you thought this would go. I'm not all bad, darling."

Angel found her voice. "I'm not leaving. Not without you both. Don't make me do this the hard way."

Leila swept her mass of hair back, keeping the gun trained on them absently, like she'd forgotten it was there. "I like you more and more. There must be something you want. Why don't you put that knife down for a minute and I'll put this silly gun away? I'm sure we can work something out."

"That seems incredibly unlikely."

"Goodness me." Leila studied her from beneath thick dark lashes. "You really are one of the good ones, aren't you?"

Angel didn't move.

Leila pouted. "Fine. Be rude, then."

A blunt, banging cough echoed round the room.

Something hot and thick spattered across Angel's face; Amir was suddenly a dead weight in her arms. She realised her mouth was open. She closed it.

"What?" Leila sounded amused. "You thought because I'm a woman you'd be able to pull some sentimental nonsense? How very tedious. So now will you talk to me? No?"

She fired again. Angel dropped, letting Amir's body cover her as she pulled out her own pistol. Leila obviously didn't care whether the neighbours heard the shots.

"Don't you think it's rather tasteless, using my dead husband as your human shield?" Leila peered over the edge of the mattress, laughing. "Come out, little one. Do you even know how to use that thing?"

She fired another shot into her husband's body. Angel swallowed her disgust and fired back.

Leila let out a shriek. Angel shoved Amir's body off her and stood up.

Leila's pretty face was grey, her lips purple. "You *shot* me!" she whimpered.

"Well? You shot him."

Leila clutched her bleeding arm disdainfully. "That's hardly the point."

Angel pulled Leila up off the bed, pressed the pistol to her back and walked her into the living room.

"Good," Hahn snapped as they entered. "You were taking –"

"Gosh." Leila shivered violently in Angel's grip. "Quite the party out here. And they sent you in there all alone, little one?"

Hahn's face was tight and stony. "You have your instructions," she said to Angel.

Angel did. She knew exactly what she was supposed to do.

What would happen if she disobeyed?

She had to. She could not be what Hahn thought she was, what the Agency demanded of her. She would be different. She would be better. She had driven a path through a wilderness before. She had the strength to do it again.

She met Hahn's eyes. She could barely feel her heartbeat at all now. She was light, clear-headed, calm.

"Listen carefully," she said, "because I'm only going to say this once. I'm not your pet killer. I'm done with all this. I *mean* it," she snapped, as Hahn opened her mouth. "You want her dead? You do it."

Hahn scoffed. "Why? Because she's a woman? You of all people should know that means nothing."

"I'm not just talking about her. I'm not killing anyone else for you."

"Wow," Leila said, still shivering. "Well done, little one."

Angel gave her a little shake. "You shut up. This isn't about you."

Hahn's nostrils flared. "I expect you think you mean it. Step away from the prisoner, please."

Angel didn't move.

"I said *now*."

Slowly, Angel let Leila go.

"Faith," Hahn said, "escort these three to the vehicle, then come back up."

Faith nodded mutely. Angel couldn't feel her body. Skyler gripped her hand, and that was her anchor.

"Well," Faith said, as they left the building. "That was... interesting."

"Don't you start," Skyler snapped.

"I'm not starting anything." Faith held up her hands. "But if you think there won't be questions... And trust me, Hahn isn't going to ask so nicely."

"It's none of your —"

"Skyler!" Mackenzie growled. "Leave her alone."

Skyler swung to him, incredulous. Angel squeezed her hand. "It's okay, Sky. She's right." She shrugged at Faith. "But I don't even know where to start."

Faith unlocked the truck. "For what it's worth, that was brave. Just... she's going to be mad, okay? So maybe just... prepare yourself."

Mackenzie froze. "What do you mean? What do you think she'll do?"

Faith chewed her lip. "I don't know."

She walked away. Angel and the others climbed into the truck in silence. The feeling started to seep back into Angel's body, a dull, radiating ache.

Skyler kissed the top of her head. "Are you okay?"

Angel leaned against her gratefully. "I feel better now."

19

TRANSATLANTICISM

It was hard to see how they were going to salvage this.

Hahn and Faith returned to the truck an hour later with no sign of Leila. Mackenzie had endured many long, awkward hours over the past three years, but the silent drive back to Copenhagen was a strong contender for the top five. When they finally escaped the truck, Hahn swept Faith off without a glance at the rest of them.

Mackenzie looked at Angel, who was ghostly pale. "You all right?"

She closed her eyes. "I need to sleep."

Skyler slipped an arm around her. "See you later, Mack, yeah?"

He sighed. "Yeah."

He understood. He did. But was it always going to be like this, now? Angel needed their support – but she didn't really need his, did she? It seemed like all she and Skyler wanted or needed was each other. So where did that leave him?

Alone again, pacing from wall to wall in his room, his thoughts looping in maddening circles. What would happen to Angel now?

And why had Hahn dragged Faith into the Yousefis' apartment? To teach them a lesson? What if Leila had shot Faith? What if Amir had overpowered Angel and Faith had been the first person he grabbed as he burst into the living room?

What if this kept happening? What if he kept putting Faith in danger?

One. Two. Three. Four. Five. Six. Seven.

Tap the wall. Turn.

One. Two. Three. Four. Five. Six. Seven.

Tap.

The aftermath of most jobs tended to look like this. Same gnawing worry, same rituals. But at least in the South he'd only had himself to worry about. He hadn't even known how it felt to be part of a team.

Was he really part of a team now, though? He'd thought so, for a while. He'd hoped so.

A knock at his door. He couldn't answer; he wasn't finished. He wouldn't be finished for hours at this rate.

"Mackenzie?"

It was Faith. Oh, no. He couldn't let her see him like this. He wanted her to know his confident, competent self, not this frightened, pacing mess, this slave to the rustling fear that occupied the dark corners of his mind. The person he really was, in other words, when everything else was stripped away.

No. Come on. You can do this.

He didn't want to be alone.

He wanted to know if Faith was okay.

He wanted to stop pacing.

Just because you feel something doesn't make it real, remember?

He'd stopped this before. He could do it again.

He took a deep breath, turned mid-pace, and opened the door.

Faith seemed to be concentrating hard on polishing her glasses on her shirt. She looked up and smiled at him, but it wasn't her usual infectious one; it was tentative, concerned. "Hey," she said. "You okay?"

He shook his head. What was she doing, worrying about him? "I'm fine. What about you?"

She squinted at him. "Are you sure you're okay, Mackenzie? You look a bit... not okay."

How could he answer that? He couldn't tell her the truth.

She kept coming to see him. Sometimes, in his more hopeful – or deluded – moments, he wondered whether that might be because she liked him, or something.

She hadn't seen the real him, though, had she?

She wouldn't want that.

"I'm fine," he repeated.

She slid her glasses back up her nose. "You were pretty amazing earlier."

"Ah –" His face went hot. "That was nothing."

"Maybe compared to your other escapades, but to this boring analyst, it was something."

Oh, the hell with it. He stepped back. "Want to come in?"

She grinned. "I thought you'd never ask."

"So you're really okay?" he asked, as she settled cross-legged on his bed. "Today must've felt pretty scary."

"I don't think I was really in any danger." She glanced up, looking troubled. "Listen... I don't know what's going to happen with Angel. Hahn can be... pretty rigid. She really doesn't like it when people throw her plans out. But I want you – all of you – to know I'm trying to get her to rein it in. I know you feel weird about what happened in Armenia. Kimura said he had to stay out of it because it was an assessment. I know him, and I know he would've stepped in if he'd thought Angel was really going to get hurt, but I doubt that means much to you. I want you to know that even though they're my bosses, I'm not on board with everything they say. There's not always a whole lot I can do – but I'm trying, okay?"

What was she *doing*? She was going to get herself in even more trouble. Hahn would punish her, and it would be his fault.

"You shouldn't," he muttered. "Just stay out of it."

"I was only trying to –"

"Well, don't! Let us take care of ourselves, all right?"

For an instant, Faith's face crumpled with surprise and hurt. Then her mouth set as though she was retreating beyond his reach. "Fine." She got up and headed for the door. "Whatever you want."

He wanted her to be safe. He wanted to know her better. He wanted to find a way to smooth away the unhappy crease in her forehead, to bring the mischievous spark back to her eyes.

She opened the door. Without thinking, he darted forward and caught her hand. "Wait –"

They both froze.

Shit. Why had he done that?

Why was he *still* holding her hand?

He looked up. Faith raised an eyebrow.

"God. Sorry." He pulled away, his face burning. "I didn't mean to –"

She sighed. "I don't get it, Mackenzie. One minute it's like we're friends, the next you're all dark and brooding and 'leave me to my misery'. I know this is all pretty weird, but I didn't have you pegged as a game-player. If you want me to stay away, just tell me."

If she stays away, you can't hurt her.

This was so *stupid*. It was just another roadblock thrown up by his brain, that looked so solid but always turned out to be nothing more than smoke. All that time wasted torturing himself over stuff that never happened. Wasn't everything that *had* happened bad enough? Did he really have to make it worse for himself?

"I'm sorry." He rubbed his hands over his face. "I'm not trying to be some brooding mysterious jerk. I just get – worried. I'm scared you'll get in trouble for helping us. I didn't mean I don't want to be around you. I do." A lot, actually.

Her face softened. "I get anxious too, you know."

Probably not like this. "You always seem so confident. Like you know exactly what you're doing."

She laughed. "I think the same about you."

That was so far from the truth it was almost comical.

She took a step closer. "We're all just faking it, Mackenzie. Most of us don't have a clue what we're doing. We're just pretending and hoping for the best."

She was smiling again. And they were closer than they'd ever been, one more step would bridge the gap, and he couldn't do it, but he couldn't remember when he'd last wanted something more –

The background hum that was his constant companion, checking and assessing and analysing every next move, had fallen silent.

And he was holding her hand again.

And she was still smiling.

Out in the corridor, a door opened. "Mack?" Skyler called. "We're gonna go get some food. Might as well make the most of it before – Oh. Am I interrupting something?"

Mackenzie dropped Faith's hand. Faith turned to Skyler, who was standing with her hands on her hips, eyes fixed pointedly on the spot their hands had been joined. "Hey," she said. "I just came to see if you guys were okay."

Skyler regarded her as though Faith had presented her with a turd in a box. "We're fine. I need to talk to Mack. Alone," she added, as though Faith might not have got the hint.

"Skyler," Mackenzie snapped. He'd made excuses for her for years – because this was just the way she was, because of what they'd both been through – because, like it or not, she was all he had. But the manner he'd grown used to seemed so much less okay, somehow, when it was directed at Faith.

Faith held up her hands. "Sure. I'll see you later, okay, Mackenzie?"

"Bye," Skyler said sarcastically. Mackenzie glared at her.

As Faith walked away, her phone rang shrilly in her pocket. She pulled it out. "Yes? Hi."

She stopped, her shoulders tensing. "Um. I can do that. But are you – I mean, what are you going to –?"

A pause. "Yeah," Faith said slowly. "Right. I'll tell her."

She turned to them, biting her lip.

Mackenzie's stomach lurched. "What's wrong?"

Faith sighed. "Hahn wants to see Angel."

20

THREAT SYSTEMS

Angel had told herself – over and over – that when she faced Hahn, she would be fine. What she had lived through had made her almost impermeable. Even the very worst Hahn could throw at her would barely register as a paper cut.

She tried to squash the little voice that kept wondering why she had to work so hard to convince herself of that. And when Faith appeared, wringing her hands like she'd come to deliver Angel's execution date, Angel's stomach tightened treacherously.

She cleared her throat. "I take it Hahn wants to see me?"

Faith nodded uncomfortably.

"C'mon." Skyler reached for her hand. "Let's get it over with."

Faith coughed. "Uh – Hahn says just Angel."

Skyler shot her a poisonous look. "Did I ask for your opinion?"

Faith just met Skyler's glare steadily. "Don't make it worse. Seriously."

"I'll be fine, Sky," Angel said gently. Of course she would. Hahn wasn't a serial killer. She wasn't a psychopath. Well, probably.

The problem was that she still didn't really know what Hahn *was*. Her face, her body language, her motivations – all were utterly inscrutable. Angel had no idea what Hahn wanted, which meant she had no idea what might happen when she walked into that office.

And what if you can't cope?

She couldn't go back to that, to all those years fighting for balance on a crumbling precipice, each moment a new terror that threatened to plunge her back into an old one.

You're not that person anymore.

She tried to smile, but her mouth didn't want to work properly. "See you in a bit."

She didn't think she could take all the worried eyes following her. "Come on, guys. How bad can it be?"

She left before anyone could answer.

Outside Hahn's office, she gave herself a minute to breathe. It didn't help much. Then she raised her chin, straightened her jacket, and knocked.

"Come in," Hahn called.

Angel opened the door, willing her hands not to tremble.

"Ah." Hahn pushed her laptop aside. "Hello. Sit down."

Angel lowered herself onto the edge of a chair in front of Hahn's desk. She didn't want to sit. She wanted to be able to run. But she didn't want Hahn to know that.

The faintest twitch of a muscle in Hahn's cheek as her gaze darted towards the door.

Footsteps in the corridor. One set. Two.

The squashy chair beneath Angel. How would she escape if she had to?

Her head was a swarm of wasps, a prickling, seething mass, each thought barbed with danger. She took another slow breath, trying to calm the frantic buzz. *She can't hurt you. That's not what this is about.*

In here, she needed to be able to *think.*

"So," Hahn said. "We need to talk."

"I was trying to talk to you before. You weren't listening."

Hahn tilted her chin thoughtfully. "Yes. You tried to tell me you've had enough of killing. You want to do something different."

"Yes."

"What I think you were really trying to say is that you want to *be* something different."

This was a trap. Wasn't it?

Angel said nothing.

"My problem," Hahn continued, "is that we employed you on a specific understanding, which you've chosen to renege on. I don't know where that leaves us. There's no room here for dead weight."

"I –" *She's trying to get under your skin.* And – worse – it was working. If Angel had to leave the Agency, she couldn't ask Skyler and Mackenzie to leave too, not with the future of the North at stake. But where would she go? And what would she do without them? "You know that's not all I can do. I thought you lot were all about helping people, anyway. Why are you so keen to have assassins on staff?"

Hahn rolled her eyes. "Are you seriously telling me you think it's possible to live in this world – to achieve the things you say you want to achieve – without spilling any blood? How many people did you have to kill to destroy that virus? And as you've found, killing can be a difficult habit to break. Keeping people alive is often a good deal less convenient. Reference our friend Leila Yousefi."

"Yes. What *did* you do with her?"

"That's not your concern. Your current concern is my concern, which is that between your new-found conscience, the fact that you seem to positively revel in doing the complete opposite of your instructions, and the fact that you froze up in Armenia" – Angel stiffened – "I'm far from convinced that you're an asset to the Agency."

Angel pressed the balls of her feet into the floor.

"So you tell me." Hahn rested her chin on her hand. "In my position, what would you do?"

Say something. This shouldn't be so difficult. Why couldn't Angel *think*?

Hahn shrugged. "If you want to stay, you'll have to sell the idea to me. But today I want to talk about something else."

"Okay." Angel kept her tone even. "What?"

"Let me tell you a story." Hahn's words were still

light, but something about them set the hairs on the back of Angel's neck on end.

"Five years ago," Hahn said, her eyes fixed on Angel, "a young girl lived in Coventry, UK, with her mother, a paramedic; her father, a teacher; and her brother and sister, who I believe were ten and seven –"

No. No, no, no, she wouldn't, she's not –

"The girl was an extraordinarily gifted ballet dancer. Her family weren't wealthy, but she won a scholarship to a very exclusive Birmingham school which was world-renowned for its dance programme."

The ringing in Angel's ears rose to a deafening whine. She couldn't make herself meet Hahn's eyes. Couldn't make herself look as if she didn't care.

"She was smart, conscientious, well-liked, had a loving family. A charmed life, by all accounts."

Angel's stomach tied itself into dark, jagged knots. She dug her nails into her palms until they stung. *Do – not – let – her do this to you.*

She tried to tune Hahn out, but she felt like a hedgehog on its back, legs kicking helplessly, soft, defenceless underbelly exposed to a circling predator.

"And she had a friend," Hahn continued, "named Erin Redruth. The daughter of – well, I suppose businessman is technically correct. A violent, ruthless man, who took pleasure in his violence."

What was Hahn doing? *Why* was she doing this?

It didn't matter. All that mattered was that Angel held herself together.

"The dancer and Erin became a couple. They came

out to their friends; the dancer came out to her family. Everyone was happy for them. And then."

Angel's throat felt like sandpaper. "Please stop," she whispered.

"Then came Easter weekend, five years ago. The dancer's family home burned to the ground. Aside from the dancer, the whole family's remains were found inside. The investigation records were lost somehow. A terrible mistake, compounding a terrible tragedy.

"The following week, Erin Redruth was withdrawn from her school. The dancer, meanwhile, vanished. There was some speculation that she might even have been responsible for her family's deaths, but she was never found.

"And then a year later a vigilante appeared on the streets of Birmingham. A young woman with surprising strength and agility who targeted violent criminals, developed a reputation for absolute fearlessness, and made clear that she had a particular vendetta against Daniel Redruth."

Angel's whole body hurt. Fearless? That had been a shell, built over years like the concrete casing around Chernobyl's nuclear reactors: a better-than-nothing barrier between her and the corrosive material she carried at her core, that would destroy her if she went near it, if she even looked at it.

And Hahn had reduced that shell to rubble in the space of minutes.

Just stay still. Just get through this moment without falling apart. And the next. And the next.

179

"And, of course," Hahn added, "the dancer has a name."

Angel was on her feet before she knew it, her chair crashing to the floor behind her. "Stop. You've made your point. Please."

Hahn sighed. "You see," she said, gesturing, "*this* is what I mean. If you can't even hear your own story, your own name, without falling apart – how on Earth am I supposed to believe you can cope with this op?"

"It's not my name. It's not my name anymore."

"Your birth certificate says different."

"You can't –" Everything was buzzing. Head. Limbs. Thoughts. Everything was moving too fast, and Angel was trapped, everything that made her *her* slipping away.

She had to make Hahn stop.

She didn't know how.

There was one way she could make this stop.

She rocked on the balls of her feet while Hahn sat with her lips parted like there was a word on the tip of her tongue, ready to fall.

Angel ran from the room.

21

MY NAME IS

After Angel left, Skyler returned to her room, muttering vaguely to Mackenzie about work. When Angel's door slammed twenty minutes later, she ran outside. "Angel?"

No answer. Skyler banged on the door. "Angel, it's me."

From inside came a muffled gasping that jolted Skyler like an electric shock. She banged again. "Angel, let me in!"

Nothing. Should she ask Mackenzie to pick the lock? "Angel, come on. Please?"

At last, Angel opened the door, white-faced, her eyes bloodshot. "I can't be with you right now, Sky," she said dully. "Leave me alone."

Skyler put out a hand to stop Angel closing the door in her face. "Yeah, that sounds like a terrible idea."

Angel shook her head. Skyler reached for her. "Please, Angel. Let me help."

"You can't help," Angel muttered, but she stepped

back and folded up on the floor, burying her face in her knees.

Skyler crouched beside her, rubbing her back. "What happened?"

"Hahn found a way to punish me."

"What? What do you mean?"

"She knows." Angel picked at a loose thread in her jeans. "She knows about – what happened. To my family."

Skyler cut off a sharp intake of breath. "What's she done to you?"

"Nothing. She just... told me the story."

It didn't sound like much. But Skyler had only ever heard the briefest sketch of what Angel had suffered, had seen how much it cost her to say even that aloud. Angel fought, every minute, not to think about the unthinkable, the uneraseable. What other motivation could Hahn have for this than punishment? She had chosen – intentionally – the thing that would hurt Angel most.

"She's a fucking monster," Skyler growled. "I'll –"

"Don't," Angel mumbled. "I don't want her to know –" She swallowed. "And... I need you here. Please."

"Okay. Okay." Skyler made herself unclench. "I'm not going anywhere."

Angel was silent.

Skyler waited.

"It's the name," Angel said at last. "The name I... used to have. She knows it."

It had never really occurred to Skyler that Angel had

once had another name. She was just Angel. But of course, she hadn't always been.

"No one knows it. No one." Angel picked urgently at the carpet, her fingers building tempo with her words. "Because... okay. The last time I heard it was... that day. There were so many things I had to get used to so I wouldn't just fall to pieces all the time, and that was the one thing I could never make myself face. And I didn't have to, because nobody ever knew. And now *she* could just throw it at me, and I might... just..." Her voice cracked. "... break."

"She's not gonna do that. I won't let her." Skyler would strangle Hahn with her bare hands first.

"I don't know what to do!" Angel dragged her hands over her head. "I can't face her again, Sky. I can't."

"Well... what did you do about the other stuff?"

"Made myself face it all. Over and over, till I could stand it. But this – is different."

"Okay. Different how?"

More frantic scratching at the carpet. "I – I don't know if I can –"

How do I do this? Angel was the one who held Skyler together. What she if couldn't do the same, now that Angel needed her?

She wanted to scream. She wanted to find Hahn and *hurt* her.

Instead, she stroked Angel's hair. "Shh. It's okay. Think about what you can tell me."

"Because..." Angel abandoned the carpet and started picking at her thumb instead. "This is... personal. The other stuff was just circumstantial. But this... it's not just the word. It's who said it, and what they said, and what it meant."

Gently, Skyler covered Angel's hands with hers. "What do you think we should do?"

"I don't know. I'm scared, Sky, I don't think I can —"

"You don't have to do anything you don't want to. But if it helped to face the other stuff — do you think that would work with this? If I helped you?"

Angel went rigid.

"I'm sorry," Skyler said quickly. "I just thought —"

Angel glanced up. "You'd help me?"

"Of course. Anything you need."

"It's not my name," Angel said quietly. "I need you to understand that. I don't want to hear anyone call me that ever again."

"I understand. I'll never use it. I promise."

Angel pressed her knuckles into her eyes, rocking back and forth. Skyler's chest ached. Was she doing the right thing? What if she made Angel worse?

Angel looked up again. "Promise you'll never —?"

"Never. I swear."

Angel squeezed her eyes shut.

"I'm gonna sit opposite you, okay?" Skyler shifted position, reaching for a calmness and confidence she didn't feel, and took Angel's hands again. "Just lift your head, okay? That's all you need to do."

Angel's eyes were glassy-bright, wide, terrified. "I..."

"I've got you. Take all the time you need."

Angel's mouth opened and closed soundlessly.

Skyler waited.

"Felicity," Angel whispered at last, and she didn't sound like Angel at all. "I... was called... Felicity."

"Good. Okay." Skyler squeezed her hands. "Now keep talking to me, Angel."

"I – I can't –"

"Remember where we are, Angel," Skyler said urgently. "We're safe. We're in Copenhagen in this weird building that looks like a hotel and it's 2034 and I'm here. Everything else is in the past."

Angel didn't move.

"It's okay," Skyler repeated. "I'm here, it's me, Skyler, and we're okay, Angel, we're safe, there's nothing here that's going to hurt us." She kept babbling, the words spilling out: *please, please, come back to me.* "Open your eyes, Angel. Look at me."

Finally, Angel's eyes fluttered open. She seemed to refocus.

"Hey," Skyler whispered, breathless with relief.

"I can't do this. I can't, Sky – it's too much –"

"Because it's not just about the name."

Angel nodded.

"Could you tell me? The worst thing about it?" Skyler hated herself for asking, and she didn't know if she could bear the answer. But if Angel needed her to hold the worst moments of her life, then that was what she would do.

"You'll hate me," Angel said quietly. "If I tell you, you'll hate me."

"I could never hate you."

Angel shook her head, her lips pressed together. Skyler touched her cheek. "If that's what you think, you *have* to talk about it. It'll never lose its power otherwise."

Angel blinked, over and over. "He – he walked into her room and grabbed her," she whispered. "Erin, I mean. But he didn't even look at her. He just stared at me. I tried to get him off her... She didn't fight back. She just kept saying, 'Dad, don't, please, don't.' And I was saying the same, I think. And she said, 'Stop, Felicity. Please. You'll make it worse.'"

She raised her eyes to the ceiling. "I didn't listen, of course. I kept trying to drag him off her, yelling at him, begging him. And when he let her go, he looked at me and said, 'Don't say she didn't warn you.'"

Angel's voice was flat, like she was telling a story about a stranger. "He walked out, and Erin sort of collapsed. She kept saying, 'You have to get out of here, right now.' I didn't want to leave without her, obviously. Then she screamed, '*Go*, Felicity, you're going to make it worse.' And I still didn't understand. But... I left. I never saw her again. I ran home. And when I got there..."

The distant glassiness was back in her eyes. Skyler gripped her hands. "You're doing great, Angel. Stay with me."

Angel's breathing quickened, sharp, frantic little gasps. "I – I can't –"

"You can. Come on. Deep breaths."

"I... I couldn't breathe." Angel screwed up her eyes. "It was Easter, and it was raining, and I was soaked, and hysterical. I didn't call my parents to come get me because we didn't have a car anymore. But if I'd just called, if I'd warned them... It was nearly dinner time, there was shepherd's pie in the oven. I ran into the house yelling for Mum and Dad, but I couldn't talk properly, I was breathing in these sort of weird sobs... And when I ran into the living room, they... He was there."

Skyler would have given anything not to have to hear the next part, to erase it from Angel's history.

Angel gulped again and again, like she was choking. "He'd brought two of his people with him. They had my brother and sister. My brother was crying – he was only seven, he didn't have a clue what was happening. My sister was glaring at Redruth like, *how dare this idiot barge in here?* And my parents... They were terrified, obviously, but they were trying not to show it. That was the worst thing – one of the worst things – I'd never seen them like that before. And when I ran in, my mum sort of yelled my name, she yelled, 'Lissy –' and then she cut herself off. I guess she thought he was going to hurt me."

Angel's mouth contorted with grief. "I *hate* that. She should've been thinking about herself and Hattie and Cam. She shouldn't have been thinking about me at all."

Of course she was, Skyler wanted to say. *She was your mum.*

Angel closed her eyes. "Hattie went, 'Lissy, this man says he knows you.' All indignant. I wanted to tell her – God, so many things. That she needed to be quiet, that I was sorry... I felt so *powerless*. I had this feeling in my stomach like something terrible was going to happen, all these crazy things were going through my head – at least,

187

I thought they were crazy. But I didn't know what to do, so –" Her voice broke. "So I didn't say anything."

She snatched her hands from Skyler's and pressed them over her eyes. Skyler pried them away as gently as she could. "It's okay, Angel. It's okay."

Of course it wasn't. Nothing about this could ever be okay.

But she couldn't let Angel stop now.

"Remember where you are," she said. "I'm here." *I'm sorry. I'm sorry.*

"Mum went, 'What's going on, Felicity?' With this little wobble in her voice I'd never heard before. And I – there were so many things I should've said. To him, to them... My dad said the same thing my mum had, but it was like I'd lost my voice.

"And then *he* pointed at Hattie. And asked me, 'What's her name?' I didn't answer. But she went, 'It's Harriet. Not that it's any of your business.'

"And he laughed. And looked at me again. 'I like her,' he said. 'I think I'll start with her.'"

Angel had gone distant again, her face blank except for the tiny tremor in the line of her mouth. "She didn't even have time to scream. Everyone else did, though. Except me. In my head, I was, but I couldn't... I couldn't..."

Skyler wanted to close her eyes, like that could block out any of this horror. She made herself keep them open.

"Then he grabbed Cam. I tried to say, *please don't,* but I couldn't – And my dad... I'd never seen him cry like that. He kept saying, 'Why are you doing this? What have we done?'

"And Redruth said, 'Ask your daughter.' And the way my parents looked at me, then... All I could think was that they must wish I'd never been born. Because none of this would be happening if it wasn't for me.

"And he raised his eyebrows. And said, 'Well, Felicity? Are you going to tell them?' And then... he..."

Angel doubled over. Skyler pulled her into her arms and rocked her as she sobbed. "That was the last thing they heard. Not me saying sorry, saying I loved them. It was my fault, and I couldn't even open my mouth to tell them... They must have thought I didn't care at all."

"They'd never ever have thought that. They loved you, Angel. They knew you loved them." Skyler bent her head. "Is that everything? Is that the part you thought I'd hate you for?"

Angel nodded, still sobbing. "I'm sorry. I'm so sorry."

"Shh. Look at me." Skyler lifted Angel's chin. "I know you loved your family. They knew it too. And I know that you couldn't have stopped him. You probably think if you'd said the right thing you could have, but it's not true. It wasn't your fault, Angel."

Angel stayed curled on the floor with Skyler wrapped around her like a portable shelter.

It wasn't your fault.

Not once in all the years since the end of her world had she let those words enter her mind.

"What do you need?" Skyler asked her eventually.

It was such a strange question. What could you need, after all, when the world had ended?

But the earth was still spinning. And Angel hadn't disintegrated.

"Can we go to your room?" she said. "Would you just – hold me?"

Skyler took her hand. "Let's go."

Apparently Skyler had some sort of previously unmentioned magic power, because she'd somehow managed to multiply the small pile of clothes the Agency had given her into a quantity sufficient to festoon every available surface in her room. Only her laptop – naturally – had escaped the chaos, to sit in a neatly protected corner of her desk.

Angel crawled into bed like she was wading through treacle. She thought she might never move again.

"Stay with me," she whispered, as Skyler pulled the covers over her. "Please?"

Skyler laughed quietly, not the scornful bark she usually treated people to, but a gentle, *you're crazy to even think you need to ask* laugh. "Of course." She climbed in beside Angel. "I reckon I make a pretty good big spoon, even if you are six inches taller than me."

Angel closed her eyes, and for the first time since she and Skyler had fallen asleep on a half-inflated air mattress in the twins' attic months ago, she really closed them. She wasn't going to open them to find herself eye to eye with a hungry wolf.

Her thoughts drifted into fragments, and she let them.

When they reformed, she was still enveloped in Skyler's warm, reassuring weight. "Thank you," she murmured, rolling over.

Skyler's eyes, as blue as the fierce depths of the sunlit ocean, were bright and alert. "How're you feeling?"

Still intact, as Angel blinked away the fog. Like she could risk taking a step without the ground falling away beneath her. "I think I'm... sort of okay?"

"When did you last eat?"

"I don't remember." It was hard to pay attention to anything her body told her other than *run* or *find a weapon*.

"Right." Skyler sat up. "You need food. You okay here for a few minutes?"

Angel nodded.

"Want anything particular?"

"Something spectacularly unhealthy, please."

Skyler kissed her on the nose. "Done."

While she was gone, Angel stared at the ceiling.

Hahn could walk in here whenever she wanted and fire the name at her like a bullet. And what would happen?

It would hurt. A lot. It would rip open a thousand bloody memories.

But it wouldn't make them happen again. The world would still keep turning. And she would still be Angel.

Skyler returned, bearing a pizza box. "You think you can manage not to get pizza in the bed?"

Angel raised her eyebrows. "I'm not sure it's me who needs to worry about making a mess."

Skyler grinned, handed her the box and plonked down beside her. Angel took a slice and ate half in two bites. "You're a genius."

"I know. People keep saying." Skyler started devouring a slice of her own. "Wow. I'd forgotten pizza was even a thing. Hadn't had it since I was a little kid. It might be the best thing about this whole bloody place."

"I reckon Mack would disagree."

"Ha. Yeah. We should talk to him about that."

She glanced at Angel, frowning. Most people interpreted that frown as being somewhere on a spectrum between irritation and rage, but it wasn't. It was fear, and the fact that Skyler hated more than anything being made to feel afraid. And behind what anyone else might mistake for a scowl was a tenderness that lit the depths of the ocean in her eyes and spoke to Angel like a lighthouse beam: that somehow, despite everything, they might both one day be okay.

"D'you think it helped?" There was a tiny, uncertain wobble in Skyler's voice. "It didn't – I haven't made you worse?"

Angel took her hand. "No. It sort of broke the spell. Now I know I can survive hearing it." She tipped her head back and sighed. "Weird, isn't it? How the idea of something can be so much worse than the thing itself? I *know* that. But all that time I spent convincing Mack to face the stuff he's scared of, and I couldn't do it myself."

"But you did do it. That's how you knew it'd help him, right?"

"I couldn't do the hardest bit, though. Not without you."

"And I couldn't do any of the scary stuff without you or Mack. It's okay to need people, Angel."

"I just... never thought I'd have the option. I figured I'd always be dealing with it alone, or not at all."

"That's how I used to feel too," Skyler said. "This way's tons better."

Angel laughed. "Agreed."

"So... what happens now?"

"Well, I'm pretty sure I've done a horrible job of convincing Hahn to let me stay." All she'd done was reveal the unstable core of the reactor, threatening to explode at any moment. Hahn feared that when she did, she would obliterate everything in her orbit along with her.

Perhaps that wasn't so unreasonable, really.

"D'you even want to?" Skyler said. "We could just leave."

God, that was tempting. They were beyond the Board's reach here. Angel was good at being a ghost, and in a country like Denmark, with plenty of electricity and no extradition treaty with the UK, she and Skyler could earn money, build a new life. They could walk out of here and never look back.

She sighed. "We can't. I want the North to be

protected. I want it to be safe for you to go home. As far as I can see, the Agency's still our only chance to make that happen."

"I'm not staying without you." Skyler's arm tightened fiercely across Angel's middle. "We've lost so much, all of us. I'm not sacrificing this, not for anything. Yeah, this lot and all their fancy shit might make things easier. But if they won't help, we'll find another way."

Angel kissed the top of her head. "I believe you."

"Angel?"

"Yes?"

Skyler sat up, her eyes burning into Angel's. "Promise me something. Promise you won't get some mental idea that you need to do, like, the noble thing or whatever and disappear on us. I *know* you, Angel. It's exactly the sort of idea you'd get."

Her tone held a familiar sarcastic thread: the vocal equivalent of an eye roll. But then, suddenly, her face crumpled. "Promise me. Please."

Angel cupped her face gently. "I'm not going anywhere without you. I know I told you that before and I broke my promise, and I'm so, so sorry. But it won't happen again. I swear."

"Good." Skyler smiled. "Then no matter what, we're gonna find a way through this."

Angel pulled her close. "You're amazing."

Skyler snuggled into her. "Yeah, I know."

They lay quietly for a while.

"Angel?" Skyler said at last. "Can I ask you something?"

"Of course."

"Where'd your name come from? Why Angel?"

"Ah." She'd never told this story before, either. So many parts of herself she never talked about. But perhaps now, with Skyler, was the right time to start piecing them together. "I didn't have a name for a while. I was just... running. Trying to hold on. I used to walk, all night, because if I slept – well. I couldn't sleep. I was out in the city one night after curfew and an enforcer pulled up. Sixteen-year-old private school kid, all on her own in the dark... I must've looked like the easiest target in the world. I tried to run, and he grabbed me and shoved me up against his car. And when I tried to scream, he laughed and said, 'Don't bother, angel.'

She tipped her head back. "You hear it all the time, don't you? Even at school, it'd already started. Angel. Sweetheart. Love. All designed to put you in your place, make you feel small, powerless. And it worked. But just then, I wasn't scared. The worst thing I could imagine had already happened and nothing else mattered anymore. So all I thought was: *fuck this*. I managed to snap his finger, and when he let me go I kicked him as hard as I could and ran like hell."

Angel smiled. "That was the first time I realised I didn't have to be powerless. And I thought..." She took a long breath. "I thought: if people are going to call me these things... I'm going to make damn sure nobody laughs when they do."

22

A CHANGE IS GONNA COME

Faith spent the night with a sick, uncomfortable feeling in the pit of her stomach, like she'd eaten about four times too much pie. Hahn had locked herself in her office after summoning Angel, and Faith hadn't been able to think of a good enough excuse to deploy the emergency key. Kimura was out, and Faith didn't dare go and check on Angel in case Skyler – possibly literally – ripped her head off.

And when she went back to knock on Mackenzie's door, he didn't answer. He was in there – she could hear him moving around – but he obviously didn't want to see her. Why would he? Especially if Hahn had done something awful.

But earlier, he'd taken her hand and his eyes had widened like he couldn't quite believe what he'd done. He'd told her he worried about her. He'd looked at her like he was longing for something.

And God, this was stupid, this was so, so stupid,

because if he hadn't thought of her as the enemy before, surely he must do now. Skyler certainly did. And Faith didn't *do* this. Sure, she sometimes went for drinks with other agents, and occasionally there was a night in someone's room, simple and fun and free from expectation and need. She didn't do feelings and mess and holding hands with boys in corridors while they gazed into each other's eyes and she tried to read their minds.

She headed for her office at six AM. She needed to get out of her room, clear her head. Then she would find Hahn and try to work out what the hell had happened and how she could possibly start repairing the damage.

But when she reached her office, a fifth pie joined the weight in her stomach. Skyler was leaning against the door, arms folded. Her stony face bore no traces of sleep.

Faith decided to aim for friendly-neutral. "Hey, Skyler. You okay?"

"Did you know?" Skyler demanded. There was nothing either friendly or neutral about her tone.

"Know... what?"

"What Hahn was going to do to Angel."

Shit. Faith hesitated. "Come inside, Skyler."

"We can do this out here."

"Yeah, well, we're not going to. Come inside or walk away."

Skyler stepped away from the door, arms still folded. Faith wondered fleetingly whether she should be more cautious about being alone with her, but it seemed unlikely Skyler would hurt her. Physically, anyway.

She leaned against her desk, resisting the temptation

to fold her arms and match Skyler's stance. This office was way too small for that kind of showdown.

"*Did you know?*" Skyler repeated.

"I honestly have no idea what you're talking about."

"Ha. Really. Shouldn't you be paying attention to the sort of organisation you work for?"

No matter what Hahn had done, Faith wasn't going to cringe and apologise for something she knew nothing about. "I'm pretty sure I know, thanks," she retorted. "But I'm not privy to every single thing that happens here. Look, something's obviously upset you. Do you want to talk about it or not?" She pushed away the guilty whisper: *you might have some idea.*

Skyler scoffed. "Honestly, I'd respect you more if you told me you *did* know. At least then you'd be paying attention. But either you're lying to me, or you literally haven't noticed that your boss is a fucking monster. And trust me, I know monsters."

She did, too. Faith had put together Skyler's file, before Skyler was real enough to her for it to feel like an intrusion. She knew about Skyler's years in Daniel Redruth's cellar. She'd put together a file on Redruth, too. It had made her want to throw up.

"That's unfair," she snapped. No matter what Hahn's flaws, comparing her to Redruth was disgusting. "Hahn's not cruel. She doesn't set out to hurt people."

"Jesus *Christ*. You really are clueless."

Faith sighed. "What *happened*, Skyler?"

"Your boss found out about the worst thing that ever happened to Angel, and she used it to try to break her."

No. She wouldn't. She wouldn't have done that.

"Yeah, that's right." Skyler's eyes locked with Faith's. "*That's* who you work for. And if you knew she was going to do that – or if you think it's in any way okay – then that tells me everything I need to know about *you*."

She wouldn't be that cruel –

But Hahn's comments after Armenia kept echoing. *You never know what someone's truly capable of until they're pushed to breaking point.*

Angel had shown herself – repeatedly – to be volatile and unpredictable. If Hahn had found a weak spot, of course she would put weight on it.

Faith swallowed. "Hahn tests her teams so she knows they're capable, Skyler. She tested me too at first. She just wants to be as sure as she possibly can that nothing's going to go wrong. She hates failing people."

And it was true. So why did Faith feel like she was making excuses?

Skyler barked a scornful laugh. "Bullshit. Yesterday was about punishment."

"That..." Could be true. Hahn had been even more livid after Aarhus than after Armenia. But she told Faith often enough to think with her head, not her heart. "No. Whatever she did, it wasn't about making Angel suffer." Although it was certainly convenient that she'd been able to kill two birds with one stone.

"You're absolutely fucking delusional," Skyler shot back. "You didn't see the state Angel was in afterwards." For a second, the hard lines of her face wavered into distress. "She's strong, Angel, she's the strongest person I know, but... No normal person would treat someone like that."

"I never said Hahn was normal. And disagreeing with you doesn't make me delusional."

"Ha. No. Maybe it just means you've been brainwashed. Hahn's certainly got you toeing the party line, hasn't she?"

For all Skyler despised Hahn, she had an uncannily familiar knack of identifying the jugular and going straight for it. "This organisation's full of exceptional people, Skyler," Faith said. "Including me, actually. Am I really supposed to believe you're the only person here with critical thinking faculties? You might not like the way Hahn works, but she's saved thousands of lives."

"I don't care what you believe," Skyler spat. "I care about Angel and Mack. I *care* that you lot claimed to want to help us, and so far I haven't seen a single piece of evidence that's actually true."

"Apart from the fact that you would literally be dead if it wasn't for Hahn? Not everyone here was up for getting involved in this, trust me. She fought for you because she knew it was the right thing to do. Don't forget that."

Skyler cocked her head. "Do you know who Daniel Redruth was, Faith?"

Wow. She was really going there. "Yes, I do. And I know –"

"Yeah, well. What Hahn did to Angel – that's exactly the sort of thing *he* would've done. Digging out the worst moment of your life and holding it over you, so you knew he could break you any time he wanted – and all you could do was wait and see whether today was the day he felt like doing it. Use your *critical thinking faculties* and see if you can imagine what that's like. Then tell me you still think Hahn's got her heart in the right place."

Faith screwed her eyes shut against her pounding heart. How dare Hahn put her in this position? This wasn't right. It wasn't fair.

"Oh," Skyler added. "And whatever the fuck you think you're doing with Mackenzie – you stop that. Right now."

It took Faith a moment to recover her footing. When she did, a flash of heat obliterated the churning in her stomach. "*Excuse* me? *What I'm doing with Mackenzie* – who the *fuck* do you think you are?"

"I'm his friend. I don't know what you're pretending to be."

"I'm not *pretending* anything –"

Something bright and deadly flashed in Skyler's eyes. But then, abruptly, she deflated. "Just... leave him alone, Faith, okay? He's been through enough."

They've gone through so much together. Of course she's protective.

But Skyler's words stung. And was Faith really going to take this shit from someone who wasn't even kind to the friend she claimed to care so much about?

She sighed. "Don't make him choose between us, Skyler."

"Why?" Skyler said tartly. "Because you think he'll choose you?"

"No. He'll choose you, because that's the right thing to do. And he'll be miserable. And you won't even acknowledge that it might have cost him anything, will you?"

Skyler's mouth opened in furious astonishment. At last, she shook her head. "You don't know anything about me. He's my friend."

"Really? Are you sure you know how to be someone's friend? Because honestly, I'm not. And that's not your fault – I can't even begin to imagine what you've been through – but I think you only know how to care about yourself. And somehow you've made space for Angel, and that's awesome for both of you – but where does that leave Mackenzie?"

There was a good chance Faith was burning her bridges with Skyler beyond repair here, but what was one more match on a bonfire? "You don't trust me," she said. "Of course you don't. But don't you trust him? He deserves to be happy. So why can't you let him have this? Or is it just that you have to be in control of everything?"

Skyler's expression was unreadable. Faith bit her lip. Maybe that had been a bit much.

Then – "Let me tell you something about Mack," Skyler said quietly. "He's kind. He's good and he's kind, and even though the world's done nothing but fuck him over, he still sees the best in people. Everything I know about being someone's friend, I learned from him. I don't deserve him, but for some reason he's still with me. And I'm trying to be the friend he deserves."

She met Faith's eyes. "He *does* trust you. That's what

scares me. I don't think you have any idea how special that is, that he can even do that. I'm scared you're yet another person who's going to let him down. And I'm scared that if I trust you, I'll be letting him down again too."

Faith took a deep breath. "I'm not going to let him down, Skyler. I swear."

Skyler sighed. "I hope not. I don't know if this is just a bit of fun to you, or if you really do like him. I hope you do. I want him to be happy more than anything. But... you talked about me making him a priority. Are you sure *you* can?"

"I understand how big a deal this is. I'm not going to mess him around."

Skyler regarded her with something like pity. "See, maybe you think you mean that. But even the fact that you can say that... It's not about *messing him around*, Faith. It's not about blowing hot and cold or cancelling dates or, I dunno, texting your ex or whatever. What are you gonna do if Hahn goes for Mack the way she went for Angel? Will you stand up for him, if it comes to it? Or will you just keep making excuses for her?"

"I –"

"Don't bother." Skyler held up a hand. "You know I won't believe you anyway. Just... think about it, okay?"

She didn't look angry anymore. She just looked tired. Somehow, that was worse.

23

WE DON'T FIGHT FAIR

A violent bang rattled Mackenzie's door. Panic propelled him to his feet before he was even properly awake. It was the middle of the night and he'd fallen asleep in his clothes.

"Mack!" Skyler yelled, as he fumbled for the light switch. "Open up!"

He stumbled to the door and wrenched it open. "Jesus. Why the yelling?"

Skyler's face was flushed, her hair coming loose from its plait. She looked angry – but then most of Skyler's emotions tended to get expressed as anger, especially when she was actually scared.

Angel was behind Skyler, looking almost as bemused as Mackenzie felt. She shrugged at him.

Skyler marched inside and slammed the door behind them. It was only then that Mackenzie noticed her laptop under her arm.

Angel laid a hand on her shoulder. "What's wrong, Sky?"

Skyler dropped heavily onto Mackenzie's bed. "You're both gonna be mad at me."

Mackenzie groaned. "Skyler, what –?" His eyes landed on the laptop again. "Fucking *hell*. You hacked the Agency's files."

Her mouth set defiantly. "Yeah."

"Oh, for –"

Angel closed her eyes. "Sky –"

"I had to!"

"Did you, Sky? Really? How the hell did you think that was gonna help?" Mackenzie swung to Angel. "Did you know about this?"

"No," Skyler snapped. "I did it on my own."

Mackenzie threw up his hands. "What happened to us making decisions together?"

"He's got a point, Sky," Angel murmured.

"You had enough on your plate. And *you*" – witheringly, to Mackenzie – "would've told me not to."

"Of course I bloody would! Why would you –"

"Because we've given them chances and chances and all they do is piss around *testing* us and not telling us anything! I tried to give them the benefit of the doubt or whatever, because I knew that's what you'd say" – this to Mackenzie, as if it were an extremely tedious character trait – "but this Aarhus thing – it's too much. We don't even know if they're gonna bother doing anything in the North, and we need to know what's happening over there. We need a backup plan."

Mackenzie flopped backwards onto the bed. "Well, you've bloody done it now, haven't you? So? You find anything?"

She nodded.

Abruptly, Mackenzie's anger solidified into something cold and heavy and horrible. He sat up. "What did you find?"

Skyler sighed. "They do have information about the North. They haven't had it long, to be fair," she added grudgingly. "They sent someone to check how things are over there."

Mackenzie couldn't breathe. "And?"

Skyler dropped her head. All at once, she looked small and sad and worried. "The Board have taken people from the settlement you were at."

It would never have been good news. But all the endless worrying and bargaining and trying to fix things, and her words were still a punch to the stomach that doubled him over, arms wrapped around himself as though that could protect him or anyone else.

Angel had gone white. "The twins. Any word –?"

"No news. Apparently they left the settlement before the Board showed up. Didn't tell anyone where they were going."

Angel picked at her thumb. "What do we do with this?"

Skyler's shoulders slumped. "I don't know."

"You shouldn't have done it, Sky," Mackenzie muttered. "Especially behind our backs. If they find out –"

"What else was I meant to do? We can't trust them. I know you've got this whole thing with Faith, but –"

"Sorry, *what*? What's that got to do with anything?"

"Oh, come on, Mack. I know she's hot or whatever, but you need to be careful."

All this time together, and she still thought he was a complete idiot. All the times he'd looked to her for guidance, all the times he'd asked himself, *what would Skyler tell me?* – and she didn't trust him at all. What were they even doing together if she thought that little of him?

"What's that supposed to mean?" he said.

"Just... don't forget whose side she's on. What if she's, like, trying to get stuff out of you?"

"Like *what*? What am I gonna tell her? And anyway – she just wants to be friends."

Skyler snorted. He glared at her. "Oh, right. God forbid she might actually like me."

"Oh, come on, I didn't mean –"

"Yeah, you did."

"Mack." Skyler laid a hand on his arm. "It's just – you've got to admit, it's a bit weird –"

He shrugged her off. "Just stop talking, Sky, for God's sake."

She squinted at him. "What's the matter with you?"

Mackenzie's throat ached. This was all too much. And there was no point trying to explain to Skyler why he was hurt. There never was.

"It's not important," he muttered. "We need to focus on the North."

"Right," Skyler said. "We need to know what the Agency are planning to do. If anything."

"Did you fancy asking me or Angel for our opinion there? Anyway, how are we meant to ask them without letting on that you hacked their system? Never mind us trusting them, you've just gone and proven they can't trust us."

"Yeah, well, if they'd –"

"D'you honestly think for a second they're gonna see it like that?" He looked at Angel. "Whatever we do, we can't let her do the talking."

Skyler scowled. "Oh, fuck off, Mack."

"Guys." Angel held up her hands. "How is this helping?"

Mackenzie sighed. Angel was right, as usual. And she had enough on her plate without having to play referee.

"We're meant to be a team," he said to Skyler. "It was you who said that! Doesn't that mean anything to you?"

"We *are* a team –"

"Bollocks. It's just you, like always, deciding you're right and expecting everyone else to fall in line. What – you expect me to just stop talking to Faith because you think you know best? Like, what about what I think? Does my opinion seriously not matter to you at all?"

Skyler gave him an all-too-familiar look that managed to communicate, very clearly, her opinion that he was being a fucking idiot. Given the circumstances, it didn't really help.

"Don't be ridiculous, Mack," she said. "You're just not exactly being objective. We're not like normal people.

We can't trust everyone who's nice to us." The pity in her tone stung more than her actual words.

"Do you seriously think I don't know that?"

"You're not acting like it."

Mackenzie looked away. His eyes stung: hurt and frustration and loneliness – and, worst of all, the fact that he'd really thought that loneliness was behind him. He should have known it was too much to hope for.

And what if Skyler was right? He wanted so badly to believe that Faith was on their side. That she liked him. That she might be thinking, like him, about the time he'd taken her hand, and whether that might happen again, and what might happen next.

But what if his instincts were wrong? What if he was just lonely and pathetic and deluding himself?

Angel sat beside him and laid a hand on his shoulder. "Sky? Could you give us a minute, please?"

Skyler opened her mouth as though she was about to snap again. Angel raised an eyebrow at her.

"Sure." Skyler sounded taken aback. "I'll see you later."

She left. Mackenzie leaned his elbows on his knees and buried his head in his hands.

Angel squeezed his shoulder. "I'm sorry. She doesn't –"

"*Don't* tell me she doesn't mean it," he said into his palms. "We both know she does."

"Well… yes. But she doesn't mean to hurt you. She's just used to doing things on her own."

"We all are. She still doesn't have to be such a dick."

Angel laughed quietly. "True."

"You think she's right, don't you? About Faith?"

She hesitated. Mackenzie sighed. "Of course you do."

"I'm... trying to be balanced," Angel said slowly. "I think Faith means well. Everyone else here, I'm not so sure about. And I don't think she can see that."

"Skyler shouldn't have hacked their system. Not without talking to us."

"I know."

He glanced at her helplessly. "I don't know what to do about this, Angel."

Angel sighed. "Me either."

24

THE WEIGHT OF THE WORLD

"This is ridiculous," Clara snapped, the next morning. She stalked back and forth in front of Hahn's desk, anger radiating from the hard lines of her face. "They've been on two ops, both of which went spectacularly wrong –"

"No they didn't," Hahn said. She was using, Faith noted, the mild tone she reserved especially for people she couldn't stand. Hahn had never admitted it, but Faith suspected that some petty instinct in her revelled in the fact that the calmer and more reasonable she was, the more incensed Clara became. "Both Virtanen and the Yousefis are out of action."

"They *cannot* pull this off. Going into the UK will do nothing but waste our time and sacrifice our agents. Honestly, Julia, I can't begin to fathom what you're thinking."

Hahn let out a *you're-testing-my-patience* sigh through her nostrils and steepled her fingers together. "I'm thinking that the North is rapidly running out of time. The Board won't start bombing in the next few days, but they're negotiating with the US for support. Once they reach an agreement, and another month or two passes without enough concrete evidence to compel the UN to act –"

"You can't save everybody. Bringing a bunch of teenagers into the Agency" – Clara's gaze flickered briefly but pointedly towards Faith, sitting to the side of Hahn's desk – "and thinking the outcome would be in any way desirable –"

Hahn's eyes narrowed. "My track record speaks for itself."

"Your decision-making regarding the UK has been totally erratic throughout. First you bypassed all our protocols –"

"Because there was no time for the protocols." Hahn spoke as though addressing a particularly dim, fragile student who needed everything explained very gently and slowly.

"Nonsense. You let your emotions drive you into a rash course of action."

Hahn leaned her elbows on her desk. "I don't know what you're implying, Clara." Her tone was pleasant, easy. "Do explain."

"You say often enough that others shouldn't be ruled by emotion. You made an emotional decision because of your past failures, and you're refusing to back down now not because you think you're right, but because you can't stand admitting you're wrong."

Hahn rose gracefully. "How lucky we are that you're

so passionate even about operations outside your remit. I'll take your thoughts under consideration."

Clara threw up her hands. Hahn stared her down until, finally, Clara scoffed and turned towards the door.

"This isn't about doing the right thing, Julia," she said, as she left. "This is about you having a God complex and bullying everyone around you into compliance. This op is going to fail. And if you're not careful, one of these days you'll take the whole Agency down with you."

"Thank you, Clara," Hahn said smoothly. "Your opinion has been noted."

Clara stared at her for a moment, her mouth half-open. Then she swept out, slamming the door behind her.

Hahn stood very still, watching the closed door. Eventually, she sighed. "That woman is desperate to get me out of here."

Abruptly, she turned to Faith. "Do you think she's right?"

Faith blinked. "What?"

"Is Clara right? Should we abandon this and cut the Northerners loose?"

"No! Absolutely not!"

Hahn raised a reproving eyebrow. "The fact that you like them and don't want to let them down isn't a reason to stay involved."

"We promised to help them!"

"But the Agency comes first. It has to." Hahn sat back down. "I need to think."

She couldn't be serious. Faith leaned forward, her

heart pounding. "Julia. You're not – you can't – We need to talk this through."

Hahn nodded at the door. "I'll speak to you later."

"But –" Faith bit her tongue. If she argued, Hahn would only dig her heels in. "Okay," she said instead. "Let's talk later."

Out in the corridor, she leaned against the wall and ran her hands through her hair. *Shit shit shit.*

She could at least warn the Northerners that the Board was hunting for them, and that their friends were in danger as a result. If the Agency took days or weeks to decide how to proceed, they deserved to be able to choose whether to stick around.

She swallowed the lump in her throat. Hahn would be furious if she discovered Faith had shared the information – and she almost certainly would find out. The incendiary device that was Skyler wouldn't care whether letting rip at Hahn put Faith in the firing line.

She was going to do it anyway, though, wasn't she?

When she reached Mackenzie's door, she didn't hesitate. She knocked and he answered, his face flushed, eyes dark with worry. Angel sat cross-legged on the bed behind him, her usual unreadable self, while Skyler was on her feet, her scowl even more ferocious than usual. "What do *you* want?" she demanded when she saw Faith.

Mackenzie swung angrily towards her, but before he could speak, Faith stepped inside and closed the door. "Shut up, Skyler. I'm here to help."

Skyler barked a laugh. "Awesome. I mean, you've been *super* helpful so far."

"Skyler!" Mackenzie rounded on her. "Stop it. I'm serious." He looked at Faith. "Sorry. We were... kind of in the middle of something."

Like that wasn't obvious. "Look. There's something you all need to know. *Listen*," Faith added, as Skyler opened her mouth again. "I'm so sorry, Angel, about what Hahn did to you. It wasn't okay. And I know you guys don't trust me – or any of us – and I don't blame you. But I do care about the North. I've cared since the beginning. That's why I'm here."

Skyler folded her arms. "This'd better be good."

Faith took a deep breath. *No going back now.* "The Board are hunting for you. They've figured out which settlement you were at, and they've taken people... They're biding their time, but when they don't find you, as soon as they think they can get away with it, there'll be air strikes."

She'd expected gasps, tears, a barrage of questions. Instead she got – nothing. Three blank faces stared back at her. Were they in shock?

Oh. No. Of course.

"You guys already know all this, don't you?"

Mackenzie winced. Angel adopted an expression that might generously have been interpreted as edging towards contrition. Skyler just met Faith's eyes steadily.

Faith sighed. "I guess we shouldn't really have expected anything different."

"Nope," Skyler said.

"I'm sorry," Mackenzie muttered.

Skyler's arms stayed folded. "I'm not."

Right. Pulling at this thread wouldn't get them anywhere. Faith cleared her throat. "The other thing you should know is that people here are starting to weigh in. Not everyone's super in favour of going into the UK." And if anyone found out about Skyler's extra-curricular activities, that would sink this ship once and for all. "I don't know how long it'll take them to decide."

Mackenzie dragged his hands through his hair. "This is such a mess."

"At least we agree on that," Skyler murmured.

Angel rubbed her eyes. "Any idea which way the wind's blowing?"

"I... honestly have no idea."

Angel nodded slowly. "All right. Thanks, Faith. Sky, I think you and I should take a walk. Maybe we all need a bit of space. Mack – we'll come back and talk about it later, okay?"

He shook his head. "Fine."

Angel and Skyler left. Mackenzie flopped backwards onto the bed and covered his face with his hands. "Fucking *hell*." He peered at Faith from between his fingers. "I don't know what to say. I'm sorry. About Skyler. About everything."

Cautiously, she sat beside him. For some reason, despite the approximately one million more important things she had to worry about, her stomach gave a sort of quiver, the kind she couldn't seem to help whenever she was within touching distance of him. "Sorry to give you such shitty news."

"Hardly your fault."

"Well, it's not your fault Skyler's... like she is, either."

He stared at the ceiling. "I could bloody strangle her sometimes. Kind of reminds me how things used to be with my sister, except Bex and I never had to overthrow a government." He gave her a rueful smile, and then it died on his lips.

Faith leaned back to lay beside him. "You had a sister?"

He nodded. "She'd be twenty now."

Would be. Faith swallowed. "I'm so sorry."

"I miss her so much," he said quietly. "My mum and dad too, of course, but Bex... We were a team. She was always the one who was there when I needed someone. When I started secondary school I got bullied, and she knew something was up, but I kept telling her I was fine. So she stalked me to find out what was going on, and one day when this kid was being a dick she burst out of nowhere and kicked the crap out of him. And then called me a twat for not telling her sooner. She was so... *alive.* Always bouncing around, you always knew exactly where she was in the house, always knew *exactly* what she was thinking." He rolled his eyes and grinned.

"She sounds super cool."

His grin faded. "Somehow it never even occurred to me to worry about her. It just didn't seem possible that she might... you know. When everything happened... I really, really thought she'd be fine. But then she wasn't."

Faith's throat ached like she'd been trapped in a smoke-filled room: because his grief was so raw, because this was all so unnecessary, because Bex had died for no reason.

And because she understood. She never talked about it; how would it help, after all? How would digging up the past she'd worked her fingers bloody to bury do anything but undermine the foundations of the new life she'd burned every last scrap of strength to build?

And yet.

"My dad," she said, and Mackenzie looked at her. "He was the one I went to. Always, no matter how stupid or embarrassing it was. He never laughed, never said it was just stupid kid stuff. My mom was... she loved me, I always knew she loved me, but she didn't really know how to listen the same way he did. Ironic, considering she was a psychology professor. I guess I relied on Dad too much, but I just kind of took for granted he'd always be there, you know? I couldn't imagine the world without him."

A beat of silence. "How old were you?" Mackenzie asked.

"Fourteen." Five years, and sometimes it was as raw as if he'd gone yesterday.

"Same as me." He gave her a twisted smile. "Shit, isn't it?"

She let out a breathy laugh. "Yeah."

"I'm really sorry about your dad."

"I wasn't trying to make it about me. It's just – I get it, that's all."

"No." His fingers brushed hers, just for a moment. "It's good to be around someone who understands."

They lay side by side, staring at the ceiling.

"That's why I can't just tell Sky to fuck off," he said. "It'd be so much easier if she was just an ordinary friend, but she's all I've got. And what she's been through, all that stuff with Redruth – you can't imagine. *I* can't imagine. And I know she tries, but God, she's fucking infuriating sometimes. She's like a tornado when she's fixated on something. She just rips up anything that gets in her way."

"She cares about you," Faith said. "A lot. Maybe she doesn't always know how to show it, but she does care."

He shot her a sad little smile. "Whatever gives you that idea?"

"Well, she came storming into my office the other morning to warn me off you, for a start."

Mackenzie let out a startled laugh. "Jesus. I'm so sorry." He covered his face again. "God, I'm gonna kill her."

"Don't be mad at her. She was just looking out for you."

"In the most intrusive, embarrassing way possible." He grinned at her through his fingers. "That would've been a very Bex thing to do." His cheeks tinged pink. "Why'd – uh, why'd she do that, anyway?"

"Because she's worried my intentions towards you are not honourable," Faith said, half-sarcastically, and instantly regretted it. Shit. What was wrong with her? Now they were going to have A Conversation. How did you even do Conversations? How did you tell a boy with bright eyes and a lopsided smile and the weight of the world around his neck – *Hey, I like you, and I think you like me too because when our eyes meet you look away like you've got no idea what to do with yourself, and I'm sorry my boss keeps tormenting your friends, I don't really know what to do about that, and I know we're supposed to be saving the world but I'm also wondering what it would be like to kiss you –*

Mackenzie propped himself up on his elbows. His gaze met hers and he looked away quickly, but she caught the smile in his eyes.

"You're gonna get in trouble for telling us this," he said.

"Probably. But it'll be worth it."

He glanced at her. "You really do care about the North, don't you?"

"Yes." She didn't know how to show him how much she cared. "I don't want you to leave, but if that's what you need to do, then you should."

He laid his hand over hers and her pulse quickened, dizzying. "Thank you."

Faith tried to smile through the knot in her stomach that was half sadness, half something else. "I'm sorry. I thought we could help you. As soon as the video arrived, I knew –"

He twisted towards her. "It was you who got the video?"

"Uh – well. It didn't come straight to me. But I took it to Hahn. I sort of... made the case."

Mackenzie stared at her. "You never said."

"It would've been like... showing off, right? Besides, I didn't really –"

He leaned over and kissed her.

Funny; she'd expected him to be shy, hesitant. But this wasn't a *not sure* kiss. It was an *I've waited too long for this* kiss. And it only took her a fraction of a second to realise what was happening and lean up and kiss him back.

Mackenzie pulled away. "Oh my God. I'm sorry. That was –"

Faith couldn't have stopped the smile that radiated from her core and spread through her. She cupped his cheek. "Mackenzie?"

"Uh. Yeah?"

"Did you want to do that?"

"Um. Yes. Like, you have no idea how much."

She pulled him towards her until she could feel him smiling against her mouth, the way she was. "Then do it again."

25

SPEAK

"It's time we moved things forward," Hahn announced.

Skyler, Angel and Mackenzie had finally been summoned to meet with her and Kimura. Faith was there too, of course, looking scared shitless. Things should have moved forward ages ago, and if it hadn't been for Mackenzie and Angel, Skyler would already have kicked Hahn's office door down. Mackenzie seemed really angry with her for the first time in a long time, though. She wouldn't always have considered that a relevant factor, but he did sometimes see things differently to her, and occasionally he was even right. And this was too important to get wrong.

That didn't make it any easier not to throw things at Hahn.

Mackenzie was sitting on his hands, which usually meant he was trying not to tap. "Move forward how?"

Faith cleared her throat. Skyler looked at her, trying to modify her glare a little. Faith had come to them with the information, she supposed. Maybe she wasn't a total doormat after all.

"We infiltrate the upper levels of the Board," Faith said. "Make it look like the loyalty of senior members is wavering. The Board's hold on the South is already weakening. More public evidence of that could undermine it to the point of collapse."

"If we could get people to have less faith in it and less fear of it," Angel said.

Faith cocked her head. "Right. Go on."

"The Board's power comes from two things. Powerful Southerners feel it protected their interests during a crisis and see the North as necessary collateral. Everyone else gets terrorised. The internet's censored, so's the media. Even a joke to a colleague or a whinge to your neighbour and the greycoats come and kick your door down. But if it became less frightening to the powerless, and less attractive to the powerful..." Angel studied the ceiling. "You'd have to make the crime lords think the Board was turning on them. That's how you get them to jump ship."

That's my girl. Skyler hid her grin behind her hand.

"Could that really work?" Mackenzie had lost the battle and started tapping the side of his chair. "Won't it take too long?"

"I asked my magic eight ball," Kimura said. "It wasn't sure. But we think it's worth trying."

"So where do we start?" Mackenzie asked.

Hahn looked at Angel. "First we need to decide who's doing what."

Skyler stiffened. Mackenzie, still tapping, caught her

eye. The message seemed to be: *keep your damn mouth shut.*

"I can help," Angel said. "You know I can. I have a brain."

Hahn's lips pursed. "Your grasp of the situation does work in your favour."

"Angel probably knows the Southern underworld better than anyone," Faith pointed out.

"Yes, thank you, Faith. I'm well aware of your opinion." Hahn's attention pinged back to Angel. Skyler glanced at her, but she was watching Hahn steadily, her back straight and her chin raised.

"There's no denying your intentions are good," Hahn said. "But when you're under pressure, when the people you care about are in danger..."

"I handled it before."

"You were a bloody mess."

"Things have changed."

Hahn sighed. "Plenty of our agents have suffered from PTSD –"

"I *don't* have –"

Hahn held up a hand "– and many of them have very successful careers. But like it or not, your ability to fight is part of your value, and I'm not convinced you're as capable as you want to believe."

Skyler bit her tongue. *Angel can handle this.*

Angel leaned forward. "This is important. I want to be part of this. I think I need to be. What do I have to do to convince you?"

"Are you sure you want to do this?"

"Yes."

"Very well. Then my concern is that I think there's something you still can't let go of. It's keeping you stuck. And that will put you and others in danger."

The colour drained from Angel's face. Skyler tensed.

"Then test me," Angel said.

Skyler reached towards her before she could stop herself. "You don't have to do this."

"Yes, I do."

"There's no shame in struggling with certain things," Kimura offered. "After what you've been through –"

"Are you going to act like you feel sorry for me now? Please. Let's clear this up once and for all."

"For the record," Kimura said, looking at Hahn, "I still don't think this is the right way to handle this."

Hahn flapped dismissively at him. "She's right. This has gone on long enough." Her basilisk stare fixed on Angel again. "Let's talk about Redruth."

Angel raised her chin. "Fine."

"He murdered your family eighteen months before the Wall went up."

"Yes."

Skyler clenched her fists. There was going to be a murder in here in a minute.

"You fell off the radar for almost a year. Hardly surprising. Then you emerged as Angel. On your own time, you tracked and executed Daniel Redruth's associates."

"You already know all this."

"When did you first meet Skyler?"

Oh, that was *enough*. "I don't see what that has to do with anything," Skyler snarled.

"Your opinion is irrelevant." Hahn didn't take her eyes off Angel. "If you want me to entertain the idea that she continues to work here, you will be quiet."

It took everything she had, but Skyler shut her mouth.

"Once more," Hahn said to Angel. "When did you meet Skyler?"

"Just after the Wall went up."

"Tell me."

"We had a mutual acquaintance, AJ. He found her ill one day and brought her to me."

"Ah, yes. I forgot about your side business as a healer." Hahn imbued the word 'healer' with the same inflection she might have used for 'rubbish collector'. "You treated her. She got better, evidently. How did your relationship develop from there?"

"I didn't see her again for nine months. Then she turned up asking me to teach her self-defence."

"Why did she do that?"

Angel glanced at Skyler.

"It's okay," Skyler said. "Tell her." Though clearly Hahn already knew. This was some sort of weird game, but Skyler couldn't figure out the goal. The idea that she had to just go along with it made her want to scream.

Angel sighed. "She was living in Redruth's cellar. It was the only way she could get enough electricity to work."

"She was working for the man who'd murdered your family. How did that make you feel?"

Skyler rolled her eyes. Was this the game, then? Trying to shit stir, like she and Angel hadn't already been through all this?

"I was angry for maybe a second." Angel's gaze flitted back to Skyler. "But then I realised she'd come to me because she was terrified. He was hurting her. More than that – he was holding the threat over her, all the time. I wanted to help her. So I gave her a gun."

"How did you feel about her back then?"

"I... liked her. I looked forward to seeing her. And I worried about her."

"You wanted to help her."

"That's what I said."

"And yet." Hahn steepled her fingers together. "While you killed plenty of his entourage after discovering that Skyler – your friend, whom you cared about – was in his home, you didn't go near Redruth. You talked about it – at length, apparently – and yet... you didn't touch him."

Kimura coughed, tight-lipped. Faith shifted in her seat. "Julia," she murmured. "I really don't think this is –"

What little colour had remained in Angel's face vanished. Her fists balled in her lap.

"You didn't go near him," Hahn repeated, and Angel lifted her head and blinked. "And that I can't understand. You knew he was hurting Skyler. Surely, if anything, that should have spurred you on. And yet – you did nothing. For months, you did nothing."

This was ridiculous. This was beyond stupid.

Except... Hahn's point had never occurred to Skyler before.

"I think you do understand," Angel said. "I think you know exactly why that happened. But in any case, it's not you I need to explain myself to."

She turned to Skyler, and she was as pale and unhappy and wretched as Skyler had ever seen her. "I'm sorry," she whispered. "Because it's true, what she's saying. I knew you were suffering, and I – I put off going after him –" a sobbing catch "– because I... was... scared. That I'd freeze. That I'd be the girl watching her family die in our living room again, and he... maybe he would've killed me, or maybe he would've just... laughed at me. I'm sorry. I had chances, and I couldn't – I didn't take them. You thought I was brave, but I wasn't. I wasn't."

She curled in on herself, crying silently. Skyler's chest filled with a tearing ache.

Everyone was watching them. It didn't matter.

She slid off her chair, knelt in front of Angel and took her hands. "It's okay," she murmured. "It's okay."

Angel shook her head violently. "It's not! It can't be."

The ache in Skyler's chest flared into white heat: half at Angel's pain, half with rage at Hahn, who for some reason seemed determined to rip them apart, to break Angel into pieces.

The hell with it.

No more secrets. No more silence. No more shame.

She glanced over her shoulder at Hahn. "Since

you've seen fit to do this in front of everyone," she said, "I guess I will too."

She turned back to the only person who mattered. "Angel. Look at me."

Tears streamed down Angel's cheeks. "I'm sorry. I'm so sorry."

"No. Don't be sorry. Listen." Skyler swallowed. "You remember, back when you gave me the gun, what I told you? What... happened to me, when I first went to the cellar? Daniel's men. What they did."

Angel gulped and nodded.

"It started on the second day and it went on for about a month. I was stupid enough to think I'd be safer in the cellar than I'd been on the streets, but..."

Her mouth was as dry as dead leaves. She couldn't really do this, could she? Cut herself open for everyone to see?

But that was what had just happened to Angel. It was the loneliest place in the world, to be trapped with a secret too awful to speak aloud. So Angel would not be alone. Skyler wouldn't let her be.

"After the first time, I thought: okay, they've got what they wanted, it's over now. But..." A painful breath. "They kept coming back. And I didn't know what to do. I mean – it happened on the streets too. At least in the cellar there was less chance the Board would catch me, I could make some money, I could..." She cleared her throat. "I was too ashamed to ask Daniel to make them stop. I... Every time it was over, I'd tell myself, *you're not going to let that happen again*. I'd tell myself, next time, you'll fight back, you'll hurt them, you'll make them stop. You'll do *something*."

She closed her eyes. "And then the next day, or the day after that, I'd hear them coming again. And I... would... just... freeze."

She gripped Angel's hands. "So you don't apologise to me, okay? Not for that. Not ever. I understand, Angel. Sometimes our brains let us down. But you never have."

She shot another glance at Hahn. "You can't get between us. Do you understand? If you don't believe me – bring it on. Let's have whatever mind game bullshit you think you've still got up your sleeve."

Hahn met her eyes, unflinching. Skyler let out a slow breath. "Are we done, then? Are you satisfied now? Because I swear to God, I am *this* close to being through with every last fucking one of you."

"So." Hahn leaned back and started ticking points off on her fingers. "We've got one unpredictable, traumatised assassin with a sudden crisis of conscience. One thief whose ability to function with what appears to be a severe case of obsessive-compulsive disorder is frankly beyond me. And one hacker whose skills are surpassed only by her breathtaking level of arrogance."

"Yeah," Skyler said. "And if you actually give a shit about doing what you claim this place was set up for, you're lucky to have us. We're the best chance the North has."

"We don't make allowances here," Hahn said. "For age, for mental health, for what a person has suffered. There are no mitigating circumstances in war."

Abruptly, Mackenzie stopped tapping.

"D'you seriously think we don't know that?" he said. "Do you think we've been doing the last few years on cheat mode or something? We've made it this far. We can finish this job. And we're gonna do it with or without you."

Every so often he threw a total curve ball. It was like watching a rabbit turn into a honey badger. Skyler just hoped Hahn wasn't about to unhinge her jaw and swallow him whole.

For a long, long moment, nobody moved.

Then – "We're done here," Hahn said. "You'd all better go with Kimura and get to work. This isn't going to be easy."

Mackenzie's mouth fell open. "All of us?"

"That's what I said. Don't make me regret it."

26

WHITE FLAG

"I really am sorry," Kimura said, as he ushered the three of them into his office. "That wasn't okay."

Angel's eyes were still red-rimmed, but she'd recovered her composure. She shrugged. "It's done now."

"You're facing huge challenges. We need to be sure our teams are solid."

"Yeah, well, hopefully we've established that." Skyler crossed her arms across her chest, trying to ignore the unsteadiness in her legs. She felt like she was missing a layer of skin. "Now shall we get on and do something about it?"

Kimura's dark eyes were on her; was there sympathy in them? "What?" she demanded.

He shook his head. "Nothing."

"Right. Good."

Kimura held up his tablet to show them a photo of a heavy, red-faced man with wiry hair. "Recognise him?"

Angel studied the image. "Isn't he the Justice Minister?"

"That's right. Anton Fitzpatrick. We need to leak a set of confidential memos from his office signalling the end of the Board's co-operation with certain businesspeople."

"The Redruth types," Skyler said.

"Exactly."

Finally, something she actually wanted to think about. "I'll get my laptop."

Several hours later, Kimura was summoned to Hahn's office and Angel went to find food. Skyler and Mackenzie were left alone. She stayed hunched over her laptop, but she could still hear him fidgeting.

If she just kept ignoring him, he was bound to get the message.

"Sky?"

"Kinda busy here, Mack."

"I know. I just – are you okay?"

"I'm fine." *Stop it, Mackenzie. Please.*

"You sure? Because that, earlier... that was –"

"*Mackenzie!*" It came out as a yell. She didn't care. "Just – *leave* it, okay? Stop feeling sorry for me, stop doing sad Mackenzie puppy eyes at me, stop looking at me like a... a rape victim! Just *stop* it!"

A horrible silence fell. Skyler's heart pounded, each thud landing in her stomach like a rock into a dark well.

She leaned her elbows on the desk and buried her head in her hands.

After a moment, she heard Mackenzie sit down nearby. "I'm sorry," he said. "I'm sorry. I just... don't know what to say."

"Yeah, well, I'm sorry if this is difficult for you, Mackenzie –"

"Skyler!" His voice was so sharp she jerked her head up. In all the years she'd known him, she could count on one hand the number of times she'd heard him raise it. "Would you *stop*? D'you think that if you're mean enough I'm going to stop caring about you or something? 'Cos sorry to disappoint you, but that's not gonna happen. So would you please just *once* let me be your friend without being a dick about it?"

He might as well have pulled the chair out from under her. Agonising and apologising was what Mackenzie did. Ripping into him was the easy option. He would take it, and she would feel better – or at least, she'd have something different to feel bad about. She didn't know what to do with this new version of him.

"Look," he said quietly. "If you want me to pretend I never heard a word of that, then I swear I'll never bring it up again. I just want you to know – I'm really fucking sorry that happened to you."

"I know," Skyler muttered into her hands. "I know. It's just – every time you and all the others look at me, you're not gonna see me anymore. All you're gonna see is what they did to me. And I can't stand it."

"Hey." He shuffled closer. "You want to know what I see when I look at you?"

She bit her lip hard to stop it trembling. "Not really."

"Well, I'm gonna tell you anyway. I see the person who rescued me from being stuck in that warehouse in Leeds on my own. The person who was by my side when I did the scariest shit I've ever done – who *made* me brave enough to do that stuff. I see someone who punched me in the face because she got bored of trying to talk me into something. I see someone I know I can trust to be totally honest because she doesn't care if she's being a dick. I see the bravest, smartest, most annoying person I've ever met. You think what I just heard changes any of that? Of course it doesn't."

Skyler tried to laugh. "You must think I'm so stupid."

"Since when did you care what I think of you?"

"I feel so... ashamed." She knotted a strand of hair around her fingers, pulled it tight. She still wanted to curl into a ball and never come out. "I *know* I shouldn't. But sometimes I think – why didn't you see it coming? Why didn't you leave after the first time? Why didn't you fight back? Like, I know it's not my fault, but sometimes... I don't *feel* it, you know? And I feel like other people will think that stuff too. That I didn't try hard enough to stop it."

"Well, if anyone ever does think that, Sky, then *fuck them*. Nothing you did or didn't do could ever have made it your fault."

"Huh. That's what Angel says, too."

"Well, then. Who else's opinion even matters?"

235

Skyler thought about the first time she'd told Angel what had happened. How she hadn't really believed until she met Angel's eyes that Angel wasn't looking at her differently.

She risked a glance at Mackenzie. He still looked upset, worried – but there was no disgust, no judgement, no pity in his eyes. The caustic heat in her blood began to cool a little.

"D'you promise to keep thinking I'm a dick?" she asked.

He laid a solemn hand on his chest. "Till the day I die."

This time she didn't have to force her laugh. "Mack?"

"Yeah?"

"Don't let this go to your head, but I actually do care what you think, you know."

He squinted at her. "You're not, like... dying, are you?"

She rolled her eyes. "Shut up."

"Can I give you a hug?"

She managed to look him in the eye for at least a couple of seconds this time. "Fine. If you need one or whatever." She would probably never admit it, but he gave pretty good hugs.

"Thank you, Mack," she murmured, as he wrapped his arms around her.

"I still think you're a dick," he said into her hair.

She wiped her eyes and hoisted herself onto Kimura's desk. Mackenzie perched beside her. They sat, swinging their legs in contemplative silence.

"So you really like Faith, huh?" Skyler said at last.

He went pink. She elbowed him in the ribs. "I'll take that as a yes."

More silence.

"Mack?"

"Yeah?"

"I'm sorry I was such a jerk about that whole thing. I never meant to suggest she didn't really like you. How could she not?"

He grinned. "Thanks. That actually does mean... Thanks, Sky."

There was a tiny, troubled crease between his brows. Absently, he started tapping the table.

He'd just done the good friend thing for her. She should do the same for him, even though she was shit at it. "You gonna tell me what's up, then?"

His lower lip caught between his teeth. "Uh. I dunno. It's stupid."

"Oh, go on. Since we're doing this whole words and feelings thing. What's the matter?"

"You mean apart from all the Board stuff? I guess it's just... The reason I was so mad at you was that you kind of hit a nerve. I mean, why *would* she like me? And even if she thinks she does, she doesn't know the real me, right?"

Skyler frowned. "Isn't there only one you? You're about the realest person I know, Mack."

He glanced down meaningfully at his right hand, still tapping relentlessly. "She hasn't seen – you know." He blushed again.

"She doesn't know about – that?" Angel called it OCD, but she'd never heard Mackenzie refer to it that way. It didn't seem polite, somehow, to label it in a way she wasn't sure he was comfortable with.

"I don't want her to know. I don't want her to think... ah, I dunno."

But Skyler understood, for once. He didn't want Faith to think he was small and weak and pathetic. "Seriously, Mack? Don't tell me I'm gonna have to give you relationship advice, because I don't think either of us are going to enjoy it very much."

He just kicked his heels together.

"Fine. You asked for it." Skyler cleared her throat theatrically. "You have to tell her."

"I know, I know. It's not fair to let her think I'm something I'm not."

"No, you bellend. You have to tell her because you shouldn't be embarrassed and you shouldn't have to hide it from someone who's supposed to like you. It's not *you*, Mack. Same as all that shit that happened isn't me. I think she'll get that. She seems nice or whatever. And if she doesn't get it, she doesn't deserve you."

"Okay, seriously, are you dying?"

"No. I wouldn't get used to this if I were you."

27

COMPASS

"So," Hahn said, later that afternoon. "What've you got?"

Angel, well aware her every movement was still under scrutiny, handed Hahn the paper she'd been scribbling on. Hahn squinted at it. "If I were being generous, I'd say this looked like a genogram."

"It is, sort of. Of the South's big players. They all have Board enforcers moonlighting for them. If we can split the enforcers' loyalties, that'll be a good start. And once the public cotton on, that'll undermine confidence in the Board even more."

"We're talking about millions of people who just sat and let them commit atrocities," Mackenzie said. "Are they really gonna give a shit?"

Angel shook her head. "Southerners aren't evil. They're no worse than anyone anywhere else. They just got pushed, an inch at a time. And once you're on that path, there's never a good time to speak up, is there? The Board got stronger and scarier, and by the time people realised how messed up everything was, there was no way to fight back."

Kimura nodded. "Everyone likes to think that when it happens on their doorstep, they'll do the right thing. Unfortunately, if this job's taught me anything, it's that people are endlessly disappointing."

"What a heartwarming sentiment," Hahn said dryly.

He shrugged. "Tell me it's not true."

Mackenzie rubbed his eyes. The heat had gone out of him since earlier; now he was subdued, dejected. Angel understood. The magnitude of what they were trying to achieve was so vast, so overwhelming, that holding all that gnawing hopelessness at bay was a full-time job in itself. "The thing is, if the Board goes, what replaces it? And how do we know whatever does will be any better?"

"It could hardly be worse," Skyler pointed out.

"Things can always get worse."

"It's a gamble," Hahn agreed. "But I'd say the odds favour the unknown."

Mackenzie sighed. "I bloody hope so."

"Course they do," Skyler said. "Anyway. We need to do something about the internet. It's censored. If we make it easier for people to communicate, share as much information as possible, the Board'll crumble way quicker."

"You think you can do something about the fire-walls?" Hahn asked.

"It'll be hard."

"Impossible?"

Skyler grinned. "Nothing's impossible."

"Of course not," Kimura said. "That would mean she'd have to pass up an opportunity to show off."

Skyler raised an eyebrow. "Don't go getting jealous, Kimura. I can teach you some stuff when all this is over."

She was magnetic when she was determined. There was a light in her eyes, a steel to the way she held herself, that made it seem like nothing could stand in her way. Angel could have watched her all day. There would never be enough time.

Mackenzie dragged his hands through his hair. "And if we just provoke the Board into bombing the North?"

"They won't." Kimura sounded confident, at least. "Once they realise you're not up there, they'll know it would be a huge waste of effort for far too high a price."

"They were worried enough before to build a biological weapon," Mackenzie muttered.

"Well, once we get started, they'll have bigger problems."

Mackenzie groaned. "I hate that I'm even thinking like this. But what if we just make everything even worse?"

Hahn let out an irritated, *this is pointless* sigh, but Kimura's face softened. "This is your first time doing something like this," he said, laying a hand on Mackenzie's shoulder. "But it's not ours. Have faith."

Angel, Faith and Hahn spent the evening poring over the South's criminal elite. It was beyond awkward, with Faith flitting around like a guilty sparrow and dropping things every time she caught Angel's eye. Hahn was acting like nothing had happened, but Angel hadn't expected anything different. She was hardly going to apologise.

Oddly, Angel was no longer having trouble meeting Hahn's eyes. The humming danger that had overwhelmed her every time she was in the woman's presence seemed, somehow, to have dissipated. Angel had faced the deadliest weapon Hahn could throw at her and she was still standing. She didn't need to run anymore.

It was past two AM when she went to bed. She'd nearly dozed off when a soft knock at her door catapulted her back into consciousness. She forced her muscles to loosen before she padded to the door.

Skyler was outside, her hair coming loose from an untidy plait. "Hey." She stifled a yawn. "Sorry. Did I wake you?"

Angel smiled at her. "I don't mind. Come in. Have you finished working?"

Skyler sat on the bed to pull her boots off. "Kimura called it a night, so I figured I probably could too. Besides, I wanted to see you."

The candle-flame flicker of warmth and pleasure inside Angel glowed brighter. "Come to bed," she said.

Curled together under the covers, Skyler reached up to caress Angel's cheek. "Are you okay?" she asked. "What Hahn did to you earlier – I could've smacked her."

That had certainly crossed Angel's mind. But what she hadn't expected was that she would be lighter for shedding her terrible, corrosive secret, the shame she'd thought she would carry forever.

She shook her head. "I'm just sorry you got dragged into it. And that I never told you before. I know I should –"

Skyler touched a finger to her lips. "No apologies, remember?"

"Thank you." Angel stroked a strand of hair from Skyler's forehead. "How're you doing?"

"Eh. I'm good. I don't care what those idiots think of me." She gave Angel a crooked smile. "All right, so I kind of wanted to throw up after I said all that stuff. But Mack talked some sense into me. I just wish you'd told me sooner. I hate the thought of you beating yourself up over it."

Was this real? Skyler didn't blame her, didn't hate her. She had seen the weakest, most flawed part of Angel's heart, and she was still watching Angel with a smile in her eyes.

Skyler shifted closer. They both leaned in at the same moment, into a kiss that started soft, that neither of them moved away from.

Skyler's fingers trailed up and down Angel's arm, leaving a shimmering shiver behind them. "You've got goosebumps."

"Uh huh."

"Interesting."

Skyler's fingertips still tracing patterns. Another enquiring kiss. An involuntary sigh from Angel.

"I thought you'd want to go to sleep," Angel said.

An edge of mischief in Skyler's voice, as her hands continued their exploration. "Suddenly I'm not so tired."

"No," Angel murmured, as their kisses turned fierce, unstoppable. "Me either."

And later, when their limbs tangled sleepily together, Skyler rested her head on Angel's chest and smiled up at her. "Okay. We're gonna need to get this whole revolution thing finished as quick as possible so we've got time for a lot more of that."

Angel laughed. "Sounds good to me."

"Angel?"

"Mm?"

"D'you ever think about... you know, afterwards? Like, what you'll do when all this is over?"

"I don't know." Angel studied the ceiling. "I never used to." All those years with no concept of tomorrow. At best she'd been indifferent; at worst, she'd hoped it would never come. But now...

"Me either," Skyler said. "I do now, though."

The idea of the future was a blank canvas, so vast Angel couldn't fathom how to picture it. It was like trying to imagine a new colour. But perhaps together they could start to sketch a map.

"What do you think about?" she asked.

"Being with you, of course. Having a flat or something – not a massive one, you know? Just somewhere that was... ours. Somewhere safe, with lots of windows."

And there it was, suddenly: a north to point towards. "Somewhere electricity isn't rationed?"

"Obviously."

"What would you do? Hacking?"

"Maybe. Be nice not to have to worry about getting arrested, though. I dunno."

"Definitely in favour of you not getting arrested."

"Oh," Skyler added. "And we'd live near the beach."

A clench of Angel's heart, but not a painful one. "We would?"

"Of course. You might even talk me into getting in the sea occasionally."

Angel pictured Skyler edging towards the waves, face scrunched against the chill of the saltwater. She smiled. "Maybe we should have two places and follow the summer."

Skyler snuggled into her. "I like that idea. Reckon we could convince Mack to come? I can't imagine not having him around."

"You wouldn't want to live back in the UK, then?"

Skyler sighed. "I don't know. Like, I feel duty bound to try and mop up all this shit, but even if we do get rid of the Board, I can't imagine ever feeling safe there." She hesitated. "I guess that's pretty selfish, huh?"

"It's okay to be selfish sometimes."

"What about you? How would you feel about leaving for good?"

"The same as you, I think. Like we'd earned some peace."

"D'you know what you'd want to do?"

That had been a question for her old life, for teachers and friends and relatives at Christmas: *what do you want to do when you're older?* It was a question that only worked when you were looking forward. Not when every cell of your being would give anything to be able to just go *back*.

Angel stared into the darkness. "I've never thought about it. I didn't even think I'd live this long."

"Is it too hard to talk about?"

Yes. But as soon as the thought appeared, it was no longer true. "It's just... different. New. I – don't laugh, okay?"

"As if I would."

"I... wonder if maybe I could get some proper medical training. Be a paramedic or a doctor or something."

"Why would I laugh at that?"

"Because I'm technically a serial killer, and they're not usually allowed to be doctors?"

"Eh. We'll figure it out."

Angel took a deep breath. "That was my plan, you know, before. Dancing is so precarious – one wrong move and your career could be over in seconds. So med school was the backup. Like..." She swallowed. "Like my mum."

Skyler held her tighter.

"I never thought there was anything I'd be able to take with me," Angel said quietly.

Skyler kissed her cheek. "Maybe you can take some of it, after all."

28

HOURGLASS

"We've got a problem," Skyler announced the next day. "A big one."

Of course they bloody did. Epic problems aside, though, she looked more alive than she had in a long time. Mackenzie had worried about her the day before, knowing how she hated her own vulnerability. But if anything, she seemed stronger now.

Hahn, at her desk with Kimura hovering at her shoulder, sighed. "We'll add it to the list. Enlighten us, then."

Skyler showed them her laptop screen: reams of code that meant nothing to Mackenzie. "I thought I'd be able to take down the firewalls remotely. I figured whoever runs the South's internet can't be any smarter than me."

Kimura's mouth twisted like he was trying not to laugh.

"We get it, you're smart," Hahn said. "And?"

"Something's changed since I was last in their system.

They've made it so everything's only accessible through one location. Within the Board headquarters."

Kimura drew a sharp breath, but Hahn just closed her laptop. "Interesting," she said mildly. "They've got someone smarter than you."

Mackenzie expected Skyler's response to be a combination of 'fuck' and 'off,' but she only snorted. "No. They've just done what I would've ages ago if I wasn't smart enough to build a system that would keep me out."

Mackenzie tried to speak through the vice round his chest. "This isn't good, is it?"

"No," Skyler said. "It's like the definition of 'not good'."

"Does it... uh, does it mean what I think it means?"

"That if I'm gonna do any of the stuff we've been talking about, I need to be inside the headquarters? Yeah."

A lurch into a bottomless pit: ears ringing, vision blurring. "We've got to go back."

Skyler's face was blank in a way that could only mean she was suppressing a tsunami of emotion. "Me, Mack. I have to go back."

What he was thinking about was safety. About warmth and places to sleep where no one came to kick your door down; about days when you didn't once wonder whether this might be your last one on Earth.

About how easy it would be to walk away from all of this and leave the UK to get on with it, for better or worse.

He shook his head. "Us."

Skyler awarded him the familiar look that communicated with perfect clarity her opinion that he was being a fucking idiot. "Are you planning to learn advanced coding in the next three days?"

"What're *you* gonna do, hack your way through a bunch of locked doors?"

"There must be other people here who can do that stuff."

"Yes." Kimura's mouth twisted thoughtfully. "Including me."

"Well, then –"

Mackenzie took a deep breath. "Sky –"

"No!" She swung to him. "If you stay here, you can be safe, you can be happy. Don't you dare throw that away."

"And what about you? Don't you deserve that too?"

She closed her eyes. "Don't make this difficult, Mack. Please."

"No, I'm gonna. You listen to me, Sky. If this is how it has to be, then you're going in with the best possible chance of coming back out. I'm the only person who's ever broken in there and got out again."

She opened one eye and glared at him. "You're being ridiculous."

His throat ached. "I was the one who got left behind before, remember? It took years for me to realise that wasn't my fault. I did everything I could to save my family. Well – now you're my family. You think I could live with myself, if I let you do this alone? You think that'd be a life worth living?"

"Mack –"

"No. Shut up." He looked at Hahn and Kimura. "How are we gonna do this?"

"Teenagers," Hahn said. "Everything's a drama." She sighed. "Skyler, find somewhere to stash your ego and go with Kimura to find Sophia Rodriguez. Have one more try with her to make sure we really have exhausted all our options. Mackenzie, let's talk details. As you say, you're the only person who's done this before."

Skyler hesitated. "Are you sure about this, Mack?"

Hahn yawned. "Goodness me. Let us assume that he's sure. Leave, please, before someone succumbs to the urge to break into song."

* * *

"I want to go with you," Faith murmured into Mackenzie's chest.

They were cuddled in her bed. The flight to England was leaving in two hours, and the minutes were slipping past with impossible speed.

"You can't." He stroked her hair. "Like, not that I'm telling you what to do. But you couldn't come into the headquarters anyway, and Kimura's sorted on the outside."

He felt her nose wrinkle against him. "Plus," he added, "Hahn made it super clear what she thought of that idea. She'd skin me alive if I tried to argue you should come."

Faith laughed. "She's really not that bad."

"She's bloody terrifying. And she's also right about this." The idea of Faith facing down a greycoat was stone-cold horrifying. "You'll have loads to do here, anyway."

"I could be doing loads over there."

"And I'd be worrying about you the entire time. Which, fine if it's really necessary, but since it's not... It'll be bad enough with Sky and Angel." He couldn't stop thinking about the night they'd crossed the Wall. About Skyler's blood on his hands and Angel taut and terrified and the weight of a gun in his hand.

Faith kissed his shoulder. "Like you need to worry about them. They're both such badasses."

And there it was: this had been a mistake. He'd let himself get carried away; because there was so little time, because he'd wanted to make the most of every moment with Faith, knowing there might never be another. He'd let himself have something good, for once, because he was about to die and it wasn't fair and he might as well do *something* with the final hours of his life, something he could share, something he could hold onto, so that he could at least leave knowing that the last few years had held a spark of something other than darkness and misery.

But that meant he'd pushed the conversation he'd intended to have with Faith aside. He hadn't told her about the worry, the rituals. What did it matter if he was never going to see her again?

But it did matter, because she still didn't really know *him*. And if this was going to mean something – to mean anything – then she deserved to know who he really was.

Suddenly Skyler's way of dealing with emotions – that was, not dealing with them – seemed a lot more appealing.

Damn.

"It's not about logic," he said slowly. "It's about feeling... responsible. That if I don't get everything exactly right, really bad stuff will happen."

She rolled over, her bright eyes on him.

Oh, no. This was a terrible idea.

Well, you've bloody started now, haven't you?

"I get... bad things stuck in my head," he went on, reluctantly. "And I can't get them out. I have to do stuff to make sure nothing bad happens. To keep everyone safe."

"Like what?"

"I don't know. Anything. Tap the right number of times, count stuff, not think certain thoughts... I *know* it doesn't make any sense. And the tapping, the counting – like, at least I know logically there's no way that stuff actually affects anything. But a situation like this, where every single thing I do or don't do could get someone killed... It's unbearable."

Faith sat up. "Oh, Mackenzie."

His insides curdled with shame. He ducked his head. "I'm sorry. I *hate* being like this. And I know if anyone can pull this off, Sky and Angel can, but –"

She grabbed his hand. "*You* can, you mean. It'll be okay. You have to keep telling yourself that."

God, this was getting worse and worse. "You know how many times I've heard that? When the power rationing started, people said it over and over. When the water went off – Mum kept going, 'It's just a cock up. It'll be back on in no time.' When they all got sick –" He choked down a surge of bitter memory. "And I used to try to believe it – but you know what? It's *never* okay. All that ever happens is that you think things are as bad as they can possibly get, and then they get worse."

Faith frowned at the bedspread. Mackenzie stared at his hands, his pulse hammering out a frantic rebuke: *congratulations, idiot, you ruined it.*

You're probably gonna be dead by tomorrow anyway so I don't know why you're even worrying about this.

"So there you go," he muttered. "I'm the furthest thing from brave. I worry all the time. About everything. I'm scared shitless right now."

"Uh, I think you're allowed to be."

He shook his head. "You don't understand. I'm trying to tell you – *this* is the real me."

Her hand was still on his, warm. "You're saying you've got OCD, right? That's what this is."

"I dunno. That's what Angel calls it. I just think I get a bit ridiculous." It felt like an excuse, calling it OCD, when really he just needed to be braver, more rational. "But sometimes my thoughts are so awful, and they feel so real – And I *know* it doesn't make any sense, but I just... can't make it stop."

She cuddled into him. Mackenzie screwed his eyes shut: *she's trying to think of a way to get out of this gracefully, considering you're about to go on a suicide mission.* He ruined everything, without even trying.

"Remember I told you my dad died?" she said at last.

253

The abruptness of it threw him. "Uh. Yeah?"

Faith took a deep breath. "Well, the bit I didn't tell you is that afterwards, my mom totally went to pieces. I always thought she was this really strong person who could handle anything, but she just... crumbled. And when I needed to lean on her, she wasn't there." Another deliberate breath, like she was trying to breathe through a suffocating ache. "Everyone we knew had this whole construct of our family. I was so... I couldn't bear to tell anyone how things really were. I didn't want to let my mom down – I wanted people to remember my family how we were, I guess. So I just... stopped. Stopped going to school, stopped talking to my friends. Couldn't even leave the house because I felt like anyone I met would take one look at me and be able to tell that I was broken."

She shrugged. "That's how come all the languages. The only people I could talk to were strangers online. The languages were just... another layer of a mask, I guess."

She flashed him a taut, bright smile. "So sorry to somehow make this all about me when you're the one who's got to go save the world, and sorry if you thought I was this totally normal person with all their shit together. But what I'm trying to say is... So you've got some stuff. That doesn't make you any less *you*, Mackenzie. Having OCD or whatever you want to call it doesn't make you any less brave. If anything, it makes you braver. Because you do the scary stuff anyway."

Mackenzie wondered whether he'd managed to invent some sort of alternate reality to make himself feel better. "Thank you," he said at last. *Seriously, you couldn't find a more underwhelming response?* "You're amazing."

"You're damn right." She grinned. "And that makes two of us."

He wanted to laugh and cry and kiss her all at once. "I don't want to do this."

"I don't want you to either. But you have to, so you're going to come back safe, okay? And I'm going to keep believing that." She sat up and kissed him, hard. "I might have something useful, actually," she added, leaning across to rummage through her bedside drawer. "If you promise not to rat me out to Hahn or Kimura."

Mackenzie was reminded, oddly, of the time his best friend Hannah had persuaded him to skip double Maths and go into Leeds to meet her favourite band. He'd spent the afternoon feeling like he was about to throw up and bolting down the street whenever he caught a glimpse of anyone who remotely resembled his parents. Afterwards, he'd been so wracked with guilt he'd ended up confessing to them – completely unnecessarily – as soon as he walked through the front door, with Bex rolling her eyes at him from the sofa the whole time.

"Um," he said, now. "What're you –?"

Faith held up a slim, flat silvery object a couple of inches long. "I borrowed this. I thought it might be useful."

Mackenzie squinted at it. "It's a... What is it?"

"A communication device. A prototype."

"Where'd you get it?"

Her grin took on a mischievous edge. "Ayodele owes me a favour."

"But they've already given us something to contact Kimura with –"

"Yeah, and if you get caught the Board'll have it off you in about a second. Not this, though. This is an implant."

"I'm not putting anything up my –"

"Dude! It goes in your arm! Here." She traced a line on his wrist. "We do a tiny incision and it just slides in. No one'll see it. You press down for five seconds to activate it, and if you speak into it I'll be able to hear you and you should be able to hear me."

Mackenzie eyed it dubiously. "Is it gonna migrate through my body and get lodged in an artery?"

"Well, it hasn't been fully tested yet, but there's like a 98% chance you're good. Besides, if you don't get caught you'll be back in a couple of days, and if you do you're gonna have bigger things to worry about."

"And how much trouble will we be in if Hahn finds out I've smuggled this cutting-edge technology into the headquarters?"

"Uh... let's say it's probably best if she doesn't find out."

"This is way worse than bunking off school," Mackenzie mumbled.

"Huh?"

"Nothing. Look, I really don't know about this –" He was well aware of the Agency's views on improvisation.

He didn't want Hahn and Kimura to decide he was more trouble than he was worth.

But Faith's face had clouded. "Maybe you're not the only one who worries," she said quietly. "If you have this, I might be able to help you if things go wrong. Otherwise – you come back, we take it out, no one ever needs to know. So – please. Please take it."

He kissed her. "You're a terrible influence."

She threw her arms around his neck. "I'm the best influence. C'mon. Let's go bribe Ayodele into fitting this."

29

WE WHO WERE LIVING

To get them into the South, Kimura was posing as a businessman visiting to discuss trade negotiations. "Japan's still on good terms with the Board," he explained, "so I've arranged a meeting with the Business Secretary. And as befits an obscenely rich business mogul, I'll be arriving in an extremely fancy private jet."

"Which we'll be squashed into the hold of," Skyler said.

"My alter ego is hardly going to arrive with a gaggle of Caucasian teenagers in tow. You can survive a couple of hours in the hold."

"I'm just saying it won't be much fun."

"The trip to Disneyland will be on the way back."

It wasn't really the time to be winding Kimura up. But if she didn't, if she actually let herself think about the reality of what they were doing, she might drown in the absolute crashing dread that threatened to sweep her away whenever she paused for breath.

There had been times – most of the last few years, if she was honest – when Skyler had really thought it might be better if she just wasn't here anymore. And then fate had said: *okay, then, if that's what you really want* – and all at once she'd realised she didn't want to die at all.

Twice, in the last three months, she'd believed she was about to die. The day Daniel Redruth had arrived to exact his revenge. And the bullet in her stomach as they fled towards the Wall.

Running so hard her lungs burned.

Cold.

Mackenzie crying.

Lydia yelling.

Angel: *I promise I won't leave you.*

A single thought, over and over. *This can't be it. I don't want to go.*

All those years of selfishness, when she hadn't even cared whether she lived or died. Now she cared, she cared so much, and she had an entire bloody country to think about. And she had more courage with Angel and Mackenzie beside her – but less, too. She would sacrifice everything they were fighting for if she had to, to keep them safe.

It had seemed best not to mention that to Hahn or Kimura.

Quiet on the plane, hands locked with Angel's in the dim hold. She didn't want to let go even for a second. If this was it – if this was all she could ever have – she wanted to absorb every last heartbeat.

She'd assumed Mackenzie would spend the whole

time tapping, but he was still and silent, and not even in the absent, distracted way that meant he was doing all the rituals inside his head instead.

"You're thinking about Faith," she said.

He looked startled, the way he always did when she managed to guess what he was thinking. She suspected he thought she was a robot.

"You're gonna see her again, Mack."

He just looked at the floor.

"Hey." She prodded him. "We're coming back out, yeah? All of us."

He didn't always like hearing things like that, she knew. He thought it was tempting fate or something. But maybe it wasn't really him she was trying to convince.

To get them into the headquarters, she'd ordered a consignment of office furniture from a pre-vetted company. She, Angel and Mackenzie would hide in the delivery crates and Kimura and his colleagues would hijack the supply lorry to drive them through the perimeter fence. They would arrive late, when the porters would most likely dump the boxes in a storeroom rather than bother unpacking them. If not, they'd have to kill whoever opened the boxes.

She prayed that, whatever happened, they wouldn't open Mackenzie's box first. She wasn't convinced he was capable of killing anyone.

She was, though. One day it would be really nice not to have to kill anyone else. Or maybe just not to meet people who needed killing.

She'd never been scared of the dark or small spaces –

Daniel's cellar would have been a whole other hell if she were – but as the plane started its descent and the lid of the crate closed over her head, the darkness felt like it was burrowing through her mouth and nose into her lungs. She might as well already be in a coffin; not that she would get one if she died today. And Angel and Mackenzie were gone, she couldn't see them, touch them, speak to them. She was adrift in the universe, with nothing to anchor her.

The darkness in her mouth tasted like iron. *I don't want to die. I don't want to die. I don't want to die.*

You're just panicking. Breathe.

This is definitely the stupidest idea I've ever had.

She'd never really understood Mackenzie's rituals. Now, though, all she could think was that she'd give anything, do anything, to know the others were safe.

The box jolted. They were off the plane.

Kimura wasn't coming into the headquarters. "The fewer the better," he'd said. "Besides, we might need someone on the outside."

In case they all got shot, in other words.

The journey felt endless: rocking, bumping, snatches of indecipherable sound. How long since she'd felt this powerless?

Abruptly, the movement stopped. Skyler held her breath as the lorry doors scraped open.

A disgruntled Birmingham accent. "Bit bloody late, isn't it?"

"Sorry. Running behind."

A grunt. *Not good enough.*

"Get these inside, then, and we can get off. Early shift'll sort it."

The headquarters were a sprawling warren, ten storeys high and over half a mile from end to end. There was no telling how near they would arrive to the computers Skyler needed to access, how many people they might run into on the way.

More jolting. Her neck prickled. She'd never itched so much in her life.

Please just let this be over with.

When did you get to be such a coward?

"Just chuck it in there. It's only cabinets or something."

"Bloody delivery drivers. Like we don't have homes to go to."

She forced herself to keep breathing, but each shallow breath sounded as loud as a gale. How could they not hear her?

She gripped her pistol. *What if I've forgotten how to shoot?*

For God's sake. She was annoying herself now.

"That's the last one. C'mon."

The footsteps retreated. A door clicked shut. Skyler screwed her eyes shut and held her breath until, finally, three soft knocks thudded nearby. Dizzy with relief, she pushed the top off her crate and emerged into darkness on shaky legs. "Are you guys –?"

A burst of light, as sharp and bright as the terror that froze her to the spot. Behind the dazzle, figures lined the room.

Greycoats.

Machine guns.

"Drop your weapons. Now."

Angel.

Mack.

Skyler dropped her pistol. A hood went over her head, blackness again, hands yanked behind her, metal biting into her wrists like frost. A cacophony of yelling. *"Get down. Don't say a word."*

She dropped to her knees with a thump. A hard, blunt point pressed against the back of her skull.

I can't go, I haven't said everything I meant to say –

No sound from Angel or Mackenzie. She couldn't feel anything. Then a safety catch clicked in her ear and suddenly she felt everything, all at once, and a sob caught in her throat –

"Now?" A woman's voice.

"Yeah, I think we –"

"Hold. Your. Fire."

That was a man: young-sounding, carefully devoid of accent.

"But Atkins told us –"

"And now *I'm* telling you that if you so much as sneeze on these three, I'll blow your damn head off. Is that clear?"

Silence.

The man heaved a sigh. "Am I going to have to make an example of someone?"

"No, sir," the first woman muttered.

"Good. Reactive idiocy, that order. Nobody likes a reactive idiot, do they?"

"No, sir."

"Search them, then take them to the lower ground. Harris and I will see them there." As rough hands hauled Skyler to her feet – "No *accidents* on the way."

"Sir."

"I know where your families live."

"Sir."

And then she was being dragged, but she was barely aware of it. Her head was a tornado.

Angel.

Mack.

They knew we were coming.

And crashing over everything else, incomprehensible, impossible –

I know that voice.

30

RIP TIDE

Too many greycoats; far too many guns. Angel was good, but no one was *that* good.

Once she might have fought back anyway, even after they'd taken her weapons. But everything was different now.

They knew we were coming.

That was the thought ricocheting around the darkness of the hood as she was dragged along. That and a frantic, silent plea that the others wouldn't do anything reckless. Mackenzie almost certainly wouldn't; his self-preservation instinct was too well-honed.

Skyler might.

Angel's mind seemed to have split in two. The terrified, helpless, useless part of her, the part that screamed and cried and begged and wished, had to stay walled up. How ironic, that she'd survived all those years wishing for death because her coldness, her detachment, had allowed her to see with perfect clarity what needed to be done in a thousand impossible situations, and to do it without hesitating.

There had never been a situation more impossible than this.

So don't feel. Think.

Twenty greycoats, twenty machine guns. There was no way to beat those odds. The solution, then, was to stay alive until the odds became more manageable.

Her brain whirred furiously. They had walked into a trap – but who had set it? And had the traitor betrayed only the three of them, or the whole Agency? How much did the Board know about them?

The three of them had made it clear – far too clear – that they were a package. Their strength would only be a weakness here, and their captors almost certainly knew that.

They stopped. Angel was dragged a few more steps, then shoved onto her knees. From either side of her came an echoing thud and a tiny hiss of pain.

Everything the Agency knew about them. Her flashbacks. Mackenzie's OCD.

She'd been far too careless.

Someone wrenched her hood off. Angel screwed up her eyes against the glare.

She was in a concrete chamber lit with dazzling spotlights, Skyler kneeling to her left, Mackenzie to her right. Greycoats with semi-automatic rifles lined every wall she could see.

Before them were two more greycoats: a woman who might have been pretty if not for the severity of her scraped-back bun and the tightness of her lips, and a man in his early twenties with cropped sandy hair, luminous hazel eyes, and a face so empty it made Angel cold inside.

The Board did something to the greycoats when they recruited them. She didn't know what, exactly, but they broke people down into nothing and built them back up in their own image, into a kind of revenant. It was a terrible fate, and sometimes she'd even pitied the greycoats, because there was no denying they were victims too. But pity wouldn't get her and the others out of here alive.

"Well." The man rubbed his hands together. "Shall we start with introductions?"

If Hahn was the informant, they had another weapon. Angel's former name.

So take it from them.

She met the man's empty eyes. "Felicity Caitlyn North." To her relief, the words came out clear and steady. "But your informants will know me as Angel."

The greycoat snorted. "I suppose that's what happens when teenagers get to choose their own names. *Angel.* Seriously?" He nodded at Mackenzie. "What do they call you, then?"

"Mackenzie." His voice trembled. "Thomas Mackenzie."

"Carrying on the family name? Aww." The greycoat raised his eyebrows at Skyler. "And you?"

"S – Skyler." Her voice shook even more than Mackenzie's, and a sharp pang of alarm drove through Angel, because that was the last thing she'd expected. "Skyler Linley." She sounded bewildered, dazed. Had she taken a blow to the head?

"Oh, of *course*. The internet sensation. What an honour. And do either of you prefer a different name? Hex, perhaps? Nightstalker?"

Perhaps the Board had pioneered insufferable smugness as an enhanced interrogation technique.

The woman coughed. "You can make this easier for yourselves if you share your plans and the names of your associates now."

Maybe they don't know everything after all. Maybe we've got some time.

"Don't be silly," the man said reprovingly. "They're *freedom fighters*. Giving up that easily wouldn't be very noble, would it?"

Now it was clear where the danger in the room was. Their interrogation was a job to the woman, but to this man, it was a game.

"No," the woman said, sounding bored, "but it would mean a lot less mess and a lot less paperwork." She looked at the three of them. "I'll put this simply. You are all guilty of treason. So you can make life difficult for yourselves, or you can give us an incentive to be lenient."

Angel steeled herself for a scornful bark of laughter or a sarcastic retort from Skyler. But Skyler seemed transfixed by the male greycoat, her face utterly still and colourless.

Instead, amazingly, Mackenzie started to laugh. "The Board doesn't recognise Northerners' human rights," he said. "You don't even think of us as *people*. And you're talking about leniency?"

"Everything's relative," the man said, as though addressing someone he suspected to be mentally deficient. "But let's be honest – we've got a thousand ways to make this whole process worse for you. You may not have many choices left, but you do have some. How much pain you and your friends spend the rest of your lives in being the most obvious."

Mackenzie's whole frame slumped. Angel hated to see him like that, but at least he understood. Outward defiance, however tempting, was a terrible idea. There was no point offering the greycoats something to crush.

Skyler's temper was the thing to worry about, especially with someone as full of himself as this guy. Angel tried to catch her eye, to implore her not to bite. But there was no tell-tale tension to Skyler's jaw suggesting she was doing her best to hang on to the edges of her temper. She looked... *lost*.

Did Skyler know this man? Had he worked for Redruth?

No, that couldn't be it. Angel had known every face on Redruth's crew.

So what the hell was going on?

"Take them away." The female greycoat waved dismissively. "Separate cells, obviously. Let them make up their minds."

As the bag went back over her head and hands

dragged her to her feet, Angel dug her nails into her palms, fighting down a howl from the shut-away part of her. There would be a way out of this. She just had to last long enough to make one.

31

EYES OPEN

Faith had spent the last two years telling herself that one day, when she finally became the person she aspired to be, that version of her would be exactly like Hahn. She'd never been able to calm the flutter in her chest when she was under pressure, like a sparrow beating, futile, against its cage. But no matter how fraught, how desperate, things got, Hahn stayed cool and detached and in control.

But Faith's captive sparrow seemed to have grown into an albatross in the last few hours, and it hurt to watch Hahn working through emails as serenely as though she were shopping for groceries while Mackenzie might be about to die. To reduce the risk of interception, they'd agreed that the Northerners would communicate only with Hahn via Kimura, but Faith was still checking her own emails relentlessly, scrutinising Hahn for any sign of news, painfully aware of the illicit communication device in a band around her wrist.

Eventually, Hahn shot her an accusatory scowl. "What's wrong with you?"

Faith stopped fiddling with her wristband. "Uh. Nothing." Distractedly, she picked up a pen and flicked it across the room.

"You're a terrible liar, Faith."

She'll understand. She's not a robot.

But ever since the incident with Angel, Faith had stayed out of Hahn's way. She had no idea how to confront what Hahn had done – and what could Hahn possibly say to justify it anyway? She clearly thought her behaviour was perfectly acceptable. To have that confirmed would send their relationship down a path there might be no coming back from. Faith wasn't sure she was ready for that.

"You're worrying about them," Hahn said, as though Faith had brought home an exceptionally poor school report.

"Aren't *you*?"

"Would it help them if I was?"

More than not giving a shit at all, probably. Faith stared at Hahn. "Don't you care about them at all?"

"Care and worry aren't the same thing. Care is useful. Worry is not."

Before the last few days, Faith's trust in Hahn had never wavered, even when her methods and her logic were as inscrutable as her demeanour. But – "How can you just *switch it off*? Surely –"

"Faith." She'd heard that suppressed current of exasperation often enough to know that Hahn was trying her best to be patient, and considered that Faith was making this difficult. "This is why relationships with colleagues are a bad idea. Instead of focusing on finishing the job safely, you're wasting half your energy playing 'what if?' Worry isn't just useless, it's irresponsible."

Like it was that easy. Faith ducked behind her laptop so Hahn wouldn't see her trying to force away the sting behind her eyes.

Hahn sighed. "Perhaps you should work on something else."

"What?" Faith cleared her throat hastily. "I'm fine."

"Nonetheless." Hahn's tone had genuinely thawed, but Faith didn't feel like acknowledging it. "Go find Rodriguez. She could use your help on the Paraguay op. I'll call you when there's news."

There was no point arguing; Hahn was about as flexible as an iron bar. Faith picked up her laptop with a sigh.

"Ah," Hahn said, as she reached the door. "There we are."

Faith spun round. "What? What?"

"Kimura says they're in and they've found the IT systems." Hahn offered her a small smile. "All's well so far. And Skyler, despite her many irritating qualities, is more than capable of pulling this off."

Faith managed a wobbly smile back. "Thanks, Julia. I know you think I'm being silly, but –"

"No. I understand. I'd be lying if I said I wasn't glad to hear from Kimura. Try to keep busy, Faith. It'll be over soon enough."

En route to Sophia's office, Faith ducked into a bathroom and splashed cold water on her face. However scared she was, it was a thousand times worse for Mackenzie. She had to be strong. She had to keep it together.

She dried her face slowly with a paper towel. *They're going to be okay. He's going to be okay.*

As she dropped the towel into the bin, the little receiver in her wristband vibrated.

She froze.

Mackenzie must have pressed it by accident. Hahn had literally just said everything was fine.

But the receiver kept buzzing insistently.

She locked the bathroom door with shaking hands and crouched against the wall. "Mackenzie? I'm here." She pressed the device to her ear, her mouth dry. *Come on, come on –*

"Faith?" His voice came through tinny, muffled. "Can you hear me?"

"Hey." She tried to keep her words steady. "I can hear you. What's up?"

"I – I can't –" His tone sharpened. "I can't really make out what you're saying – Faith, say 'yes' if you can understand me, but don't say anything if you can't, okay?"

"Y – yes."

"I don't have much time. They were waiting for us inside the headquarters – I don't know how – but – they knew."

No. No. She must have heard him wrong, he must be confused, there was no way –

"They knew we were coming," he repeated.

"Someone sold us out, Faith. They've separated us, they've taken all our stuff... I think... I think we're really in trouble."

She took a ragged breath, wiped away scalding tears. This was no time to cry.

"I don't think they'll kill us right away." Mackenzie's voice was quiet, matter-of-fact. "But I don't know how long we've got, and I don't know how bad it'll get before... I don't even know if you can do anything. Please don't put yourself in danger, okay? Please. But... if you do happen to have any bright ideas..."

Somebody here did this.

Faith stared at the wall, numb, dreamlike. This was how dreams went, after all: making no sense but carrying on anyway, relentless.

"I've got to go," Mackenzie said. "I don't want them to – Listen. Faith..." He sighed. "You made me believe... that the world could be good again. And I didn't think I'd ever feel like that another day in my life. So what we... What you gave me..."

There was a long pause. She pictured his face: the wry little smile and flippant tone he used to help him say the things that mattered most. "Thank you, is what I'm doing a terrible job of trying to say. It meant something. More than I could ever tell you."

She squeezed her eyes shut. "I hear you," she whispered, even though she knew he couldn't hear her. "And I'm going to help you. So hold on, Mackenzie. Okay? Hold on."

"I'm going now," he said. "Before I say something totally ridiculous and die of embarrassment."

Don't go, she wanted to say. But he was out of her reach.

She curled into a ball on the bathroom floor, digging her nails so hard into her forearm she thought they would break the skin. Deep down, she'd really believed it when she'd told him he would be fine, that they would all be fine. Yes, their job was difficult, but no more so than dozens of things they'd already survived.

'A relentless optimist,' Hahn called her sometimes, usually in a way that suggested this was rather tedious; how tiresome, that Faith was constantly inclined to see the best in things. "I'll see you soon," she'd told Mackenzie firmly, gripping his hands before he boarded the plane. And he'd hesitated, and kissed her on the cheek, and said, "I hope so," with an achingly sweet, sad smile that said, *I don't think so.*

He knew. And Faith had forgotten, had allowed herself to forget, the fragility of the world, the way you took for granted that there would always be another meeting, another kiss, another chance to right wrongs, to say the things you'd meant to say. You clung to the lie that *soon* would always come, because how could you move through the world bearing the truth that one day it wouldn't?

But the world where soft, sad, mischievous boys rolled over and kissed you like they'd waited all their lives for that moment was, after all, the same world where people set out for a perfectly ordinary day at work in the morning and never came home again.

And Hahn had been right: worrying was pointless. You could worry for a thousand years and still be no better armed against the very worst life had to throw at you. It was just another delusion, that you could innoculate yourself against misery, that you could wrestle a veneer of control from the uncontrollable, the unbearable.

And yet... Faith *did* have some control here, didn't she?

Mackenzie was still alive. Angel and Skyler most likely were too. And hadn't this been the whole point of giving him the transmitter?

She gave herself ten seconds. Then she got up, blew her nose, and went back to Hahn's office.

When she walked in, Hahn's face pinched with irritation. "I told you to find Rodriguez."

"I... think she's out." *Steady. Come on.* "Julia – have you – have you heard any more?"

Hahn's expression lost its last semblance of patience. "In the last twenty minutes? No."

Please let me wake up now. Please let this not be real.

"For God's sake, Faith –"

Kimura's lying to you. She opened her mouth to say it –

And stopped.

Kimura and Hahn had been partners for fifteen years. This would tear the Agency apart.

Kimura's lying to you.

Or –

A black hole opened in her stomach.

Or Hahn was lying to her.

"Well?" Hahn demanded. "Spit it out."

"N – nothing." Faith swallowed. "Sorry. Sorry. You were right. I... need to step away."

Hahn's face softened. She laid down her pen. "You've been working very hard. Go, have a rest. I'll call you when there's news."

Faith just about made it back to her room before she threw up.

She crouched over the toilet bowl, gasping. She had to get a look at Hahn's messages. That was the only way to figure out who was lying.

She retched again. *God*, how was any of this possible? Why would either of them do this? She remembered the night Skyler's digital package had arrived: Hahn snatching her laptop to examine the files, already on the phone to Kimura. An hour later, their helicopter had been in the air.

But the Northerners were not what the Agency had expected – and while Hahn had many talents, admitting when she was wrong wasn't one of them. Clara was right about that. If Hahn had decided that bringing the Northerners in had been a mistake, perhaps she'd also decided the simplest solution was to just... get rid of them.

No. She wouldn't do that.

How many times had Faith told herself that over the last few weeks?

She always says you do whatever you need to get the

job done. And the number one job is protecting the Agency.

What about Kimura, then? He'd been just as ready to jump in that helicopter. He seemed to like Skyler, despite his grumbling. He'd told Hahn more than once that she was being too hard on Angel.

Faith wiped her streaming eyes. There was nothing else for it. She had to go back and face Hahn.

But ten minutes later she'd been back and forth to her bedroom door a dozen times and she still didn't have a clue what to say.

You're wasting time they don't have. Open the goddamn door.

Instead, she pulled out her phone and dialled.

"Hello, Faith," Kimura said. "Is everything okay?"

Faith blinked hard, suddenly light-headed. "I – uh, just wanted to check in."

"Isn't Julia keeping you updated?" He sounded confused, but not overly exasperated.

"She's... busy. The Croatia thing kicked off, and – look, Ren, I know I'm probably way over-involved, but I just... need to know."

"Ah. Of course. They're fine, as far as I know." There was a smile in his voice. "Last contact must've been twenty minutes ago. They'll be out before morning, I'm sure."

Her stomach convulsed. She doubled over, swallowing a sob.

"It's only natural you're worried," he said. "Maybe don't let on too much to Julia, though."

"I... yeah." Faith's voice sounded weird even to her. "I know. Thanks."

"How about I copy you in next time I update her?"

"Y – yeah. Thanks." Faith coughed hard. *Get it together.* "Sorry. Just been a stressful day, you know? Thanks again, Ren."

"Sure. Take care, Faith."

Faith's legs buckled. She landed with a bump on her bed.

Well, she had her answer. Now all she had to do was break it to Hahn that her closest friend and colleague had intentionally fucked up an op for God knew what reason.

She'd have to admit to borrowing that comms device, too. Hard to know which bit of good news to lead with, really.

This time when she reached Hahn's door, she didn't knock. She just turned the handle and –

The door was locked. That was weird. Faith rattled the handle, frowning, but no sound came from inside.

Knocking would be pointless. "A locked door is a useful hint," Hahn was fond of saying. Even when she wasn't actually rolling her eyes, she'd perfected a tone that conveyed the same effect.

Faith swallowed, fighting the urge to vomit again. Time to deploy the emergency key, then.

She found Hahn seated behind her desk, her shiny hair still pinned as neatly as it had been first thing that morning, a single bullet hole in the centre of her forehead.

32

HISTORY

Inside the blackness of the hood, everything was heightened. Skyler fought to keep her footing as she was dragged along, fingers digging into her arms; there would be bruises, if she lived long enough for them to form. Her captors were silent, but the greycoat's words were still ringing in her ears.

She'd seen his face, heard his voice, but she didn't trust what her senses told her. *You're imagining things. Who you think that is – that's impossible. You* know *that.*

She'd come untethered from her body somewhere around the time they'd searched her and taken the flash drive which held the programs she would have used to break into the computer systems. She was a sailor washed overboard in a shipwreck, growing cold and numb as the current swept her out into a vast, empty expanse.

Then a voice – *the* voice, the imposter – barked, "Take the others down there. I've got this one" – and terror ripped through her like a bullet through her stomach, and the others – the others –

She bit the inside of her cheek so hard to stop herself calling out to them that her mouth flooded hot and coppery. The impossible person holding her stopped abruptly. "I'll take it from here."

A buzzing whine rang in her ears. She bit her cheek harder still.

"Uh –" A different man. "It's not protocol, sir –"

The man holding Skyler's arm shifted; a step towards the second speaker, perhaps. "You took your keys with you when you signed out on Tuesday." A dangerous undercurrent rippled beneath his casual tone. "Ah – don't bother denying it. And you didn't sign in again till next morning, so I guess you just couldn't be bothered to come back when you realised, hmm?"

Silence.

The same voice, soft, deadly. "Is that protocol?"

"N – no. Sir."

"Harris not super keen on security breaches, is she?"

The second greycoat said nothing, but the first seemed satisfied with whatever reaction he'd seen. "So we'll keep one or two things between us, shall we?"

"S – sir."

"Fuck off, then, there's a good chap."

The hand on Skyler's arm hauled her a few more steps. A door slammed. She stood in dizzying blackness, wrists burning, her heartbeat filling her ears, filling her world.

Then she was in the light, blinded, frozen. She screwed up her eyes against the glare.

Stared at the man in front of her.

He'd had long hair, before. Now it was cropped, severe. He was still taller than her; six years between them, he always would have been. But not as tall as she remembered.

Hazel eyes, eyes she'd mourned, knowing she would never see them again. Skyler's eyes came from a man she'd never met, but his came from their shared blood, and the sight of them splintered something at her core into shards that stabbed at her lungs.

He was so absurd with his machine gun and long grey coat he might as well have been playing dress up. In the last few years, she'd fled like a frightened rabbit at the merest glimpse of one of those jackets.

His stony face had made him almost unrecognisable in the interrogation chamber. But now, as he stared back at her, the hardness crumbled and disintegrated, leaving something wondering and grief-stricken and terrified.

"Sky?" he said.

And this time, when he spoke, she knew.

"Sam –" she whispered, and that was all she managed before the ice in her throat melted into a flood of tears.

And then he'd dropped his gun and was clutching her to him, and he was crying too, his face pressed into her hair – "Sky. Sky. Don't cry, little sis. Please don't cry."

She gasped for air. He pulled back with a shaky laugh. "I never could stand to see you upset. Remember when you were little? All you had to do was turn on the waterworks and I'd let you on my computer as long as you wanted." He started abruptly. "Christ! Your wrists – let me get those off you." He fumbled the cuffs off with a watery smile. "We've got so much to talk about."

"I – you –" Skyler flailed for words, but they were as impossible to form as this new reality was to grasp. And then she remembered where she was, what was happening, and before she knew what she was doing she'd grabbed the sleeve of the grey jacket that symbolized terror and pain and death – "Sam – the others – Angel – Mack – please, you've got to make sure they're okay, don't let anyone hurt them, please –" She was sobbing now. "Please, Sam –"

"Hey. Hey." He gripped her shoulders. "Don't worry. Nobody's going to touch them without my say so, they're all scared shitless of me."

"I don't understand – Sam, I thought you were dead, I thought you died in Leeds – How did you get in here? Who are you working with? What're you – posing as a *greycoat*? That's – Jesus, I thought what we were doing was dangerous –"

He just kept watching her. She dashed her sleeve across her eyes. "Sam. Tell me what's going on!"

"You look different," he said. "You – your face –" He gestured at the scar under her eye.

"A sociopath tried to kill me. Sam! We need to figure out how to get out of here –"

He ducked his head. And Skyler, staring at him, saw what she hadn't been able to before.

The crumple of his expression. Defeat in the line of his mouth.

Misery. Regret.

Shame.

"No." She backed away, cupping her hands over her mouth. "Oh, no, no –"

"Sky, listen to me –"

"You're one of them. You're a greycoat!"

"Skyler –"

She turned away, drew a breath that turned into a juddering sob.

"Sit down," Sam said. "Let me explain."

She straightened her back, but she didn't trust herself to turn around. "What, is that an order?"

You can't talk to him like that. You don't know who he is anymore.

"Stop being a brat and sit down." He still sounded like her brother, though, and that made it all so much worse. "Please?"

She forced herself to face him.

The cell was no more than six feet square. Concrete walls, concrete floor, a single strip light in a high ceiling, a keypad by the door.

And Sam's gun, discarded on the floor.

She sat as near it as she dared, but he sat beside her, between her and the gun.

"I don't understand," she said, because she had to start somewhere. "You *hated* the Board."

He took a deep breath. "The year the Wall went up.

That was my second year at Oxford, remember? I'd come home for Christmas."

How could she forget? She'd counted down the days from the moment they'd dropped him off in October.

"I stayed at Jayesh's one night, about a week after I got home. I doubt you'd remember."

But she did, of course. Because he'd been gone when she got home from school that day, the day before her world fell apart, and it meant she'd never had the chance to say even a small, temporary goodbye to him.

"I was walking home the next morning – bit hungover, you know – and a van pulled up. A bunch of greycoats jumped out, shoved a bag over my head and bundled me inside."

"Wow," Skyler said, before she could stop herself. "I wonder what that felt like."

Perhaps she'd just wanted to see his reaction, to see whether her brother was still in there. But she couldn't tell whether he was amused, or whether she was just wishing desperately that he might be.

"They took me to some warehouse," he said. "And they made me an offer."

Everything about this hurt. "What... kind of offer?"

"They knew what I could do with computers. They wanted me to work for them. I was ready to spit in their faces... and then they went, look, something big's coming, and you're not going to want to be up here when it does. They said I had so much potential, it'd be a waste not to give me a chance."

"They'd rather have had you inside pissing out than outside pissing in."

He gave a short, humourless laugh. "That was never the choice. As soon as they started talking, I knew I wasn't walking out of that room. It was inside pissing out, or in the ground."

"How could you –?" This didn't make sense. It wasn't the Sam she knew.

"I nearly told them to go fuck themselves. Thought I'd die honest. And then I thought... I thought..." He hung his head. "I said I'd do it. If they took you too."

A stinging, ringing shock, a plunge into freezing water. "You – what –?"

"It was a tough sell," he said, and he was still there, her Sam, her idol, whom she'd loved and grieved so fiercely. "I mean, you were only thirteen. But then they looked at some of the stuff you'd done and said they'd take us both South there and then."

She hadn't thought this could possibly hurt any more. She'd been wrong. "They came to my school."

"Yes." Sam's voice was bitter, coarse. "But you were gone."

She tipped her head back against the chilly wall. "I... saw them arrive. I thought they'd come to arrest me. I thought –"

His voice cracked, like hers. "You ran."

The tears leaked through her eyelashes, scalding. She nodded.

"I didn't know what to do," Sam said. "You were the whole reason... and you were... And I – My life was over.

I begged them to look for you, but they weren't interested. So... you were gone, and I – I could hold to my principles, or –"

"Or you could live."

"If you can call it living."

A terrible hope flared, searing and unbearable and already too late to banish. "When you were negotiating with them – did you – did they –?" She could only whisper it. "...Mum?"

He squeezed his eyes shut and his knuckles white, and she had her answer.

"But you don't – Sam, you're not really with them, are you? You can't really –"

"That was the plan at first," he said painfully. "I figured I'd take them down from the inside. But they're smart – it was over a year before they left me alone, even to go to the bathroom. And eventually I realised... we bring stability. Dividing the fuel and power we had available across the whole country would have sent us back to the dark ages. If we wanted any hope for the future, there was never any other way."

That was her Sam too, that authoritative tone: *I'm right and there's no point arguing.* She never had been able to stop herself biting. "And the virus? There was no way other than genocide? Really?"

"The UN were asking too many questions. There was too much unrest in the North. And there've been so many sacrifices – believe me, we know what people have sacrificed for the greater good. If the Board falls, all of that will have been for nothing."

For the greater good. For a better tomorrow. Mantras she'd recited at school, that she knew off by heart. Everyone did.

"You don't really believe that," she said, and she'd meant it as a challenge, but instead it came out as a plea.

He met her eyes and a chill seeped through to her bones like she was sprawled on freezing tarmac, bleeding into the snow. "I absolutely believe it."

"Have you been to Leeds, Sam? To Seacroft? Since they put the Wall up?"

He shook his head. "They said it would be unfair. That it would be too hard for me to be objective."

"Well, *I* went back. After the Wall went up, I lived on the streets in Birmingham for three months, and then I went back for you and Mum. And guess what I found instead? The fucking apocalypse. Our flat – People rioted when they realised the Board had left them to die. They burned down our block."

Sam let out a long sigh. "I wish I was surprised. The South was always more civilised."

"*More fucking civilised?* What the fuck do you see when they let you outside, Sam? Because it wasn't a Northerner who gave me *this*" – she jabbed at the scar under her eye – "or *this* –" She wrenched up her shirt. Sam's mouth twisted and wobbled when he saw the snarled red web of scar tissue, but then his face went blank again like a screen going dark.

She wanted to hurt him now. She wanted him to *wake up.* "Mum's dead, Sam. She burned to death in that fucking flat, all on her own waiting for us, and you – you

289

had a fucking choice. You could've done something, you're practically a fucking genius and you *left her there* and joined the people who murdered her, and what've you got to say for yourself? *Oh well, can't be helped – Fuck you, Sam.*"

"For you," he said quietly. "I did this for you."

"Don't – you – *dare*. Don't you fucking put this on me."

They sat in silence. Skyler fought the tears, but she couldn't make them stop.

You can't let him see you vulnerable.

Bit bloody late for that.

She choked back a sob. "What now, then? You're gonna take me outside and shoot me?"

She felt him flinch. "We'd still take you in. There's no one like you, Sky. The virus that took down our systems – I still can't believe my kid sister did that. I was so bloody proud when I realised it was you."

Breathe. Breathe.

Say something.

"So – what? You want me to help you drop bombs on people who've done nothing wrong? People just like us?"

"It's nature," Sam said distantly. "It's Year Seven science, Sky. When a population gets too big to sustain itself, some of it has to die off. Until the rest have enough resources to survive."

"We're not talking aphids and fucking ladybirds, Sam. These are *people*."

"And so are the people here in the South. The death toll would've been so much higher if we hadn't –"

290

"*We*? Would you fucking listen to yourself? The Board isn't on your side, Sam!"

He sighed. "You've been given a certain picture. That lad who stole the drive from us, the people who dragged you into all this, their agenda..."

"I haven't been *given a picture*! Blowing up the lab, doing all this – that was *my* agenda. I can see the truth, and the Board needs to be stopped."

He shook his head sadly, like he was resigning himself to something he'd been trying not to accept. "You always were naïve. An idealist."

"You used to be, too."

"And then I grew up."

Into a monster. But she couldn't bring herself to say it.

"So you don't agree with everything we stand for," Sam said slowly, and she bit back a hysterical yelp of laughter at the understatement. "Does that really matter? It's *me*, Sky. You and me."

Her brother. For the first thirteen years of her life, the centre of her world. And she'd dreamed of this moment, despite her best efforts, despite the excoriating burn of knowing it was something she could never have.

She'd got used to breathing through pain. To enduring, in spite of everything.

But not like this.

No more running. No more fighting.

Safety.

Sam.

She swallowed. "I... need to think."

"About *what?* This is it, Sky. Everything's going to be all right now."

She bit her lip. He raised his eyebrows. "Oh. The boy and the girl."

Oh, no. Too late, she remembered her frantic begging.

He already knows you care about them. There's no point pretending.

But it was still dangerous. "If I go with you, what happens to them?"

He shrugged. "They're criminals. Murderers and traitors. Why do you even care?"

"*I'm* a fucking criminal, Sam. How do you think I survived, all those years when one of your mates might've put a bullet in me any time I stepped outside? I'm alive *because of them.* In Leeds – when I saw – you weren't there, Sam, but Mackenzie was. When Daniel Redruth was torturing me, when one of your pals shot me in the fucking stomach – you weren't there, but Angel was. And you think I can just –"

"I understand." He nodded slowly. "Friends are important when you don't have anyone else. And it's sweet that you're worried about them – but c'mon, Sky. This is me and you, now. Family."

But they are *my family.* Mackenzie had been right: she and him were bound together. And Angel...

I love Angel. It hit her like a wave, the truth she'd known all along but hadn't had the words for: that fierce, aching, all-encompassing joy and hope and need that ran in her bloodstream, that lit up a place inside her that before had only been dark and hopeless and helpless.

I love Angel. And I never even got to tell her.

No more tears, now. She had to find a way out of here.

How could she let go of any of them?

"Sam," she said urgently. "You could come with us. The Board trust you – you know them inside out – we could –"

His hand shot out and grabbed her wrist. "Stop," he said through gritted teeth. "If you keep talking like that, I'll have to –"

His fingers dug into her flesh. Skyler stared at him, her heart thumping.

There must be a way to get through to him. He's just scared. Everything he thought was true has just been turned upside down.

Except... that wasn't right, was it?

He'd known for months that she was behind the attack on the lab.

He'd had months to think this through. To pick a side.

"You really mean it, don't you?" she whispered.

His jaw tightened defiantly. "Your friends are as good as dead, Sky. I'm sorry, but it's true. And I... I don't want you to go with them. I don't think you do either. So think fast, okay?"

She couldn't do this.

He picked up his gun and stood up. "I might," he said slowly, "if you join me... Maybe I could get one of them out. I'd never manage both – but one, perhaps –"

Her stomach gave a sour lurch. "You're saying you'd save one of them. If I join you."

"You wouldn't be able to see them, of course. But they'd have a chance." He winced, like he had a delicate favour to ask. "Of course, you'd have to tell me..."

"Which one I wanted you to murder?" Her voice came out so bitter she didn't even recognise it. "Who the fuck do you think I am, Sam? That little kid who worshipped the ground you walked on? She's dead. I... You have no idea what I've lived through since you saw me last. And if you think you can show up and turn me into a monster, make me feel like you're all I've got, that there's no other place for me... No."

She still couldn't read him. Which made sense, because he was walking around in her brother's body, using his name, but he wasn't her brother at all. "If you're going to do that to them – to me – if you're going to take away everything good in my world – you bloody well choose."

He stood very still, head on one side. "All right," he said at last, turning towards the door. "As you wish."

A white-hot tumult, fear or rage, she couldn't tell anymore. "I dreamed about this, you know." She hurled the words at his back and he froze. "Since the moment I saw Seacroft, this is all I've dreamed about." Hard, like granite, the words, the way she'd had to make herself all these years. The only way to survive such wildfire devastation was to turn to stone.

She thought about Angel and Mackenzie watching their families die, about how bitterly they must wish, every day, for a miracle like this. About how fucking unfair everything about this was.

"I would've given anything," she said. "*Anything*. I wished for this every fucking day of the last three years. And it turns out it would've just been better if you'd been dead all along."

Silence. Stillness. Her heart pulsing in her throat.

She thought perhaps his shoulders slumped, just a little, but she didn't really know.

He walked out without looking back.

33

TRUST EXERCISES

Mackenzie would have given anything to keep talking to Faith, even though he couldn't hear her reply, but he couldn't risk the device being discovered. So there was nothing to do but stare at the wall, wondering what was happening to Skyler and Angel and how long it would be before the pain started. And, increasingly, whether he would have to resort to emptying his bladder on the floor.

Strangely, he had no urge to tap or pace or count. The idea that the right rituals might get them out of this situation alive seemed, unfortunately, implausible.

By some miracle he actually managed to doze off after a few hours, propped in the corner with his head crooked awkwardly onto his shoulder. The next thing he knew, the cell door was opening. He shot upright, nerves flaring into sharp, shiny urgency, as the male greycoat from the interrogation room closed the door and leaned against it, studying him.

"Making yourself at home, I see," he said.

What could Mackenzie do? Beg? Plead? Like that would help.

"Gotta tell you," he said, meeting the man's eyes, "your interior design skills could use some work."

"Oh, good." The greycoat smiled, tight and grim. "A sense of humour. I'd hold onto that if I were you."

"Is this where the torture starts, then? Or are we still in the menacing stage?"

The greycoat yawned. "People are so *unimaginative* with interrogation. They think it's all hot pokers and jumper cables. Which is just messy, frankly. Not to mention ineffective. A few pokes with a cattle prod and most people'll say whatever they think you want to hear."

"Are you seriously telling me the Board's seen the error of its ways?"

"I'm telling you we appreciate efficiency. Because you know something interesting, Mackenzie? It turns out if you get someone distressed and confused and disorientated enough... well, then the truth *does* tend to slip out."

Mackenzie did his best to pretend his mouth hadn't gone dry.

"What, you don't think that's interesting?" The greycoat sat opposite him, cross-legged. "I would, if I were you."

Mackenzie made himself lift his head. "What's that supposed to mean?" he said, but a constricting hopelessness was wrapped around his neck, suffocating him.

"I'm pretty sure you know. We've heard a *lot* about you." The greycoat raised his eyebrows. "Obsessive-compulsive disorder ring any bells? With particular concerns around contamination and protecting others?"

Shame curdled inside Mackenzie like rotten milk. He looked away.

"It's always interesting to see how long people last," the greycoat added. "It depends how, uh, mentally strong they are, of course. But here's the thing: everyone breaks eventually."

You won't. You won't let them down.

The greycoat sighed as if he were looking at something rather pitiful. "I understand. I wouldn't want to admit it either. You're the weak link in this little ensemble."

He's trying to get inside your head. Don't listen.

"I must say, though, Mackenzie – I expected more. It was you who started this whole thing, after all, breaking in here and stealing that drive. Very daring. You must really have some strong feelings about the Board to have gone to all that trouble."

Actually, Mackenzie had been paid to steal something completely different and he'd had no idea what was on the drive when he stole it, but there didn't seem to be much point correcting the greycoat's narrative.

"So I suppose you put the others up to all this," the greycoat added.

That was a weird assumption, though.

"Though actually, now I've met you, I'm not so sure you've got it in you." The greycoat cocked his head. "Funny. The stories people tell, anyone'd think you were a proper hero."

Mackenzie stared at the floor, but he could feel the greycoat's eyes burning into him. "You've fooled people into believing in you. But they don't see everything, do they? The hours you spend washing your hands. All those nights staying up doing the same ritual over and over. They don't see inside your head."

Mackenzie closed his eyes.

"There it is," the greycoat said cheerfully. "You're a cheap facade, Mackenzie. One strong gust of wind and it all falls apart. I see you. And we both know how this is going to go."

You don't know anything about me. You don't.

But then how was it that the greycoat could see so clearly all the needling, parasitic little doubts latched to Mackenzie's heart, that he tried so desperately to ignore?

"You're going to break," the greycoat said, almost kindly. "And you could save your friends a lot of pain and yourself a lot of humiliation if you just accepted that and told me what I need to know."

No. Don't listen.

"Are you really going to let Skyler and Angel suffer, Mackenzie? Don't you care about them at all?"

Of course he did. That was why he was here. He hadn't been able to bear the thought of Skyler doing this alone.

But what if he'd screwed up? What if he'd brought this down on them?

No. It wasn't right, what the greycoat was saying. Talking wouldn't help the others.

Would it? What if he was just deluding himself because he was scared? Like he always was?

What if talking *was* the right thing to do?

"See?" the greycoat murmured. "You're selfish, and a coward, and you're going to make the people you claim to care about suffer because of it. And it'll all be for nothing in the end, because you're going to break anyway. But who knows what state *they'll* be in by then?"

Mackenzie wanted to cover his ears, but he was stuck. *You need to hear this*, the poisonous voice hissed. *You could stop this. If you weren't such a fucking coward.*

You need to not – fucking – listen. The Board won't let the others go if you talk.

Think how much it would hurt them, losing you.

Yeah, right. They don't need you. They've got each other.

They're better off without you.

The greycoat got to his feet and stretched lazily. "Have a think, eh? But time's running out for them, don't forget. It's all on you."

He punched the code into the door, then glanced back. "Oh. You're probably wondering what you're going to do about the toilet. And, well, we *could* give you a bucket... but that would rather defeat the point of what we're trying to achieve here, wouldn't it?"

He gave a little grin and a shrug, and closed the door behind him.

* * *

Faith had fallen through a black hole into a nightmare.

This could not be real. Julia Hahn could not be dead.

And yet.

She'd seen enough bodies to know there was nothing to be done. The glassy eyes, the waxy pallor, the way Hahn's head slumped on her shoulders – Faith swallowed a bitter rush of bile. A sour, coppery smell hung in the air, blood and brain matter and the indignity of death, and it was too awful, that anyone might see Hahn like this, she would hate it –

And it was Faith's fault. Kimura must have guessed that she was onto him and that she was about to tell Hahn.

But he was in England. He couldn't have shot her.

Which meant he'd had someone here do it. And they would come for Faith next.

What would Hahn tell her to do now?

She's fucking dead, she can't tell me anything –

She'd tell you to cut that the fuck out, for a start.

She fixed her eyes on the floor. If she looked up, reality might hit her, and she couldn't afford for that to happen.

She should raise the alarm, put the building on lockdown. And by the time the killer was found and everyone had calmed down enough to even think about what was going on in England, it would be too late.

She shook her head. Hahn was dead, and nothing was going to bring her back. But Faith could still help the Northerners.

Not on her own, though, she couldn't. And she couldn't trust anyone in the Agency either.

Think.

The killer was probably hunting Faith right now. The building was huge, though. If she could get out unseen, she might have a chance.

She made a decision.

She switched her phone off and left it in Hahn's desk, shoved her laptop and a collection of files into her backpack, and rummaged through Hahn's safe in the corner of the office until she found what she was looking for.

Hahn's pistol was in the safe, too. Faith's hand hovered over it.

She'd learned to shoot when she'd joined the Agency, but she'd never carried a gun. She'd never shot at a living creature. She'd never really believed she would have to.

Eventually, handling it like it might bite her, she tucked the pistol inside her jacket.

She listened at the door. When no sound came from the corridor, she darted out, locked the office, and hurtled down the service stairs to the lowest level of the basement, the shadowy corridor half the Agency didn't even know existed.

When she reached the steel door at the very end of the corridor, she stopped.

Okay. If you can think of a better idea in the next thirty seconds, you don't have to do this.

Her brain gave her nothing but tumbleweed.

Faith leaned her forehead against the chilly metal, trying to calm the battle-drum thumping of her heart.

When that didn't work, she pulled out the key she'd taken from Hahn's safe and opened the door.

"*Finally*," a voice drawled from inside, as Faith flipped the light on. "You people *really* need to work on your customer service."

Huddled in the corner of the cell, one hand shielding her eyes, was Leila Yousefi.

"*Well.*" Leila sat up straighter. "You're not the usual one."

She'd lost a startling amount of weight since Faith had last seen her in her Aarhus apartment. Her injured arm was in a sling, cradled to her chest. In her dirty grey tracksuit, her hair hanging in limp, greasy locks, she was almost unrecognisable.

Leila cocked her head. "You broke into my apartment."

Faith found her voice. "Yes."

"Goodness. What an unexpected pleasure. That German bitch is your boss, then? I remember you watching her like a sheepdog waiting for orders. Has she sent you to have a go at boring me to death?"

The mention of Hahn was a stab to the stomach, a swift and vengeful blade from the dark. Faith shook herself. "No. I – I'm here because I need your help."

Leila burst into peals of laughter. After a while, when Faith didn't move, she stopped. "Oh, my," she said. "You're actually serious."

"Yes."

"Clever of that harpy to send you down here all wide-eyed and innocent, then. Transparent as air, obviously. But cleverer than coming herself."

"She didn't –" Faith screwed her eyes shut. "She didn't send me. She... she's dead."

That set Leila off cackling all over again. Then, abruptly, she stopped. "Good," she said, deadpan. "I'm absolutely delighted to hear it."

She studied Faith appraisingly. "You must be in real trouble, then. Haven't you been warned about me?"

Repeatedly. "Yes."

"*Fascinating.* Why aren't your little friends helping you?"

Giving too much away would be dangerous. Faith could already feel the ice cracking beneath her feet.

"What happened to your boss, little one?"

"She –" Faith's voice broke. She coughed.

"You're telling me just as much by what you *don't* say, darling. You think one of your little friends killed her, don't you?"

There was hardly much point lying. Faith nodded.

"Dear me." Leila sounded like she was trying not to laugh again. "So what do you want from me?"

One step at a time. "We need to get out of here first."

"Maybe *you* do. I've got all the time in the world, sweetpea. And I can virtually guarantee I'm not going to give a toss about whatever's got you in such a flap."

Faith took a deep breath. "What's it going to take to get you out of here with me in the next thirty seconds?"

"Oh, darling, didn't your boss teach you *anything*?

Never show your whole hand up front. Now I know how desperate you are, I've got all the power."

"I don't care about power. I care about –"

"Good Lord." Leila looked at her pityingly. "You really are dreadful at this. Very well." She got to her feet. "A shower, some clean clothes – *decent* clothes, thank you, not another tracksuit – and a cheeseburger."

"What?"

"That's the price of admission. You can work on your pitch while I'm in the shower. I'll hear you out over the burger."

"Fine." Faith gritted her teeth. "But could you hurry up before we both get shot, please?"

She was so terrified as she ushered Leila up the stairs towards the accommodation quarters she felt like she was in a bubble, listening for footsteps, for the sound of a gun being cocked, wondering how the hell she would explain who Leila was if they ran into anyone. She shoved Leila inside an empty bedroom on the second floor, locked the door before Leila could argue, and ran down the corridor to the room where dead agents' belongings were stored.

The Agency became people's whole lives; many agents didn't have anywhere – or anyone – to return their possessions to. Rifling through boxes for an outfit Leila wouldn't turn her nose up at, Faith tried to suppress the thought that kept sidling persistently to the forefront of her mind: that Julia's things would end up here, too.

Had Hahn even had a family? She'd never mentioned one. Faith had often wondered whether, like her, Hahn had joined the Agency to escape another life; whether she'd chosen Faith because she'd sensed some shared experience between them.

What did it matter now?

She grabbed a towel, some clothes and a bag of toiletries, sending up a silent apology to their former owners, and ran back to Leila.

She was half-convinced Leila would have managed to escape in the time she'd been gone, but Faith found her reclining on the unmade bed, hands linked behind her head like she was sunbathing.

"Here." Faith thrust the bundle at her. "You've got ten minutes."

Leila opened one eye. "Is *that* what you think?"

"If the wrong people find us, we're both screwed. Trust me, now is not the time to be making a point."

"Oh, well, since you asked so nicely." Leila swung herself off the bed and strolled to the bathroom. Faith hovered by the door, straining her ears over the hiss of the shower for sound from the corridor.

Fifteen interminable minutes later, Leila sauntered out wrapped in a towel. "I need a hairdryer."

"Tough. Hurry up."

"I'm not terribly keen on your attitude, sweetpea." Leila held up the black shift dress Faith had given her and wrinkled her nose. "Or your fashion sense, come to that."

"Listen, if you don't put that on right now you're going back in that cell and I promise there won't be any cheeseburgers."

"*Ughhhh.* Fine. I want extra fries, though."

"Uh –" Faith bit her lip. "Is there any chance you have a contact who could give us a lift?"

Leila let out a startled laugh. "You really don't have any idea what you're doing, do you?"

With considerable misgivings, Faith had retrieved Leila's phone from Hahn's safe. She held it out. "Have them meet us two blocks away."

"You're the boss, darling." Leila took the phone and winked at her.

34

HOPELESS OPTIMIST

Okay. All we have to do is get out of the building. That's fine. That's fine.

It wasn't remotely fine. Faith had always felt at home in the Agency. Now, as she dragged Leila through the quiet corridors towards the fire escape, she felt like a fugitive.

A door clicked open behind them. She froze.

"Faith?" It was Ayodele, sounding confused.

"Oh dear," Leila said under her breath.

Shut up, Leila. Faith turned to Ayodele, achingly conscious of the unnatural stiffness in her face. "H-hey." Her voice was nearly as bad; it came out as an odd squeak. "You all right?"

He shot Leila a puzzled frown. He hadn't been involved in the Aarhus mission, though; with any luck, the frown was *I don't know your face*, not *shouldn't you be locked in the basement?* Faith gestured helplessly at her. "Just taking this one to Hahn."

Ayodele relaxed. Hahn's name was pretty much magic: tell someone she wanted something and it got done without question. She commanded respect.

From most people, anyway. What had *happened*?

She forced a brittle smile. "Better get going. You know what she's like if you keep her waiting."

He grinned. "You better move. Catch you later."

Faith grabbed Leila's wrist again and hurried away. When she checked behind her, Ayodele had gone.

Could he be involved in this? It seemed impossible – but so did everything else that had very definitely happened. She stumbled down the stairs towards the exit, dizzy with terror again, bundled Leila outside and set off at a run.

This late, the district was quiet and peaceful. None of the few people she and Leila passed looked twice at them.

"Tell me you know where we're going," Faith gasped, two blocks from the Agency. "Your contact's going to come through, right?"

Leila's eyes glittered in the glow of the streetlights. "Don't you trust me, darling?"

Faith would have laughed if she hadn't been so convinced she was about to get shot.

"Ah." Leila raised a hand at a battered Volvo rolling down the street towards them. "Our chariot awaits."

Faith hung back as Leila swooped towards the driver, a man wearing a baseball cap and a surly expression. He lowered the window and his face brightened as Leila bestowed an effusive flurry of air kisses upon him. He shot Faith a quizzical glance. Leila giggled and said something in Persian.

Faith didn't speak Persian. *Damn.*

"Well?" Leila held the back door open for her. "Get in, princess."

There was a good chance Faith was going to get kidnapped or murdered if she got in this car.

She got in anyway.

Leila and the driver ignored her as they drove across Copenhagen, descending instead into animated conversation punctuated with laughter. Faith couldn't shake the suspicion that most of it was at her expense. She'd vowed not to give Leila the satisfaction of looking frightened, but that resolution only lasted fifteen minutes that felt like an eternity before the words "Where are we going?" slipped out. Damn again.

"Burgers, darling," Leila said, as they pulled up outside a late-night fast food restaurant. "You did promise. Oh, don't sulk. I do all my best thinking on a full stomach."

Faith was not at all sure whether Leila at full capacity would be a good thing or not, but she had indeed promised her a cheeseburger. She watched a little awestruck as Leila ordered what seemed to be half the menu, pointed imperiously to the laden tray and sashayed across to a table in the corner. Faith followed with the tray, trying not to feel too grudging. It was the Agency's fault Leila's arm was in a sling, after all.

"I thought you'd have more expensive tastes," she commented, as Leila unwrapped a burger one-handed.

"Simple pleasures, darling. I've had three weeks of nothing but that gruel you people claim counts as food." Leila eyed the burger lovingly and took an enormous bite. "Right," she said, when she'd more or less swallowed. "Give me the sob story, then."

Shit shit shit. How did you convince someone with no apparent morals to do something both selfless and dangerous?

"You're aware of the situation in the UK?" Faith said at last.

"Oh, yes," Leila said, through a chicken nugget. "They love me over there."

"I bet they do," Faith muttered. She sighed. "Three of our agents are over there, trying to take down the Board. They've been... compromised." *Don't cry, for God's sake.* "I need to get them out of the Board headquarters."

"Well, you've got a building full of secret agents at your disposal, little one."

Faith's fraying patience snapped. "You're being deliberately obtuse."

"I think *you're* the one being selective with your information. It's not much good being coy, darling. But if I'm reading the situation right – and I usually do – not all of your little friends think this mission was a good idea, yes? And I'm guessing *someone* felt strongly enough about it to remove your charming boss permanently from the picture. I'm sure I can't imagine why. She seemed like such a delight."

Two cheeseburgers in and apparently Leila could read minds. Faith needed to fight back, find the right buttons to press. Leila might be a people trafficker, but she was still a human being.

"The Board are doing terrible things in the North, Leila," she tried. "We've got evidence of –"

Leila yawned expansively. "A word of advice, darling: I wouldn't bother appealing to my social conscience if I were you. I don't have one."

"I kind of got that when you shot your husband. That and the whole people trafficking thing."

"Then do us both a favour and stop being such a terrible bore. Which of your agents have the Board got?"

"Why does that –?"

"Because I want to know." Leila was suddenly cold and sharp as steel. "Because if they're the ones who've been keeping me awake for days on end or flushing my head down the toilet, I might not find myself feeling *terribly* helpful."

Oh, fuck.

"I'm waiting, little one." Leila's voice was a blade through silk. "And I'll know if you lie."

If this was a dead end, it was better to know now. Faith sighed. "They were part of your... arrest party."

"Don't you mean my *false imprisonment party*? I'm not getting a trial, am I? I've just been shoved in a hole while you people use a range of ploys straight out of the Board's playbook on me. And you're seriously telling me you sent those three children up against the greycoats? They never stood a chance."

"They were the best people to –"

"Do try to remember I don't actually care, sweetpea."

Leila dipped a fry into her milkshake. "Why are you asking me for help, anyway? You can't be dense enough to think any of this interests me."

Because you're smart, insanely well connected, and I don't have a damn choice. All right. Half-truth time. "You've got contacts in the upper levels of the Board. You've got resources. I thought we could work out a deal in exchange for your freedom."

Leila laid a sympathetic hand on Faith's. "Oh, you poor child. You've *given* me my freedom. There's nothing stopping me killing you and leaving you in the gutter."

Faith's mouth was like cotton wool. Whole truth time, then. "I know. I'm trusting you not to." Even as she said it, she knew how ridiculous she was being. Trusting a psychopath not to kill her?

"Oh, you really *are* that dense. How charming." Leila's mouth twitched. "Which one are you sleeping with?"

"Excuse me?"

"Darling." That metallic edge again. "I have a very short attention span. Which one?"

You shouldn't be telling her this.

You shouldn't be doing any of this, idiot.

"The guy," Faith said reluctantly. "The dark-haired one."

Leila sniffed appraisingly. "Well, he was okay, I suppose, in a nerdy sort of way. Whatever floats your boat, I guess. So. He and the girls went off to save the world, and one of your delightful colleagues screwed them over. And now you want me to help fish them out of some Board hellhole."

At least she was succinct. "Pretty much."

"Despite the fact that the four of you put me in *your* special super-secret hellhole."

"I... guess so, yes."

Leila chased the last of her fries through a blob of ketchup, stuck them in her mouth and chewed with exaggerated care. Faith clenched her fists, every nerve twanging like piano wire, and tried not to scream.

Leila picked up her soda and took a long slurp.

Faith counted to ten inside her head.

Leila wiped her hands daintily on a paper napkin. "I'll do it."

Faith jerked her head up. "Huh?"

"I *said*, I'll – do – it."

"But – why would you –?"

Leila snapped her fingers in front of Faith's nose. "Remember we talked about my attention span? Oh, very well, if you must know. I liked the little redhead. She was cute, and all full of righteous indignation. Imagine how cross she'll be when she finds out she owes me her life. Plus you're desperate, which is *super* fun, and you'll spend the entire time paranoid that I'm about to stab you in the back, which will be terribly entertaining."

"I don't suppose you feel like giving me some reassurance on that score, do you?"

Leila raised a reproachful eyebrow. "Where's the fun in that?"

Well, it had been worth a try.

"I suppose we're going to England, then," Leila added, pulling out her phone and cradling it between her chin and her shoulder. "Any bright ideas about how to rescue the Three Musketeers?"

"Uh." Faith tried to shake the feeling she was failing a test. "I'm not exactly –"

"Good grief. Don't tell me I've got to bring all the brains too." Leila held up a hand as Faith bristled. "Darling, bring the car back around, will you? And tell Tariq to get the helicopter ready." She pushed back her chair and sauntered towards the door. "Say what you like about the dark side, darling, at least we're efficient."

"Are you crazy?" Faith hissed, hurrying after her. "We can't just –"

"*I* can do whatever I like. And if you want my help, you're going to play by my rules." Leila gave a one-armed shrug. "Or you can waste the next three days figuring out how to even get into the same country as your friends."

Infuriatingly, she had a point. Wasn't that exactly why Faith had come to her?

Ensconced once more in the back of the Volvo, Leila pulled her phone out again and dialled. From the other end came the rumble of a male voice.

"Anton!" Leila spoke as though she were greeting an old friend at a party. "Dear heart, how *are* you? Listen, I'm on my way to your fair country. Business, you know. I would just *love* to catch up."

She wrinkled her nose. "Oh, you heard right, sadly. Amir is gone, bless his heart. Terribly tragic... Thank you. Do keep him in your prayers. Life must go on, though...

Yes, it's what he would have wanted..." Leila rolled her eyes and mimed sticking two fingers down her throat. "Listen, my sweet – I shall have a companion with me. She's lovely. Not the sharpest tool in the shed, but charming nonetheless."

She threw back her head and cackled. "I couldn't possibly comment. I trust it won't be an issue? Of course. Cross my heart, petal. I'm ever so grateful. Ta-ta."

She dropped the phone theatrically. "All sorted."

Faith's mouth fell open. "That was *Anton Fitzpatrick?* The Justice Minister?"

"I told you the Board love me. Now, don't get pouty. I'm about to save your friends' lives."

"But they hardly let anyone into the UK! You need all sorts of paperwork! And you just call him up and suddenly we're on the guestlist?"

"That's how the world works, darling."

"It's not how *my* world works."

"Well, that's what you get for sticking to all those silly rules. Even I can't just swan into the headquarters, though. We need a plan."

Faith's head throbbed. She screwed her eyes shut. "We can't smuggle ourselves in. That's what the others did – the Board'll be wise to it. And besides, that wouldn't get them out."

"Hmm. Muscle won't work either. You look like you'd wet yourself if you had to point a gun at someone."

Faith ignored this. "So either we break in another way, or we talk our way in."

"I'm not going to be scaling any buildings with this arm, darling. How about bribery?"

"No good. We'd have to bribe loads of people. And maybe money would sway a few greycoats, but most of them are pretty indoctrinated."

"So that leaves walking in with our heads held high." Leila clapped delightedly. "That'll be *much* more fun."

"You have a really strange concept of fun."

"And you have a really strange concept of morality, darling, but you don't see me judging, do you? Anyway, this is going to take more than the two of us and you're going to have to think of something clever, because I don't know anyone who'd want to bite the hand that feeds them."

"I've... got some ideas." Okay, one idea. And so long a shot as to be virtually invisible, but Leila didn't need to know that. "I think there might be someone. If we make the right case."

"I admire your optimism. Let's hear it, then."

Faith pulled up a photo on her tablet of a tall woman of about nineteen, with blue eyes, an artful pile of glossy caramel-brown hair and smooth tanned skin from a lifetime of expensive products and holidays on far-flung beaches. The picture had been taken at a party: the woman's black cocktail dress was elegant, understated, and was probably worth a month of Faith's salary. Diamonds glittered in her ears and at her throat. Her lips curved in a smile that didn't reach her eyes or smooth away the tiny crease between her brows.

Leila's face lit up. "I know her!"

Faith blinked. "You do?"

"Oh, ever since she was a little girl. I knew her father *very* well."

Which, actually, was not the least bit surprising.

Leila studied the photo fondly. "Well, she's rich and connected, so it's not a completely mad idea. But tell me, darling – what on earth makes you think Erin Redruth would have the slightest interest in helping your scruffy little band of renegades?"

35

DRIFTWOOD

Angel had expected the noise, a discordant, ear-splitting howl that blared at irregular intervals so she never quite knew when it was coming next. Sometimes it lasted a few seconds, other times a minute or more. Her cell was pitch dark, though she thought there was an infra-red camera in the ceiling.

She didn't try to sleep. She refused to give them the satisfaction of seeing her jerk awake. Instead she positioned herself in the middle of the floor, legs crossed, back straight. Each moment was almost bearable if she took them one at a time.

When they came for her, she would be a wall: impassive, unassailable.

No – not a wall. Walls crumbled eventually. She would be an ocean.

The door opened. The lights came on.

The male greycoat, the one Skyler had seemed transfixed by, leaned against the door like he was sunning himself. No gun. He'd be trying to goad her into lashing out, then.

"Very Zen," he said. "Had any sleep?"

I spent years sleeping in half-hour intervals, you moron. Back when the nightmares had been at their worst, Angel had kept herself awake for days on end. When sleep became inescapable, she'd set alarms, hoping they would wake her before the flashbacks hit. Things had got better, until the North, until her dreams filled with Skyler and Redruth and blood on her hands and being too late.

"You must be wondering how the others are," the greycoat said. "The boy's doing his best, but it's not pretty. We haven't really started on the girl yet."

Had his voice changed, just a little, when he mentioned Skyler? Or was Angel imagining it?

"I had a good think about what we should talk about," the greycoat added. "All sorts of misery and mystery in your past, apparently. But I think you're ready for that, *Angel.* I don't think that'll touch you."

Damn. He was right. She'd been counting on them fixating on that.

"So. You've spent the last four years running around offing baddies, all on your own. But the other two matter to you now, don't they? And what happens, Angel, when someone like you – someone who's turned themselves into a monster – starts to care about people?"

You're the sea. You're the sea, and if this idiot thinks he can get the better of you, you'll swallow him whole.

320

He peeled himself away from the wall and crouched in front of her, too close, close enough to make her skin crawl if she'd let it.

"They want to change," he said. "And you know what? That might just be the most pathetic thing of all. You made some friends, and you started to think... what? That they might not realise what you really are if you could just scrape together a veneer of humanity? I mean – that's what this was all about, right? Trying to be *good*?"

His lip curled. "Well, look where that's got you all. And the thing is – the others will be dead soon. And you'll be left behind." He considered. "Or something will be, anyway."

They're just words. Just sounds, spoken and gone. They don't mean anything.

"People think you're strong, but they don't get it, do they, Angel? Strength isn't turning into a monster when things get tough."

He's guessing. He's got a few pieces and he's throwing them out, trying to land a hit. He doesn't know anything.

"So the others will be gone – and you'll get to watch, don't worry – and you'll be left behind. And you'll sit in here and tell yourself you can get through it, you're not going to be the monster... but we both know the truth."

Jesus, doesn't this guy ever blink?

"It's kind of sad, how hard you're trying," he said. "Considering it's all going to be for nothing."

He laid a hand on her forearm. She could have grabbed him, choked him, broken his wrist. She didn't move a muscle.

"We're not going to kill you," he murmured. "Remember that."

He left. The lights went out.

Angel stared into the blackness, and kept breathing.

36

BAD BLOOD

Skyler slept, for a while. She'd been given a camping mat, a plastic jug of water, and a bucket. Nothing to eat. She'd grown too used to regular meals over the last couple of months; her stomach was protesting loudly and irritably.

She was dreading Sam's return. It wasn't that she didn't know what to tell him. She just had no idea how she was going to get them all out of here alive afterwards.

The cell door opened. She jerked her head up, fear spiking hot and sharp in her bloodstream.

"Sorry about the bucket," Sam said.

"Are you shitting me? You're sorry about the *bucket*?"

"Well, and the other stuff. You know."

"You're unbelievable."

He grinned impishly, and for an instant he looked like her brother again and she had to choke back a sob. "Made up your mind, then?"

Skyler squinted at him, searching for traces of irony. Had he really forgotten her parting shot? Maybe she had another chance after all. Maybe it wasn't too late to do the double agent thing. How hard could it be?

"I know you're not going to join me," he said, ruffling her hair. "That offer's off the table, I'm afraid. But you still have decisions to make."

For fuck's sake. Maybe if you actually thought before you opened your mouth for once, you could've got them out.

No. Even if he'd let them go, he'd have shot them as soon as they were through the gates.

Still, it stung.

Sam pulled her upright. "C'mon. I want to show you something."

She opened her mouth to tell him to fuck off, then remembered her resolution. He cuffed her hands with an apologetic grimace. "Bad form if anyone saw you without them. Can't have people thinking I'm playing favourites."

This could still all be an act, his behaviour. Perhaps he had to prove his loyalty all over again now his sister was in front of him. Perhaps any moment now he'd whisper, "*Play along. I've got this.*"

She tried to drown the thought, but it kept bobbing to the surface, hopeful and irrepressible, as Sam ushered her down a featureless corridor and a flight of stairs into a small, windowless office containing a desk and two chairs.

And a computer.

Her pulse quickened. He'd brought her to a computer.

She stood, achingly rigid, as he urged the machine into life. The screen filled with a grey-green image of a small, empty cell. Inside, a lone, motionless figure sat cross-legged on the floor.

The air froze in Skyler's lungs.

Sam sat back, gesturing at the screen. "She's been like that for ages. Not sure if she's completely dissociated or what, but that definitely doesn't look normal."

Skyler drew a quiet breath. *She's all right. She's fine. That's just how she looks when she's in business mode.*

"She's got a great poker face," Sam went on. "Shame it's all an act. Apparently she's been a real mess lately. Pretty pathetic, right?"

Skyler's throat constricted. "What – what did you say to her?"

"Oh, nothing she doesn't already know." He patted her on the shoulder. "Don't worry, kiddo. We're not going to kill her."

"No." Skyler stared at Angel. "You're going to kill us and make her watch."

Sam grinned. That grin had helped him get away with so much when they were young; you couldn't help but grin back, no matter how mad you were at him. It turned her stomach, the perversion of something that for her whole childhood had made her light up with joy.

She held herself still, fixing her sights on a lighthouse beam of logic through the storm of grief and terror. *Angel's too strong to let him get inside her head. If we were together, we'd be laughing at him for thinking it was that easy.*

Sam clicked to a different screen. "And Exhibit B."

This cell was dimly lit and completely bare. Inside,

Mackenzie paced back and forth with rapid, measured steps, tapping the wall each time he reached it. As Skyler watched, he balled his hands into fists, dragged them over his face and set off again, each movement more frantic than the last.

She hadn't seen him this bad for a long time.

And... there was no bucket in his cell.

"He's in quite a state," Sam said, as though he were showing her an interesting piece of code. "I think he did eventually relieve himself in the corner rather than piss himself, but it was a close call. And the pacing's just got worse and worse since. Imagine what he'll be like in another couple of days."

To her horror, Skyler's throat was suddenly thick with tears. Mackenzie could so easily have stayed in Copenhagen, but he'd insisted on sticking with her, even though all she'd done was snap at him and give him shit for finally finding a little bit of happiness.

He'd been doing so well. He'd tried so hard to hold her and Angel together. And now he was all alone in his own personal hell.

And her brother, her Sam, had deliberately selected the worst thing he could have inflicted on Mackenzie. And he looked *satisfied*.

"Please stop," she whispered. "Please, Sam. Don't do this to him."

"I mean, this is kind of the point of torture, Sky." He was studying her, analysing her reactions and filing them away. She was making things worse for all of them.

In the years after the Wall had gone up, when every

breath hurt and every word out of her mouth, every emotion she betrayed, was ammunition for Daniel to use against her, she'd shoved it all into a dark, bottomless box and sealed it away. She needed that box now. She needed to treat Sam the way she'd treated Daniel.

"How long d'you reckon before these two completely lose their shit?" Sam asked. "I mean, solitary confinement fucks with even the sanest people eventually, and I wouldn't exactly call either of them mentally stable."

He shot a glance at her. "Is this what you're holding onto, then? These two pathetic creatures? You're so much better than this, Sky. Just put them out of their misery and move on. It's the kindest thing you can do."

She didn't even have the energy to be angry anymore. Her brother was gone, and the realisation enveloped her like a lead sarcophagus.

"What do you even want to know?" she said dully.

He started ticking the points off on his fingers. "Where the other three are who helped blow up the lab. How you got out of the country and back in – who helped you, and why. What you were trying to do in here. Your fallback plan."

She tore her gaze from Mackenzie's desperate pacing, bit the inside of her cheek until she tasted blood.

Sam shrugged. "Or don't tell me. A few more days make no difference to me. It's them who have to live with the consequences."

Don't – give – him – anything.

He laid a hand on her arm and she flinched before

327

she could stop herself. A shadow of regret flickered across his face.

"I hate to see you like this," he murmured. "I don't want to cause you any more pain, Sky. Let me help you."

When she said nothing, he sighed. "Come on, then," he said, pulling her upright. "Back you go."

37

THE FAUST ACT

Despite Leila's assurances that her driver was *terribly* discreet, Faith insisted on putting the conversation about Erin Redruth on hold until they reached the helicopter waiting for them outside Copenhagen. In the meantime, sitting in the back of the Volvo staring out into the blackness, all she could think about was whether Mackenzie was in darkness too.

She hadn't heard from him again.

Leila greeted their pilot – Tariq, apparently – with a caressed cheek and a dazzling smile, flapped at Faith as if to say there was no point bothering to introduce her, and, as they got airborne, settled into her seat as though reclaiming her throne. "Details please, darling."

At least she'd said 'please'. Faith sighed. "Erin has... history with one of my colleagues."

"*Does* she, indeed? Which one?"

At the back of Faith's mind, Hahn's words chimed like a warning bell. *People like Yousefi are expert manipu-*

lators. Give them nothing *about yourself, however inconsequential.*

But she and Leila were, against all possible reason, a team. Besides, Leila had made it perfectly clear that her help was entirely contingent on Faith playing along with her. Faith had to let her believe she was in control.

"Angel," she said. "The redhead."

"The one who shot me?"

Faith winced. "Yes. She and Erin were in a relationship at school."

Leila frowned. After a moment, her mouth fell open. "You're insane, darling. Why on earth would you open *that* can of worms? You do know what Daniel did to that girl's family, don't you?"

"How do *you* know?"

"Oh, he told me. He was really quite pleased with himself. I thought it was a bit much, personally. I could hardly have told him that, though, could I?"

A bit much. Faith couldn't swallow her disgust, either at Leila or at herself for forgetting what Leila was. "I'm surprised you even cared. You're just the same as him, after all."

Leila raised a chiding finger. "Now that's unkind, darling. That's not fair at all."

"Really? You said yourself you don't have a social conscience."

"Which makes me callous, sweetpea, not cruel. Other people's suffering may not mean anything to me, but I don't revel in it. Not like Daniel, bless his heart."

"Jesus *Christ.* You know what he was! What he did to

a fifteen-year-old girl who had the temerity to fall in love with his daughter. How could you ever associate with someone like that?"

"Well, he threw a hell of a party." Leila laughed uproariously at Faith's expression. "Oh, don't look like that. Daniel was useful. Being on his right side opened lots of doors."

"Do you have any idea how fucked up that is?"

"You associate with murderers and torturers too, darling. I'd come on down off that high horse if I were you."

"That's different —"

"Is it? Pain is pain, no? Suffering is suffering."

"The Agency protects people." Faith didn't want to admit she'd been shocked by the state she'd found Leila in. Or that she wasn't sure how keeping someone in a pitch-dark cell for weeks counted as protecting anyone.

"Is *that* right? Well, take it from me that some of your colleagues enjoy their *enhanced interrogation techniques* a little more than they should."

The Agency doesn't torture people. You'd know if they did. "We help people," Faith repeated through gritted teeth.

"And I help myself, petal. If all human life is equally valuable, why is it wrong for me to protect myself, but not for you to protect others?"

"Forgive me if I'm not convinced that selling people into slavery is *entirely* necessary to protect yourself."

Leila yawned. "Now, if you're going to get all preachy, I think you'll find me rapidly losing interest in your little scheme. Let's talk about something more interesting."

Faith tried to pull herself together. They were wasting time with every word. "Right. Right. Any idea how we convince Erin to help?"

Leila's skewering stare ran straight through her. "That's not quite what I had in mind, sweetpea."

Christ. Just get through this as quick as possible and get her back on track.

Faith raised her chin. "Fine. What do you want to talk about?"

Leila twiddled a shiny black lock of hair. "Would you consider Daniel Redruth an evil man?"

"I –" Faith's headache wasn't getting any better. This was a really, really stupid gamble, and she was going to reveal all sorts of things about herself in the process.

"You have to play, little one." Leila's voice was sing-song, chiding. And she was right. Faith couldn't think of a single alternative.

"I don't think evil is a useful concept," she said at last. "It has all those religious connotations – it's... reduction-ist. It doesn't account for the complexity of human nature. But Redruth was sadistic. He did horrific things for his own entertainment. If evil people do exist, I think he was one of them."

"I see. What about me, then? Am I evil?"

"Well, I haven't seen any evidence that you take that kind of pleasure in other people's distress." Though she was definitely enjoying Faith's discomfort. "But you're indifferent to it, and you've caused a lot of suffering because of that. I think ultimately people should be judged by their impact on the world."

"Oh, *interesting*. People often say actions are the measure of morality, but this sounds more like you think the end justifies the means. Isn't that the Board's philosophy too?"

Faith's whole body was humming with tension, each discordant heartbeat driving a frantic urge to flee through her brain and limbs. She was hundreds of feet above the ground with a woman who'd made it abundantly clear that all she cared about was herself. If Leila got bored, she might well consider it perfectly justifiable to throw Faith out of the helicopter in mid-air. Faith must have been broadcasting her unease like a signal flare. And Leila, by contrast, was languid and relaxed, watching Faith as though she were a jester summoned for Leila's amusement.

"It's the same argument," Faith conceded, resigning herself. "But the Board are selfishly motivated."

"And selfishness is bad?"

"Not always. But sometimes."

"All right. Next question: do you think people like me and Daniel are born the way we are?"

Faith felt like she'd followed a trail of breadcrumbs into a dark forest, over-confident she'd be able to find her way back out. Somewhere along the way she'd taken a wrong turning and now all the trees looked the same, the paths had disappeared and she'd lost sight of the sun.

"No," she said. "I think people are mostly products of their environment."

"Tell me, then – what kind of environment produces a person who's had to switch off their capacity for empathy? Someone so desperate for control that they're driven to torture and kill to guarantee it? Is it safety and validation and unconditional love that creates that?"

"I... no." As Leila's lips curved triumphantly, Faith added, "*But* none of that means people don't still have choices. Redruth knew he was hurting people and he chose to do it anyway."

"But doesn't that imply every choice is equally accessible to everyone? Which surely isn't the case. Not if your experiences haven't equipped you to be able to take them. So when does a child you pity turn into an adult who deserves to be locked up and made to suffer?"

"I don't think anyone deserves to suffer. I *do* think some people are so dangerous other people need to be protected from them. Especially if they're not willing or able to change."

"Like me, you mean?" Leila sounded amused.

Faith met her eyes. "Yes."

"At least you're honest. You think I'm irredeemable, then?"

It suddenly felt important that Leila saw Faith as a worthy opponent, not just someone who would roll over and try to placate her. "You don't seem to have any interest in changing."

"And that means I should die?"

"I'm not sure."

"Daniel, then? What about him?"

"I don't think he would ever have changed. I think it's better that he's dead."

Leila nodded thoughtfully. "I can't say I disagree with your first point. Imagine how it would feel to develop a conscience after the things he'd done. It would be unbearable."

"Tell me about Erin." Faith willed her voice not to betray her thumping heart. "You said you've known her a long time?"

"Oh, I suppose you did play nicely. Very well. Daniel wanted Erin to take over the family business one day – or wanted her at his side, at least. He trod a difficult line with her. He needed her to fear him, like he did everyone – and she did, believe me – but he needed her to adore him, too. To never quite be able to believe his monstrous side was the real him."

"You seem to understand a hell of a lot about all this."

"I've met a lot of monsters, darling." Leila bit her lip, then seemed to catch herself. "I imagine she'll still be devastated. He was all she had, after all – he made sure of that."

She cocked her head. "Now, sweetpea – it occurs to me that Daniel wasn't at *all* the sort of person your Agency would approve of. Which leaves me wondering whether any of your friends had a hand in his untimely demise?"

Shit. How would Hahn have answered that?

Faith tried to make her face neutral. "It wasn't the Agency." Well, it was true. Angel hadn't been working for the Agency when she'd killed Redruth.

"Something you'll want to bear in mind," Leila said, in her teasing-but-not-really voice, "is that environments that produce people entirely focused on their own needs *also* tend to produce people who are exceptionally good at reading others. It's an adaptive function." Her smile turned wolfish. "Wait. Let me guess."

"Can we just focus on this whole Board thing, please?"

Leila gave her a reproachful look. "Don't rush me, darling."

Faith wanted to scream. Why had she ever started this?

"Just let's do this one thing and then we'll play your game." Leila patted Faith's knee as though offering a placatory treat to a child. "Do your poker face again, won't you? It's cute."

Faith glared at her.

"*So.* You don't want to tell me the truth, which means you *do* know who killed Daniel. And if it were irrelevant, you'd just have told me. You're tediously inclined to honesty. *But* you were also trying to justify your answer as a technical truth, so..." Leila's face lit with a luminous smile. "Oh, this is *too* good. Of course it was the redhead. There's poetic justice for you." She laughed delightedly. "I've got to hand it to you, little one, your audacity is absolutely breathtaking."

She flicked her hair over her shoulder, clasped her hands on her knees, and made a show of arranging her face into seriousness. "Right. Let's talk business."

38

TELL IT SLANT

They landed in a Board airfield north of Oxford as dawn broke. Faith had heard nothing from Mackenzie, and the horror of the last twelve hours kept coming in waves, and with every passing minute she felt as though she was locked in a coffin listening to soil rattle down on the lid.

Leila swept past the airfield's greycoats in a whirl-wind of air-kisses and radiant charm to a gleaming SUV driven by another of her apparently endless list of contacts. Faith trailed behind, trying to summon Leila's aura of careless arrogance instead of her own suffocating nausea.

Well, in a way, this is right where you're supposed to be.

It helped, a little.

"We don't call ahead," Leila told her as they set off. "And let me do the talking."

Off the top of her head, Faith could think of about a

thousand things that might go wrong with this. "I'm not sure that's —"

"Darling, I am so dreadfully uninterested in your opinion. Don't worry. I'm ever so good at manipulating people."

"That's not really what we're aiming for, though, is it?"

"Well, let's see. You want to convince this young woman to do something fantastically dangerous for the sole benefit of you and your friends, and you've chosen her specifically because you're hoping to play on her emotional connection with the redhead. Do explain how that's not manipulation."

While Faith flailed, Leila shrugged. "Just because you attribute honourable motivations to something doesn't mean there's not an ugly word for it. I'm not judging. Manipulation is ever so useful."

Christ. Was Leila's world view actually starting to make sense?

Redruth's estate was visible from a good mile away, hemmed in by a towering red-brick wall at the front and an expanse of woodland spilling out behind. "Why doesn't the wall go all the way round?" Faith asked as they approached the wrought-iron main gate. "Surely those woods aren't very secure?"

"Oh, that was just Daniel's sense of humour. He quite enjoyed when people tried to break in. It was a good way of eliminating his competition."

Faith's eyes burned. She felt like she'd been awake for days; at some point, her brain had simply stopped processing. Something similar had happened at the age of fourteen, when she'd got home from school as a police car pulled up, around the time her father should have gotten home from work, and the officer had taken his hat off when her mother answered the door and asked, "Is it Mrs. Jackson, ma'am?"

She didn't remember the words the officer had used to explain what had happened. She only remembered the way her reality had splintered, the way a mirror fractures on impact with the floor, so that in its reflection everything was suddenly both the same and utterly incomprehensible. For days afterwards, in the leaden numbness that descended after the initial tears, the words had played on a loop in her head: *Dad's dead. Dad's dead*, as her brain tried to absorb a new version of reality that she hadn't asked for and didn't want and was trapped in nonetheless.

She'd been on autopilot then, trying to hold the fragments of her life together: school, homework, grocery shopping. Now there was no comfort to be found in routine. She was a stranger in a strange land, and when she looked in the mirror there was nothing, not even a distorted, fragmented version of the world to try to make sense of. Only an empty frame, and darkness.

And she had to find a way to hold onto herself as they climbed out of the car and Leila pressed the intercom button on the gate.

A male voice answered, terse and unfriendly. "Yes?"

Leila screwed up her eyes as though trying to recall

something. "Is that... Jacob? It's Leila Yousefi, darling. How *are* you?"

"Leila?" The voice changed. "How the hell are you?"

"I'm marvellous, darling, bless you. I've just landed, and I simply *had* to come and pay my respects to little Erin. Is she around?"

A pause. "I'll see if she's up to visitors. Why don't you come in and wait?"

"That sounds wonderful. I have a friend with me, incidentally. Can she tag along?"

"Any friend of yours, Leila."

The gate swung open. Faith followed Leila up a sweeping tree-lined avenue to a red-brick Georgian mansion with enormous shiny black front doors. A middle-aged man in a dark suit greeted them; he'd once been muscular, perhaps, but was now running a little to fat. He embraced Leila and Faith returned his proffered handshake stiffly, trying not to wonder what those hands had done on Daniel Redruth's orders.

The entrance hall was cavernous, with a huge, hideous chandelier suspended from the ceiling, laden with actual candles. The candles were an affectation; Redruth could easily have afforded electric bulbs.

Skyler had lived in the cellar of this gleaming, echoing building for almost three years. Faith thought about Leila's commentary on Redruth, the notes in her file, and shuddered.

"Erin's getting ready," Jacob explained, leading them into the drawing room. "Would you like a drink?"

Faith didn't want to touch anything in this place, but

Leila accepted a crystal tumbler of orange juice and she knew she couldn't afford to appear rude, so she took one too.

The drawing room had floor-to-ceiling windows over-looking sweeping lawns, magnolia trees and fountains. Behind it all, the shadow of the woods lurked.

What must Erin Redruth's life here be like? This place was luxurious, but it wasn't a home. It was more like a museum. Or a mausoleum.

"Is Liliana around?" Leila asked, perching on an enormous leather sofa and sipping her juice.

Jacob settled into an armchair. "Liliana's abroad. Thailand. Needed to clear her head."

"Understandable." The ice in Leila's drink clinked against her glass. "And how's dear Erin?"

"She's... erratic." Jacob winced delicately. "I keep telling her we've got a business to run – I can keep things ticking over, of course, but it's not the same, we need a Redruth at the helm. But she can't seem to focus, and Liliana's not much help. She's never had anything to do with the business and she doesn't want to start now." He waggled his eyebrows hopefully at Leila. "Perhaps you could have a chat with Erin?"

Leila smiled. "What a good idea."

The drawing room door opened. Faith looked up.

The woman in front of them was the girl from the photo, but different: wan, no makeup, messy bun, over-sized hoodie wrapped around herself like a blanket. When Leila embraced her, Erin's attempt at a smile fell away like a post-it note fluttering to the floor.

"Darling." Leila assessed her at arm's length. "Thank you *so* much for making time to see me. I can't tell you how sorry I am about your dear father."

"Thank you." Erin's words were toneless, as tired as her eyes.

Leila gestured at Faith. "My new associate. I think you'll get on ever so well."

Faith shook Erin's hand, wondering whether there had ever been a more awkward greeting in the history of humanity. Erin was still trying to be gracious, but the effort was clearly taking everything she had.

Leila turned to Jacob, dazzling again. There was something genuinely magical about being on the receiving end of her attention, like you were the only important person in the world. "Now, darling," she said conspiratorially, steering him towards the door. "I think Erin and I should chat woman to woman. You understand, of course."

"Of course." Jacob returned Leila's smile, but it didn't have the same effect; it was more reminiscent of bad taxidermy. "I hope our paths might cross again before you leave England?"

"Count on it, darling." Leila stood on tiptoe to kiss him on both cheeks, and Faith could have sworn he blushed. Erin was still clinging to the ghost of her smile, but it was fixed and slightly puzzled, as though she knew she had to be polite but was trying to work out what the hell Leila wanted.

As soon as Jacob disappeared, Leila guided Erin towards the sofa. "Quick question, darling," she murmured. "Are any curious listeners likely to be hanging around?"

Erin blinked. "Uh – no. No. The room's sound-proofed. My dad valued his privacy."

"Smart man, your father. What about bugs, hmm? I'm sure your father's men think they're being ever so helpful, but us girls need our privacy, don't we?"

"Um..." Erin's face clouded. "I – I don't think –"

She sat very still for a moment, as though some kind of tug-of-war was happening inside her head. Then, abruptly, she stood up. "I... know somewhere private."

Leila winked at Faith as Erin unlocked the French doors to the patio. Faith pretended not to see.

Erin led them across the manicured lawns all the way to the woodland. It gave Faith the faintest glow of satis-faction to watch Leila's dainty nose scrunch with distaste as her feet squelched into the dead leaves and mud. "Not that I mind, darling," she called after Erin, picking through brambles, "but are we going somewhere in particular?"

Erin stopped in front of a sprawling oak. They followed her gaze up to a treehouse nestled amongst the budding leaves.

"I haven't been up here in years," she said. "It won't be bugged now."

It was the fanciest treehouse Faith had ever seen: glass windows, fairy lights, beanbags; even a hammock. The instant they were inside, Erin turned to Leila with her hands on her hips.

"Let's get one thing straight," she snapped. "If bloody

Jacob's brought you here to talk me into running the business, you can piss off. I'm sick of hearing about what my father what have wanted."

Leila held up her uninjured hand. "I assure you, darling, I've got zero interest in your father's business."

"Oh, please. I know how much your work here was tied up with him."

Leila settled delicately into a beanbag. "I've had other issues on my mind of late. Perhaps you haven't heard about my dear husband's passing?"

That took the wind out of Erin's sails somewhat. "Oh." She sat with a bump into a beanbag of her own. "I'm – I'm so sorry."

Leila waved the apology away. "How are you keeping, darling? Your father's death must have been a terrible shock."

"Yes." Erin's eyes went dull again. "It was."

"And I imagine since then you've learned some things that might have unsettled you a bit."

Erin laughed bitterly. "Like the fact that my father was the biggest drug dealer in the South? Or that he was extorting half of Birmingham? Or that the reason he had so much Board support was that he'd bought half of them off? Yes. You could say that's *unsettled* me."

Leila's face softened. "I'm sorry, petal."

"You're sorry? My father was rotten to the core, propping up a corrupt regime, everyone was terrified of him, and I'm just supposed to be a good little girl and pick up his mantle? And you're *sorry*? I –" Erin covered her mouth with a little gasp.

"You don't know what to do without him."

She nodded.

"He told you how to think, didn't he?" Leila said gently. "But you still had your own ideas, your own values – and it turns out the most important person in your world had completely opposing ones. And there's no one you can talk to about it, because he was all you had, wasn't he? He never let you near anyone who might have offered you a different opinion."

Erin's eyes filled with tears. "He was just – protective. I was his only child... he didn't want me to grow up. He didn't stop me –"

"Oh, he did, darling." Leila was still soft, sympathetic. "The first sign that you were developing a little independence, a world apart from him... He didn't like that, did he?"

Erin hunched in on herself like a cornered animal.

"I know it's hard." Leila spoke with such kindness and sincerity that she sounded like a different person. "I know you feel disloyal. And scared, I expect, even now. But he's gone, petal. He can't hurt you."

Erin shook her head violently. "He would never –"

"But he did, darling. You're stronger than you realise, you know. Your father's men, the Board – they've been pushing you, haven't they? Jacob's got a whole list of demands, I bet. But you haven't given in. You know what you believe, deep down."

Erin's gaze darted away. "I –"

"I'm not going to shop you to the Board for speaking your mind. Consider this a safe space."

"I... know all the arguments," Erin said slowly. "My father always said the Board had their flaws, but they were better than the alternative. And they were good to us, and I should be grateful. But... there's so much that doesn't feel right."

"You've got instincts for a reason, darling."

"I... I want to do some good. I don't know exactly why everyone was so scared of my dad, but I don't want people to be scared of me. But he worked so hard to build all this – he always said it was for me and my mother, and I – I don't want to let him down."

"Oh, darling. I understand. It's so difficult to make sense of all this when you're grieving someone you love. My Amir –"

Erin snorted. "Oh, please. You didn't even *like* Amir. I heard you say it often enough. I wouldn't be surprised if you'd killed him yourself."

For the first time since Faith had met her, Leila actually looked nonplussed. It was more than a little satisfying.

"And now you want something from me too." Erin's eyes narrowed. "Don't give me that *paying your respects* bullshit. You're just like the rest of them."

Silence fell. Faith clenched her fists. They were teetering at the edge of a ravine, and Erin was sharper and angrier than she'd expected – and, apparently, than Leila had.

And Faith knew exactly how Erin felt.

"Erin –" she began.

Erin swung to her. "And who the fuck are you,

anyway? Leila's latest bit on the side? Do you really think I give a shit what you think about any of this?"

Faith met her furious gaze steadily. "Of course not. And you're totally right. Leila didn't give a shit about Amir, and she doesn't have a clue how you feel. But I do. My dad died five years ago, and all I wanted for years – all I still want, honestly – is for him to show up and tell me, 'This is what you need to do. This is how you make everything okay.' And when I moved away from home I felt so awful, because I knew I was breaking my mom's heart all over again."

Erin hesitated. Some of her roiling anger seemed to drain away. "You left anyway, though?"

"Yes. I did."

No matter how many times Faith told herself that staying at home wasn't helping her mom, that it wasn't fair to sacrifice her own life and future, that the mire they'd got stuck in was killing both of them, the guilt never dulled or faded. All she could do was push it away and try her best to ignore it. The hurt on her mom's face when Faith had told her she was leaving was burned into her brain in tight, shiny scar tissue, and she would never forgive herself.

"How could you do that?" Erin asked. "How *did* you do it?"

If there was ever a time for honesty, this was it. "I realised I'd been letting all the shit that'd happened control me. I'd stopped believing I had choices. I kept finding reasons not to change – because I was scared, because of my problems, because my mom needed me..."

Faith sighed. "Then someone offered me a chance to take control of my life. And I almost didn't take it. But then I decided to be brave."

Hahn. Hahn had seen something worthwhile amongst the misery and grief that had become Faith's world; had taken a chance herself, because she'd believed Faith could be something more. And her conviction had allowed Faith to believe it too.

"Do you still feel bad about leaving?"

Every day. "Sometimes."

"D'you ever regret it?"

"Not even for a second."

Erin examined her trainers. "Why are you both here?"

Leila gestured at Faith as if to say, *oh, go on, then.* Faith took a deep breath. Time to jump into the ravine and find out if she was wearing a parachute. "You... had a girlfriend a few years ago."

Erin went rigid.

"Felicity North," Faith pressed on. "Except now she goes by Angel."

All the colour drained from Erin's face. "My father and his employees used to talk about someone called Angel," she whispered. "He put so much energy into hunting her..." She cupped her hands over her mouth. "That was *Felicity*? That – that's crazy."

"No. It's true. I know her."

"He was so angry when he found out about us," Erin said into her hands. "Not because she was a girl – he just

– I don't know, I don't think he thought anyone was good enough for me."

"No, darling," Leila said. "He didn't want anyone in your life who was more important than him."

"No – that's not –"

But she didn't finish the sentence.

"You said the Board's corrupt," Faith persisted. "Angel thought so too. She and two others were working with my agency, trying to destabilize them. They got caught. They're in the headquarters, and – well." She couldn't stop her voice catching. "You know what's happening to them."

Erin looked up. "That building that got blown up back in February..."

"It was a lab. The Board were storing a biological weapon there. They were going to massacre everyone north of the Wall."

"But... *Felicity*? I mean – she was a ballet dancer, for God's sake! What *happened*?"

Faith and Leila exchanged glances.

"You – uh, you don't know?" Faith said carefully.

"I – no. No. My dad made me change schools, I had to delete all my social media... I felt awful, but I couldn't do anything. I thought about trying to get a message to Felicity, but I didn't dare. My dad had such a temper and he could've really ruined her life – she was on a scholarship and he could've got her thrown out of school or anything..."

Leila's eyes were glinting in a way that suggested she

was enjoying this a little too much. Faith felt sick. How could Erin be so blind to her father's cruelty?

But then what about the things Leila had accused the Agency of? Sleep deprivation. Waterboarding. Faith wanted so desperately to believe Leila was lying, or that Hahn hadn't known about any of it. She'd have seized any tiny scrap of hope that spared her from confronting the truth: that the organisation she'd given everything to wasn't what she thought it was; that the woman who'd saved her hadn't been either.

"You want me to help get them out," Erin said.

"Yes."

"How?"

"We're... not sure yet."

Erin glanced at Leila. "Do you work for this agency too, then?"

Leila burst out laughing. "Christ, no. I'm in this purely for entertainment. Winding up Lawful Good here might be my new favourite hobby."

"Oh, God." Erin covered her mouth again. "What they'll be doing to them..." She shook her head. "I – I don't know about this. It's all so –"

"It's a big decision," Leila said kindly. "Of course it is. It's terribly difficult and dangerous, what we're asking. And of course, we *are* talking about the woman who killed your father."

Faith and Erin both snapped their heads up in horror. Leila covered her mouth in mock-dismay. "Oh, I'm sorry. Was that supposed to be a secret?"

"What the fuck are you doing?" Faith hissed. She swung to Erin. "Erin, listen —"

Erin jerked towards her, her mouth contorted with grief. "Get. Out. You come into my house and ask me to risk my life for my father's murderer? How *dare* you?"

"Well, he did butcher her entire family, darling," Leila said. "Fair's fair."

Erin slumped back into her beanbag like all the life had drained out of her. "No. No, no, he wouldn't —"

Leila sighed. "Now look, sweetpea, I was really very fond of your father. He was an excellent businessman, and he was ever such good fun when he wasn't stringing people up by their ankles and torturing them — but let's not pretend he was anything other than an absolute monster. God, even I was scared of him, and I can tell you *that* doesn't happen very often. You can't just go around murdering everyone who upsets you and expect there'll never be any consequences. He created the instrument of his own destruction — and frankly, darling, that little girl did you a huge favour. Your father didn't see you as a person, he just saw you as an extension of himself. What better way to find out who you really are than to do something that would have made him absolutely furious?"

Erin stared into space, motionless.

"Besides," Leila added, "even if you balance out a life for a life, that still leaves your family *considerably* in debt."

Nothing.

Faith opened her mouth to plead with Erin — she had no idea how — but Leila held up a cautioning finger. *Wait.*

She had less than no reason to trust Leila, but she also had no idea how she could possibly salvage this. She closed her mouth.

Leila watched Erin with the same hunger and intensity she'd fixed on Faith in the helicopter. Faith tried to stop the sucking wound of hopelessness in her chest collapsing into a black hole, tried not to think about how desperately she'd failed Mackenzie and Angel and Skyler.

Finally, at last, Erin looked up.

"Okay," she said. "How are we going to do this?"

39

GET UP

Seven steps across the cell. Seven steps back.

Breathe in when you look at the wall. Breathe out when you look at the door.

Don't look at the corner. Don't look at the corner. Don't look at the corner.

At some point someone had delivered a plastic jug of water and a beaker. Mackenzie's mouth was dry and tacky, his lips cracking, his head fuzzy – but if he drank the water, he'd have to urinate again. Besides, the greycoat would almost certainly have put something in it designed to make his situation even worse: laxatives, hallucinogens, some sort of truth drug – were those even a real thing? Anyway, there was no way in hell he was risking it.

Even without the intermittent clanging of the bell, he wouldn't have slept. He couldn't stop pacing.

He didn't even know what he thought would happen if he stopped. Only that the burning itch in his brain, the shapeshifting monster that morphed with every other heartbeat into a new horror, wouldn't leave him alone.

The worst was coming. It was inescapable. And what if he, with his determination to convince himself that a thought was just a thought, had caused it?

Your fault. Your fault. Your fault.

There's no point doing any of this. You're all going to die anyway.

Faith knows you're here. What if she could've helped and you fuck it up because you stopped pacing?

What if you can keep the others safe as long as you do everything exactly right?

Vision blurring. Head throbbing. Christ, he needed a drink.

If you drink that water, they'll all die.

And the vilest thought of all, that kept clawing its way back to the surface like a reanimated corpse no matter how desperately he tried to bury it: *what if Faith did this?*

He didn't believe it. He didn't really believe it. And he would be punished; she would be taken from him, Skyler and Angel would be taken from him, because how monstrous must he be that he could even think it?

But what if it was *her?*

And what if the greycoat was right? What if he could save the others by sacrificing himself?

The part of Mackenzie that still had access to logic, choking and suffocating in toxic clouds of dread, spluttered, *Don't be so bloody stupid. That greycoat is not trying to help you.*

But. But. But.

His thoughts spun and stung and spiralled, a tangle of brambles snarling round his limbs. He was losing his mind. The greycoat would be back soon, and Mackenzie wouldn't be able to control what came out of his mouth. He was too scared, too fuzzy, too frantic, he couldn't think, he couldn't –

The cell door opened.

Mackenzie spun round. The dark hiss in his head rose to a scream: *you broke the pattern, you broke it, you have to fix it –*

"How's it going?" the greycoat asked.

You're not strong enough for this.

He started pacing again. *One. Two. Three. Four. Five. Six. Seven. One. Two. Three.*

"This is getting kind of pathetic, Mackenzie." The greycoat sounded kind, amused. "Look, you've done much better than I expected. But come on now. Enough is enough." He sat on the floor and patted the concrete beside him. "Have a rest. Drink something."

Mackenzie shook his head frantically. *One. Two. Three.*

The greycoat poured a beaker of water and held it out to him. "Really, Mackenzie, at this point you're basically doing this to yourself."

"Shut up," Mackenzie mumbled.

"Oh, now, that's not very friendly, is it?"

I wasn't talking to you.

Maybe I was. I don't know.

"There's nothing in the water, you know. I do have

limits."

Mackenzie let out a bitter laugh before he could stop himself. The greycoat sighed. "I'll give you one more chance, Mackenzie."

Perhaps the water really was okay. The guy sounded like he meant it.

One. Two. Three. Four. Five. Six. Seven.

Mackenzie's legs shook as he set off again. *Jesus, don't fall over. Not in front of this guy.*

Strange. That didn't sound like the hissing darkness – the OCD, as Angel called it. It sounded more like his own voice.

One two three four –

"How long d'you think you can keep this up?" the greycoat said. "I mean, really? It's been twelve hours, Mackenzie, and you've lost the bloody plot."

Christ. Twelve hours? It felt like days.

That couldn't be a good sign.

"You've gone mad, Mackenzie. You knew you would."

I'm not mad.

You're hardly acting sane, are you?

"Skyler's seen the state you're in," the greycoat added conversationally. "She thought you were pathetic." He heaved a theatrical sigh. "Imagine how disappointed she must be, finally seeing the real you."

He lowered his voice. "She's exceptional, Skyler, isn't she? Fierce. Even if by some miracle you both made it out of here – d'you really think she'd want to spend one more minute around *this*?"

The putrid blister of shame swelling inside Mackenzie burst abruptly. Skyler had seen him, in this terrible, weak moment. Perhaps she thought he'd already broken, already betrayed her. She would think he wasn't worth saving. She was right.

But then the tiny part of him that was still *him*, weakened and fading as it was, staggered through the clouds of poisonous gas waving its arms and gasped, *Hang on a minute.*

Something about the greycoat's words didn't make sense. And if Mackenzie could just *think* for a second between the greycoat's needling and the nightmare in his brain, he might be able to figure out why.

He set off across the cell again.

Suddenly the greycoat was in front of him, pulling a thin metal rod from his belt. "Oh, Mackenzie, Mackenzie." He shook his head sadly. "I did try to help."

He jabbed the rod into Mackenzie's ribs.

The next thing Mackenzie knew he was in a twitching heap on the floor, limbs screaming like they'd been flayed. He thought he'd cried out, but his mouth didn't want to work properly. Even his shuddering gasps hurt.

The greycoat crouched over him as if he were a laboratory mouse who'd yielded some unusual results. Through the buzzing mist, Mackenzie saw every school bully, every gang member, every goon who'd ever taken one look at him and written him off as weak and worthless and pathetic.

And the current coursing through him was, abruptly, different.

He met the greycoat's eyes. "'m not fucking telling you anything."

The words came out slurred, through unexpectedly rubbery, unco-operative lips. Not quite the effect he'd been going for, but it would do.

The greycoat grinned as though he'd been given an unexpected treat. His hand shot out, grabbed Mackenzie by the hair, and dragged him towards the corner he'd reluctantly used as a toilet. Mackenzie couldn't struggle; his limbs felt like jelly filled with stinging nettles. All he could do was hold his breath against the acrid smell of his own piss as the greycoat held his nose an inch from the half-dried puddle.

"How long do you think you can hold your breath for?" the greycoat asked, like it was an interesting theoretical question, and the rod dug into Mackenzie's ribs again a millisecond before the pain returned, searing, and obliterated everything else.

When the agony faded, his face was pressed to the floor, the sharp, rancid smell flooding his nostrils, coating his tongue. He gagged, let out a sob.

"You're a mess," the greycoat said, contempt hard in every syllable. "And if you think for a second you're capable of standing up to me, I promise I'll show you how wrong you are. You probably think you can't get any lower than this. I guarantee you that's not true."

Mackenzie couldn't have answered if he'd wanted to; the second shock had torn any remaining control from his muscles. He could only lie, the greycoat's weight hovering over him, face down in his own piss.

The greycoat was right. This was bad. This was really, really bad.

But as the pain ebbed away, something odd was happening. His brain was no longer crowded and noisy. The hissing monster recoiled like a snake from burning metal, and in its place was one clear thought:

The greycoat was wrong.

Mackenzie was about to die. Everyone he cared for was about to die. He had failed, and now thousands more people were going to suffer and die too. And like all that wasn't enough, now he was lying in a literal puddle of piss.

And yet – there'd been times when the OCD had been much worse than this. Okay, so he'd spent the last twelve hours pacing and counting and suffocating in spiralling paranoia. But he remembered being on the run with Skyler and Angel: taking three days to navigate a flight of stairs and a hallway. Cleaning a single floor tile until his hands bled.

And Skyler had seen him like that, at his lowest and most wretched. Okay, so she'd had no idea what to say – but she *knew* that part of him. And if she hadn't turned her back on him then, she wasn't going to now.

This was bad. This was really, really bad.

But it wasn't as bad as the greycoat wanted him to think.

He wasn't alone.

And he wasn't broken yet.

40

BORN TO BE

Erin strode towards the mansion, her stance suggesting it would be either a very brave or very stupid person who tried to get in her way.

"Where are we going?" Faith asked, trying to keep up and finding herself forced instead to break into a rather less sophisticated jog.

"Come with me." Erin marched past an astonished Jacob up the marble staircase, leading Faith and Leila along a landing lined with gilt-edged mirrors. In front of a heavy oak door, she fished a key on a long chain out from under her hoodie.

"My father's study," she said, ushering Faith and Leila inside. "He kept the key hidden in my room. He didn't trust anyone completely, even my mother or Jacob. When he died, I hid the key before anyone else found it. There's no way this room will be bugged."

Heavy footsteps pounded on the staircase. Jacob appeared on the landing.

"Erin," he panted, lumbering towards them. "What on earth are you up to?"

Erin's expression was a mask. "I'm becoming who I was born to be," she said.

And she shut the door in his face.

"Well done, little one," Leila murmured.

Faith had to admit she was impressed too.

She'd half-expected bear traps and cattle prods, but Redruth's study was oddly serene, with modern art adorning dusty-blue walls, an antique desk, and a large window overlooking the gardens and woodland. A drinks cabinet sat in one corner, and several leather armchairs were scattered around the room.

Erin stared around. "I haven't been in here for years. He used to let me play in here sometimes when I was tiny."

"You really knew you'd made the inner circle if he brought you here," Leila commented, running her fingers over the desk's intricate inlay. "I must have known him five years before I saw this room."

Erin's gaze hovered on the high-backed chair behind the desk for a moment before she lowered herself into an armchair instead. Faith took her own seat gingerly, in case she activated a trigger that would pitch her through a trapdoor into a dungeon.

"Right." Erin drummed her fingers on the arm of her chair. "Time to pool our resources. Tell me about your agents. What can they do?"

Faith, aware that identifying Skyler by name would burst open yet another can of worms, decided to start with Mackenzie.

Erin nodded slowly. "He's exceptional, by all accounts. My father would have liked to put him on a retainer, but he never went for it."

Thank God.

"Lawful Good here's sleeping with him," Leila supplied helpfully.

Faith flushed scalding. "That is *not* relevant."

"It's the whole reason we're here, darling. It's quite relevant."

Rise above it. Faith shook herself. "So he can pick pretty much any lock, and he can break codes. Plus he's ridiculously agile – you shut your mouth," she added, as Leila's face lit up gleefully. "And Angel's smart and tactical, and she can fight and shoot. I think she could use pretty much anything as a weapon."

"Assuming either of them are in any fit state," Leila murmured.

Faith swallowed. She'd been trying not to think about that.

Erin massaged her temples. "I don't think I'll ever get used to you calling her Angel."

"Well, you'd better," Faith said. "*Don't* call her by her old name, whatever you do."

Erin sighed as though filing this away under things she couldn't or didn't want to think about. "And the third person?"

"Uh." Faith rubbed her neck. "Yeah."

Erin's eyes narrowed. "Why do I get the impression I'm about to hear something else I won't like?"

Oh, for Christ's sake. They'd come this far. Faith steeled herself. "Her name's Skyler. She's a hacker."

Erin's expression clarified into stony understanding. "You're fucking kidding me."

"What?" Leila demanded, as though she'd just missed a really good piece of gossip. Which, to be fair, was sort of the case.

"She shot my father," Erin snarled.

"I don't mind admitting I am *so* confused, darling."

"She worked for him. He really went out of his way for her, he said, and then she broke in one night and shot him. Some vendetta over a work thing. He nearly died. In fact, he let almost everyone think he had, so he could go after her. And then" – Erin's lip quivered – "he turned up dead anyway."

Faith sighed. "Erin –"

"That was one of the worst things, you know." Erin's face hardened to match her tone. "When he died, everyone else already thought he'd been gone for weeks. Try explaining *that* to people."

Faith had always prided herself on her patience. When she'd reinvented herself, reconstructed herself, it had been one of her few original attributes she'd considered worth keeping. Now, with Mackenzie and the others hovering like ghosts at her shoulder, it occurred to her that perhaps there was such a thing as too much patience.

"Look, Erin," she said. "We've already established that your father was a total psychopath, so shall we just not do this whole soul-searching thing again? Skyler didn't *break into* your house. She lived in your cellar for nearly three years and he terrorised her the entire time. She had to shoot him to escape."

"Bullshit," Erin fired back. "Three *years*? I would've known –"

Wordlessly, Faith got out her tablet, pulled up a photo of Skyler and thrust it at Erin.

Erin went white. "I... recognise her."

"Yeah, probably because she *lived in your damn cellar.*"

"I – I saw her running across the grounds a few times. I just assumed she was a gardener."

Faith managed to stop herself rolling her eyes. Erin had spent her life being fed an endless stream of lies by her father. Everything she understood about the world, her home, her family, had just been shattered.

Faith knew exactly how she felt.

Erin stared at Skyler's picture with a faraway look on her face, as though she was trying to find a way to assimilate this new information into the equation and still come up with the same answer. At last, she shook her head and dragged her hands over her face.

"Right," she said, untying and retying her bun. "So she's a hacker. An amazing one, apparently. Can she do any of the stuff Fel – the other two can?"

Faith recalled Mackenzie describing the time he'd talked Skyler into climbing down a drainpipe. "I think we'd best assume not."

Erin chewed a fingernail. "Breaking all three of them out would be virtually impossible. Finding out where they are, getting past that many greycoats..."

Faith went cold. "But –"

"Less of the angst, please," Leila told her sternly. "Erin's right. We need to get to one and give them the tools to rescue the others."

"Mackenzie," Faith said at once. "If he had a lock-picking kit –"

"You said the Board use electronic locks."

"Even so, he could –"

"You're being irrational, darling. That would be a colossal waste of time. If we get the hacker in front of a computer, she can reset the codes to the entire building."

Faith's eyes stung. *Dammit.* "It's just –" *Don't cry. Don't prove her right.* "I think... I think he needs to know help's coming."

"You think he'll break quickest."

She hated herself for thinking it. She nodded.

Leila wrinkled her nose. "He sounds like the sort who'd get all hand-wringy about shooting someone."

Faith thought about Mackenzie, his kind eyes, the way he never sat still, the way he carried the past like a millstone around his neck.

"That's a yes," Leila said, as if that brought the matter to a close. "Besides, if he's in that much of a state, he's not the one you want to give all that responsibility to. Sorry, petal. You're outvoted."

"There wasn't actually a vote –"

"Hush." Leila flapped at her. "We already know the hacker can shoot, and if we can get her to a computer she should be able to find the others. The question is, how do we get to *her*?"

Faith chewed her lip raw, trying to shape a miasma of half-formed ideas and all-too-defined fears into something solid enough to grasp. "Could you convince the greycoats to let you see her alone?"

"I doubt it. What reason would I give?"

"I could," Erin said quietly.

They turned to her. She gave them an icy smile. "The Board are just as desperate as Jacob for me to pick up where my father left off. If I asked the right person for twenty minutes alone with the girl who killed him... they'd give it to me."

41

STILL WATERS

Angel had tuned out the alarm a while ago. At some point, someone had delivered a plastic bowl of gluey grey porridge, a spoon and a cup of water. She'd drunk the water, forced down a few mouthfuls of the porridge, and returned to the middle of the floor.

Drifting. Waiting.

She could use any of the items they'd left as a weapon. He would be expecting it, though.

The light came on. She didn't move.

The insufferably smug male greycoat squatted down and waved a hand in front of her face. "Hello? Anyone home?"

She looked through him.

"Had a chat with Skyler," he said.

A skip, a catch in the steady lull of her heart. Skyler.

"Not as good as you at keeping her mouth shut, is she?"

There was, unfortunately, no denying that.

"She was really worried. Frantic, actually."

In. Out. Little waves lapping at a quiet shore.

"Funny thing, though... she barely mentioned you."

The sea always wins.

"She cares about the boy, though, doesn't she? It was him she was begging me to spare."

He held out a phone with a video on the screen. Angel stared straight ahead, willing her pulse not to quicken in response to Skyler's voice, heated, frightened: *"Please stop. Please don't do this to him."*

The greycoat rewound the recording. "See – this is her when she saw you." He zoomed in on Skyler's impassive face. Angel thought back to the afternoons in her cellar teaching Skyler to fight, the way something behind Skyler's eyes shut down at any mention of Redruth.

"But when she saw the boy..." The greycoat played the first clip again, his eyes still fixed on Angel.

Angel didn't move.

After a few moments, the greycoat tucked the phone away. "I thought you deserved to know," he said kindly. "What you really mean to her."

Angel closed her eyes. Uncrossed her legs. Drew her knees up to her chest.

The greycoat patted her shoulder. "Just think about that for a bit, eh?"

Footsteps on concrete. The door opening, closing.

Lights out.

Tucked inside her cocoon of darkness, Angel grinned.

42

LEGACIES

Erin made the calls. It didn't take long; as soon as she dropped her name, she was passed in a panicked flurry to a senior greycoat called Governor Harris.

Her whole demeanour changed while she was on the phone. Gone was the hesitant speech, the bowed head, the fretful picking at her nails. Her voice was smooth and level as she said, "I believe you have something that belongs to me."

A pause. "I quite understand that national security takes precedence. I've been thinking about how to honour my father's legacy. There's been too much unrest in the city of late, and I fear his passing has contributed. He was a loyal supporter of the Board, and he did much to maintain order. I'd like that collaboration to continue."

Another pause. Erin smiled, the small, calculated, satisfied smile of someone well versed in the art of getting what they want. "Of course. I just have one request – a personal favour. I would very much appreciate a private conversation with the girl who murdered my father."

A shorter pause. Erin gave a short, mirthless laugh that sent unease crawling through Faith's stomach like worms. "I'll make sure she can still be interrogated afterwards. It might even work in your favour. It's much easier to get the truth from someone who's already frightened and in pain – I'm sure you don't need me to tell you that."

She was so *convincing*. Just as convincing, in fact, as she'd been up in the treehouse, wide-eyed and vulnerable. Faith studied her intently, searching for some tiny tell that would assuage the creeping worms in her stomach – but Erin might as well have slipped on a second skin.

"Twenty minutes should be sufficient. This afternoon? Thank you, Governor. You'll find me extremely grateful."

Erin ended the call and stood for a long moment, staring at her father's empty chair behind the desk.

Then she flashed Faith and Leila a bright, chilly smile. "Well, that's that taken care of. She practically bit my hand off."

She glanced down at her oversized hoodie. "I can hardly turn up looking like this, though. Give me half an hour."

"What are you going to wear?" Faith asked. "We need to make sure we can hide the wire –"

"I'm not wearing a wire."

"But –"

Erin shook her head. "Too risky. I don't think they'd dare search me, but you never know, especially if there's some young over-enthusiastic idiot on the gate. Besides, I won't need it."

Her face was still unreadable. Faith opened her mouth to protest, and Leila laid a cautioning hand on her arm.

Purely in it for the entertainment. Leila might have just as much fun watching Faith's world collapse around her. Then Faith would be trapped with two sociopaths, having exhausted all her resources, all her options, and the Northerners would be out of time.

"Are you sure you feel okay about this, Erin?" she tried instead, as Erin headed for the door.

Erin turned to her, expressionless. "I feel fine."

Half an hour later, Erin was transformed in an elegant black trouser suit, heels Faith wouldn't have been able to walk more than a few metres in and a tasteful platinum necklace so simple it had to be worth enough to feed half the city for a week.

She looked even more remote and frightening now, striding down the stairs with Faith and Leila in her wake. The lost girl from the tree house had vanished entirely, and Faith couldn't help but want her back.

Her hands had trembled a little as she handed Erin the equipment she'd smuggled out of the Agency: a thin transmitter bar like Mackenzie's, plus a tracker implant, a tiny disc no more than five millimetres in diameter that would help them direct Skyler to an escape route.

Assuming the equipment made it to Skyler. Assuming Skyler was in any fit state to move. Assuming –

"Erin." Jacob materialised from nowhere, blocking the front door, and Erin stopped dead. "I'm so glad you're looking more like yourself." He nodded at Leila. "I don't know what you've said to her, but it seems to have done wonders." He sounded more accusatory than appreciative. "And now you're off somewhere?"

In her heels, Erin was the same height as him. "Yes."

"Wonderful. I'll give you a lift."

"No, thank you. I'll take care of my own business."

Jacob's mouth opened slightly, and then a hint of smug satisfaction crept across his face like an indulgent parent watching their child pack a bag and announce their intention to run away from home. "I don't want you overdoing it. You haven't been yourself for months, you've barely been out of the house, and now all of a sudden you're running around to goodness knows where with people you barely know?" He eyed Faith and Leila with the manner of someone who suspects their child's friends of being a Bad Influence. "I'm so pleased you're thinking about your father's legacy. Really. But you mustn't go rushing in. You need guidance from people who know the business."

Erin lowered her gaze.

Jacob gave a tiny jerk of his head. A man and a woman in dark suits, both of whom looked as though heavy masonry had featured in their lineage, melted into place either side of him.

Erin's shoulders stiffened. She didn't look up.

Faith held her breath, not daring to move. Suddenly she wanted Scary Erin back.

But Erin had spent her whole life being trained to follow orders, to think what she was told to think. Could she really shake it off just like that?

Beside Faith, Leila's lips parted thoughtfully, but she said nothing.

"You can't stop me leaving," Erin said, but she sounded hesitant, uncertain.

The gleam of amusement in Jacob's eyes turned flinty. Faith tensed. Was this the point where she was meant to get her gun out? She still had no idea if she was actually capable of shooting anyone, but it was looking more and more like she might have to.

"Come on, Erin." Jacob's tone said he was working hard to be avuncular. "You're not thinking clearly. Your father would have wanted me to look after you."

All at once, Erin's marble visage snapped back into place. "I don't give a shit what my father would have wanted. Get out of my way."

"Erin..." A warning. *Do as you're told, young lady, or there'll be trouble.*

Erin's laugh was as hard and humourless as her eyes. "Do you really think that tone works on me? Do you think after nineteen years under *his* roof I'm scared of you and your idiot minions?"

"That's *enough*," Jacob snarled. "I've been patient because you're grieving, but this –"

"You're not my father, Jacob. You're not anyone. This is my house, and you're going to leave it. Now."

The minions exchanged uncertain glances, but Jacob just snorted. "Or what?"

Erin gave him a smile like an iceberg. "My father didn't trust anyone. Even you, no matter what he let you think. The dirt I've got on every one of you could ruin you three times over. And there's backups, before you start getting ahead of yourself."

She took a step closer. "What do you think *you're* going to do? Kill me?" Her tone was mocking. "Lock me in my room?"

Inches between them now, Jacob's expression growing stiff and brittle, and Erin was unflinching, cold and sharp as a crystal blade. "You know what he was, Jacob. His blood runs in my veins. So go ahead. Try me."

"You ungrateful little bitch," Jacob hissed. "I'll –"

Steadily, Erin pulled out her pistol and levelled it at him.

His ruddy face paled. "You don't have it in you."

Leila flicked her glossy hair back. "Oh, you know I do, though, darling," she said, pulling out her own weapon. "Especially when I'm bored. And you're being *very* tedious."

"Leave," Erin said. "Don't come back."

Jacob's eyes darted from side to side. Erin cocked her pistol. "I'm going to count to three. And then I'm going to make an example of someone."

The man beside Jacob shifted nervously. "Boss?"

"One," Erin said.

"Fuck this." The woman turned for the door. "She's lost it."

"Two."

The man at Jacob's side backed after his counterpart.

"On second thoughts" – Erin's head tilted thoughtfully – "do stay, Jacob. Give me an excuse."

Jacob's mouth was an ugly twist of anger. "This isn't over, Erin."

"Three."

He turned and bolted.

Erin stared at the open door, her pistol still raised, as an engine revved outside and gravel crunched on the driveway.

Leila patted her on the back. "Well done, little one."

Erin's shoulders sagged. "He was always a bully. I really thought I was going to have to shoot him."

"I thought so too," Faith admitted. "I just wasn't sure I'd be able to."

Erin tucked her pistol away and pulled out her car key. "I'm pretty sure I could have."

43

MONSTERS

By the time the cell door opened again, Skyler had just about had enough. "This is getting really boring, you know, Sam," she snapped. "If you're here to gloat again, why don't you just fuck off and – oh, *shit*."

It wasn't Sam.

Skyler shot backwards into the corner as the woman in the doorway turned to the unfamiliar greycoat behind her. "Twenty minutes," she said, her voice cool and level. "As agreed."

"Nothing life-threatening, remember. We still need to question her."

A humourless smile. "Surely she doesn't need all her fingers for that."

Skyler considered screaming, but who would possibly come to her rescue?

"Don't worry," the woman added. "My father taught me well. You'll get her back in one piece. More or less."

The greycoat nodded approvingly. "Nice to see his spirit's still alive."

"Quite. Do excuse me. I'd like to make the most of my time here."

The greycoat disappeared. Erin Redruth turned to Skyler.

Skyler scrambled to her feet. "I'm not sorry," she spat, as Erin strode towards her. "Your father was a monster and he deserved what he got. He deserved worse than he got."

Daniel's daughter – for Christ's sake, could this *possibly* get any worse? – backhanded her across the face, grabbed her by the throat and pinned her against the wall. In a flash, Skyler was back in Daniel's mansion, pulse fluttering vainly against a tightening hand, those same icy blue eyes boring into hers while she thought, *this is it, this is how I'm going to die.*

And then the present returned with a crashing jolt and it was rage, not terror, driving her blood through her veins. "If you're trying to fill his shoes," she growled, meeting Erin's eyes, "you'll have to do better than that."

"We'll see," Erin said grimly.

But Skyler wasn't listening. She was too busy thinking: *I can speak.*

She's not actually choking me.

"You killed my father, you little bitch," Erin said loudly. As Skyler stared at her, trying to process something that made no conceivable sense, she put her mouth to Skyler's ear and hissed, "I'm here to help. Play along."

Skyler tried to make a convincing choking noise

through her confusion. "He – he would've killed me," she gasped. "I had no choice –" She dropped her voice. "Who sent you?"

"Faith Jackson," Erin murmured. Then, louder: "You're going to die, and I'm going to watch. But in the meantime, you're going to suffer."

Under any other circumstances, Skyler would have rolled her eyes. It was still tempting. Erin seemed to have got her lines from the playbook of a pantomime villain. "Why are you –?"

"Save it," Erin snarled, and Skyler realised she was right. Whatever Erin's reasons for helping her – assuming she actually was helping, assuming Faith wasn't in fact the traitorous bitch Skyler had written her off as, that this wasn't some horrible elaborate ploy to take fucking with her to the absolute next level – the heart to heart could wait.

Erin wrenched her away from the wall and shoved her, rather half-heartedly. In the spirit of playing along, Skyler threw herself down as hard as she dared and let out a genuine yelp of pain when she landed on the arm Erin's father had broken three months before.

Erin grabbed Skyler's other arm and twisted it behind her back. "*Listen.* We haven't got long."

Skyler gave a sobbing cry. Erin's grip loosened. "Shit – sorry –"

This time Skyler did roll her eyes. "You're not hurting me, idiot. I'm playing along."

"Oh, for –" Erin's hand tightened again. "Listen. I'm going to give you a weapon. It's like a Taser, but smaller.

Use it to get a gun. There's a tracker and a communication device too. Faith'll help you get to a computer so you can find out where the others are and change the door codes to get to them. Then we'll figure out an escape route and pick you up outside."

"Lot of wishful thinking in that plan."

"Or you can stay here and let the greycoats cut pieces off you if you prefer. We'll try to create a distraction."

"Yeah, well, you'd better make it a good one –" Erin jerked her arm and Skyler remembered she was supposed to be in pain.

"You're really annoying, you know," Erin said over her cries. "I can see why my father didn't like you."

"That was a low blow," Skyler muttered.

Erin slipped something hard and rectangular into her waistband. "Taser."

Skyler screamed. "Hurry *up*," she hissed.

"Good. I'm glad it hurts. I'm going to show you what real pain is, you little –"

"Oh my God, shut up," Skyler mumbled. "You're terrible at this."

Erin grabbed her hair. "You'll fucking speak when I say you can," she said levelly, and suddenly there was a familiar edge to her words that made Skyler's blood crystallise into ice.

"Better," she murmured. She raised her voice. "Please – please don't hurt me –"

"The tech stuff goes in your arm." Erin's knee dug into Skyler's back. "Like, under the skin."

Does it have to? "Fine. Just get it in. You got a knife?"

"I –"

"For fuck's sake, just do it –" Skyler cried out again, for real this time, as the flesh of her wrist stung and parted, warmth and wetness spilling out, and then something shoved into the wound with a crash of sickening pain and she choked down a scream.

"I'm sorry," Erin whispered, as Skyler moaned into the concrete. "I'm sorry –"

"Keep going," Skyler hissed.

"What?"

"You can't just do one cut, it'll look weird. Ah – fuck –" The sting again, and again, but she was okay, she was okay, and –

"The tracker's the round thing," Erin breathed. "The transmitter's the long one. If you press on it for five seconds, it'll go live."

Skyler gritted her teeth. "Right. Anything else?"

"Keep the connection live. Faith'll tell you when to move."

The pressure on Skyler's back relented. She rolled over, blood trickling down her arms, and met Erin's eyes. She'd meant it as a challenge, and it was – but it was also, she had to admit, fascination.

"That all you've got?" she gasped. *Remember who you're supposed to be*, she mouthed.

Erin recoiled. "I – I don't know if I can –"

However Skyler had imagined Daniel's daughter, this wasn't it. "You've got to get your money's worth." She wiped an arm across her face, smearing it with blood.

Every little helped. "It's what *he* would've done. Just – I dunno, kick me or something."

Erin swung her foot clumsily into Skyler's abdomen, curling her into a knot of white pain around her scar. Well, she supposed she had literally asked for it.

She'd caught glimpses of Erin during her years in the cellar. Long before she'd had any idea that this was the girl Angel had once loved, she'd had a construct of Daniel's daughter in her mind. And though she knew, logically, that Erin was as much a victim as she or Angel or dozens of people who'd had the misfortune to cross Daniel's path, Skyler had still resented her.

But while Erin had been born into his house, Skyler had put herself there. And now, when she looked at Erin, all she felt was pity.

"I'm sorry," she whispered as Erin kicked her again, and this time she had no idea whether she was acting or not. And Erin hesitated like she was about to speak, but then –

The cell door crashed open. Sam stood framed in the doorway, chest heaving, his features etched with freezing rage. And in a rush of numbing horror, Skyler realised she could see far more of Daniel in him than she could in Erin.

Sam pointed his gun at Erin's head with trembling hands. *Shit.* He might actually shoot her.

But Erin didn't flinch. Calmly, she stepped away from Skyler. "Sam." She pulled a tissue from her pocket and began wiping her hands. "What a pleasant surprise. We've met several times, you recall, at my father's house."

Skyler would have laughed if she hadn't been so terrified. Sam was as shell-shocked as he was furious. He had absolutely no idea what to do.

He lowered the gun and tried to plaster on a neutral expression. "Ms Redruth. Of course. Forgive me – I didn't expect – You understand, the person who let you in here is guilty of a... uh, a breach of protocol. Access to this prisoner is highly restricted."

"Yes. Governor Harris was very kind to grant me access. She understood it's what my father would have wanted."

Governor Harris was, by Skyler's best guess, several rungs above Sam. That was a smart name drop.

Sam was trying to match Erin's marble coldness, but he couldn't quite get there. "I was under the impression you were, ah, still in mourning. Otherwise it would have been my pleasure to inform you of this development. I didn't realise you were... taking up your father's mantle so soon."

"It's my civic duty to help the Board restore order to the city. This" – Erin jerked her head at Skyler, who was still curled on the floor, holding her breath – "seemed a good place to start."

She extended a still-bloody hand to Sam. He hesitated, then took it.

Erin gave him a glacial smile. "Rest assured the Board can rely on my continued support. As I'm sure I can yours."

"Of course." He dropped her hand. "But for now, I

must ask that you let us escort you out. I trust you've got what you came for?"

Erin glanced down carelessly at Skyler. "Oh, I'd say so."

Left alone, Skyler rearranged herself into a suitably cowed pose. What the hell had possessed Faith to go to Daniel Redruth's *daughter*? There was still a not insignificant chance Erin was playing them. It was exactly Daniel's style: go to extravagant lengths to convince her he was on her side, just so he could be there to drink in the moment she realised she'd never had any hope at all.

But as much as her gut screamed that she could never, ever, trust a Redruth, Erin's performance had been pretty damn convincing. No one was *that* good an actor.

God, she hoped not, anyway.

She fumbled for her wrist, swelling blue and pink where Erin had shoved the transmitter in, gritted her teeth and pressed down on the thin bar under the skin. "Faith?" she hissed. "Please, God, tell me you can hear me."

An agonising wait, her chest crushingly tight – *please let this be real, please let this work* – before Faith's muffled, breathless voice came out of her arm. "Skyler? Can you hear me?"

Jesus, that was weird. Skyler closed her eyes against a flood of relief. "Yeah. Listen, I can't talk much, but I'm gonna leave this live. Don't contact me till I tell you it's safe. And I've got no fucking idea where I am, so I'm gonna need you to find me a path to a computer as soon as it's quiet. Can you do that?"

"Yes. Yes."

"Who was it, Faith?" Like she had to ask.

But there was another torturous pause. "Kimura," Faith said at last, her voice thick. "It was Kimura."

It was, unexpectedly, another kick to the stomach. Of them all, Skyler had liked him best.

"Right," she said, clearing her throat. "Well, if you see him, do me a favour and shoot him in the fucking face. I'm going now. Sam'll be back any minute."

"Huh?" Faith sounded confused. For once, Skyler couldn't blame her. "You – do you *know* one of the greycoats?"

Skyler swallowed painfully. Once she said it out loud it would be real, she'd have to accept that, and everyone else would want to weigh in on this whole bloody mess. "Don't get excited. It's not good news, and no, I don't want to talk about it, and no, I'm not interested in your opinion. He's... he's my brother."

Faith, thankfully, said nothing. Skyler slumped against the wall and dragged her hands over her face.

When Sam burst back in a few minutes later, his eyes were still wild. He stumbled across to Skyler and knelt beside her. With an unbearable stab, she noticed the little case in his trembling hand. A first aid kit.

Fucking *hell*.

"Sky," he said urgently. "Are you all right?"

She buried her head in her arms. "What do you care? She didn't do anything you and your pals aren't going to."

"Hey." He smoothed her hair, so gently it tore at

something inside her. "Come on, now. I haven't hurt you, have I? I haven't let anyone touch you."

She wanted to scream, *there's more than one type of pain, Sam, and you fucking know it.* But there was a weapon in her trousers, a transmitter in her arm, and Sam's composure was brittle, threaded with spiderweb cracks. She would do better to play up her vulnerability.

"I – I thought she was going to kill me," she whispered. "Please don't let her come back, Sam. Don't let her hurt me."

He touched her arm and she flinched. "Hurts," she mumbled. Which was true, at least.

"Sorry. I'm sorry. Let me help you."

Her heart was going to break all over again if she had to sit there and let him act like her brother. Because she knew, now, that her brother was gone. This man wore his face and spoke with his voice, but he wasn't Sam.

But it was better to have him protective of what he saw as his, all that icy anger radiating outwards, away from her. Just like Daniel.

So she didn't scream or yell or shove him away. She didn't beg him to tell her this was all pretend, that everything would be okay. She just let him clean the blood from her face and bandage her arms, and the scalding tears that spilled, that kept spilling, wouldn't stop, couldn't have been any more real.

44

THE THING WITH FEATHERS

Faith spent most of the ninety minutes waiting behind tinted windows in Erin's opulent Land Rover – top of the range, obviously, and even more expensive considering how scarce motor vehicles were in the South – wondering just how badly she'd fucked up.

"How're you holding up, little one?" Leila asked from behind a pair of enormous designer sunglasses. Faith jumped. She'd thought Leila was asleep.

"Oh, please," she said. "Like you care."

Leila lowered her glasses. "I'm interested in people, sweetpea. And you've had an interesting night."

Faith sighed. She needed to talk to *someone*. "I'm... scared." Hahn's warning hummed again – *never show weakness* – but Faith was exhausted, and the weight of grief and confusion and fear was crushing her, and she'd already made herself so vulnerable; she didn't have the energy to care about this too. "I haven't heard from Mackenzie for hours, and his receiver didn't work properly, so I couldn't even tell him I was coming. I couldn't even tell him that – that it wasn't me. That I didn't betray him."

Leila eyed her curiously. "Are you in love with him?"

When Faith squinted sideways at her, she laughed. "I think we're past small talk, darling, don't you? Don't worry, I'm not going to do anything spiteful. I'm not Daniel."

Unspeakably naïve though it was, somehow Faith believed her.

"I... don't know," she said. "It's a big word, isn't it? I've only known him a few weeks. But I care about him. I like him. A lot."

Leila slid her sunglasses back up her nose. "I've never been in love."

Faith blinked. "What? Never?"

"Nope. Don't get me wrong, sex is wonderful –"

"I literally can't tell you how much I don't need to know about your sex life –"

"– but all those feelings everyone goes on about? Tedious. Much better my way, if you ask me. You get all the fun with as many people as you like, and none of that messy stuff."

"You married Amir," Faith pointed out. "Although I guess you did kill him, too."

Leila sniffed daintily. "It was a marriage of convenience."

A current of sympathy stirred. "Was it his idea? The whole people trafficking thing?"

Leila snorted. "That'd be much more palatable for

you, wouldn't it? Poor little Leila, so vulnerable, that wicked man made her do such *terrible* things. Well, sorry to disappoint you, darling. I was the brains of the whole operation. Amir was just useful. He was rich and handsome and amoral, and stupid enough to do as he was told. Especially if I let him think it was his idea."

"Why'd you shoot him, then?"

"*Was* useful. He'd outgrown it. The little redhead gave me a decent excuse. I owe her, really."

Before Faith could think of a response other than *what the fuck,* one of her transmitters buzzed. She shot upright, her pulse speeding up to one long continuous hum as Skyler's voice crackled out: "Faith? Please tell me you can hear me."

"Skyler? Can you hear me?" *Please.*

"Yeah," Skyler said, and Faith's eyes burned with tears of sheer relief. She ignored Leila's inquisitive stare as she blinked them away.

When Skyler had gone, she and Leila sat in stunned silence.

"Well," Leila said at last. "That's an interesting development."

Faith rubbed her hands across her face. "Fuck."

She jerked upright again as Erin appeared at the end of the street, marching towards the car with her chin raised. When she got in, her cheeks were flushed, her manicured hands stained red. Faith's stomach flipped upside down.

Looking faintly nauseous, Erin pulled a packet of wipes from the glovebox and started scrubbing her hands.

"How did it go, darling?" Leila said.

Erin's shoulders slumped. "I've... never hurt anyone before."

"Are you okay?" Faith asked.

A faint, puzzled frown spread across Erin's face. "Uh. I think so?" She started the engine. "Didn't quite get the full twenty minutes, though. A greycoat turned up – and Christ, he was furious. I haven't seen anyone look like that since –" She shuddered.

"He's her brother," Faith said. It was still beyond surreal. "That greycoat. He's Skyler's brother."

Erin's hands jerked on the steering wheel. The car veered and almost clipped the kerb. "Sorry. Shit. Are you serious? Sam Linley is Skyler's *brother*?"

"That's what she just said. You know him?"

"He used to come to my father's parties. My father liked him. Thought he was a rising star." Erin shivered. "I tried to avoid him, to be honest. He gave me the creeps."

All things considered, it said something pretty disturbing about Sam Linley that there was no trace of irony in Erin's words.

"Skyler seemed pretty certain he was Board through and through," Faith mused. "You think there's any chance he might come around? I mean – she's his little sister."

Erin shook her head slowly. "You can spot the greycoats who've really embraced it all a mile off. He's a true believer all right. And you know what they say – new converts are the most zealous. If he's involved... honestly, things are even worse than we thought."

Great. Just what they needed. Faith sighed. "How did Skyler seem? Was she hurt?"

"Don't think so. She seemed... angry, mostly."

So normal Skyler, then.

"You know," Erin added, "I actually kind of liked her."

As they sped back towards the mansion through lanes laden with bright leaves and snowy blossom, Erin checked the rear-view mirror and her knuckles whitened around the steering wheel. "Uh, guys? I don't want to alarm anyone, but I think maybe we're being followed."

Faith whipped round, her pounding heart snatching the air from her lungs. Leila turned too. "That's not the Board," she said, peering luxuriantly over her sunglasses. "Erin, darling, is this one of yours?"

"No." Faith's stomach had plummeted to somewhere round her knees. "This one's for me."

Erin glanced at her. "What do you want to do?"

Cry. Run. Drive him off the fucking road. "I'll talk to him."

"Are you sure?"

"Yeah."

Erin shrugged and stopped the car. Clutching her pistol with numb fingers, Faith climbed out into the dazzling spring sunshine.

She'd reinvented Kimura overnight: added a coldness to his eyes and a cruelty to the line of his mouth that had never been there before, that wasn't there now. He was just Kimura, still: her mentor, her friend.

He seemed to be alone, but there could easily be someone in the car with sights on her. He wasn't holding a weapon, though, and his mild face sobered into shock when she trained hers on his chest.

Skyler would probably just have shot him. Mackenzie would talk to him, hear him out. Faith no longer had any idea what Hahn would have done.

And she – what was she going to do?

Kimura's brow was wrinkled. She'd had no idea he was such a good actor. "What are you doing here, Faith?"

"What are *you* doing here?"

"I heard you were missing from the Agency. You left your phone, but your laptop's still trackable."

Shit. She hadn't thought of that. How *stupid*.

"Why did you do it?" she blurted. "Why did you betray them?"

He sagged. "I didn't want to. Honestly. I like them. But I felt I had no choice."

"What the fuck? *Why*?"

"When we first got involved in this, I let emotion blind me. Julia was so passionate, I knew how much it meant to her... and truthfully, I couldn't resist the idea of recruiting such talented people. But when I had time to reflect... History has shown us over and over the chaos that follows when external forces remove dictatorships. Infrastructure crumbles, economies collapse – The instability can last for years. Here, the crime lords could easily take over, or another extremist group. More people would die. Perhaps many more. How would that be any better?"

Faith forced down a violent surge of nausea. "So you just handed them over to be tortured? They *trusted* you, Ren!"

That hurt him. She could see it in the way his face crumpled. "I – and others – tried to persuade Julia to bow out, but you know what she's like. She carried the pain of the last op's failure for years, and she was so determined to make amends that she couldn't – or wouldn't – see that this one was doomed to fail too. I didn't want to hurt anyone, but this had to come to an end."

Faith had been willing herself not to cry – but all at once, she knew she wasn't going to. "You're wrong. The UK is heading for a revolution with or without us. They just needed a push."

Kimura shook his head. She knew that expression: *you're too young, too naïve. There's so much you don't understand.* "I must say I'm disappointed in Julia, sending you to fight her battles. Where is she, anyway?"

It was like he'd slapped her. "Are you – are you fucking kidding me?"

"I don't know what you mean."

This had to be part of the game. She didn't know how or why, unless he really was crueller than she'd ever thought possible. But she would spit the words at him like arrows, and hope they pierced him somewhere. "Julia's dead, Ren."

He laughed. He actually *laughed.* "What? That's – *what?*"

"She's dead. Someone walked into her office and shot her. Right after I spoke to you."

"Oh, this is unacceptable. Did she tell you to say this? Where is she?"

Anger.

"I'm not lying." Faith's mouth quivered around the words. "I saw her."

"Don't be ridiculous. You must be mistaken – there must be some – are you *sure*?"

Bargaining.

Faith stared at him. "You really didn't know? You didn't order it?"

"No! How could you – I would never, ever hurt Julia, no matter what our differences. She's my friend."

It's still your fault. "Well, someone took matters into their own hands." She hardened her tone; it wasn't difficult. "When I called you, you realised I knew, didn't you? And you told someone in Copenhagen."

He nodded, hands over his mouth.

"Who?"

He said nothing.

"*Who*, Ren?"

"Clara," he said distantly. "I told her to... to distract Julia. To keep her out of your way."

Somehow the fact that he'd betrayed Hahn by allying with Clara was almost as awful as everything else. Faith wanted to retort that she wasn't surprised – but when you fell out with colleagues, you stormed out of their office and sent them emails signed 'Regards'. You didn't *kill* them.

"Well, Clara walked into Julia's office and shot her in the head," she said. "So congratulations, I guess. You got what you asked for."

Kimura shook his head frantically, over and over.

Denial.

"I'm surprised you even care," Faith added bitterly. "What's one more sacrifice, right?"

"She's my friend," he said into his hands. "She's my friend."

"Was," Faith said quietly.

Kimura was crying, she realised. And, impossibly, she wanted to comfort him. "That wasn't what I – I didn't mean for this –"

"But you started something you couldn't control. And now Julia's dead, and Mackenzie and Angel and Skyler are going to die too. And what are we going to do? Keep running around like we own the place? I know what the Agency's been doing, Ren. Torture, illegal detention... We're no better than the Board, are we? We've just convinced ourselves we know best. But what do we know? Fifteen years, you and Julia worked together, and you still couldn't figure this out. What right do we have to decide who lives and who dies?"

"We were helping people. Protecting people."

More denial.

"We didn't protect the Northerners, did we? We're just behaving like some lives are worth more than others. That's what Clara did – decided it was okay to kill Julia because she was *in the way*. How many people have we done that to?"

Kimura stared at the tarmac, his eyes red and glassy.

Depression.

Faith had never seen him cry, never seen him or Hahn look lost. She'd always believed they knew exactly what they were doing, like she had her parents when she was a kid. None of it was true, though, was it? Her mom hadn't been able to cope with her dad's death, hadn't been able to guide her through it. Kimura hadn't been able to contain the terrible consequences of his decision.

"I didn't want to cause any more suffering," he muttered. "Please believe me. I didn't mean –"

Faith was going to scream if she heard that one more time. What did good intentions count for when the result was so much pain?

She believed him, though – or at least, she wanted to. It would be so much worse if he'd set out to be deliberately cruel.

So maybe intent did matter after all.

"You have to make this right," she said.

Kimura didn't answer. She thought she knew what he was thinking: *how?* Suddenly, she understood what Mackenzie had been trying to explain to her, the myriad potential consequences he saw unfolding with every action. How could you ever take another easy breath when you could see all of that? How could you ever dare make any choices?

Mackenzie had made choices, though. He'd chosen to put his trust in her, in the Agency. *He's kind,* Skyler had said. *He's good and he's kind. He still tries to see the best in people.* And they had taken that and destroyed it.

Faith had resented Skyler's mistrust, the fierce accusation in her eyes. But she had seen something, after all, that Faith hadn't been able to.

And Kimura was still dazed, speechless, and Faith had had enough. Enough of people crying and feeling sorry for themselves, of being so consumed by their own misery that they lost sight of the real people who still needed them.

She put her gun away. "I'm going to make this right," she said. "I'm not coming back to the Agency. You – you can go back, I guess, and cover up what you did, or whatever. But I'm going to help them. And I swear to God – if you try to get in my way, I'll do whatever I need to do to get you out of it."

She didn't know what kind of response she wanted. *Sorry's not good enough,* her mom had been fond of saying when Faith was a kid, and Faith had hated that, the feeling that every mistake, no matter how innocent, was a permanent scar. She understood now, though. Some wounds couldn't be healed.

She walked back to the car.

There was something like sympathy in Erin's face, but Leila eyed her with pure fascination.

"Are you okay?" Erin asked.

Faith shook her head.

"He's the one who betrayed them?"

"Yes."

"What do you think he'll do now?"

Faith glanced back at Kimura, still standing in the road like a sleepwalker. "I've no idea."

"You should probably get rid of him, darling," Leila said brightly.

Don't tempt me. Leila had a point, probably. Faith wanted to believe Kimura would stay out of her way, but so much of what she believed had turned out to be a catastrophic degree of wishful thinking. It would be safer to kill him.

But it would also be vengeance. Once again, her deciding who should live and who should die.

Leila sighed and held out her hand. "Give me the gun."

"No." Faith took a deep breath. "Erin – just – drive. Please? Just drive."

45

HURTING DISTANCE

Erin had left the headquarters just after two in the afternoon, according to Faith. Still hours to go until the building would be emptier, until Skyler could risk her escape. Left alone, the thought of all the horrors that might erupt in those hours crawled over her skin like ants: *what if, what if, what if?*

She had no idea what Sam might do next. There was a danger he might go after Erin, even. That would be at odds with his allegiance to the Board, though – and besides, presumably Erin could look after herself. Possibly, anyway. She'd probably cry if she had to shoot someone.

In the end Sam returned only a couple of hours later, with no visible trace of the panic and fury that had blazed in him earlier. Instead he strode towards Skyler, as blank and remote as he had been in the interrogation room when she'd first come face to face with him again.

Something was different. Something was wrong.

She opened her mouth to ask what was happening, but before she could speak there was a hood over her head, cuffs biting into her wrists.

"Sam?" she said, as he hauled her to her feet. "Sam, what's going on?"

"Come with me," he said.

Skyler stumbled blindly, dry-mouthed, fighting to keep her balance as he hurried her along. What was going on? Had he seen something on the cameras? Had he figured out what Erin was really doing?

"Sam?" she whispered again, but the only reply was silence.

Finally, they stopped. Skyler stood rigid: *what if, what if, what if –?*

"Don't be scared," Sam said in her ear. "I thought I had it all figured out, but I had to... re-evaluate a few things. There – you don't hear me say that every day, do you?"

Skyler screwed her eyes shut, her breath coming fast, shallow, a frantic stream of oxygen to her muscles. Fight. Freeze. Flee.

How would any of those help?

"I thought I could treat you like any other prisoner," he said sadly. "But seeing you in there... you're still just a kid. Still my little sister."

A bright, horrible flare of hope. Had he changed his mind?

"I'm going to fix this. I'm going to help you, Sky. Don't worry. Everything's going to be okay now."

Oh, thank God.

She'd ached for years to hear those words, that voice. Fantasised about it, during the nights and years alone in the cold and the dark. She bit her lip hard, swallowing a sob. "Sam – you –"

"I can't hurt you." His tone was almost rueful. "I can't let anyone hurt you. I know it's a bit – people might disapprove, but they don't know you like I do."

Wake up. This wasn't a fairy tale. This wasn't her fantasy.

No. This was too good to be true.

"Sam?" she whispered. "What – what are you going to do?"

"I figured it out when I saw how you reacted to those videos." There was a note of pride in his voice. "It's the boy you really care about. So I'm going to get the girl to talk."

An icy spear drove through Skyler's stomach.

"It won't be hard, the state she's in." He said it so casually, as though it was a minor favour, while Skyler shook, forcing herself not to double over. "Then I'll talk Harris into giving you a chance, and we can put all of this behind us. I know how smart you are, you've just been... misguided. It's not your fault. You'll see things the right way soon enough."

No, she wanted to scream, *you've got it all wrong, you don't understand –*

But that would only give him more ammunition, and then he would change the game again. She clenched her jaw. *Play along. Get to Angel.*

"I realise this might still upset you a bit," he added.

"But you can't make an omelette without breaking a few eggs, isn't that what Mum used to say?" He patted her shoulder and she started violently. "Don't say I never do anything for you, little sis."

He guided her a few steps, then pulled the hood off. Skyler blinked. And then her lungs filled with earth.

She was in a high-ceilinged concrete chamber with Sam at her side. In the middle of the room, two plastic chairs stood opposite each other. One was empty. Tied to the other, motionless and black-faced, was Angel.

Skyler bit down hard on the inside of her cheek to stop herself crying out. The need to say *something* to Angel – anything – burned a hole through her.

Sam pushed her into the unoccupied chair and cuffed her wrist to the chair leg. Skyler was too fixed on Angel to think of resisting, willing Angel to meet her eyes, to give her some sign, any sign, that she was okay – but Angel's empty gaze only flicked towards her momentarily, then darted away again.

"She's not doing great," Sam said conspiratorially, like Angel was a *thing*, like she couldn't hear or understand anything he was saying. "Dissociated, I guess. But we've got ways of dealing with that."

She's not dissociated. Skyler remembered Angel on her bedroom floor in Copenhagen, glassy-eyed, rigid, as though her body was in the room but her mind was locked in some personal hell a million miles away, her terror and isolation radiating across all that distance. This looked similar, probably, to someone who didn't know better. But Angel was still in the room. Skyler was sure of it.

Sam produced a thin metal rod from his belt and pressed a button on the handle, setting blue-white sparks crackling at the tip. An answering buzz of dread shot through Skyler: *no no no no no* –

Sam touched the tip of the cattle prod to Angel's leg. "Rise and shine, Angel."

Angel jerked. Skyler choked down a scream.

"Well, now. That got your attention." Sam squatted in front of Angel. "I've brought you a visitor."

Angel's chest heaved. She said nothing.

"Had a chat with some of your Northern pals," Sam went on. "Apparently you were a real mess up there. Not knowing whether Skyler here was dead or alive was tearing you apart, they said. Gosh. You must really care about her, huh?"

Angel stared into the middle distance. Sam heaved a sigh as if she were inconveniencing him enormously, and pressed the rod to her thigh again.

Skyler watched, hot and cold with horror, as Angel's face whitened and her body shook. Her mind buzzed like a trapped insect, helpless: *make him stop. You have to make him stop.*

Sam lowered the rod. "I asked you a question, Angel."

Another painful pause. Angel swallowed hard. "Yes," she whispered. "I care about her."

"Wow. It must really sting to see how little she cares about you, then. She didn't even flinch when she saw the state you were in yesterday. Doesn't seem too bothered now, come to that."

She can't believe that. She knows how I feel about her, she wouldn't –

Another crackle of electricity; the smell of scorched fabric filled the air. Skyler tried desperately to meet Angel's eyes, but Angel was vacant again, looking through her.

"Y – yes." Angel's voice caught. "It hurts."

A longer jab, a stronger smell of burning: skin as well as cloth. Angel convulsed with a choked whimper. When Sam took the rod away she slumped on the chair, eyes closed, breathing in ragged gasps.

"Look at her," Sam ordered.

Angel didn't move. Sam raised his hand and slapped her across the face. Skyler, straining against her cuffs, felt the crack of the blow as though she'd taken it herself, hating Sam, hating herself.

With a visible effort, Angel opened her eyes.

"Look. At. Her," Sam repeated. "She's watching you writhe in agony and she doesn't give a shit. If it were the other way around you'd be begging me to stop hurting her, wouldn't you? You'd do anything."

He sighed theatrically. "And all she has to do to make this stop is answer a few simple questions. She *knows* that. But she won't."

That's not true, Angel, it's not true – What should Skyler *do*? Begging Sam wouldn't stop him hurting Angel. If anything, he might redouble his efforts if he thought Skyler was close to breaking.

But if she did nothing... If she did nothing...

Angel wouldn't break, but what would be left of her by the time Sam figured that out? And if she survived, would she ever forgive Skyler?

"You can make it stop, though." Sam hovered the rod above Angel's thigh. "*She* won't help you, but you can help yourself. All you have to do... is talk."

Angel's eyes drifted shut again. Sam watched her for a few seconds, then pressed the rod back against her leg.

This time he held it there for what felt like hours, until Angel let out an awful moan and slipped sideways, her limbs spasming. Skyler bit the inside of her cheek until her mouth flooded metallic as Sam turned to her, eyebrows raised.

Behind him, Angel's eyes fluttered open. They were bloodshot and cloudy with pain, but she looked straight at Skyler and gave a tiny shake of her head.

Despising herself with every bone in her body, Skyler reached for the flat, numb insolence she'd worn as a mask in front of Daniel. She had to let Sam believe he was right. If he thought for one moment that she was going to choose Angel over him, he would take the choice away from her for good.

Sam spun back to Angel. "Fancy talking yet?"

Angel's breath rattled in her chest. "Dunno," she whispered. "Hate to interrupt you enjoying the sound of your own voice."

Sam stood very still, the muscles in his neck clenching. Then he jabbed the rod back against her leg.

Angel screamed, a raw, terrible scream that went on

and on, echoing round the room. Skyler had never heard her scream before, and nothing – not a broken arm, not a bullet in her stomach – had ever ripped through her the way that sound did.

When Sam finally took the rod away, Angel pitched sideways and vomited onto the floor. Sam stretched his arms over his head in a leisurely sort of way, and every nerve in Skyler's body went sharp with terror.

"She was always selfish," he remarked to Angel, who was gasping, barely upright. "Single-minded, if we're being charitable – but I'd call this pretty damn selfish, wouldn't you? Now. I know you're feeling sorry for yourself, but I want you to pay attention."

Angel didn't open her eyes. Sam tapped her arm reprovingly with the length of the rod. "That wasn't optional."

She opened one eye. Skyler tensed.

But Sam didn't raise the rod again. Instead, he strolled behind Skyler's chair.

Perhaps he was going to kill her after all.

"Watch carefully," he told Angel.

The cuffs around Skyler's wrists sprang free.

Skyler sat frozen as Sam re-emerged to stand between them, turning his back on her. "See?" He dangled the cuffs in front of Angel's nose. Skyler's mind whirred furiously: this had to be a trap. Could he really be this arrogant? "There's literally nothing to stop her coming to your rescue now. But she won't."

He dropped the cuffs on the floor. Skyler held her breath, watching his back. Could she really do this?

Should she do this? What if she blew their chance? What if –

Sam took a step towards Angel, and terror tightened like a vice around Skyler's chest. Inch by painful inch, she reached behind her. At last, her fingers closed around the weapon in her waistband.

Angel's breath rasped in her throat.

Sam raised the cattle prod.

Skyler leapt to her feet, fumbling with the slim black oblong – *fuck, how does this thing work –?*

Sam whipped round, eyes wide with astonishment, as she hurled herself at him. She jabbed the weapon against his chest, and he jerked backwards and hit the floor with a yelp that rose from shock to pain. Skyler dropped to her knees and held the black box to his side until his eyes rolled back and the noise that came out of his mouth was one long awful inhuman moan.

When she finally pulled away he was limp, his breathing stertorous and irregular. She stabbed her finger into his sternum and he didn't even flinch.

She lurched towards Angel, but Angel shook her head. "Him... first," she mumbled. "Cuffs. Weapon."

Skyler rolled Sam over and cuffed him with clumsy, trembling hands. He stirred and her stomach lurched. Fighting down bile, she pressed the box back against his chest.

"Radio," Angel croaked.

Skyler grabbed Sam's radio and the cattle prod and searched him for other weapons, finding a knife with a double-edged, serrated blade, and something that looked like a corkscrew and which she didn't want to think about even for a second. No gun. She could have really used a gun.

She scrambled towards Angel, whose arms were raw and bloody where she'd convulsed against the ropes. The cattle prod had scorched through her trousers, leaving a weeping reddish-orange burn on her thigh.

"I'm sorry." Skyler sawed frantically at the ropes, the words spilling out through hot, violent tears. "I'm so sorry, Angel, it's not true what he said, I swear, I just didn't know what to –"

Angel lifted a shaky hand to cup her cheek. It flopped back down almost immediately. "Shh. I know."

Skyler cut the final rope and Angel toppled into her arms. Skyler cradled her carefully, the way Angel had held her all those months ago when their roles had been reversed. "Please don't die, Angel, please –"

"Not... gonna die. Just... need a minute." Angel gulped. "What the hell's going on, by the way?"

"Long story. We have to find a computer, Angel. We have to get to Mack."

"Know where... he is?"

"No. But Faith managed to get some sort of tracking communication thing to me."

Angel raised a wobbly eyebrow. "...Not her, then?"

"Apparently not." Skyler forced herself to check on Sam. He still seemed properly out of it, but she'd seen too many people play dead to be convinced. Past experience had taught her that erring on the side of optimism in such situations was a terrible idea.

Which meant...

But if she killed Sam here, his colleagues would find his body before long. Then they would know she and Angel were coming for Mackenzie, and they would move him.

If Sam regained consciousness, on the other hand, he would want Skyler to find Mackenzie. Because when she did, he would use Mackenzie to punish her.

Whatever she did, she was gambling with Mackenzie's life.

Angel was pressing her forehead against her knees, flexing trembling fingers. Skyler couldn't ask her to help decide.

"I think we have to leave him alive," she said at last. "He'll make sure we find Mack."

Angel seemed to understand, or at least was too disorientated to disagree. Skyler peeled back the bandages on her wrist. "Faith. Faith!"

"I'm here, Skyler."

"I've got Angel. I need you to find me a computer *now*."

"It's only six o'clock, Skyler, it's too early. You can't –"

"Does this sound like a debate to you?" Skyler scanned the room frantically. The door was locked, like all the others, with an electronic keypad. "We can't get through the door, and we don't have a decent weapon." *We're fucked.* "We need another way out. Now."

46

BEST FOOT FORWARD

"Okay. Okay. Hang on." Faith took a deep breath. "Let me figure out your location. Are either of you hurt?"

"Angel is. She –" The words caught in Skyler's throat. "He kept shocking her."

"Shit. Is she conscious?"

"Here," Angel said faintly.

"Can you walk, Angel?" Faith asked.

"...Think so."

"Try for me, okay?"

"Give her a minute," Skyler snapped.

"You haven't got a minute. Angel, try to walk, please." Reluctantly, Skyler let Angel roll out of her arms.

"Skyler," Faith said. "Is *he* with you?"

Skyler hesitated. "Yeah."

"Dead?"

"...No." She wasn't at all sure Faith would be on board with her plan.

Faith, fortunately, let it go. "Tell me about the room."

409

Skyler tore her eyes from Angel, who had grabbed a chair and was hauling herself to her feet, her face scrunched with pain and concentration. "Uhh. Concrete floor. No windows. Two chairs. No air vents or anything else useful. Keypad on the door. Um, the ceiling's those plasterboard square things you get in offices, but it's too high to reach."

"And you're sure you can't, like, rewire the keypad or something?"

"I'm a hacker, Faith, not a magician."

Angel took a couple of wobbly steps and folded up onto the floor. Skyler's heart hurt, watching her.

"Skyler," Faith said urgently. "How high is the ceiling?"

"I don't know. High? More than normal ceiling height."

"Could you get up there if you stood on a chair?"

Skyler tried, standing on tiptoe. Her fingertips brushed the plasterboard. "I'm not tall enough. Angel might be, just."

"How long d'you think you've got before someone shows up?"

"Probably a while. I doubt Sam will have told anyone he was bringing us here. He wouldn't want to let anyone else near me."

Angel, dragging herself upright again, stopped dead. Fuzzy realisation dawned on her face as she frowned between Skyler and Sam's prone form.

Skyler looked away, her chest aching. She had to

explain to Angel somehow who Sam was, but how could she possibly find the words?

Faith timed her interruption well. "I'm looking at Mackenzie's notes from when he broke in before. There's a crawl space between each floor about three feet high. You can get into it through the ceiling tiles. That's your only route out other than the door, so Angel, you're gonna have to get up there and pull Skyler up after you." She hesitated. "Can you do that?"

Angel looked like she'd expected this. She took a deep breath and climbed to her feet again, a little steadier now. "To get out of here? Easy."

"You holding up okay?"

"Had worse."

Skyler was not at all sure this was true.

"Okay," Faith said. "I've got your location superimposed on a blueprint of the headquarters. The good news is I'm pretty sure there's a computer on your floor. The bad news is it'll take you at least twenty minutes to reach it. *Don't* rush. If anyone hears you –"

"Faith, if I don't get to Mack before the greycoats realise we're coming for him, he's going to die," Skyler said. "Do you understand? So I need you to be really, *really* fucking sure about this."

There was a long silence. "I understand," Faith said at last. "Get up there."

Skyler looked at Angel, who was swaying on her feet. She wanted to tell her – everything. Everything that had happened, everything she felt, everything she'd thought she would never get a chance to say.

Angel reached out and brushed her cheek. "Later," she murmured. "There'll be time later." She nodded at the chairs. "I'm not going to get enough height from those. Fancy giving me a leg up?"

Skyler clambered onto a chair and slammed the handle of the cattle prod into the nearest ceiling tile until it buckled and lifted. Uncertainty trickled across Angel's face as she stared up into the darkness.

Skyler scrambled down and grabbed her hand. "Hey. We can do this."

Angel squared her shoulders. "Course we can."

Skyler locked her fingers together to make a foothold and pushed Angel up, her arms burning with the effort. Angel wobbled, scrabbling, but then her foot slipped and she slid back down.

"Shit," she mumbled, sagging against Skyler. "Sorry."

Skyler cradled Angel's head against her shoulder. "It's okay. Breathe."

"Try again."

"You sure?"

Angel nodded, her face set with determination. This time, she managed to grab something inside the crawl space and swung wildly for a moment before dragging herself up with a groan.

"Okay?" Skyler whispered, as Angel's pale face appeared against the blackness.

"Never better. Here – don't try to hold the plaster-board, it won't take your weight. I'll grab your wrists and I want you to jump as high as you can. Sort of throw your-self in."

Skyler had a brief mental image of what Mackenzie's expression might have looked like had he been there to hear this suggestion.

Angel gripped her wrists. "On three. One, two –"

Skyler jumped, gritting her teeth as pain tore through her shoulders. She launched herself forward as Angel hauled her up and hooked her arms around a beam. Angel let go of her and toppled back, breathing hard.

Gasping, Skyler found her balance on her hands and knees and took stock of their surroundings. Their path through the building was a network of intersecting wooden beams that stretched away into blackness. Below them was a layer of the ceiling tiles Skyler had just punched through: flimsy and definitely not soundproof.

"All right?" Faith said out of her arm. Skyler yelped. If they made it out of here, she'd be having nightmares about talking body parts for years to come.

"Which way?" she asked Faith.

"Um. Which way are you pointing?"

"How the fuck should I know?"

"Fair enough. Just – move a few metres so I can figure it out."

Skyler crawled along the beam, getting her hands full of splinters. After a few seconds, Faith said, "Turn around. Not quite 180 degrees. Left a bit. No, the other left."

"You mean the right?"

"Just... the other way, all right? Keep going till I tell you to stop."

Skyler looked at Angel, who was deathly pallid in the

gloom. "What if I find you somewhere to hide and come back for you?"

"No." Angel shook her head frantically. "I don't – Don't leave me. Please."

Skyler scurried back to her, ignoring Faith's hiss of "Wrong way!"

"I'm not leaving you," she said fiercely, pressing her forehead against Angel's. "I'm not going anywhere without you."

Angel kissed her. "Let's go get Mack."

Between her thundering pulse and the whining terror in her ears, Skyler had no idea how much noise she was making. The only clues to their position within the building were the periodic bursts of sound that echoed far too clearly up through the ceiling: voices, footsteps, the odd chuckle. Each time Skyler froze, holding her breath, until the sound faded and it seemed safe to move on.

Then came a rumble of conversation: several different voices that grew louder as Skyler and Angel shuffled through the darkness. Skyler's heart turned to ice in her throat. There must be a room full of people beneath them. People who might easily notice a strange rustle or creak overhead, and turn to the person next to them, and ask, "Hey, did you hear that?"

Inch by painful inch along the narrow beam. Why was it that the harder she tried to be quiet, the more she moved like a concussed elephant? When this was over, she and Angel would live somewhere they could jump on the floorboards, run up and down the stairs, sing and shout. They would make a home somewhere they never had to be quiet or scared.

Skyler had never tried to ease any of the awfulness of the last few years by imagining the future. There had been no conceivable future – at least not one any better than whatever she was currently enduring. But now she reached for the tiny spark of hope, the possibility of something better, and held it close. There would be an afterwards.

The muffled buzz of conversation below fell silent. All Skyler's muscles locked together: *they're onto us, the alarms will go any moment* –

A male voice made a short remark. A woman replied. There was a ripple of laughter.

From behind, Angel touched her leg gently. *Keep going.*

A thousand years later, Faith murmured, "You're nearly there. The room's about three metres to your left."

Skyler manoeuvred herself into position, holding her breath, and felt through the darkness for the ceiling tiles beneath the beam she was balanced on. She'd hoped they would simply lift off, but they gave a little resistance. She fumbled for Sam's knife in her belt and prised the tile away.

She was light-headed as bright artificial light bled into the crawl space– but no sound met them, no indication they'd alerted anyone to their presence. When she peered through into the small office below, sure enough, a computer sat on a desk waiting for her.

"Are you in the right place?" Faith demanded breathlessly. "Is there a computer?"

Skyler exhaled. "Yes and yes. Nice one, Faith." Thank God Faith's sense of direction was better than her own.

The ceiling was lower here; evidently this was an area prisoners were never meant to see. Skyler dropped down into the office, still holding her breath, and turned to the computer as Angel followed her.

The terminal was logged on, but locked. Skyler prayed the process for administrator access was the same as it had been last time she'd hacked into the Board's system. She set to work.

The process hadn't changed. The terminal window looked just the same. Skyler grinned to herself. "There it is," she murmured. "I –"

The office door opened.

One second for the greycoat in the doorway to register the presence of intruders. One more to raise her gun. In the same moment, Skyler leapt to her feet, wrenching Sam's knife from her belt. In the next Angel was in front of her, snatching the knife –

– and the blade was buried in the greycoat's chest before her cry for help ever reached her mouth.

Angel didn't look at Skyler as they dragged the greycoat's body inside the office, but Skyler saw the tremor in her hands as Angel retrieved the dead woman's gun.

"We'd better move fast," Angel said, still not looking at her. "There might be another one along in a minute."

Skyler nodded shakily. "Faith?" she said, as she

started scouring the system. "If I give you a room number, can you find us a route to Mack?"

"Yep. Go ahead."

Where is it? Where is he?

Mackenzie, Thomas. Her stomach knotted painfully as his terrified countenance appeared on the screen. *Known Associates. Vulnerabilities. Family: Confirmed deceased. Legal status: None.* And a red flag that had her forcing down bile: *For enhanced interrogation. Supervision of Officer S. Linley.*

A couple of taps and Mackenzie's file was gone. She searched for Joss' and Lydia's next. *Current whereabouts unknown,* the files read. *Believed to be at large in the North.*

"Oh, thank fuck," she breathed to Angel. "The twins might still be okay."

She deleted their files, then her own and Angel's. If only everything could be so easy.

She turned her attention to the 'Site Security' settings. A warning box quickly informed her that administrator privileges were required to access the system that controlled the lock codes. This was annoying, but not unexpected, and Skyler was familiar with the necessary process – she'd built a similar program a couple of years ago for an international client whose motives she'd chosen not to examine too closely. And, of course, Sam had designed these encryptions. How many times had she hacked his computer when they were kids?

Apparently her skills had evolved more in the last three years than his. There had been nothing else she'd been able to bear thinking about. Sam had clearly been extending his interests into other areas.

Single-minded. His words to Angel rang in her head: *she was always selfish.* It hurt, absurdly. Was that really how he'd seen her?

Did it matter anymore?

"Faith?" she said. "It's not just the rooms that lock, is it? Different corridors and areas are locked off too."

"That's right."

"Okay. Got it."

She opened the terminal window and took a deep breath, waiting for the command prompts to appear.

"Fuck," she said.

Angel was at her side immediately. "What's wrong?"

Skyler stared at the lone command prompt: *enter passphrase.* "I... don't know what to do."

"Of course you do." Angel squeezed her hand. "This is what you *do*, Sky."

Skyler shook her head furiously. "You don't understand! I can't just – I need other programs to crack the password, and I don't have – they took my flash drive. I haven't got anything." Tears of pure frustration stung her eyes. "I could try to write something, but even if I got everything right first time it'd still take way too long – Fuck, why didn't I *think* of this?" And it was too late now. Too late, it was all over, they'd never reach Mackenzie in time, all three of them would die in this building –

"I'm sorry," she whispered, burying her head in her hands. "I'm so sorry, Angel, I can't –"

"No." Angel's voice was as strong and clear as

Skyler had ever heard it. She crouched beside Skyler, gripping her arm. "Look at me, Sky. Right now. Look at me."

Skyler lifted her head, tears spilling down her cheeks. "Angel –"

"You called him Sam."

Skyler closed her eyes. "Yes."

"Oh, Sky..." Angel's hand brushed her cheek, wiping away her tears.

"Doesn't matter." Skyler pressed her lips together. "It doesn't matter now."

"Yes, it does. Think, Sky. Is it possible he designed this part of the system?"

"I – I don't... Yes. Probably. I recognise his designs."

"Right. Okay. So... maybe he set the passwords?"

"Uh." Skyler scrubbed her face with her sleeve. "Maybe? It's possible."

"So, think. Was there anything he used when you were growing up? What was he interested in? Did you have any family jokes?" Only the faintest unsteadiness in Angel's words gave any hint at the pain behind them.

Skyler frowned. "I mean – I can think of a few things, but surely he'd never..." He wouldn't be that stupid, would he? Even if he'd held onto any part of his old life, his old identity, surely he'd have changed the password once he realised she was a threat?

"Try them," Angel said. "You said he was full of himself, right? I mean, if earlier was anything to go by..." Her lips twitched, just a little, but Skyler couldn't bring herself to smile back. "He already shut down remote access to the system. Maybe he thought that would be enough to keep you out."

Skyler nodded, though she didn't really believe it. But a final, defiant spark of hope flickered in Angel's blood-shot eyes, and Skyler had to try. If this was going to be the end of everything, she had to go knowing she'd fought for Angel and Mackenzie to her last breath.

Stupid sibling in-jokes. Secret code words they'd made up. The names of group chats with family and friends.

She kept her face blank and her movements controlled as she tried each one, desperate not to betray the way her heart pounded faster, sickening, with each failed attempt. She couldn't look at Angel. She couldn't meet her eyes and admit how badly she'd let her down.

Then she remembered the program she and Sam had written together before he left for uni. Operation Awkward Peregrine, which somehow had seemed hilarious at the time. It was nothing ground-breaking, just another chat program – but it had been secret, and it had been theirs, and they had used it all through his first year in Oxford and she had treasured it.

She almost couldn't bear to type the words.

She did it anyway.

She braced for the inevitable as she pressed return, already swallowing a sob of despair –

And a list of commands appeared in the terminal window, scrolling down the screen.

"I'm guessing that's good, right?" Angel said after a moment, as Skyler began to laugh through her sobs.

Skyler pulled Angel close and kissed her. "Yes. This is good."

She examined the commands, querying them to give her more information. At last, she found the ones she needed.

Carefully, she typed the new commands.

```
>> LOCKDOWN --global
>> ACCESS:DOORS --keypad only
```

She squinted at the screen. "Faith? I've locked down all the doors, changed the key codes and disabled the universal override system so each door has to be opened one at a time. Am I missing anything?"

"Disable lift operation, darling."

Skyler stared at her wrist. "Did you just call me darling?"

"That *wasn't* me." Faith sounded acutely embarrassed. "I... had some help from a friend."

"Aww. We're friends now," the strange woman said. "How delightful. Disable the lifts, sweetpea."

"On it."

"I must say," the strange posh woman commented, "I'm impressed. You think the hacker would work for me?"

"What, helping you sell people into slavery?" Faith said. "Probably not."

Skyler ignored them, her fingers hovering over the keyboard. She'd thought of one more thing.

```
>> ACCESS:SYSTEM
--local-only
--terminal=DTK852659
```

Now the whole system was locked down. If anyone wanted to change the door codes back, they would have to do it through this terminal.

She took the gun from Angel. "Stand back," she told her. "Cover your ears."

She fired into the base unit. It exploded in a shower of sparks and scraps of metal.

Somewhere nearby, an alarm began to howl.

47

THE LAST TIME

Skyler and Angel hurtled through corridors, fingers slipping against keypads, Faith yelling directions over the blare of the alarms – "Left at the end. Two floors up. Next right – no, not that way –"

Angel seemed determined to stay in front, but she was slower than usual and her legs shook every time she slammed up against a door. They reached the staircase that led to Mackenzie's floor and Skyler tried to dart ahead, but Angel hauled her back by her shirt. "Don't even think about it," she gasped. "I'm still the best bet in a fight."

"We'll come back to that later –" Skyler called, hurling herself after Angel. Then Angel opened the stairwell door, and a barrage of gunshots met her.

Skyler bolted up the last few stairs, burning lungs forgotten in an explosion of sharp, shiny terror. "Angel? Are you okay?"

Angel had already slammed the door on the hail of

bullets. "I'm fine." She studied the door, frowning. "That's... not ideal, though."

Skyler dragged her hands through her knotted hair. "Fuck. What do we do?" Their only path to Mackenzie was through that door, and if Sam had got to him before the lockdown –

Angel tilted her head thoughtfully. All at once she was in control again: calm, measured, certain. "Reckon there's five greycoats through there. Only two guns, though."

Skyler refrained from pointing out that two guns were more than enough.

"We'll have to use the door as a shield," Angel said decisively.

"You think that'll work?" Confident or not, Angel's reflexes were nowhere near as fast as usual.

Angel shrugged. "Done it before."

"Angel –"

Angel gripped Skyler's hand, holding her gaze. "We're all getting out of here together, Sky. End of story."

She was grey-faced, soaked with sweat, the bloodshot whites of her eyes an alarming contrast to her forest-green irises. She was the most beautiful thing Skyler had ever seen.

She pulled Angel close and kissed her, hard and urgent. "Together."

Angel kissed her back. "Together."

The thundering shots resumed the instant Angel cracked the door open and started firing blind, but it was clear no one on the other side dared get close to it. The door shook and rattled and splintered under the onslaught, but it was still on its hinges by the time the greycoats' final shots died away into ringing silence.

Skyler opened her mouth, but Angel raised a cautioning hand and closed her eyes.

Skyler held her breath.

At last, Angel held up one finger. *Behind the door*, she mouthed.

Skyler tensed, ready to shove Angel aside and launch through first, but Angel had already slammed the remnants of the door open and been rewarded with a grunt and a *thud* which was presumably the sound of someone taking a large piece of wood to the face. As Skyler followed her into the carnage of the corridor, the last surviving greycoat staggered out to meet them.

Angel spun into a high kick, sending his pistol sliding across the bloody floor, then kicked him again in the stomach. He was probably only Sam's age, Skyler thought as he slammed into the wall, which was no age at all, really, was it? Barely even a life.

Perhaps Angel was thinking the same thing, because she hesitated as she raised her gun. The greycoat was surrounded by the bodies of his colleagues, soaked in their blood, and the hatred in his eyes as he stared at Angel and Skyler was sharp and dark and bottomless.

For several long, breathless seconds, nobody moved.

Then the greycoat twitched towards Angel. She responded with a fluid, swinging right hook that sent him crashing back into the wall, then to the floor.

Stillness descended. Angel flexed her hand and grimaced.

"I didn't want it to be like this," she said quietly.

Skyler laid a hand on her shoulder. "I know." Her voice trembled. "We just have to get through this, and then it's over. I promise."

"Two more doors," Faith said into the quiet, and Skyler shook herself. "You're nearly there."

Nearly there.

And then, at last, they were outside Mackenzie's cell.

Skyler stopped dead.

"Why've you stopped?" Faith demanded.

"Just... shut up a minute, okay? I'm thinking."

There was a good chance Sam was already in that room. That when she got through that door she might not find Mackenzie behind it at all, but only his body.

She had been so certain, just hours earlier, that Sam would wait for her; that he, like Daniel, would want to make her watch as she lost all hope. But what if she was as wrong about him as he'd been about her? Skyler knew – not even that deep down – that she could be just as arrogant as Sam. And look where his arrogance had got him.

If she got this wrong. If Sam hurt Mackenzie. If she failed him as she had so many times in the last three years ... she would never forgive herself.

"What d'you think we should do?" Angel asked.

Skyler swallowed. "I guess... I guess we just walk in."

But Angel wasn't okay.

And she and Mackenzie had suffered so much, and it

was Skyler's fault. And maybe there hadn't been any way Skyler could have stopped it earlier – but right here, right now, there was.

"Don't come in with me," she said urgently, gripping Angel's hand. "Wait out here."

"Like hell –"

"No. I mean it. You're exhausted. I can't risk him hurting you again." She cupped Angel's cheek desperately. "Please, Angel. Please do this for me."

"You're sure?"

"I'm so sure."

Angel nodded slowly. "Here." She pressed Erin's Taser into Skyler's hand. "Shout my name, and I'll be right there with you."

"I know."

Angel kissed her gently. "See you on the other side."

48

THICKER THAN WATER

"Hey, little sis," Sam said, as Skyler opened the door. "Fancy seeing you here."

He was standing behind a pale, rigid Mackenzie in the middle of the cell, one arm hooked around Mackenzie's neck. His free hand, hanging by his side, clutched a pistol.

Skyler edged towards them, raising the cattle prod. "Sam –"

"Ah, ah –" Sam pressed his gun to Mackenzie's head. Mackenzie looked rather like he'd expected this. "Don't come any closer, Sky, or your boy's going to wish you hadn't."

"I dunno about the *your boy* thing," Mackenzie said through gritted teeth, "but he's definitely right about the other bit."

Skyler froze, her brain running a thousand frantic calculations. Sam was dishevelled, his eyes bloodshot, his face drawn and tight like Angel's had been. And he was watching her greedily, hungrily – but it wasn't him she was thinking about.

She met Mackenzie's eyes. "I'm so sorry, Mack," she said. "I'm so, so sorry."

She launched herself towards them. Everything happened at once.

Mackenzie yelled. Sam's gun fired into the ceiling. All three of them hit the floor in a shower of plaster dust. Skyler's foot tangled in someone's leg, wrenching at an angle it was almost certainly not supposed to as she struggled free, and a bolt of nauseating pain shot from her ankle all the way through her body. A nauseating *crack* resounded over the howl of the alarm that could only be the sound of a skull smashing against concrete –

And there was blood on the floor, seeping into the dust.

"Mackenzie?" Skyler screamed, scrabbling for Sam's gun through the starbursts of agony exploding in her vision. *"Mack?"* The cattle prod was no longer in her hand, shit, she must have dropped it –

She wrenched the horrible black box from her waistband instead, but Sam's arm slammed against hers and the box flew across the cell. And Mackenzie was crumpled on the floor, why wasn't he getting up, why wasn't he *saying* anything –

Sam's gaze landed on him, filled with a mix of grim determination and bitter vengeance that shot a bolt of dark, bloody rage through Skyler, as fierce and ugly as anything she'd ever felt. She punched him in the jaw and grabbed at his gun with a stinging hand. But he held it out of her reach, and no sooner did she have him pinned than he fought back again. She threw her weight into forcing his gun upwards instead, sending a stream of bullets into the ceiling and more plasterboard raining down on them, dust filling her nose and mouth, cloying, suffocating, and Sam was too strong, she couldn't keep him down –

Resorting to a trick that had almost worked for her on at least one occasion, she seized his weapon hand in both of hers and yanked his little finger back. He yelled, and she snatched the gun triumphantly as his grip loosened.

But she'd had to shift her weight to win it. Sam shoved her in the chest, throwing her off him, and lurched upright. As Skyler staggered to her feet, coughing, he looked down at Mackenzie's prone form and a calculating, satisfied grin spread across his face.

Steadily, holding Skyler's gaze, he lifted his foot and hovered it over Mackenzie's neck.

Skyler whipped the pistol up, training it on Sam's chest. "One more millimetre, Sam, and I'll put a bullet in you. I *mean* it."

He barked a scornful laugh. "Do you have any idea how ridiculous you sound?"

"Because you still think I'm the same kid you left behind. Just your little sister. But I'm not."

"Oh, don't be such a drama queen. I get it, Sky. Why you got caught up in all this – with all *these*." He cast a contemptuous glance down at Mackenzie. "You needed something to latch onto. But you've got me back now."

"You *don't* get it. When I started all this, I wasn't

looking for anything but a way out of Redruth's cellar. It wasn't me who needed something to latch onto, Sam."

His forehead creased, just a little. Carefully, he put his foot back on the floor.

Skyler knew better than to relax. For thirteen years, Sam had been her everything. And she wanted this conversation – she owed herself this conversation – but she wasn't going to pay for it with Mackenzie's life.

"You always had to be right," she said. "I *know* you, Sam. You were so convinced the Board were irredeemable, and then you sold out to them. For me. I can't imagine how devastating that must have been. And you couldn't bear it, could you? So you had to convince yourself you'd done the right thing."

She understood it all, in a fierce rush of terrible sympathy. Not for the man she'd seen do so many unforgivable things, but for the part of her brother who'd been so lost and so desperate that he'd turned himself into a monster to be able to keep breathing, and didn't even realise that was what he'd done.

She'd always believed, deep down, that he was better than her: smarter, stronger, braver. That if he'd endured the things she had, he would have coped so much better.

But here they were.

Sam's lip curled. He sniffed. "Very profound, little sis. Very deep."

"I know it hurts. I'm sorry."

He stared down at Mackenzie. Skyler held her breath, her finger hovering on the trigger of her gun.

"D'you remember when you were five and I was

eleven?" Sam said at last. "You were fascinated with coding even then. I'd sit you on my lap and show you stuff, and Mum'd go, 'Don't be daft, Sam, it's not gonna make a blind bit of sense to her.'" He gave a sad little chuckle. "But I always knew. I remember the first program you ever wrote. It was only simple, but you were chuffed to bits. And Mum went, 'Bloody hell, our Sky's gonna be trouble, isn't she?'"

Skyler couldn't move, couldn't speak, couldn't breathe.

"And when you started Year Seven. I'd see you wandering around on your own, all lost... I heard the other kids making fun of you. You were always good at looking like you didn't care, weren't you? Like a hedgehog, I used to think. All prickly, so no one would realise there was something soft underneath they could get at. And I'd walk home from school with you. My friends thought I was nuts at first, letting you hang out with us – but after a while they thought you were pretty cool, didn't they?"

Those were the things Skyler thought about too, the memories she'd clung to during the long years when she'd thought the sun would never rise again. "They were kind to me," she said distantly. "I was heartbroken when you all went off to uni, but they still messaged me. Sent me little memes and articles and stuff."

Sam's lips twisted into a crooked smile. "D'you remember the day you and Mum dropped me off at Oxford?"

How could she ever forget? "I cried and cried. It was

such a massive deal, a Northerner getting a scholarship like that... I knew I should be happy for you, but every time you looked away I just started crying again."

"Ha. I know. You weren't very subtle. And d'you remember what I told you when we said goodbye?"

She swallowed, but it didn't ease the jagged lump in her throat. "You said, 'No tears, little sis. I'll be back before you know it. And then you and I are going to take over the world.'"

Another flicker of a smile: not his impish, charming one, but one that was gentle, full of pain. It hurt her too, like a torn muscle in her heart.

He hadn't always been cold and hard and cruel. That wasn't the real Sam. If she found the right words, if she could only work out how to reach him, surely he would find his way back to her.

"And of course," he said, "you remember our little secret program. You remember Operation Awkward Peregrine."

The words took on a strange echo. Suddenly, everything seemed to be happening a long way away.

"Don't you get it, Sky? I wanted you to see. I wanted you to know, when you hacked the system. I never let you go."

And with a crash, it all made sense. "You... you weren't being careless." Skyler's lungs ached with something harsher than dust and debris now. "It was a message. You – you *wanted* me to see it?"

He laughed. "Credit me with a bit of sense, kid.

You're still my sister. It's still you and me. It always has been."

It always has been.

But her eyes were on Mackenzie again, limp and bloody at Sam's feet.

And she was making up a story, a fantasy to comfort herself so she wouldn't have to accept that she had to grieve for her brother all over again. Because this wasn't fair, any of it; hadn't she had enough pain? Wasn't there a quota somewhere that said she'd paid her dues, that nobody should have to mourn the same brother twice?

But fairness was a fairy tale too, the one people all over the South told themselves to justify turning a blind eye to the Board's actions. The one Sam told himself because he couldn't face the truth.

Skyler would not be that person. She would keep her eyes open, she would see truth, not fairness, because how could you ever hope to ease the pain in the world if you pretended it wasn't there?

"You tortured them," she said. "When you showed me what you were doing to Mackenzie – you were *pleased* with yourself. And the way you talked to Angel, earlier... You enjoyed it. You enjoyed hurting her."

Sam shrugged. "Are you telling me you didn't feel the tiniest bit satisfied when you blew up that lab? Four people died in that explosion, you know."

"I didn't fucking *gloat*! Even when I shot Redruth, after everything he did to me, I didn't *enjoy* it."

Sam stood very still, head cocked. Eventually, he sighed.

434

"I was... unfair on you," he said slowly. "You were always so grown up, I guess because we spent so much time together – sometimes I forget how young you really are. I hoped that if I gave you the chance to think things through sensibly, you'd be able to understand. But I see now that was too much responsibility for you. And I'm sorry, because this is going to cause you more pain, now, and that was never my intention. But it's my job to look after you. And even if you don't understand now, you'll thank me in the end."

He met Skyler's eyes, and dread filled her veins with the bite of frozen mercury. This wasn't vengeance. He really believed he was right.

No. This was vengeance, *and* he believed he was right.

"I understand why you did what you did earlier," he said. "I won't pretend I'm not hurt, but I accept that I made mistakes too, assuming you were more mature than you really are. So I want you to know, Sky – this isn't a punishment. I'm your brother, and I have to keep you safe. And that means teaching you that unacceptable behaviour has consequences."

He was looking at Mackenzie again.

"Sam," Skyler said. "If you even breathe on him, I'm going to pull this trigger."

He shook his head sadly. "You have to learn, Sky. There's only so much I can do to protect you if you insist on being difficult."

Skyler thought of the burnt-out tower block in Leeds, of Mackenzie crouching at her side as she crumpled onto

435

the freezing tarmac; of how she'd felt, in that moment, like she would never be whole again. Of the endless nights huddled in Redruth's cellar, forcing herself to focus on her laptop to keep from disintegrating, to keep from dreaming that Sam might burst in and carry her away. Nights when he'd been right upstairs, drinking and laughing with the man who'd tormented her.

"Listen to me, Sam." She forced the words out clear and steady through each discordant heartbeat. "You will *never* have me back after what you've done. Even if you take everything away from me – I'm never, ever coming back to you."

Sam stared at the floor, his face unreadable.

"Back in your cell," he said at last, glancing up at her. "The first time I saw you again. You told me you'd spent years dreaming about that moment."

She closed her eyes. "It was true."

"Well, then," he said quietly. "Don't you think that I did too?"

All the noise, all the pain, all the chaos faded away. The world narrowed to a pinpoint, the whole universe in this single tiny cell.

Don't cry, little sis. Please don't cry.

She'd cried so many tears for him. No more, now.

"Come on, Sky." Sam spread his hands. "Enough of this. I'm your family."

But he didn't look so sure of himself anymore. He looked like he was processing a new version of the world. And Skyler had thought she would be unsteady, hands shaking, stomach churning. But she wasn't.

"They're my family," she said. "They're my family now. And I won't let you hurt them."

"Skyler –"

Eyes open. No turning away from this.

"Sky –"

She met his eyes. "Goodbye, Sam."

49

FIRESTARTERS

The ring of the gunshot swept away Angel's haze of pain and exhaustion like a tornado. She shot to her feet, punching at the keypad on the door with clumsy, desperate fingers: "Skyler? Sky?" *No, no, no, please no –*

The door flew open. Skyler, her skin and hair chalky with dust and debris, fell into Angel's arms, sobbing. "Oh, God, you're okay. You're okay."

Angel pressed her face into Skyler's neck, her heart pounding. "I'm okay. But –"

Two bodies lay on the floor behind Skyler. The grey-coat, the one who'd tortured her, was very definitely dead. And Mackenzie... Mackenzie...

"There's something wrong with Mack," Skyler whispered. She stumbled over to him, crouched down and shook his shoulder. "Mack? *Mack?* Please, Mackenzie –"

Mackenzie, caked in bloody dust, sat up. "'M okay." He raised a hand to his neck. "Ow. Am I bleeding to death?"

Dizzy with relief, Angel peered at the three-inch laceration below his ear. "No. You're going to have a good scar, though."

Skyler wiped her eyes and smacked his arm. "You scared the shit out of me, you idiot."

He gave her a slightly concussed grin. "I was awake for most of it. Just a bit useless, so it seemed like a good idea not to let on to *him*. I was gonna do something cool like jump up and whack him, but then I kind of thought my head might explode, so..."

"Can you move now?" Skyler held out a hand to haul him up, keeping her eyes resolutely averted from the grey-coat – Sam's – body. "Because I'd *really* like to get out of here."

"Sky –?" Angel murmured.

"I'm fine." Skyler tried to put her weight on her right foot and gasped. "Except my ankle might be broken. Fuck."

"Sky –"

Her eyes were filled with deep, endless weariness as they met Angel's. "I had to," she said.

Mackenzie put an arm around her and she sagged against him, or at least they sagged against each other. "Please tell me you guys have some idea how we get out of here," he said.

Angel considered this best left unanswered.

Skyler raised her wrist to her mouth. "Faith, now would be an *awesome* time for some good news."

"Get to the roof," Faith said out of Skyler's wrist. Mackenzie yelped and almost dropped her.

439

Skyler scowled. "I was sort of hoping we'd get out of here alive."

"Just shut up and get to the roof."

The headquarters were ten storeys high. Mackenzie's cell was on the third floor, and although she was gritting her teeth and trying not to show it, it was clear the stairs were hard going for Skyler. Angel stayed close behind her, keeping a hand on her back. She'd lost touch with her own body hours ago, sealing the pain and the weakness off somewhere they couldn't get in the way. There would be a payback, but that was a problem for tomorrow, if tomorrow ever came.

Finally, finally, they reached the door to the roof – Christ, Angel hoped it actually did lead to the roof. She seized Skyler's hand, stabbing at the keypad with clumsy fingers, and slammed her body against the door as hard as the remnants of her strength would allow. Some distant part of her started to laugh, an exhausted, semi-hysterical laugh of sheer relief, as it gave way under her weight.

The three of them tumbled out onto a flat roof in warm twilight air and promptly collapsed in a heap.

"Brilliant." Skyler's tone was as dry as it was possible to be whilst threaded all the way through with pain. "Was there a next bit to that plan, d'you reckon?"

Angel forced herself to sit up and scan the horizon. Chaos had erupted on the ground outside the headquarters: dozens of dark figures milled around, their yells faint by the time they reached Angel's ears. To the west, a glowing sliver of orange was all that remained of the day.

To the south lay the thicket of barbed wire that protected the headquarters, and beyond it, the city of Birmingham.

And to the North was the Wall: twenty-metre-high concrete slabs adorned with razor wire, stretching as far as the eye could see. The squat oblongs of the watchtowers were dotted at intervals along it, their searchlights sweeping the barren ground either side.

After all that, they were still no closer to bringing the damn thing down.

Mackenzie lifted his head and sniffed, frowning. "Hey. Can you guys smell burning?"

Angel tried to connect herself back to her body. There were definitely more than a few wires loose – but Mackenzie was right. Something thick and acrid was drifting through the twilight air towards them.

She stumbled to the edge of the roof, ignoring the stabs and twinges that suggested her body was getting back in touch to communicate that enough was just about enough. Sure enough, dark, bitter smoke was billowing from the windows below.

"What's happening?" Mackenzie asked, as she limped back to them.

Angel tried to piece together the limited information her brain was prepared to offer her. "The computer," she said at last, to Skyler. "You shot the computer."

Mackenzie looked impressed. "Sky shot a computer?"

The air moved around them. Angel snapped her head up, back in her body with a crash as a rhythmic, clacking whir drowned out the distant yelling from the ground.

All three of them stared at the dark bulk of the helicopter hovering above them.

"Fucking *hell*," Mackenzie said.

Skyler's face had gone blank, as though this was one thing too many to process. Angel grabbed her hand. "This isn't over, Sky. Do you hear me? I won't let it be over."

Rattling bursts of machine-gun fire echoed upwards. A hatch opened in the side of the helicopter.

Wait. Why would the Board fire at their own helicopter?

A rope ladder dropped from the hatch. Faith's head appeared, holding her glasses on with a finger. "*Get in!*" she yelled.

They scrambled to their feet. Mackenzie held out a hand to Skyler. Angel jerked herself out of her stupor and shoved him towards the ladder. "We've got this. Go."

He hesitated, then catapulted himself across the rooftop. Concussion robbed his movements of their usual grace, but he swung himself up the ladder as easily as if it were a climbing frame.

Angel wrapped her arm around Skyler. "One last push. Stay with me."

"You first," Skyler gasped, as they staggered towards the ladder. "If I'm too slow, you need to –"

"Not a fucking chance. I'm right behind you."

The ladder swung wildly under their combined weight and Skyler's clumsy movements. Angel could feel the last of her strength leaving her body like water down a drain as she dragged herself up, staying as close behind

Skyler as she could get so that Skyler would feel her there, would know Angel wasn't going to let her fall.

Faith grabbed Skyler's arms and heaved her inside. A sob of relief rose in Angel's throat.

Just a couple of feet to go. God, she was so *tired*. The final rungs might as well have been a thousand-foot climb; it was taking every last scrap of energy not to simply open her fingers and let everything fall away.

Firm hands gripped her wrists. She opened her eyes.

"I've got you," Skyler said. "I've got you."

And then she was in Skyler's arms, and someone had slammed the hatch shut. Beside them, Faith and Mackenzie clung together, half-laughing, half-sobbing.

"Aww," a dry, posh, and oddly familiar voice drawled, as the helicopter took flight. "Almost makes me want to cry."

Angel looked up and froze. But in the next second, the shock of being confronted by Leila Yousefi's sarcastic grin vanished like water on a hotplate.

"*Erin?*" she mumbled.

"Sorry," Skyler said wearily. "Wasn't really time to explain."

Mackenzie looked between them all, wide-eyed. "I have so many questions," he said.

50

BREATHE

There was a *lot* to process.

Through the sheer overwhelming amazement that everyone was actually still alive, Mackenzie was a little ashamed of just how relieved he was to see Faith. As hard as he'd fought to convince himself she would never have betrayed them, the fear had lingered, the nuclear weapon in the arsenal of his treacherous doubt: *what if you got it so, so wrong?*

It wasn't exactly the best feeling in the world finding out Kimura had betrayed them instead, but it definitely felt a lot less personal.

The discussion about what exactly they should do next happened in a blur between Faith, Leila and the tall, posh woman who was apparently Erin Redruth and yet somehow appeared to be an actual human being and not a murderous supervillain. At one point the idea of retreating to Redruth's mansion was floated, at which Skyler raised her head just long enough to state flatly,

"No offence, but I'm not setting foot in that bloody place," before flopping back down.

Leila, it turned out, had a town house in Oxford, which seemed as good a place as any to hole up and wait for the apocalypse to arrive. Erin pointed out that all of them probably needed a doctor, but Angel mumbled, "Just need fluids and sleep. I'll splint Skyler's ankle when I can think straight."

By the time they were all stood, swaying with exhaustion, in the hallway of Leila's house, the air was thick with unspoken words. Mackenzie could barely stand, even with Faith propping him up. All he wanted to do was shower, eat, and then sleep for about a thousand years. It turned out the aftermath of an event nobody had expected to escape alive was something of an anti-climax.

"Think we'll be safe here?" he managed eventually.

"For now." Leila put her dainty nose in the air and sniffed. "Good Lord, go take a shower, all of you. Nobody's using my sheets in this state."

"Charming," Skyler muttered.

Leila bustled off down the hall. "My house, my rules, darling."

Angel turned to Faith. "Thank you," she said. Then, to Mackenzie's – and, from her expression, Faith's – utter astonishment, she hugged her.

"Yeah," Skyler said. "Thanks. Sorry about all that shit I gave you." She looked for a moment like she might follow this up with another, less heartwarming sentiment, probably along the lines of, 'but obviously I was right about the Agency all along.' They were never going to hear the end of *that*.

Fortunately, she seemed to decide instead that she'd done enough talking. She and Faith eyed one another.

"Uh," Faith said. "Do we hug too?"

Skyler gave her a look Mackenzie knew only too well. "We don't hug."

"Ah. Right. Of course."

Leila reappeared with a stack of enormous fluffy towels. "Rooms are that way and that way. En suite, obviously."

"Mack," Skyler said quietly, as he and Faith set off down the hall.

He turned back. "Mm?"

"Don't get stuck in there, okay? In the shower, I mean. Just... you know."

He did know. And once upon a time he would have been ashamed, even humiliated, that she'd mentioned it – but the only thing in his friend's eyes was concern, not contempt, and when he met them, the only thing that stirred in him was gratitude. "Thanks, Sky."

In the end, his body's increasingly persistent demands trampled the poisonous little hiss until it was barely audible. When it did grow louder as he shut the shower off, he paused for a moment with his hand on the tap and thought: *seriously, what do you actually think is going to happen if you get out?* The most likely scenario seemed to be that he might get a drink of water that definitely wasn't poisoned, and the opportunity to be horizontal as quickly and for as long as possible. Neither of these things seemed like a problem.

"Hi," Faith murmured, when they were finally face to face in one of Leila's impossibly comfortable beds.

Less than three days since they'd parted in Copenhagen, and she'd grown so much older and wearier. It wasn't just lack of sleep haunting her features. The world looked different to her now, and it could never go back to the way it had been before.

He reached for her hand. "Hi."

"I'm sorry," she whispered. "I didn't know, I swear. I didn't know what Kimura was going to do."

"Hey." He wrapped his arms around her. "You've got nothing to apologise for. You saved us."

"I was so stupid –" Faith's voice cracked. "I just bought everything they told me."

He stroked a curl from her forehead. "What happened in Copenhagen?"

"You really want to know now? You should sleep."

But he didn't want to sleep. He'd been so close to losing everything: Skyler and Angel, Faith, his mind, his life. And now everything was safe and quiet for a few precious, fragile moments that might be over in a heartbeat, and he wasn't ready to let go of any of it, even temporarily. Not when it could so easily be permanent.

"Tell me the story first," he said.

Faith laughed in the way that people did when they were trying not to cry. "Christ. Where do I even start?"

"Well," Mackenzie said, when she reached the bit about Kimura. "Fuck that guy."

"Ha. Skyler said something similar."

"I bet." He pressed his forehead to hers. "I'm so sorry about Hahn. I know she meant a lot to you."

Faith shook her head. "After everything you've been through, I shouldn't be... It's ridiculous. I shouldn't be upset about this."

"Uh, *what*? The woman who was like a mother to you gets murdered by her closest colleague, they were both up to their eyeballs in all kinds of morally dubious shit, and that's just supposed to be nothing? Bollocks. I haven't got the monopoly on angst, Faith. There's plenty to go around."

She laughed, a little, but then her face clouded. "Hahn... saved me. I was stuck in this miserable little hole of an existence, and she believed I was worth more, and she made me believe it too. And then..." She blinked rapidly. "I poured my whole life into the Agency. I *trusted* her and Kimura. If they could be so wrong... I don't know who I'm supposed to be now, Mackenzie. What does it mean that Hahn chose me?"

"It means that she could see you were remarkable. She didn't choose you because you were cruel, Faith. She didn't even tell you the truth about what the Agency was doing. She knew you wouldn't be okay with it."

"But maybe she hoped I'd turn into someone who would be."

"Do you really see that happening?"

He was bursting to reassure her, to tell her whatever she needed to believe to feel better. And it would have been so easy – but it would have been meaningless to her.

She would have found a way to dismiss it, to convince herself he wasn't seeing some fundamental part of her that made it all a lie. She needed to be able to say it to herself instead.

"No," she said at last. "I'm never going to be that person. I would never have been that person."

He kissed her lightly. "I believe you."

A smile flickered across her face. "I know you do. Anyway. How are you?"

Great. Now he had to talk about himself. And what was he going to do? Hide behind sarcasm, make a flippant joke about concussion?

Or was he going to be honest?

"I really thought I was going mad," he admitted. "They... that guy..." He couldn't get his head around the fact that the greycoat who'd tortured him had been Skyler's brother. "He knew about the OCD, and Christ, he *really* figured out which buttons to press. I thought I was going to lose my mind."

"But you didn't."

"I've no idea how. The OCD was so... It drowns out everything else, when it's that bad. There's this tiny bit of you flailing around underneath going, *uh, hang on, this is a bit nuts* – but it's like you can't trust anything you think you know. He almost convinced me to tell him everything. I don't know how I held on."

"I do." She said it with absolute certainty. "It's because you're stronger than it is. You're so much stronger than you think."

He had never been able to believe it. How could carrying such fear and doubt be anything but a weakness?

But maybe fighting it had made him stronger.

"Well," he said. "I guess that makes two of us."

"Mackenzie?"

"Yeah?"

"I know you probably wondered if it was me who'd sold you out. That's what I would've thought. You worry so much about stuff being your fault, and the transmitter didn't work, I couldn't tell you... Don't say anything," she added, as he began to protest. "I just want you to know that I get it and it's okay, and you don't need to feel guilty or apologise. Okay?"

He thought about it; about denying or explaining or apologising anyway.

Then he nodded. "Okay."

"Okay. Awesome."

He stroked Faith's cheek. "You were so, so brave. I mean, I didn't have a choice. You did, and you basically threw yourself headfirst into the scariest shit imaginable."

"It wasn't a choice. I couldn't have lived with myself if I'd left you all there. I've never been so scared in my life. Especially the whole Leila thing. I honestly thought I'd gone mad too."

"That was *such* a badass move. How'd you even convince her to help? Hahn made her sound like a total sociopath. I guess we only got half the story, huh?"

"No." Faith sounded thoughtful. "I think we got the whole story. Leila said herself she doesn't have a conscience. I don't know why she helped. I don't think she'd ever tell me the truth anyway. I've got a feeling she might disappear now all the fun's over."

"She's grown on you, hasn't she?"

Faith smiled. "I know she doesn't give a shit about me, but we wouldn't have stood a chance without her. And she was good with Erin. I think she got her, somehow."

"That..." Mackenzie shook his head. "You are incredible. Going to Erin Redruth? That's even scarier than Leila."

"It was the only way I could think of to get to you quick enough. So I figured I'd put all my money on that."

He raised his eyebrows. "You've never gambled in your life, have you?"

She laughed and buried her face in his shoulder. "Not even once."

Sleep. Skyler and Angel fell into a bed the size of a small country, and Angel was asleep in seconds. Skyler kept jolting awake, echoes of screams and gunshots fading as the fog cleared, a new stab of pain piercing her ankle every time she moved – but all that was nothing but background noise. It was Angel she reached for each time she surfaced, her heart thudding urgently until she'd reassured herself Angel was still warm, still breathing, still nestled in the curve of Skyler's body. Only then could she fall back into sleep, wishing for some spell to preserve this cocoon of warmth and peace and safety.

Twelve solid hours later, Angel rolled over in Skyler's

arms and a slow, sleepy smile spread across her face like the late morning sunshine streaming through the gaps in the curtains.

"Hey." Skyler touched her cheek. "How're you feeling?"

Angel stretched and groaned. "Really sore, but a million times better. I'm starving."

She was so pale she was virtually translucent, her face drawn with the shadow of pain, but some of the light was back in her eyes. She was still Angel.

Skyler smiled back at her. "Well, that's got to be a good sign."

"How're you doing?"

"Fine. Just glad you're okay. Ankle's a bit sore." Her ankle was killing her, but that was irrelevant.

Angel gave her a look that said, *you're not getting out of it that easily.* "I didn't just mean physically."

Damn. "Yeah, I know. I'm still fine."

"You don't want to talk about it."

"Not right now." Preferably not ever. "Hey, I'm sorry I didn't tell you about Erin. It must've been a hell of a shock."

"In the circumstances, I think I'll get over it." Angel shook her head. "I can't believe Faith actually went to her and Leila. That took some nerve."

"I know. I feel a bit bad for giving her such a hard time." Annoyingly, she might have to consider the possibility that Faith was good enough for Mackenzie after all.

She hesitated. "I think maybe you should talk to Erin, you know."

"Urgh. That'd be the world's awkwardest conversation."

"Uh huh. You should still do it."

"Hmm. I'll think about it."

"You know I'm right."

Angel kissed her on the nose. "No comment."

"Angel..." Skyler took a deep breath. It would have been nice if she'd had any sort of clue what to say next, but since all she knew was that she desperately needed to say it, she was going to have to wing it. "I –"

A soft knock at the door, and she didn't know whether to be grateful or disappointed. "Come in," she called.

Mackenzie shuffled in, and relief unfurled in Skyler's chest like new leaves into sunlight. She grinned at him. "Get over here. How're you feeling?"

He plonked himself down on the bed. "Concussions are the worst. They're like a hangover without any of the good bits. There's food downstairs, though. We should've partnered up with the dark side sooner."

He sounded pretty normal, but as he fiddled absent-mindedly with the bandage on his neck, Skyler's insides were suddenly knotted with wire. How could she possibly make amends for what Sam had done? *Hey, sorry my brother tortured you* – how the hell did you start *that* conversation?

"Are you okay?" she asked instead. "I was worried about you."

He grimaced. "Not gonna lie, it was a bit dire. But you know... I don't think I went mad. Actually" – he grinned – "I kind of feel like I could handle anything now. I'm more worried about you."

He and Angel were both eyeing her in a way she couldn't make any sense of. The wire round her organs tangled and snarled. "I'm sorry," she said, knotting a strand of hair round her fingers. It was so *inadequate*. "I'm sorry Sam was... I'm sorry he hurt you both. I'm sorry I didn't stop him. I'm sorry –" *I'm sorry he survived when you both lost everyone. I'm sorry everything's so unfair.*

"I'm sorry your brother turned out to be such a dick," Mackenzie said cheerfully, and Skyler lifted her head in amazement. "C'mon, Sky," he added, as she let out a startled laugh. "Don't you think we know you're not him? I'm just sorry you had to –"

"No. Don't be. I did what I had to do." She glanced up at them. "He would've come after us. After you. I meant what I said. You're my family now. I'm never going to regret that decision."

"Ugh." Mackenzie gave an exaggerated eye-roll. "I guess this means I, like, owe you my life or something. There's easier ways of getting me to owe you a favour, you know."

Angel giggled, and it was exhausted, but it was real, and all at once there was hope in the world again. Skyler grinned and pushed her hair back from her face. "Where's Faith, anyway? Any word on what's happening outside?"

"She's downstairs with Leila and Erin, trying to get

online. They all seem to be getting on weirdly well. I haven't been down yet. Want to come?"

"Sure. Uh, we'll come find you in a sec, yeah?"

Mackenzie hopped off the bed with a knowing grin. "See you."

He closed the door behind him. Angel stretched and sighed. "I guess we do need to go face reality, huh?"

Skyler brushed her arm. Her heart was fluttering again; it still couldn't tell the difference between *fucking awful scary* and *possibly exciting scary*. "Wait a minute?"

Angel looked at her. "Everything okay?"

"Yeah. Um. I was just – before, I was thinking about all the stuff I didn't say before we left Copenhagen, that I didn't know how to say, and how I wished you knew that stuff, and – well, I still don't know how, but I want to say it anyway, if that's okay, before all the shit hits the fan again. Is that okay?"

Angel raised her eyebrows, a hint of amusement at the corners of her mouth. "Go for it."

"Right." Skyler swallowed. Why wasn't there a program for this stuff? Maybe she should write one. "Well. Angel, you – I – Okay. For a really long time, I didn't think I'd ever be capable of feeling... certain things. Everything was so awful for so long, and I had to shut myself off just to keep going – I know I don't have to tell you, I know you understand that. And then all this happened, you and me and Mack, and..." Why couldn't she feel her legs? How was this somehow nearly as terrifying as facing down a greycoat? "And it's like... I found the last good thing in the world. Like I walked

455

out of a bunker in the middle of a nuclear winter and found something growing. What I mean is – I love you, Angel. I love you. And I love Mack too, obviously, but in, like, a *totally* different way. And I just... needed you to know."

Finally, thank God, she'd run out of words. She stared at the sheets, every inch of her brain a perfect storm, until Angel's fingers brushed her cheek, coaxing her head up.

Angel's eyes were bright, luminous, like she was holding back laughter, like she was so full of joy she might burst. "I love you too," she said quietly.

Skyler threw her arms around Angel and kissed her. Angel responded enthusiastically. After a minute, she pulled back, grinning. "And I love Mack too, of course, but in, like, a *totally* different way..."

Skyler laughed and rolled her eyes. "Give me credit for trying, at least."

Angel leaned in again. "Oh, you definitely get credit for that."

51

DAYLIGHT

Angel and Skyler emerged into the hallway hand in hand. There was a glow in Angel's chest, like a ray of the morning sun had found its way inside her.

She didn't want to face reality. She wanted to stay in this bubble with Skyler and pretend there was nothing else in the world. But they still had work to do, and all of them knew it.

Skyler squeezed her hand. She looked up.

Erin was hovering halfway up the stairs, her hair spilling from an untidy knot. "Oh." She shifted from foot to foot. "How are you guys? How's your arm, Skyler?"

"Terrible," Skyler said, deadpan. "Probably needs amputating."

Erin's lips twitched like she wasn't sure whether she was allowed to laugh. "And you, Angel?"

Angel had no idea what to say. "I'm... okay."

Skyler squeezed her hand again, then let go gently.

"I'm gonna go annoy Mack." She raised a meaningful eyebrow and disappeared before Angel could protest.

Angel and Erin stood, not quite looking at one another.

"Thank you," Angel said at last. "For what you did."

Erin fiddled with her ponytail. "Leila's got a balcony through the master bedroom. Fancy some fresh air?"

Not really. Angel had dreaded facing Erin once the murk of exhaustion and pain had cleared; she'd expected it to bring a whirlwind of terror that would sweep her from the present, pitch her back into the horrifying unknown. But here Erin was in front of her, and Angel was tense, uneasy – but she was anchored. She was still herself.

She could do this.

They emerged into a warm spring morning. Angel leaned against the balcony railing, staring at the blossom and bright new leaves below.

After a moment, Erin leaned against the railing too.

"I know," she said, glancing at Angel. "In case you wondered. I know what you did."

Angel said nothing. What was there to say?

"And... I know why. I can't imagine it'll make any difference to you, but I didn't know that... about what he did... until Leila and Faith told me yesterday. And I'm so sorry. I'm sorry I was so blind. I'm sorry for what I caused you."

Angel found her voice. "No." It was Erin's eyes that she'd feared most. But when she looked into them, she didn't see Redruth at all. Erin was just Erin. "You're not responsible for what he did. I don't want you carrying that."

Silence.

"I can't tell you I'm sorry," Angel told a pot of snapdragons on the patio below. "I can't apologise for what I took from you."

"I know."

"Skyler told me what you did. You were brave. And to do that for us, knowing what we'd done. Knowing we'd hurt you."

"Not as much as he hurt you both." Erin sighed. "So how about neither of us apologise?"

Angel managed an almost-real smile. "Deal."

More silence.

"Hell of a way for me to meet your girlfriend," Erin said at last.

Angel laughed. "You know, I kind of think you two would get on."

"I've got a feeling you're right. She's fierce, isn't she?"

"That's one way of putting it."

"It's wonderful," Erin said softly. "That you have something good. I'm so glad."

"So what happens to you now?" Angel asked. "What will you do?"

Erin snorted. "Probably get arrested. I've no idea."

"Well, I'm sure Leila could pull the necessary strings to get you out of the country."

"She says you shot her."

"Ah." Angel winced. "Reckon she's still mad about that?"

"Strangely not. She seems quite taken with you. I reckon if you ever wanted a career change, she'd sort you out."

Angel grinned. Eventually, when Erin didn't say anything else, she turned to head back inside.

"Angel?" Erin sounded uncertain, like the name was strange and unfamiliar to her.

Angel stopped.

"I... have no right to ask this," Erin said to her back. "I know that. But – I think you'll understand..."

Angel closed her eyes.

"You feel lost," she said. "Your life as you knew it is over, and you don't know where to start picking up the pieces. Or even if they're worth picking up."

"...Yes. Something like that."

Angel turned to face her. "You're not him, Erin. You know that, don't you?"

Erin let out a long sigh and lifted her face to the sky. "I never thought I was. I just thought I was... his. That that was all I'd ever be."

And Angel had thought maybe she'd be consumed with rage. That she would blame Erin, for all she knew, logically, that none of it was her fault.

But she didn't.

"I don't have an easy answer," she said. "I wish I did. All I know is... it happens by putting one foot in front of the other, one by one, over and over. And on the days when it's too hard to do that, you stand still, and you focus on breathing until you've got the energy for another step. And at some point, you realise you don't have to concentrate so hard on where you're putting your feet, and you can look up and figure out where you're going.

"It's not magic. It's hard. It's so hard sometimes it feels like it's going to kill you. But in the end... it doesn't."

* * *

Skyler and Mackenzie found Faith and Leila sitting at an island in a huge kitchen full of sunlight and chrome, a vast pot of what must have been eye-wateringly expensive coffee and an array of bread and cereal spread out on the counter. Faith's laptop was open in front of her.

Skyler hoisted herself onto a stool and grinned at Mackenzie as he cut her a massive chunk of bread. A small, bright bubble rose inside her as Angel slipped into the room. She looked calm, somehow: no wide eyes or bloodless face, and the sight of her settled something in Skyler too.

"Any news?" she asked Faith, as Angel limped towards them and put an arm around her.

"Well, all the Southern TV stations are out," Faith said. "No surprise there. The power's been on and off, too. It's on right now, though, and – well."

She turned the laptop towards them. A Canadian news channel was playing, the reporter sombre as she announced: "An emergency meeting of the UN Security Council has voted tonight to engage in military action against the government of the United Kingdom, after fresh evidence emerged of serious human rights abuses carried out by the regime. Air strikes targeting military bases are expected to begin by morning. Following the vote, the UN Secretary General gave this statement..."

Skyler put down the jam jar in her hand. All the feeling seemed to have disappeared from her legs, which was quite impressive considering the state of her ankle.

"Um." Mackenzie ruffled his hair in a bewildered sort of way. "Did... did they just say what I thought they said?"

"Loud and clear, sweetpea," Leila said. "Faith's already played that clip seventeen times, just to be certain."

"But... how? How come they suddenly have the evidence to act, after all this time?"

"Kimura," Faith said distantly. "He must have handed over the Agency's files. Everything they could have needed was in there."

"He put things right," Angel said.

Faith sighed. "He tried."

"Plus," Leila interjected brightly, "that fire you started in the headquarters... Wasn't the whole reason you went on that ridiculous mission that they'd central- ized all their IT systems? There was a *lot* of information in that building."

"Like everyone on every watch list," Skyler said slowly.

"Holy shit." Angel's eyes widened. "You're right."

Leila yawned and stretched. "Smart move, little one. You've just wiped the entire country's slate clean."

Skyler opened her mouth to tell Leila exactly what she thought of being addressed as 'little one', and then decided maybe that wasn't an immediate priority. "If anyone asks," she said instead, "it was totally intentional."

"They'll have backups somewhere remote," Faith mused, as Erin came in and pulled up a stool beside Leila. "But I expect those will be in some sort of secure location..."

"Like a military base," Angel murmured.

Skyler was oddly numb, like everything might fall apart in the next whisper of breeze. This couldn't really be happening. Could it?

"So what happens now?" Mackenzie said. "What do we do?"

"Well." Leila placed a solemn hand on her chest. "I for one feel like this whole experience has really made me re-evaluate things. It's time I made some changes. Devoted myself to making the world a better place."

They all stared at her.

"Wow," Faith said at last. "You actually almost had me for a moment there."

Leila laughed. "I expected you to go straight for that. I don't suppose you'd like a job, would you? I think we make a good team."

Faith looked for a second like she might actually be considering it. "No," she said, finally. "I mean, thanks – I think – but it's time I went my own way."

Leila shrugged. "Any time you change your mind, sweetpea."

Skyler looked at Erin. "What about you?"

Erin's lips twisted. "Well, I can't go back to the estate."

"Sure," Faith said sympathetically. "It must be full of awful memories."

"I suppose." Erin gave them a crooked smile. "But also... I might have just told the UN that the Board are storing weapons there."

As one, Faith and Leila burst out laughing.

Angel gave Erin a small smile. "Well played."

The corner of her mouth twitched. "It seemed like an effective solution to a lot of problems."

"Well." Angel turned to Skyler and Mackenzie. "What about us?"

Skyler hesitated. What about them? The idea that they might all make it this far had seemed so wildly inconceivable that now they were here, the only real option seemed to be, as ever, 'keep making it up as we go along'.

She reached for Angel's hand. "I really, *really* wish we were done with all this." God, how she wished they were done. "But I don't think we are yet, are we?" She looked at Mackenzie. "Remember what I told you before? That we'd come back one day and take the Wall apart?"

"I remember."

"Well, maybe that's not gonna happen today. But I think we'll get there, don't you? Maybe even someday soon."

Mackenzie grinned. "Absolutely."

Angel squeezed her hand. "Me too."

"Right," Skyler said. "Then let's go and get that bloody wall down."

EPILOGUE
MAPS FOR THE GETAWAY

Skyler had thought Mackenzie was mad when he first suggested it.

"What're you on about?" she'd said. "What would we even do?"

"Not much, probably," he'd retorted. "That's kind of the point."

A holiday. Going on a trip with the sole intention of relaxing and having fun. Skyler couldn't begin to imagine it. But maybe that was the point, too.

"Besides," he'd added, "you guys might be moving away soon."

"Not that far. You'll still see us loads." He was right, though. It wouldn't be the same. She didn't even see that much of him now, what with how hectic everything had been.

Three years since they'd escaped from the headquarters, almost to the day. Three years since the air strikes, since the peacekeeping forces had arrived. Since they'd torn the Wall down. She'd been right; all that had only been the beginning. They'd barely stopped to draw breath since.

But normality was finally trickling back. Elections were being held next month. She and Mackenzie would actually be allowed to vote. Perhaps, at last, they could breathe.

So she'd shrugged, and said, "Yeah, okay. Why the hell not?"

Now she stretched out on a blanket, the warmth of the sun soaking into her limbs, watching the light bounce off the waves in sparkles and flashes. A reddish dot bobbed amongst the turquoise ripples; Angel had dived for the water the second they arrived on the beach. Skyler's breath still caught every time she looked at her.

She glanced at Mackenzie, lying beside her with his hands behind his head. "Okay, you win. Maybe this wasn't a totally ridiculous idea."

He nodded sagely. "Remember that next time you get the urge to pull the *you're a fucking idiot* face."

"Hey. I haven't called you that for *years*."

"I can still tell when you're thinking it."

She gave him a half-hearted shove. "On this occasion, I'll concede that you're not, in fact, a fucking idiot. It was just... a weird idea, you know? Kind of felt like – I dunno. Tempting fate or whatever. But I think you were right. I mean, it looks like the election's going to be okay. I still can't get used to Joss doing his politician thing, though."

"He's doing an awesome job. And it looks like they're gonna get in – but even if they end up as the opposition, I reckon it'll be okay. At least there'll *be* an opposition. And Lyd's in charge of the regeneration either way."

"Joss still on about you working for him?"

"Mm. Yeah."

"You gonna do it?" Of course he was. He was Mackenzie; the urge to do the Right Thing was basically encoded into his DNA. Skyler, on the other hand, didn't want to work for anyone but herself ever again.

"You're doing the face again," he said.

She tried to rearrange her expression. "I'm not doing the face."

"You're so doing the face."

"Yeah, well, just remember you've got a life of your own to live. You've given plenty, Mack. You don't owe anybody anything."

He just smiled at her. For a long time, she hadn't even known what his smile looked like. She saw it more and more lately.

She shielded her eyes to watch Angel, still gliding serenely through the water. "So Faith's coming out on Tuesday? Did you remind her we don't do hugs?"

Mackenzie rolled his eyes. "It's been three years."

"I know. I just like winding her up, to be honest. Sorry." After things had settled in the UK, Faith had returned to Canada for a while, and travelled a lot now. She and Mackenzie had made the distance work. It had been good for both of them, Skyler and Angel agreed privately, though Skyler knew she'd hate it if Angel moved across the Atlantic. "She heard from Erin recently?"

In defiance of all apparent logic, Faith and Erin had formed a kind of friendship. Angel had pointed out that this actually made a lot of sense; both of them had spent the rescue mission dismantling their framework for how they understood the world, had had to figure out who they were supposed to be, who they wanted to be, without it.

"They write to each other. Heavy on feelings, light on facts, Faith says."

"Ha. Figures. Probably a bad idea for Erin to write down all the illegal shit her and Leila are up to and send it to someone who works for Interpol."

Mackenzie laughed. "I get the impression Erin's sort of keeping Leila in check. Nothing too out-and-out villainous. You guys ever hear from her?"

"Not till recently. She wrote and said the insurance from when the UN bombed the estate finally paid out and she thought we should have some of it."

Mackenzie's eyebrows disappeared into his hair. "Really? What'd you do with it?"

"Okay, this time you do get the face. What d'you think we did with it? I figured the least that money could do is pay for my therapy. Besides, do you have any idea how expensive med school is? Leila wrote a note saying to get in touch if I ever change my mind about working for her, but I'm sticking to legal stuff now and it doesn't pay nearly as well. Not really looking to get put in prison at this point."

Mackenzie's eyebrows stayed raised. "You're going to therapy?"

Of *course* that would be the bit he picked up on. "Well, you and Angel both kept banging on about how useful it was or whatever, so I figured I might as well give it a try."

"How's it going?"

"Oh, God." Skyler rolled her eyes. "The first one – you should've seen the absolute panic on his face when he asked whether I'd had any *traumatic experiences*. The guy Angel used to see recommended someone in the end. It's all right, I think. She doesn't patronise me and she doesn't look like she's going to cry when I tell her something horrible, so, you know. It's not exactly fun, but I guess it's not supposed to be."

It had taken her a long time to concede that there might possibly be some benefit to therapy, but hadn't she just reminded Mackenzie that he had a life to live? And although the prospect of opening up to anyone except him and Angel about the last six years had been less than thrilling, she'd eventually decided that if her life was going to be about more than just surviving, she might as well try to have the best one she possibly could.

"Hey." Mackenzie nudged her. "I'm proud of you."

She scowled at him. "Shut up."

Angel emerged from the sea. Skyler watched her as she jogged up the beach towards them, pale limbs bright in the sunlight, face alight with happiness as she wiped saltwater out of her eyes, and thought: *this was definitely not a stupid idea at all.*

As Angel reached them, Skyler grabbed her hand and

pulled her closer. "You'll get soaked," Angel protested, giggling.

"I don't care." Skyler threw her arms around Angel's neck and kissed her; she tasted of salt and fresh air, sunshine and hope and happiness.

Mackenzie coughed pointedly. "Don't mind me."

Reluctantly, they drew apart. "Sorry," Skyler said, not very sincerely. "Anyway, you haven't seen Faith for like three months, so I'm sure you'll be getting your own back in a few days."

"I believe," Angel said, with an edge of mischief in her voice, "that there was talk of getting you two into the sea at some point."

Skyler and Mackenzie exchanged glances.

"How cold is it?" Mackenzie asked.

"Not very?"

"Well, that sounds like a lie."

"You'll get used to it in no time. Then it'll be amazing. Honest."

He was definitely going to break first. It was only a matter of time. "Oh, come *on*," Skyler grumbled, as he got to his feet. "I thought you'd at least hold out a bit longer than that."

"I decided to bow to the inevitable. C'mon."

"Uh –" But he and Angel had each grabbed a hand and pulled her upright, and now Angel was tugging them towards the sea, lit up, bright and beautiful, and Mackenzie was laughing too as they reached the water's edge.

"I've literally never been in the sea past my ankles,"

Skyler confessed, as a wave broke over her toes. "Oh, it's freezing! I don't even think I remember how to swim."

Angel was already ankle-deep in the foam. "No time like the present."

"Okay, okay." Skyler took a deep breath. "As long as you promise to make sure I don't drown."

Angel darted forward and kissed her. "I promise."

Skyler looked at Mackenzie. "We're gonna do it together, right?"

He grinned at her. "Don't we always?"

THE END

ACKNOWLEDGEMENTS

There are so many people for whom a "thank you" is an entirely inadequate acknowledgement for their help and support with the process of getting this book out into the world; nonetheless, I hope they'll accept my sincere gratitude. My deepest thanks, then, to:

Faith and Gwen, for your wisdom, your cheerleading, your on-point critiques, and most importantly, for your friendship.

To Judith, Tess, Arianna, Chel and Hannah, for your invaluable feedback on various stages of the manuscript, and to Annie, Kyle, Mike and everyone at River Exe Writers.

To every single person, friend or stranger, who has reached out to tell me that Blackout spoke to you in some way, to tell me how excited you are for this sequel, and who has waited patiently for it to arrive – you are what makes all of this worthwhile.

To my parents, who remain my biggest supporters,

and the rest of my family, whose support, interest and encouragement I am so grateful and fortunate to have.

Finally, to Ann. You're not only the best technical advisor and fangirl any author could wish for; you're the North on my compass. I'm so lucky to have you by my side.

ABOUT THE AUTHOR

Kit is 34 and lives in Bath, UK, with her girlfriend and two small, fluffy, and very helpful editors. She writes speculative fiction about underdogs and girls who like other girls, and has a secret alter ego who works as a mental health nurse. Her debut novel, Blackout, was shortlisted for the 2016 Mslexia Children's Novel Award and longlisted for the 2016 Bath Children's Novel Award.

 twitter.com/kitkattus
instagram.com/kitmallorywrites